LOVE
CONQUERS
ALL

Hung Bui

Author's Tranquility Press
ATLANTA, GEORGIA

Hung Bui/Author's Tranquility Press
3900 N Commerce Dr. Suite 300 #1255
Atlanta, GA 30344, USA
www.authorstranquilitypress.com

Ordering Information:
Quantity sales. Special discounts are available on quantity purchases by corporations, associations, and others. For details, contact the "Special Sales Department" at the address above.

Love Conquers All / Hung Bui
Hardback: 978-1-965463-05-5
Paperback: 978-1-964362-62-5
eBook: 978-1-964362-21-2

DON'T BELIEVE
IN TEARS

A NOVEL | HUNG BUI

Dear Reader,

I hope you enjoyed **Don't Believe in Tears.** A story about the pain of losing a loved one, but being found by love and fate. The story-line for it has always been one of my favorites, and I really found a lot of inspiration in Jefferson's family. The newly found American relative, the quite a story that was with Brian and Jennies are the two of my favorite characters who you've read and spent some time with.

Family means different thoughts and things to different people. Having a good family can be both a challenge and an effort of the place where life begins and love never ends.

In one's life, what is the most important thing? Is it money, status or joy? The truth is that all of these cannot be compared with love. Only time will be able to prove that love is the most important one. Without love, intelligence will only hurt yourself. Joy will not be lasting. Status is just a fake, and money does not bring happiness. It's like we wear sunglasses and go around, seeing only darkness, and through that, we can't see the beauty of love. Because love is God. And it's when we learn to love and be loved that we reflect the love, the true love of God in our lives.

Therefore, a sweet ending to a new beginning that why I am pleased to bring you my new novel in the sequel, Love conquers all, or The beauty of Love. It is a story of next Jefferson's generation who had inherited the power from Jefferson Bush and bonding blossom their childhood into the love of a lifetime to find out what family is and making it and preserving it.

Every family has a story. Jefferson's family is circle of strength and love, formed by fate, joined in unexpected love and this new togetherness teach them that their closeknit bound is strong enough to withstand anything. That is how this book has come to be in the name of love.

If you've enjoyed my first novel **don't believe in tears** and if you like mystery, thrillers and romance, then you're sure to love this one. So check it out.

Warmest regards,
Hung Bui

Acknowledgement

Life goes through different stages and circumstances, but it becomes more difficult by prejudices, classes, or bond of relationship. However, whatever is combined with love is actual getting the true happiness in the end. Love is always overwhelming in this world. And a story about of love is a work and taking such a long time to write that many sources of inspiration need to be created before it becomes a book. But my pleasure was intensified by the enthusiastic support of my lovely wife. And it seems that the second book I write, that's why there are more people I would like to express my thanks and appreciation to them who helped me to finish my story.

Thanks always to God for not only loving me, giving me the gift of writing, helping me to be a better writer, and living my dream of becoming an author. But also, his blessing gets the glory for each story. Next to my amazing publisher, I cannot believe how lucky I am to have you back this time! Thank you for making everything so easy and much better. Again, thanks to my brother-in-law Duy Binh who has created a beautiful cover and arranged for my book. Thank you to my family for being so vociferously proud of me. I owe a big thank-you to my wife, Ngân Nguyễn who still supports me and for the book. Love you, dear. And my heart felt appreciation to my friends who gave me many valuable feedback and very kind comments on Facebook, and finally, thank you to you, my wonderful reader family who personally encouraged and vigorously support for buying my first books, for reading them, for recommending them, for your reviews. You are all the reasons keep me doing this. Words aren't enough and I couldn't do this without you.

As always, I welcome your comments and letters. You can reach me in variety of ways. Through my website at authorhungquocbui.com, and I'm also on Facebook.

God is love.

1 JOHN 4:8

Because God is love, once we realize God's love, there is no truer or more perfect way than to love God's way.

Love conquers all

Prologue
Life is decided by fate, but love can change it.

Have you ever asked yourself that why you were born in this family and the country where you were living? If so, I would have guessed that your life was miserable, and your family had financial trouble. Who should say money was not everything to meet all needs, nor was there any class division? It's very important in life and had a big impact on society. But on the other hand, at the age of twenty-eight, Bush Jefferson Jr had a life that most people would envy. He often thought about these things in the luxurious office that was ii his grandpa's workplace in the past, because he was lucky enough to grow up in a wealthy and famous family in the Stage of Florida of America. He had a large and happy family with total ten members. Although his parents were both of Vietnamese, settle here and lived most of their long life away the land of their birth, still had relatives in Vietnam, but they were American citizens and completely Americanized. He had no recollections of their country. Nor did he know about the events of the loss of country on 30th day of April 1975, which forced his father's family to flee their country. But his parents had explained to him that was God's plan, not for the political struggle, by using the words in the Psalm 33:12 has been written. "Happy is the nation whose God is Jehovah. The people He has chosen as His own possession." Although, many Vietnamese people were still fighting for freedom for the country of Vietnam which they didn't grow well in faith, seeing everything from the point of God's view. That's why they're able to live in this free country, but were immersed in the regret of the past. They recounted everything to him when he was old enough and took him with them visited Vietnam couple times. Bush Jr enjoyed visiting, ate Vietnamese food, learned Vietnam history from his father, and the language from his parents, who spoke only Vietnamese when they were alone. But he could also speak Spanish as well.

Bush Jr was the youngest one and the only child in his family. He matured early, at his six one tall, had big, workingman's hands, like his father's, on the ends of long skinny arms, and his mother's thick black hair and luxuriant lashes. He liked to wear that hair slicked back in the style of his father used to. His seven other siblings were also Vietnamese and adapted by his great grandpa before he was born. Yet despite their different natures, they lived extremely close and grew up under same roof as if they were blood relates. Obviously, they loved each other deeply, and lived in wealthy circumstances. However, each of them had different qualities that were raised by their parents through their personalities and therefore they experienced life from their perspective when they grew up. All of them were educated and supported well by their parents and were aware of and deeply grateful to their lovely grandpa who loved and raised them. He was a man worthy of respect and was easily loved by anyone who got to know him. He also was a man of compassion, integrity and courage was a strong example for them to follow. He taught them what honor, courage, care and responsibility towards others were. To them, he was a mountain, a shooting star, a consolation for every disappointment, the embodiment of joy. Therefore, they always followed his instructions seriously, because he always taught about discipline and hard work.

However, even though they lived in a comfortable and wealthy lifestyle, they were educated to work hard and earn money by taking on miscellaneous chores around the house or odd jobs during summer holidays, and using bad language was strictly prohibited in the house. *If you want to achieve great things, you must start small things. Small things can't do, how can you do great things?* They all loved him, of course. How could they not? That's why they all bear his surname, Jefferson, but except for Bush Jr, his grandpa was much closer and loved him more than others because he always attached to him.

He owned everything to his grandpa. He raised him from birth, sending him to study at prestigious schools, and in his early years in college, he often discussed the company's business issues and his grandpa valued the knowledge which he was majoring in economics in school, making his grandpa more interested in him. He even helped Bush Jr again by buying him the beautiful luxury house that he owned and lived in today. His grandpa had never once asked him even to consider paying him back, even when he tried hard to do so. Like him, Bush Jr valued independence. He didn't want to have what he hadn't earned, although he was very satisfied his grandpa's help.

Bush Jr was not only crazy, but also idolized his grandpa when he was a child. "I want when I grow up, I will be like you, grandpa."

That was a big decision in life. That's why in recent years he'd been fascinated by everything his grandpa did and had copied every move from him, from gestures to speech. Bush Jr learned many values from his example, listened to what he said, and paid attention to his edicts, wisdom, or request. In particular, his intuition about business world had been tempered and often followed him to the construction sites and saw how to operate and take advantage of saving every penny. From those simple actions, frugal lifestyle, and meticulous ideas indirectly taught him about the nature of business economics. That was not just formality to make money, to get whatever they wanted, but also was an appreciation for not wasting any resources. It meant that ambition for the great commercial issues should not disregard other smaller concerns. In addition, *success is not about how much money you have, but more importantly how much you can help others. How many people are graceful because of you and successful because of you? Those who receive our helpings will also begin to do the same on their own. Invest in the eternal value of life which is giving, spreading, because it is the most valuable investment. Being smart is just a nature talent. Honesty is the choice.* A person with great ambition wanted to do the great things should understand this.

Thanked to that, he also became proficient in reading architectural plans and structures easily, and quickly to come up with creative ideas and solutions to problems. Therefore, those experiences helped him a lot in pursuit of his political economic degree, studied hard and excelled in academic programs that his grandpa set up so that he could later work in the family business of buying and selling companies since the day he graduated from college. He started business of buying and selling real estate, especially manufacturing facilities. His degree had come in handy, with the real estate were his first love and passion, and the skill of wheeling deals came naturally, slowly seeped into his blood. Bush Jr always remembered his grandpa's advice. *If you've a dream, go after it. Life's too short for cowards. Use the money, Bush Jr, and made something out of yourself, for yourself.* Therefore, the stock market was his game table just like his father and brother, James. They knew how play to win. He never intended to play it too safe, because safety came with boredom. By twenty-five years of age, his individual business had caught the attention and astonishment from his family and developers. In the opposite direction while the real estate market was falling, Bush Jr bought Riverside Hotel in Miami. It was a business that lost money in the economic crisis and the three million price tag made the owner happy after declaring bankruptcy many times. This was his personal business that had attracted attention and growth, wanting it to become a five-starts East Air hotel.

It was one of those lucky trades that fell from the sky, and was something every broker dreamed of. A solid buyer had the money, a good offer, and a real seller wanted to get rid of the property and consider selling. Bush Jr transferred money from his bank into an escrow account. And five days later, they completed all the inspections. The structures were sound, the title was clear. The deal went off without a hitch, and fifteen days after his proposal was accepted, the hotel belonged to him.

That was great success in business and brought fifty percent of total profits and was a famous success nationwide. The chances he took paid off. But he didn't stop there, any opportunity that came, he took it. He had made several wise investments after that and had turned a large fortune into an even large fortune. His grandpa was very impressed by his success, but Bush Jr never forgot how and where it all began, or how lucky he was to be blessed with success.

His grandpa was a resident of New York, he went from being a poor man to becoming a millionaire thanks to his sharp intelligence. Later he moved to this state to live. He knew what extreme poverty looked like, and all he wanted was to provide a better life for his family. But his grandpa was not a slave to money, even though over the years he had suffered the loss of his son, his wife, and his daughter. That had a big impact on his life, and he understood loneliness more than ever. So, he used the money, used it as a maid. Money equaled power, and power was a weapon that he'd used to build an empire that stretches across the fifty states. And in the process had become a wealthy man. But the loneliness and emptiness made him feel that those things were meaningless. Until he had it all, his mother appeared. She was the perfect antidote, ending his loneliness. Since then, his grandpa had been working from home, managing his investments, spending as much time as possible with them. He was also a visionary, so he had no difficulty seeing his grandchildren had absorbed what he'd molded and building on it. It was impossible to have an empire without a family to share it with. And most importantly, always took his guideline and applied it in life. Dignity, virtue, person, family or nation are all built up starting with the only trust.

Bush Jr seemed to be the successor to his grandpa's legacy. He had closely followed his grandpa's successful footsteps. Other than that, he had no idea why, or maybe he had his full name Jefferson Bush. Junior. But his parents told him when he once asked them why he was named like that, instead of taking his father's surname. His father just smiled and his mother tearfully explained proudly that for first time when his father placed him with red-face and crying in his grandpa's arms. He's not bothering to blink the tears from his eyes. From that moment, they realized that the male succession of the Jefferson's family had been fulfilled. That's why they took Jefferson's surname and named him. Furthermore, his parents respected and honored him whom they loved, admired and was important to them. They also wanted everyone to always remember him from generation to generation, whenever they heard this name.

"You've been programmed all of your life, being told you are very similar to your grandpa, From words to actions. You've grown up believing that you've inherited his strength, stamina, intelligence, and business acumen. He's been all around you since the day you were born. He is an indispensable part of you, just as you are an indispensable part of him."

His mom often told him that, and smiled passionately. "So, whenever you're stressed or worried about something, the mood and gestures shown exactly the same as your grandfather did all his life."

That suited Bush Jr, and it was true, after his grandpa passed away two years ago, at the age of eighty-eight. Everyone got emotion whenever they called Bush Jr, even his parents, besides, there was a strange coincidence that he acted and behaved like his grandpa. Bush Jr wasn't sure because all of these facts that why his grandpa left him a significant fortune, when his grandpa's lawyer gestured to the items laid out on large desk. "It's a will recording his last wishes, a descriptive letter he asked me to keep, an envelope with a little bag of jewelry, all valuable items, and his deed to this house. Oh! There are two bank books of his saving accounts."

He paused for a moment, and then slid a large sealed envelope across the desk, toward to Bush Jr. "Here you go, Mr. Bush Jr. Mr. Bush Jefferson gave it to me to keep in this condition."

The envelope was thin, as if it contained no more than a few sheets of paper. Inspecting it, his index finger pushed open the envelope's seal, and pulled out a two-page document. His breath caught when he saw the first page was a deed for the entire business. It was executed by Bush Jefferson with his signature was at the bottom, notarized by the lawyer who read the will. The name at the top, above the line for the company's new owner was Bush Jefferson Jr.

The second page was about legal description of the company with his grandpa's autograph writing that. I've thought carefully about it for a long time. I believe I've come upon a solution. At this moment when you're reading this letter, I'm handing over the reins to you, Bush Jr. You will take over my position as chairman of the board of directors, and the shares of this company will also belong to you.

"My God!" Bush Jr exclaimed with his eyes wide open in surprise. He didn't expect he was a big winner in the Family Fortune Sweepstakes.

"You sound like a complete nut, Mr. Bush, Jr?"

Bush Jr turned his attention to him and stared as if he couldn't quite believe what he was hearing. He couldn't answer. His throat was locked tight, swollen with emotion.

What did he do to deserve such a great gift? The company grew steadily and flourished under his grandpa leadership, instead of being left to his dad or to their oldest brother, James Jefferson whom they lovingly called him by the nickname Fatty? Because he was obese when he was young, but there was no evidence that he was still obese now, with a great figure. He was tall, handsome and athletic, having earned a doctorate in economics from Harvard University seven years before him. In addition, he also had many good qualities such as being virtues, reliable, conscientious, responsible, honest, trust worthy, hardworking, kind. He had been an investment banker ever since, and married to Linda, the daughter of Vietnam's foreign minister. They bought the big house in Merritt Island when their first daughter, Maggie was born. She was nine years old now, and looked exactly like her mother, whereas her six years-old brother, John, looked like his father, but they had the same sweet nature and easygoing style. Both of them, James and Linda were currently working with their dad.

Mr. Roth-well noticed that Bush Jr seemed uncomfortable with his joke, but he could reply. "I'm honored."

The right to inheritance belonged to everyone in the family, but his grandpa left the most of the assets, and Jennies Foundation for Bush Jr's parents, also left a large sum of money to his brothers and sisters.

After gathering the papers, Mr. Roth-Well put them back into his briefcase and closed it with a click. "Does anyone want to object to anything about today's appointment?"

Everyone looked at each other and no one seemed to object, because they had simply never cared about money, and always thought that whatever they had was enough. He stood up. "Very well, if anything comes up in the future, please call me." He said, shook each person's hand congratulate them, and Bush Jr thanked him.

"We appreciate everything you've done, Mr. Roth-well." Brian added and led the man out of the room and to the front door.

All members of Bush Jr's family didn't seem to be disappointed about that. Instead, tears filled Bush Jr's mom's eyes, and his dad hugged him tightly, saying proudly of his inheritance. "I'm happy and admire your grandpa's decision, son."

He knew his father-in-law's body had been aging, but his brain was still operating at full speed, because he'd come from a long line of warriors, living by intelligence as well as by sword. His pride in his career was as fierce as his ambition. That's why he had the foresight to see his career path would continue strongly. Brian was always honest with his son whenever he was with him." You're becoming everything I ever hope for."

Even his brother, James, a conservative man with money, firmly squeezed his hand to congratulate him happily without any objection.

They knew that Bush Jr was the most loved person in the family and always had been. He was clearly the heir, and they completely understood why. He was a true Jefferson in appearance, the best looking and had always been a classic type-A personality, following in his grandpa's footsteps as if they were created by God. Furthermore, Bush Jr could be said the smartest and brightest person in the younger generation of this family. Even without trying, people still loved him. Even strangers quickly fell under his spell. But he deserved to win this position, and valued it.

Thoughtful, he pondered. No one can escape their own destiny. His lifestyle became more luxurious as if he were on top of the world. His smile could melt the world, and so many other things to smile about. As expected, he was now grown stronger and stronger, just like he always imagined.

Bush Jr was the company's third-generation, the CEO of a Fortune 500 company, but he refused to move his CEO role to New York where the speed of development was very fast, and people had to move in a hurry, jostling on the roads to adapt to life. So he chose Florida as his base and the life he wanted to enjoy. He divided his time between his private beachfront mansion in Melbourne, and his home in Orlando where most people considered his twenty-room house a bit too much for just him to live in. He didn't care about that because he always remembered what his grandpa once told him. The house, with its tall windows and gleaming floors with many rooms would tell the statement of the successful businessman who had presence and owned it. Besides, this was not a matter of being rich or not, but of the need to enjoy and benefit at work.

Also, Florida wasn't simply the place of money or power that he wanted to seek to control, but the factors and privileges that this state was bestowed with. The full of sunlight and a rich and fertile land that was very good for growing crops and raising livestock. Besides, seafood was available all year round. So it had attracted not only domestic people but also tourists from all over the world came here to enjoy, making the tourist industry able to develop in all seasons, where many people had come to visit and ended up staying for years. Therefore, it helped the economy became prosperous. That's why the state of Florida suited him perfectly. And with his new company and new position, Bush Jr had gathered a huge amount of fixed capital from large and small investors, with promises of extraordinary profits. Talent recruitment, prohibition of bad competition between employees, enhanced recreational activities, always encouraged and rewarded members with good creative achievements.

His father and brother were still involved in the work, however, despite they were under Bush Jr's power command, but he never made them feel inferior. He used his money wisely, his brother, James had a knack for getting the job done seriously, plus his father's marketing skills, together, they had made a formidable team, and had built one of the most successful corporations in the city of Orlando. He was happy because they always agreed to the plan, even though they knew that his way of thinking was done instinctively. Instinct told them that his plans would increase the company's business and reputation. Not for glory or personal gain, but because it was expected. Bush Jr was not only a very logical man, but this quality was also a tradition in the Jefferson family. The three of them not only worked together and do everything as perfectly as possible, always discussing, looking for the best solution to win all the contracts as if a business family, but also together they were even more successful than when they worked separately. And most at all, he wanted to prove to his grandpa whom he had worshiped since he was a child, that he was grateful that he had not failed him when he let him inherit the legacy.

Bush Jr's siblings didn't have much in common during their teen, but they had become closer as adult. They always pursued their own dreams and each of them was on career path. He loved what they did and they became the successful in various businesses that provided them with a very comfortable lifestyle, and many luxuries. Justin Jefferson was his second brother who had a nickname was Question Mark. Precise and consistent with his personality. That's why he had decided to study law when he was fourteen years old. "I think business would be too boring," he said half teasing, half serious. "Especially with all the numbers that will make my eyes roll back in my head. I love working with people and I'd like to be a federal prosecutor when I grow up." That was pretty tough one, but he knew exactly where he was going and what he wanted out of life. So, he graduated from Harvard Law School, spent a few years in the district courts, and even became a lawyer eventually, with eloquent and started practicing for himself. He was also a handsome man, not pretentious or imposing and seemed extremely straightforward and natural, which they liked very much about him.

Spencer entered his life after she graduated and became an attorney at the same illustrious law firm where they worked and lived in Boston, Massachusetts. In just a few days, he realized that this was the woman he wanted to marry, and became the mother of his children. Justin was happily married with his wife and had two adorable children. Jimmy was seven years old and Dorothy was at five years old. Spencer and Justin Jefferson had been married for eight years and still acted like they were on their honeymoon.

But the prettiest girl in their family was Jennifer Jefferson, and Smiling was the nickname that everyone used to call her instead. She grew up to have the same beauty as her mother, Jennies. Warm, affectionate, kind, good-nature, and a talented fashion designer. She was attracted to her mother's fashion design, and had followed her since she was young, always listening to her mother's advice. *"Even the smallest thing still needs heart, patience and great effort to be able to create masterpieces and it touched the heart of others. The beauty of creative arts is the beauty seen in the heart of the creator."*

By the age of eighteen, she had a master's degree in fashion design. Smiling worked for her mother's company for a time as a design director.

She did research for her mother and found fresh inspiration for her product line that made the collection interesting and effect. There was no detail too small for her to overlook without meticulous attention. She emphasized. Accessories and fashion always had an impact on life. It wasn't necessary to design a dress, a coast, T shirt or hat and to be done, but must turn them to meet life's needs. She was passionate about what she did, and infused her vision and energy into her mother's company, and that turned up on the runway when they showed their clothes. Although she had designed many perfect modern styles at that time, but her recent designs had created a revolution in the fashion world. Additionally, she had the ability to develop her own fashion style or she could start her own company and turn it into a big company. However, she still didn't feel satisfied because it seemed like she was missing something. Until Smiling was noticed by Vogue in some photo shoots for other magazine with the elegance outfits she designed that made her famous during Fashion Season in New York. She decided to leave and didn't hesitate to work for them as not only a consulting designer and photographer, but also as a model. Everyone said she was crazy, and it wasn't because of a huge salary they paid her. But remarkably, the support what she was interested in pursuing it came from her family, especially from her mother, who secretly told her that. *"The future belongs to those who believe in the beauty of the dreams they follow."*

The best thing about Smiling was that she loved what she did. This was what she dreamed of, bringing fashion into the work fields. It's not just about designing beautiful dresses for famous models to wear, but about becoming one of them, to truly experience and perhaps generate new creative ideas for fashion models suitable for life. and making it meaningful and memorable. Especially closely following the trend that all women wanted to own.

Fashion had been her passion ever since, helping her climb the seemingly endless ladder that would eventually leaded her to a famous designer and model. And shortly after she accepted the job, Smiling met Mathew Neilson who always said it was fate. They said they specialize in Chinese restaurant then. He was one of biggest people in the fashion business, charming, successful and approachable. They fell in love almost immediately. And she hardly had time to catch her breath when he became her manager and kissed her before asking her to move in his house. She was currently living with her fiancé in London.

Unlike the rest of his family, Jeremy Jefferson who was called Steady and was a very special girl, also was as sophisticated and beautiful as Smiling. She was closer to their father. Because their feeling for each other secretly made her feel more comfortable. Perhaps because she was a disabled person, born without arms. But it was that reason that created a source of motivation for her to become a determined, independent, and brave person. Her father paid a huge amount of money to plastic surgeons successfully reattached her human arms when she was sixteen years old. You would never know it when you see her, because she looked like a normal people. But you would be stunned when you know about that, and admiring her even more if you saw her, sitting on the bench in the front of the piano, fanned her fingers an inch above the ivory keys, and then slowly lowered them onto the keys, coaxing the musical instrument to life with delicate chords, and you would immerse yourself in the climate and most the aching notes of the most beautiful music. Surely, that might sound like it was made up or exaggerated, but stories about her were written on People Magazine. She absorbed music from her father from a young age, and with her music talent, she quickly learned the piano under her father's guidance and was taught by other good teachers. That's why she played the piano beautifully. Not stopping there, she was also very passionate about literature and art. She lived in luxury with enough conditions to not have to work for her life's needs. She'd had to work for her own gratification, her own sense of ethics. Her financial base had allowed her to choose the course of her career path and establish a business that expressed her interests. Those ethics, and her own skills, effort, and shrewdness had made the business flourish. However, she decided to live with her parents, and worked with her mother at the company.

Hope Jefferson was Bush Jr's third sister, but she contracted meningitis and passed away when he was two years old. All of his memories about his sister were vague, he could only see through the pictures of her in the family photo album. Now she was resting peacefully next with her stepmother Jennies and grandpa and in the warm hard ground of Heaven Cemetery graveyard. The family always came together for the annual memorial celebration every year after their grandpa passed away three years earlier. It was a tradition, and it was held at their parents' house on the weekend of Independence Day. Today was the last day of June.

Chapter 1
Love never fails. 1 Corinthian 13:4-8

After signing the documents and completing the meetings, Bush Jr returned by his private helicopter parked on the roof of Jefferson Enterprises building.

And when he entered his office, he sat behind an enormous and elaborately carved mahogany desk that now belonged to him, and glanced at the computer screen on the desk that displayed Top portfolios in currency market trading today on the Dow Jones index. The green numbers that appeared, making him happy and very satisfied, making him look up at the array of pictures hanging on the wall.

Many generations of successful families smiled with him. A black and white photo in the frame of his grandpa Jefferson Bush and his wife, Samantha together when they were young, back in the early sixties. They were wearing their best outfits, standing in front of the building they just bought that later became the Florida Institute of Technology, smiling brilliantly for the camera. Next to it was a photo of his beloved stepmother, Jennies before marring his father, smiling and sitting in her office. In another photo, his father and mother were posing and smiling together for the camera at Jennies Foundation. But the best one was his grandpa standing in front of this building, posing with everybody in the family gathered around and beaming. A caption below was read *Love will lead you to Success.*

What a wonderful love! Love, Success and Money had come to him early in life, and some of them made him more mature than he actually was. Even though his grandpa had passed away and was no longer around to see his achievements, Bush Jr still wanted to make him proud. God, he missed him so much when he looked at his grandpa's framed photo placed on the desk in front of him and silently communicated in the spiritual world. *Hey, Grandpa, look at me moments. I don't disappoint you.* That made Bush Jr smile, but the sound of Skype from his desktop computer chimed, distracting his great spirits.

He thought it might be his mother calling, because she often called him to come over to their house to have a dinner with them. He loved talking to her, and called her as often as he could. Thinking of her made him smile to himself again, but he lost it when he saw Jessie's smiling face on the screen. That was his older sister who was nine years older than him.

"Hello, my dear lady." He said merrily.

They really cared about each other. Jessie Jefferson had been close and firmly attached to Bush Jr since his birth. Her nickname was Gloomy and everyone always called her by that name. Gloomy was pretty, funny, fun to be with, and intelligent, and was also happy in marry. She currently lived and worked in San Francisco, California, and had an adorable daughter, Cathy who was six-years old, and her wonderful husband, Bill Nguyen. She was an ER doctor of San Francisco Memorial Hospital, and Bill was a successful architect. He had opened his own architecture office, after seven years of working for a company. Bush Jr often missed her and called her to check on each other.

"Hi there, my sweet brother. How's work going today?" Gloomy asked when she saw him on the screen.

"Busy as usual." Bush Jr answered with a smile. She was his favorite among his siblings.

"Good for you." Gloomy infinitely proud of her little brother, he was a star in her eyes, she smiled inwardly, as she sat on the edge of her bed with her suitcase propped open and since she heard what he said, her spirit became more excited. "And how's the weather in Melbourne, by the way?" She asked, because Florida was beginning hurricane season, but the weather in San had been good.

"It's been hot and sunny all week. By the way, what about your job at the hospital?"

Most people thought of hospitals with dread. To them, they meant sickness, even death. But for her, they were places that brought life back and hope. The hours she worked there each week only made her more determined to save more human life. That determination made her job as a doctor worth it. "Busy just like you."

"Where are you now?"

"I'm at home and packing for the trip. We want to go to the airport early."

"Is Bill coming with you?" Bush Jr asked thoughtfully, and his sister sighed sadly. "He tries to, but he has a big presentation coming up next week, to an important client. Therefore, he wanted to work according to plan. Bill already called Dad and Mom and explained the reason."

Bill was not just an architect. He often participated in public debates, and he acted as consultant to several large architecture firms, and they were extremely pleased with the way he handled, with complex contracts better than them. Bill loved what he did, and eventually he opened his own company. But what pleased Bush Jr about Bill Nguyen was that he was also Vietnamese and respected his parents very much, and getting along with his wife's sibling, unlike Mathew. Still, he liked both of them, and frequently playing golf, tennis, and dining with them wherever his businesses were there, and attending business parties with them, where he met some movie stars, big producers, and important agents.

"I understand that well, sister. Business sometimes comes above everything else," Bush Jr reassured Gloomy. "But the family will be happy to see you and Cathy in Florida. I've arranged the limousine at the airport to pick you up."

Feeling the same way, she sighed as she put Cathy's folded pile of clothes such as, the sweaters, dresses, underwear, and several pairs of jeans into her suitcase. "I wanted to talk to you longer, brother, but Bill is coming and taking us to the airport. You know, the traffic here is often congested. I'd better go now." Gloomy announced as she checked the time on her diamond-studded Cartier watch that her father had given her for her eighteenth birthday, then added her belongings in the suitcase. They had to leave within an hour if she and her child were going to arrive at her parents' house tomorrow morning on the schedule.

"I'll call you when I get there." She said as she tightened her suitcase and called Cathy. "Don't try to work too hard. Well, I have to go, love you."

Bush Jr heard the sound of a car horn, reminded them that Bill was waiting in the car, and he glanced down at a twenty-page contract on his desk for the next board meeting. "I'll try, depending on how the next one goes. I love you, too. Call me when you can."

Gloomy snapped the suitcase closed. "I will do, brother. Take care."

"Same to you. We'll see each other soon. Goodbye, sister."

He clicked off the screen, then went back to work, but the intercom beeped and his secretary said in her most annoyed voice. "I'm sorry Mr.

Bush Jr. I know you told me you're not to be bothered, but Ms. Tiffany is on line two and she insists on speaking with you right now. Even though I told her you were busy and leave the message."

"It's okay, Lilah. I'll take the call." Bush Jr picked up the receiver, and answered. "Hello."

"I know I can find you at work." Tiffany said on the phone. Her voice was cheerful, but Bush Jr wasn't. She never called him at work. "You broke the rule, Tiffany." He said in disappointment.

"Please, don't hang up on me."

"I'd told you not to call in my office."

"I'm sorry, Bush Jr. But you're hurting my feelings." She said petulantly.

"How could I do that to you?" He said, leaned back in his chair, closed his eyes, and wondered. How different his life would have been if he hadn't met her?

And from that point, suddenly a scene from the past appeared in his mind where he transported himself back to the day when he first saw Tiffany by chance on his way to Tallahassee for an important meeting five months ago. From then on, they became romantically involved and had a serious relationship.

He had arranged for the annual meet to be held in that city. Instead, his driver would take him there, but because sometimes his job lasted many hours, and because of the habit of traveling here and there and not wanting anyone to interfere with his privacy at night, even his bodyguards. So he used one of his favorite cars to drive himself. And when his car was rolling along Route 520 East toward Orlando. He was trying to sort out the details for his new clients in his head, and was too concentrating to react when suddenly a large animal ran across the road. Wild boar or deer? Or another creature? The objects were detected by the car's sensors, so the automatic emergency braking made the car slow down, and stopped before he had time to curve. His heart flew to his throat as he stared at the animal running quickly into the bushes around which there was a traffic sign CAUTION DEER CROSSING. But through the windshield, he saw the oncoming car on the other side slammed on the brakes, the tires were trying to hold the road surface to avoid colliding with the animal and the car wobbling, swaying like a fishtail. That meant they lost control and their car was coming straight into his car...

"Oh no, no, no!" He muttered in panic, and once again his heart flipped. "Shit!"

According to his instincts, to avoid a collision, he slammed down the gas pedal, cranked hard on the steering wheel too far to the right, causing his Mercedes Maybach 6 car began to skid helplessly with the warning beeping sound and it's getting louder and louder as the car rushed straight towards the guardrail. Frantically, he yanked on the steering wheel hard again to the left to avoid hitting into it, and trying like hell to keep the car on the road. But it was too late, his rear of the car swayed and the car rammed into the guardrail. Bam! His body jerked hard against the car's motions, but his seat belt pulled tight, helping to keep him from being thrown out of the seat when the car stopped immediately. No mass of air shot at him, no balloon trapped him against his seat. Instead, he heard himself screaming.

He sat there like a lost soul, unable to move or speak, but through the windshield, he watched in horror the oncoming cars as if they were hitting his car again, and just kept going. Cars jolted side to side, and no one stopped, nor did they pay attention to him.

His hands clenched in a death grip over the steering wheel, his legs shaking, and his heart pounded in his ear. Fighting his fear, he took a deep breath to calm his wildly racing heartbeat, tilted his head back, and tried to concentrate. "Okay, I'm okay. I'm not hurt."

To maintain that state of mind, he gave himself orders until the fear passed. Someone would come to help. The best thing he could manage was to see what happened. Flat tire, he thought. If so, great. Sighing, he got out of the car to inspect his car and discovered the damage. "Oh, great! Just great! That's not possible." He muttered as he saw the iron bar of the roadblock had cut a long line from the front tire to the rear tire, and the scratches on the body of the car. "Damn, both tires were cut."

He looked up at the beautiful. cloudless blue sky which he noted bitterly, expressing personal insult under the circumstances. He would definitely be late for the meeting, but he couldn't leave his car here. He could damn well have changed a flat tire if he had to, he mused. But his car didn't have spare tires.

"What a lucky day you have for me!" Frustrated, he said sarcastically, then got back into the car to get his cell phone and called for roadside assistance triple A to come tow the car. And because he was still agitated, he decided to wait, allowing himself to regain his composure for few minutes before calling his dad. Luckily, his dad was already there. He told his dad what happened. "Dad, I had an accident on Highway 520."

His dad immediately panicked, but he quickly reassured him that he was unharmed, and decided to wait for tow truck to arrive and he would take taxi to the meeting. But to be sure of effect, Bush Jr told him to run the meeting for him, and gave him a list of partners' names in case if he's late. It was more efficient that way, and also made him feel more secure after hanging up on his dad for arranging everything.

Looking back at the situation, he pondered. The tow truck would arrive in perhaps thirty minutes, during that time, he could call his secretary to send his driver to pick him up and take him to the meeting, if he was lucky.

Before he could come to a conclusion, he heard the roar of an engine came from behind on the highway. His eyes glanced at the rear-view mirror. A motorbike was coming with the sound of its engine whirring as it passed. However, it made an illegal U-turn and pulled up behind his car. The biker dressed in black from helmet to boots, turned off the engine, turned on the emergency lights, pushed off the kickstand, and swung out of the bike.

He told himself to be alert as he quickly opened the door, got out of the car to tell the biker that he'd already called for help. But to his surprise, he immediately dismissed the idea and stopped, *Holy...!* In that moment, as fast as the blink of eye, for the first time in his life, Bush Jr found himself speechless and his heart simply stood still, could only stand there and stare, because he couldn't control it. What caught his eyes was a beautiful woman who was taking off the black helmet. Her blond hair came tumbling her shoulders and down her back seemed to catch every ray of sun as she hooked it onto the handlebars of her Harley Davidson motorbike.

Dear God, he couldn't move because he was so captivated by those piercing blue eyes surrounded by long black eyelashes, making it impossible for him to look at the other, and there was a force that drew him to her like a magnet. He used to make eye contact with others all the time, and he'd simply never had so much trouble maintaining eye contact with anyone as in this case. From the moment he looked into those gorgeous, sparking blue eyes, he realized that she was a troublemaker and someone to be wary of. However, she also exuded friendliness. And his bemused thoughts were interrupted by her deep voice interacting with her attractive appearance. "Hello Mr. Looks like you're in trouble."

She said as if she'd known him all her life, and her voice had French romance mixed with English severity. He analyzed and observed her while she assessed the situation with the sunlight making her long blonde hair shine. She wore a black T shirt, black leader jacket and black jeans torn at the knees, tucking into black cowboy boots, further enhancing the image of sexy bad girl with a sinful body. Woman liked that would make men crazy and their brains become stupid. But to keep his expression natural, he blinked, nodded, and looked straight into those blue eyes when she stood in front of him.

"Need help?"

He had ever known a woman who could change his moods so quickly. Especially a stranger. Thinking about it carefully, he felt that there seemed to be some strange relationship that connected them together. It was as if they'd met before and recognized each other. He straightened his shoulders and reminded himself he could handle any situation that arose. "I appreciate that, but you don't have to do it."

She couldn't help, but stared at him kindly, and secretly evaluated him. He summed up the best, handsome, looking attractive, and had a muscular body. Five feet seven tall, she'd never considered herself short, but this man dwarfed her. His style easily attracted everyone. With broad shoulders, relatively long legs, lean-muscled, a V-shaped body in proportion to his height. But his face was an oval shaped, smooth facial skin like a child's. No. that was a sensual face. High cheekbones, strong chin, black eyebrows were almost straight over transparent brown eyes. His mouth was a bit long but beautiful shapes. His nose was high and straight. Stylishly trimmed hair and highly polished Italian leather shoes. She also noticed that he was dressed very elegantly in a luxurious, expensive dark blue suit, without tie over the collar of an unbuttoned light gray silk shirt, and gold cuff links on the sleeves were definitely designer's signature. Looked at each seam, the skillful stitch that perfectly fit his massive physique, emphasizing his broad chest, flat stomach and strong, muscular legs. Probably Versace or Prada, she guessed. He was definitely a wealthy and fashionable man, specializing in famous and expensive items. Driving a Mercedes Maybach 6 at his age, she firmly believed that he was a businessman, in an important position because his whole body exuded nobility, majesty and authority.

She'd never had any impressed of rich men, especially rich, cocky and good-looking men, because she thought these types of men were usually the ones who only knew how to have fun and debauchery. He represented everything she detested in men. But rethinking, she shouldn't have judged him so quickly if she didn't know anything about him. Besides, there was just something about him that attracted her immediately. That was she concerned now and realized she'd made the right decision as she looked at the wide, intense and suspicious pair of brown eyes.

"Just an offer, and are you hurt?" She said, in a way that seemed also to carry an explanation as to why she was here.

Strangely enough, Bush Jr relaxed and smiled politely first. Accepting help from a stranger was against all his principles, but he adjusted that way of thinking. She didn't seem dangerous to him. "No, I'm okay and thank you for your kind offer, but you don't know me."

His words seemed to show his reluctance as he looked at her. But those eyes, the kind of eyes that seemed to sear to her soul, eyes that were twinkling with that sexy kind of mischief that she found impossible to ignore. "Neither do you. But seriously, I saw you were in trouble, so I just wanted to show my concern for you. Maybe this is how you'll understand me better." She explained, managed a grin and offered a hand attractively to demonstrate. "By the way my name is Tiffany Stanley. And you are?" Bush Jr introduced himself as he shook hands with her.

The hand holding hers was big, hard as rock, but extremely gentle. Her palm began to itch. "It's nice to meet you, Bush Jr." She said, trying to leave an impression of him coming and going, and looking inside the car through the rolled down window. "The vehicle's safety airbags were not deployed."

"Yeah," Bush Jr felt a lot more relaxed having her to talk to. The situation was unusual. He hardly ever began conversations with strangers just to talk. It was not a matter caution. For him, a conversation had a straightforward business, and also had a professional function. He had never minded having a long conversation if it was to ferret out facts. "I wasn't going that fast. I didn't hit anything, just avoided getting hit by a moron who swerved to avoid a wild boar or deer, then kept coming at me. I had to cut toward the rail and…" he motioned to the wheels. "That's how it had happened."

"Where is he, the other driver?"

"He just kept going. How can anyone do that?"

Probably because they didn't want to get involved as luxurious as you. She almost said that. But instead. "It must have given you quite a scare."

"Yes." Bush Jr replied, trying to smile at her. "But the fear is over now."

Without further ado, she turned around, walking back to where her motorbike was parked, poked through the saddlebag of it, then came back and gave him a bottle of water. "Here, sit down and drink some water." She counseled him. "You will feel better."

"Thank you." This was a good girl, he thought. Never before had he felt so quickly at ease with her. And to indulge her, he offered a smile, sat sideways on the front seat, twisting the cap on the bottle of water, and realized how dry his mouth was.

He swallowed a few sips of water then looked up at her. "I'm okay. Just a little angry."

She gave a gentle smile. "I don't blame you."

"I don't worry about that right now," he said honestly, paused to glance at the thin gold Patek Philippe watch worn on his right wrist which was his grandpa had given him years before, showed him it was half past eleven. He frowned, because right now, the only thing bothering him was how he got there. "Oh, this is just perfect."

"Something else wrong?"

"I'm going to be late. I hate being late. I have an important marketing project at Tallahassee Conference in two hours. I'm not going to make it. I hate ...." he paused. Why did he have to tell her? So he turned around, looked back at the road and saw a tow truck approaching in his direction. That was fast. He smiled as an idea flashed in his mind. If the driver could get him there, he should make the meeting right on time.

Her eyes caught the delighted grin on his face. "What are you smiling at?"

"I'll ask the driver to take me there."

"Are you afraid to ride a motorbike, Mr. Bush Jr?" She asked him bluntly. It wasn't sympathy, just a question, and he hesitated for a moment, and turned his glance towards her motorbike.

It looked unsafely small and fragile. Bush Jr considered ignoring that idea, but otherwise he would prove himself a coward. "Of course, I'm not." He lied. "Why do you ask?"

"No reason," but she volunteered. "Just because I thought it would be helpful if I'll give a lift there."

"You don't have to do that." He didn't want her involved in his problems. "It's out of your way."

"Of course I don't. But let's just say I want to finish what I start," she tried to persuade him, but again saw confusion in his eyes as he looked at her skeptically. "Actually, I'm going that way too."

She was different from the kind of woman who usually attracted him, and truthfully, she was motivating him. "Why are you being so nice to me?"

Thinking about what he just asked. I'm a nice girl. *Well, wait, that wasn't true and wasn't completely honest.* She wanted be nice with him because she genuinely liked him, and because she felt a bondage, something she hadn't experienced in a while, that excitement of this man's attractiveness, and despite her best intentions, it drew her in. "The problem here is that you need help and I'm the one willing to help."

That's right, he realized that problem. She was clearly trying to do everything she could to help him and was willing to involved what would happen, but he hesitated, not knowing whether he should trust her or not. "Actually, that sounds wonderful, but I'm not sure I want that." At this point, he raised his hand to block the sunlight that was shining into his eyes, and stared at her, looking to see if any hint of calculation appeared on her face. "These days a Good Samaritan is hard to find."

"Believe me, I'm not that kind of person." At least that wasn't a lie. "But actually, I realize, I just made you worried and suspicious, isn't that right?"

Bush Jr tried to reaffirm her personality. There was no pretense about this woman. Fraud, conspiracy or tricks didn't belong to her. Because he had eyes for people and could read their thoughts. That was one of reasons that helped him run his company more effectively. He had good ability for that. But hell, this would be the first time he'd misjudged this woman. He had nothing to fear from her. Was there any reason not to trust her? She was trying her best to help him.

"No." It was a blatant lie, but he thought he had to be honest. "Let's say you're really so enthusiastic that makes me nervous, and I'm the cautious type." She liked his honesty. "Come on, Bush Jr. What do you have to lose?"

Just my heart. He swallowed hard. "Nothing."

"Then let me take you there," she suggested. "I promise I won't take advantage of you or intentionally trick you."

She said so and although he was still concerned, he finally didn't refuse and told himself to forget the thoughts in his head. Being too cautious would not help in this case. "If so, I'm really thank you."

"That's not necessary," she said, looked up to the driver in the cockpit as the tow truck pulled in front of his car... "Bush Jr. Wait here, I know the driver. Let me handle this matter on your behalf and do the paper work."

Nodding in agreement, he watched Tiffany walked to the tow truck. Relieved and grateful while she was talking with the driver, he took a sip of the cold water again, enjoying the sunshine, and heard the sound of motor started to pull his car onto the bed of the truck. Once the car was secured, Tiffany filled out the paperwork, and when she walked back to him, she was holding a black helmet. "You need to wear this. Better safe than sorry."

Because he hesitated for a moment to accept it, so, she put it on his head, and didn't bother to hide the grin. "Cute."

He looked at his car with the sound of the truck's engine fading in the distance.

"What's about my car?"

"Don't worry, everything has been sorted out. Mr. Tom took pictures of all the damage and report back to you. This is the company that will repair your car. Your insurance should pay the cost, minus the deductible and they will call you after your car is repaired." She explained briefly and clearly.

His intuition told him that this woman was indeed very smart and skillful, able to trust and talk. Taking a card, he smiled and didn't have to worry about it. "Honestly, I really like your communication skills."

She smiled back, swung a leg over, straddled her bike, twisting her hair behind her head before putting on her helmet. "We better get going," she ordered and started the engine.

The engine roared, causing him to stare at the shiny Harley and exclaim. "Oh, my God!"

His demeanor made her unable to control the smile on her face. "Be bold, Bush Jr. I won't let anything happen to you. I promise."

She made him laugh at the way she spoke and her cool composure in which he could see the passion in her eyes, giving him confidence that he would go anywhere with her without any hesitation or doubt.

"Fine, let's do it." He managed to climb on behind her, gripping her shoulder then pressing his legs against her body as his chest pressed against her backside.

She gave the engine a couple of muscular revs. "Have you ever ridden a Harley, Bush Jr?"

"No. Why do you ask that?"

"Because you have to hold me tight." She answered, and Bush Jr did, but only placed his hands lightly on either side of her waist.

Tiffany wasted no time. She revved the engine again, releasing the clutch, accelerating that had he screamed mixed with her laughter as the metal horse jerked forward then they were flying down the road.

He knew damn well she did it on purpose. His heart skipped and scrambled as he slid closer, and his arms immediately tightened around her waist, resting his chin on her shoulder, and then he wondered why anyone would want to drive something so noisy, so dangerous.

Through her jeans she felt the muscles of his thighs grip hers, and his breath was warm against her head.

Bush Jr lifted his head, intending to firmly tell her to pull over and let him off. But the truth was that even though he was so scare, he no longer had that feeling. On the contrary, he thought he felt a real growing excitement when the bike rolled. In addition, Tiffany seemed to enjoy driving, taking it easy on the speed limit. The chill had vanished, and now that he let himself begin to relax and realized that there was nothing different like driving a car. It was primitive and beautiful and thrilling. The scenery passed by, the wind blew cool, balmy and gorgeous over every inch of him, and lashing her hair to his face as the Harley horse suddenly was no longer small, or fragile, but became powerful, just a little dangerous and breathtaking as it ran fast and smooth. Plus holding so close the woman who was driving it, was the most magnificent woman he'd ever seen. He smelled the scent of grass mixed with the leather of her jacket, the vibration of the engine between his legs, the warm of her body, and wished to God please take away the feeling of her round buttocks rubbing intimately against his crotch. Sex, he admitted. Add arousing to that terrifying thrill which was surely the reason people enjoy driving them so much. "Wow!" That's all he said and could definitely adapt and ride this kind of Harley.

As if Tiffany could read his thoughts, she asked loudly along with the wind. "Feel better?"

"Yeah," Bush Jr replied and asked. "You're enjoying this, aren't you?"

Pleasing and knowing what desired effect, she turned on the music, and the vocals were from a Rock band Gun N' Rose screamed loudly from the speakers. But they listened in silence.

Bush Jr leaned his head against her back, enjoying the pleasure of holding her in moments like these and remaining that intimate feeling until Tiffany stopped and cut the engine in front of the Convention Center about an hour and a half later. He climbed off her bike, glanced at his watch and was satisfied with the transportation that brought him here so smoothly. "Thank you very much. I must hurry in, or…" "You'll be late." She said for him, conveniently removing the helmet from his head.

"I really appreciate the help, Tiffany. Thanks to you, I was able to arrive in time for the meeting." He said solemnly, and she smiled.

"It was nothing. Don't worry about it."

But with his personality. He didn't like to owe a favor to anyone who had helped him, especially a stranger he'd just met. In addition, this woman's behavior was very interesting, and the way she cared for him showed that she was a compassionate person. So he told himself that she was the perfect woman for him to invest more time in intimate contact and learning more about her. "I've to go, but before I go, I'm curious to ask you. Are you here for business or for fun?"

She smiled at his question. "Oh, a little for both, I just hang out with other riders, and go shopping. Why?"

Traveling with her brought him many indescribable emotions, he even felt more attracted to her. He loved women, all women. If he was honest and he was, he'd admit that most women were attracted to him. To be fair, he was also attracted to them. Short, tall, plump, thin, old or young, he found them a source of passion, interest and love. Additionally, he respected them, perhaps only because he was a grown man surrounded by many women in his family that he was able to do so. But respecting them didn't mean he couldn't enjoy them. And he'd never been one to shy away from danger. In particular, he didn't pursue a woman without compassion or one who was sending out mixed signals. When a woman he met was attracted to him, he would let her know it. Frankly speaking, no tricks and no pretenses. He really liked Tiffany. "The reason I ask is because I'd like to invite you to have dinner with me tonight."

"Is that right?" She hesitated. "I think you did it because you want to repay me. Why is someone like me invited to dinner by you?"

He smiled, looking straight into her eyes, and she could see the glimmer of amusement in them. "Ah, Miss Tiffany, please keep things simple. That's my way of showing appreciation for your help. Honestly, I like you, and I want to talk to you. Besides, I'm not an easy person to miss opportunities when things were going well, and then suddenly let them disappear. Somehow it seems so futile." He said enthusiastically. "Furthermore, my personality is very clear. If a man wants to get to know a woman, he asks her out for a dinner. It quite a common practice around the world. Unless, you can't, I mean if you have work to do."

His straightforward words made her feel comfortable with the surrounding sunlight. She certainly didn't look like a nervous woman or give any impression of herself to any man. And for a long time, she'd been interested in any other man. However, she reminded herself that this was exactly why she was here, and this seemed so much more important. It would be nice for her and Bush Jr had things to find out about each other, a story to tell, a mission to accomplish. And that would give her a great deal of pleasure. "No, and I find you a difficult man to refuse." She accepted his invitation.

Satisfaction was clearly visible on his face. "Really? We don't necessarily want to go to luxurious, romantic restaurants. We could go Firehouse, grab some subs, eating and talking to each other. I leave it to you to decide."

"Okay, either way is fine. I'm not a picky person. Give me your phone." He obediently took out his cell phone from his vest and gave it to her.

"Great, I'll text or call you when I leaver the meeting." Bush Jr said after Tiffany saved her phone number on his iPhone and gave it back to him. Hanging out with her meant a lot to him, because he wanted to know more about her, her job, her life.

"What about yours? You know, just in case anything happens." She took out her phone, but Bush Jr reached into his inside suit jacket pocket, pulling out a small leather wallet from which he pulled out a business card and handed it to her. "All my contact information is in there, if you want to contact me."

When she took a look with all his phone numbers and email addresses on there, he added. "Text or call me at any of those numbers, including my private cell phone number, but please don't call me at my office."

"Okay." She smiled, understanding what he meant as slipping his business card and her cell phone back into her jacket pocket. "I promise."

"Good. See you later, Tiffany." Should he kiss her or let she kiss him to said goodbye? Because that was a way to test it and would please both sides. But he decided to make a quick kiss on her cheek to show politeness, and reminded himself to keep good manners. Didn't let her have a bad impression of him.

They had only just met each other, but their communication had become more intimate and deeper, and their emotional relationship would surely develop quickly.

"Okay. See you soon, Bush Jr." She said, looking into his eyes again to find the answer there, but he turned around and went into the building.

❧ ❧ ✳ ☙ ☙

No response, she hated this so much. Proving that she was a pathetic woman who only knew how to whine and beg him to see her. That just wasn't her style. "Bush Jr, are you still there or are we disconnected?"

Still immersing in that line of thought, he thought that was how they found each other. Why did she come to mess up his life, so he couldn't get her out of his mind since then? "Hello."

Her voice started him. "Hum? What?" He himself escaped from that cycle of recollection and returned to the present, and grateful for the line that separated them so that she couldn't see he smiled happily at the memories. "Sorry, what were you saying? I was so deep in thought that I didn't listen to what you said."

Hearing he said that, her anger subsided. "I texted you many times, but you didn't respond."

"Oh, is that so?" Bush Jr picked up his cell phone, thumbed the power button on it, and checked the message on screen. There had been more than ten messages from her, and the latest one was. Where R U? Call ASAP!

"I'm sorry I wasn't able to read your messages. I thought I turned it off." He excused for himself. Because he always did that when he went to the meeting. He also didn't want any interruptions or bothering others in the meeting room. He just wanted to give everyone his full attention.

She knew that's his habit of carefully turning off his phone every time he was in the meeting or any other social situation. Because he was very sensitive to disturbing or annoying others. But on the other hand, he often forgot to turn his phone back on right away. "I understand why you did that."

"It's good you understand, Tiffany. But why did you call me many times?" Bush Jr asked her in worried mood. "What's matter?"

A week had passed without a word from Bush Jr, because he had to leave town on business. Tiffany knew he had been working hard, and she kept telling herself that she would be happy and relieved whenever he had to work far away. The more Bush Jr preoccupied himself with work, the more preoccupied her heart became with him. Her feelings for him were quite strong since their relationship became inseparable. Sometimes their respective jobs required them to be temporarily apart for a while, but experiencing the pain of missing out silently killed her. "No. It's nothing important." She replied with the feeling of making excuses for herself. She just wanted to hear his voice and see him. "It just a week without you that makes me miss you like crazy. Do you miss me?"

Bush Jr relented, placed his cell phone back on the desk. He felt guilty for not calling her, but this wasn't the first time. Since they had a serious relationship with each other.

They always respected each other's work. "Yes, I miss you, too. But you also know what my business is like."

Sometimes she forgot that. "I know, but sometimes I feel like you don't love me."

That sulking hurt him. He wanted to share his feelings more than any woman he knew. It wasn't because he always acted like he was perfect, but women were attracted to him because of his human personality. He wouldn't make fun of their feelings. He knew some girls had been pursuing him since high school, and had a crush on him because he was Bush Jr. Then there were the girls in college, and in Melbourne had seemed to smell his wealth. Not so, they were gold diggers. He once brought two girls' home to meet his grandpa and family. Each and every one had tried to cozy up to the old man. Also, his grandpa never liked a biker girl with leather jacket and jeans, worn-down boots type and riding Harley Davidson.

But Tiffany was different. She didn't care about the wealthy and reputation of the Jefferson, nor did she care that he was one the most powerful men in all of Florida. "I miss you, too, baby," he confessed. "But because I don't want to attract anyone's attention."

On the other end of the line, Tiffany bit her lip, stunned because his words gave her a feeling of hurt and anger. "What the hell is that supposed to mean?"

She was getting irritated, he could feel it. Their love had blossomed, becoming a secret treasure, which he had carefully kept to himself, but that was an issue he had not yet been able to open to his family about their relationship since they met. It was not he didn't want to, it's just that everything hadn't turned out as he expected. So he decided to keep it a secret, waiting for the right opportunity to surprise them. He loved Tiffany, and he knew without a doubt that his parents, brothers and sisters would be extremely shocked by a woman three years older than him and especially the tattoos on Tiffany's arm. But he didn't care about that. Anything could happen and that's who he loved. In true love, age should not be determined, but rather the feelings both had for each other. And his family's prejudices were what made him worry. The men in Jefferson's family always set rules for choosing people to maintain the breed and lineage. He had no intention of breaking that tradition, so he was afraid that Tiffany would be hurt by that. However, he thought his parents would have the open mind and wisdom to let him establish his own happy paradise, opened up to Tiffany willingly and happily. So he would take it step by step, and she must wait.

"I didn't mean any," he said shortly, didn't want to say what was bothering him. "I know how you feel."

She couldn't figure out what was bothering him. Bush Jr was always so thoughtful, he did everything possible to make her comfortable, and he knew how reserved she was. Thousand times in the past six months, he'd shown so much love and care for her that it didn't take long for her to give her heart to him. During that time, he brought her into his world. He often took her to the Country Club and had taught her how to play golf and tennis.

"No, stop saying that." She said, trying not to sound annoyed. In fact, she wasn't angry at him, but very sad and a little hurt. She thought, when the relationship became serious, the next step was to move on that you had to learn about the family background of the person you love, as well as found out the feelings of their loved ones towards you. She was no exception. But it's hard for everyone to know that she was Bush Jr's lover if their relationship wasn't made public which she mentioned to him on the Valentine's Day was unfair to her. "We've known each other for a while now. Are you embarrassed about me?"

"What? Why do you say that?"

"Because you always keep our relationship a secret?"

Tiffany had been dying to meet his family, he understood the sudden anxiety. That was the whole point. But what she wanted he couldn't explain. She was what he had always thought women should be, but couldn't have defined if he'd had to put it into words. Gentle, loving, patient, understanding, interested in all his doings, compassionate, funny and kind. She was like an unexpected gift in his life, so it was time for him to deal with that. Tonight was a good opportunity for him to talk to Tiffany and explain why.

"No, it's not what you think." He said, trying to calm her anger, and made the decision to surprise her. "Actually, I thought publicizing our relationship should start with the fact that IO will bring you home to meet and introduce you to my family."

And with those words, Tiffany broke into a broad smile, forgetting her dissatisfaction and complains a moment ago. "Really! When?"

"Soon, very soon, I promise."

She was so relieved to hear that. He excited her immediately. "That's wonderful," she said happily. "And I want to celebrate with you about that. I'll prepare dinner at your house so we can say everything we want to say. What do you think?"

Tiffany was one of famous chefs, specializing in French cuisine. She graduated from Culinary Institute, then spent two years in Paris at the Cordon Bleu. He knew quite a bit about her background because of her talent in cooking delicious and healthy dishes. He not only enjoyed but also spoiled by the dishes she made. They usually had a good time together, no matter what they did. That was also the reason made Bush rethink and decided to introduce her to his family on the upcoming holiday. And he could feel her joy through her words. "It seems like a good plan. But I think we should choose a place with private and romantic atmosphere."

He heard she laughed and said. "I knew you would say that. But we will have a private and romantic space for ourselves. Please believe me. Besides, I have important news that I need to tell you."

Need, she had said *need*. "You seem mysterious." Bush Jr asked tentatively. "And what you will serve me tonight?"

She could hear the excitement in his voice, although he sounded to calm and steered the conversation in another direction. "I can explain and discuss with you over the phone. Besides, I don't want to spoil the surprise. Our dinner tonight will be a meal that you'll never forget."

Confusing, but he still complied with her wishes. "Fine. I said that but you can cook any dish, as long as we eat it together." He gave her a set of keys and the security code of his house, because he allowed Tiffany come to his house whenever she wanted. "You have the house keys so please come in yourself."

"I will, see you later."

"I'll bring wine then." He said pleasantly.

"I love you, Bush Jr."

Her words made him want to reach through the phone and touch her. Smooth back her hair. Trace the luscious curve of her body, kiss her lips. "I love you, too, Tiffany. I can't wait to see you tonight."

He rarely said that, except in bed, and suddenly she wondered if her wishes were coming true. "So do I. Drive safe."

"I will. See you in a bit."

They hung up and Bush Jr grinned, envisioning a wonderful meal, intimate conversation, and expressing all their longings through lovemaking. Life was a pretty good deal. He had everything he wanted. More than he ever imagined since he met Tiffany.

Not long ago, his weekends had been spent in the company of any number of attractive, interesting women, having dinner at some new hot spot, an evening at the theater or a concert, and if the chemistry was right, a quiet Sunday brunch in bed. And there had been so many women in his life-erotic, talented, passionate women that he could woo and win, but none of them swayed him or rocked his world as Tiffany did in his life now. A woman came to him in the first difficult situation in his life. Not only was he desperately attracted to her, but he also considered her his ideal lover. She made him suffer what he was realizing. *Dangerous women are for pleasure. Just make certain you require nothing more of them than that.* Why should she seem different from any other woman he'd never experienced before? Why should she seem more alluring? And why should her presence make it so difficult for him to keep his mind on the business, thinking about her often, and stopped whatever he was doing just to wonder what she was doing?

Love, that was the way to explain and a logical conclusion. If so, he was caught in a love trap. Because with Tiffany, he'd found a woman he could laugh with, talk with, argue with and make love with. Their days together had been golden, filled with clear blue skies and warm sunshine. The day was peaceful, the night was passionate. She shown him many interesting things in love and sex, the best wines and delicious dishes, and how to enjoy them. With her, everything was so bliss, something that they not only simply enjoyed together but was also a wonderful thing for both of them. But if he chose a long-term relationship which he thought was at least a decade away. And marriage was a direct result of love.

Marriage, home and family, had just been too confining, and these words bounced around in his head, not entirely pleasantly. But he reminded himself that they were living together, but not yet husband and wife, something he hadn't thought about yet. Could what he was doing to her make her think it would lead to a permanent, legal marriage? That's right, in love, everyone wanted stability, vows, and companionship in life.

He wasn't ready for marriage yet, he insisted. Marriage was defined as being together for a lifetime, family happiness depended on the future, and he remembered his father's advice. *Don't marry a woman unless you're damn sure of her.* Yes, this was the first step everyone must take before entering a new stage. It's simple but it weighed heavily on his decision. Because after all, no one could plan the future. Happy endings didn't exist for anyone. But there was a chance, someday in the not-too-distant future, he might be ready to finally settle down. Leaning back in his chair, he asked himself. Could two people share a life, share a love and not share what was most vital to them? Would everything change once they get married? Probably. It's always been like that. Therefore, he tried to visualize that scenario, drawing in his mind a picture of what his future family would be like when he had children.

Coming home with a bouquet of tulips in hand and smiling to himself as he went to the front door, where the warm family home with scent of flowers wafting around the house. And then the door opened, and she stood there. Her hair pulled back in a sleek ponytail, her lips curved in a welcoming smile, and she cradled his pretty, dark-haired baby on her hip, their baby giggled and held out his pudgy arms. He cuddled the baby, kissed the top of his head and smelling talc along with his wife's subtle perfume.

What was going on? But that never happened as his cell phone rang at that exact moment and eased both his conscience and mind. Before he looked at the iPhone screen, he checked his watch. "Hello, Mom. What's new?"

Like as always, she asked him how his work was today, and then she told him come for dinner. But he turned her offer down and said sorry to her that he already had a dinner date. He hated lying to his mother, but that was a convenient lie, because he tried not to mention Tiffany to her. He knew his mother well, and didn't want to hide anything from her. She was more like a friend than a mother, she rarely scolded him, always making wise comments. At the age of sixty-two, she still looked chic and youthful, with an open mind and extensive knowledge of art that she had always shared with him, attractive creative ideas. She was never afraid to tackle difficult or controversial issues, which sometimes brought her more interesting things. He trusted her, excluding secrets about Tiffany. They had been nearly inseparable for the past six months, and the relationship was really going well. Just because he didn't want his mother responded instantly with amaze.

Jennies always understood her son and assured him she wasn't upset about it at all. "Don't worry about it. I know it's just because of your work."

His mother always knew how to praise. At her age, she still worked harder than anyone he knew. That's why she understood and sympathized, as well as she was proud of all of everyone in the family, and in their own way, each of them was doing well. More importantly, they were all happy in their suitable position. She never compared them to each other, even when they were young, and saw each of them as individuals, with different talents and needs. That made their relationship with her much better now. And each in their own way loved her more. She was like a best friend, but never lose a mother's love. They had her unconditional love and approval. Bush Jr liked it that way.

"Thank you for understanding, Mom. I would like you say sorry to father for me. At family reunion dinner, I will come and bring a surprise gift for the family."

"Okay, I will do that."

In her voice that reminded him that she knew him better than he knew himself that was why he smiled happily for having a very nice mom every time he talked to her and he stared at the phone after hearing the sound of click in his ear, and was grateful to his mother.

Chapter 2

Family is like branches on a tree, we grow in different directions, but the strength of our roots still holds us together.

The atmosphere at the Ocean Resort in Paris was fraught with applause in the majestic hall where music mixed with the flashing lights of cameras recorded scenes of models walking the catwalk with perfect legs, faces as beautiful as angels, long necks, and skin tone for the performance which was going well. The most famous faces in the fashion world were in attendance, sitting in the front row, staring at the unique fashion pieces that were launched with the concept of Season of Grace on the runway. As expected, Smiling and Mathew had been busy presenting a new style for this season, choosing the model duo in an unpopular opinion, but fitting perfectly love the transparent material, combined with leaves, water droplets, could see through the beauty inside of the body, added with long, wild, wet hair hanging down the shoulders, and hay branches attached to their hair and shoes, collaborating with new fashion models, accompanied by additional jewelry, it created a seductive and attractive appeal, and turned the rare appearance for the show to become a worthy breakthrough on the runway. Smiling smiled happily, standing at the back of the hall after the last model in the collection of beautiful see-through lace dresses that could see her naked breasts and much of her body's curves and was the final fashion design for the show. With a satisfied smile, Michael, the director of the show bowed to the guests on the runway, hurried over her and kiss her cheek, and whispered her ear.

"You impressed me again, Smiling! Your fashion show today was amazing, truly a masterpiece."

He took her hand and they quickly ran out onto the runway to join the models in resounding applause, and they bowed once more.

Her next show was in two hours, at the Prada Resort, but she had already canceled for her flight tonight. Currently, Smiling had asked for half a day off to arrange her plans. She hurried into her dressing room to take off her elegant outfit and changed into her street clothes. A simple pair of skintight jeans, white T-shirt that probably showed off too much of her figure, matching with Michael Kors Debbie leather and cork platform sandal. And as she walked across the lobby of the hotel, a tall, good-looking man was waiting for her and took her hand. She turned around and smiled at him. That was her fiancé, Mathew. He followed her through the hotel doors to the side of the street where the limo was parked and driver waiting for them.

And after Mathew got into the car and sat next to her, he leaned in and kissed her. "Great show, Smiling. I loved the last three dresses at the end. So did the crown. Stuart Nielsen was smiling from ear to ear." He was the most important fashion journalist in journalism. "Also, you're really amazing when you're on the stage."

To return the compliment, Smiling kissed him on the cheek. Mathew looked lovely, and he had loved her since the first day they met. He always told her that it was fate, and in the end, she believed it. That feeling now came to her again as memories of the past reappeared in her mind.

⁕⁂ ✳ ⁂⁕

Standing up with other tourists in line to approach the ticket counter, Smiling suddenly felt like someone was looking at her. Turning to her left, she focused on a tall, elegantly dressed man, who was brazenly focusing on her. But she didn't feel awkward, instead it made her more excited. She knew the soft silver-gray color of the natural fox fur coat did wonders for her blond hair, and the fresh raspberry silk blouse with its complementary wool skirt accentuated the pink color of her cheeks. Although the black boots were still feeling tight on her feet, they were the finishing touch to her outfit.

She was ravishingly beautiful, with straight shoulder-length blonde hair. Big brown eyes on an oval face. Gently curved cheeks and heart-shaped mouth, thick lips without lipstick. Even though she had a little makeup, she still looked as delicate as a fairy.

The man dressed in a dark brown suit, with a luxurious overcoat of brushed suede, continued to stare appreciatively at her. It felt good to see that it made her blush. With this gesture, she knew that if she kept looking at him, she would encourage him to come closer to her. She wasn't used to making flirtatious glances at men at the airport, so she forced herself to look away. She's not so bad that she had to flirt with a total stranger. However, there was something radiating from this man that made her wonder where she saw him? It's true that she'd met him, But where? Through the advertising department at Vogue, she wondered.

"Excuse me, Miss," a gentle touch on her arm accompanied by a warm, deep masculine voice broke her doubts and surprised her. "I believe you dropped this." He held up one of her slim leather gloves.

Searching in her coat pocket, Smiling realized he was correct. She flashed him a smile. "Thank you. I often lose my gloves. I should pin them to my sleeves like my mother did for me when I was a little girl." She said, looking into his startlingly clear blue eyes that made her smile turn awkward, and realized with certain alarm that this stranger was still holding the hand and pressed her glove in her palm. He was tall, good-looking, and his obvious concern for her was admirable.

Where did he feel he had seen this face before? She looked like someone walking on a fashion runway somewhere that he couldn't remember right now. "By any chance could you spend a few minutes chatting with me over a cup of coffee, if you don't mind?" He asked her naturally. "Because I feel like I've been struck by love at the first sight."

His gentle and lovely eyes made her heart flutter. His confidence and boldness show that he was someone who knew how to immediately seized the opportunity of what was coming and could set the direction for it. Words like 'Charisma' and 'Power' kept bouncing through her brain. She thought she that she would enjoy a cup of coffee and conversation with this strange man, a man she found more interesting than the other men she'd known.

"I really want to," she told him honestly. "However, my flight will depart soon. I'm going to New York." Why had she told him that?

His disappointment was clear on his face. "Maybe I have to hope that we will meet again. What do you think? Here let me give you my business card." Reaching into his inside pocket of his jacket, taking it out then handed it her. "Please, call me." He looked at her expectantly as she flipped the card over between her fingers.

The ticket agent seemed to have to interrupt by asking Smiling. "How can I help you, Miss? Do you want to get a ticket and register to go?"

Flustered, Smiling stepped up to the counter. "I'm sorry. I must go. Nice to meet you." She said, slid his card into her bag.

"You have my card, call, won't you?" A small salute and he was gone.

The ticket agent smiled warmly, knowing the situation between she and the handsome man who was now walking out of the terminal. In purchasing her ticket, she pulled her passport and American Express card out of her bag and offered them with her most brilliant smile to him. But Smiling never knew that when she took them out, she accidentally dropped his business card on the floor there. And ironically, the two of them never knew their name.

During the flight to New York, Smiling thought about her encounter with the stranger. It felt good to be admired. Just a bit of harmless flirting, she told herself, feeling slightly regret missing that opportunity, knowing that if she had time, she would drink coffee and chat with the stranger. What a fool, she told herself. Why was she thinking about that strange man? He was a very special person. There was something very mature, and very childish at the same time. Curious to know who he was and what he did for living, she rummaged through her handbag to look for his business card. It was gone. She couldn't find it, she lost it, and a pang of regret that told her she was losing more of a hold than just a card handed her by a stranger.

❧❧ ✳ ❧❧

The driver took them to the restaurant on the Avenue Montaigne where they sat outside under a large umbrella to shield them from the June sun as people passed by their table and stared. They didn't care about that, and it was obvious that they recognized not only Mathew, but Smiling as well. Notably, they could see her firm breasts visible through her thin silk white T-shirt. It was the current fashion trend that she had brought and was also the reason why she had become such hot rage in the fashion world without or need bras. Her breasts were neither small nor really big. Just full, soft and perfect, doing so well for her delicate body which reminded him of when he hurried by on his way to a meeting, and something made him stop. He couldn't believe he'd actually run into her again. Before that, he had called himself a fool a hundred times for missing the opportunity to get to know her the first time he saw her at the London Airport. Now she was here, running around the models in the outfits for the summer collection that could show off their naked breasts, directing them to pose for the photo session in front of the square. His old urge had now returned. He was a man who always went after what he wanted. He was completely convinced that their meeting was not accidental or coincidental, but was arranged by fate.

Seeing that she was directing the models, so it was inconvenient to come over and say hello, he just stood there and waited.

"Okay, change the posture, but keep your eyes straight. That's right."

Mathew stood nodding happily, slightly pursed lips in the smile and walked toward her as she stopped to review the photos. And she turned to face him. When their eyes met, she looked surprised and exclaimed. "You!"

"Destiny," he said, pleasing far more than he wanted to admit, but teasing her. "I gave you my card, but I don't think you'll call me."

She held out her hand to him and the shook hands happily. "I did try," she intentionally lied to defend herself, because she lost his business card. "But I just wasn't ready, because, you know. I'm not looking for date."

"I see. How about now? When can you have a cup of coffee with me?" He asked her constantly, trying to hide his concerns. What if she said no?

The request was simple, the meaning clear. And he was a stranger, but she immediately realized he was a nice guy, although a little nervous to talk to her, which made her a little wobbly. She met and knew a thousand of all kinds of men like him, but none of them attracted her attention like he did. Even though they were professional and lovely. Everything about him was interesting and different. She liked talking to him.

"It depends on how long it takes us to finish filming," she said vaguely. "But after this, I have to drive to the hall to arrange the props to match the outfits. I'll the last one to leave."

He might offer to drive with her, but he didn't want to hinder her work. "What's about the weekend? Is there any chance?" He asked bravely and hoped out of worry that he wouldn't let her slip away again as he realized there was something unusual about her, and he had to resist the urge to reach out and touch her.

She shook her head with a look of disappointment. "Pretty busy. Saturday and Sunday, I've got three filming sessions in a row." The only free time she had was in the evening, but at night was when she could be quiet to get inspiration for her sketches. "I'm also a magazine stylist, which means I'm in charge of a lot of photo shoots the models, for the back pages of the magazine and the fashion section."

He nodded, trying to understand what she meant, but he did. And it's hard for him to concentrate when he looked at her big, beautiful brown eyes, her smile, and her luscious lips. He couldn't figure out if she was trying to refuse him or if she was really as busy with work as she said.

"Do you have any day off?" He didn't give up, looking at her hopefully. Because there was something about her that attracted him. He had no idea what it was, but she seemed somewhat attracted to him. They both lived in London, working in related fields, and had many similar views. But no matter what, he must try all means.

"Yes, once in a while. Not very often. It's like I married to my job. But I'll take summer time vacation."

Her busy schedule proved it, but made him even more curious. "Do you like the work you do here?"

"Like?" She looked happy as she said. "I love it. This is my passion."

"Even turn down my offer?" He joked, and she laughed.

"Not really," she said honestly. She didn't want to be unfair to anyone, not to him. "You can come to one of my photo shoots if you want. We have two on-set in the studio next week, and one at C&L Country Club. We rented it for one night, and I've got four supermodels that night. They're flying from French and Milan. I'll probably get a dinner break around eight PM. You can pick me up at that time, and we can go for a walk, or go to the funny China Town where we can eat. Even though it's crowded and noisy, but food is delicious."

It sounded interesting, and he really looked forward to it coming. "I can't refuse your arrangement." He admitted, and she told him where to meet on Tuesday night, and then he thought of something he needed to know urgently. "But I don't even know your name."

She met his eyes, and smiled. "I'm really sorry. My name is Jennifer Jefferson. You can call me at Vogue if anything changes. I have a pager that I only use for work." She never gave out her phone number arbitrarily.

He recognized her name immediately and satisfied. "I won't call, Jennifer Jefferson. See you Tuesday night. Have fun on your photo-shoot this weekend."

She nodded, sensing his good intentions. He was decisive, but didn't push anyone. "See you on Tuesday. It's kind of funny we met like this."

"No big deal, but I've just been looking for you for the past month," he explained with a smile. "And like I said it was fate."

"I suppose so. And I'll see you on Tuesday, night," she reminded him with a wave as he turned around and walked away.

"Do you know Mathew Neilson?" Her assistant, Shirley Thomson asked. The person who was by her side full time. Shirley was a beautiful woman, who grew up in the fashion industry, and was also an advertising model. They had met when Shirley was working as a model for photo shoot while she was at Vogue. During that time, she really needed an assistant and Shirley was eager to work for her. She was twenty-two years old and full of ambition, willing to do any assigned job and hungry to learn to become a famous designer.

That's Mathew Neilson! The name made her aghast, but she turned her face away for afraid of revealing her expression, and tried to answer calmly. "Of course, I do."

Meanwhile, Mathew was smiling all the way to his conference office, and he could hardly wait to see her again. He had to admit that fate had been kind to him in arranging it for him.

❊❊*❊❊

"I ordered the food for us in advance." Mathew said across from her. He knew what Smiling liked to eat.

"What will I have for lunch?"

"Half a turkey sandwich with split pea soup and mineral water."

"Perfect." Smiling said as the waiter brought out two lunch plates along with two tall green bottles of Perrier.

And after the waiter left, she reached for her half sandwich and Mathew asked. "Do you think you can come back early for the couture shows next week?"

She took a bite of her sandwich, ate it deliciously, then drank the mineral water. "Sorry, Mathew. You know, going home to my family and coming back in time for the show is impossible. For this year, I think I will stay there a couple weeks to have fun with relatives and family. We've arranged everything, so why do you expect me come back before the show?"

Couple weeks without her. The hot summer was going to move even slower until she returned, and he realized how empty his life would be without her unexpected visits, phone calls and some surprises. "Yes, it's true. But I hope you will consider." He tried to convince her. "I really want your presence in that show."

"That's not a reasonable expectation, Mathew. What are you worried about?"

"Because without you, I'm not very confident. But why is that so important to you?"

Smiling couldn't believe her ears, she stopped eating the sandwich halfway to her mouth by his unreasonable question. Mathew seemed annoyed. Logically, he had to go with her, but he accepted another show. She was not only disappointed by that, but also upset because of his domineering personality.

Gathering with the family on the Fourth of July every year was her duty, as well as her siblings must return home by all means to pay homage to their beloved grandfather. That's difficult situation for her this year, because this was the busiest time for the fashion world to start promoting their brands, and it would become big throughout the month of September. With one collection following another, it was hard for her to leave because there was so much work for her to do, she hated to pull herself away, and delay her work, even for two weeks to leave, Mathew. They had been nearly inseparable for the past six months, and had traveled all over the world together. Their relationship was really strong well, but like her siblings, her homecoming was important to them all, especially, she didn't want to disappoint her parents, who looked forward to seeing their children and grandchildren, thrived and full of joy to have all of them to come home at the same time.

"Important because it's my family."

He didn't seem to accept her answer. Therefore, she'd explain so there would be no any disappointment or misunderstanding later. The holidays were sacred time for all of them. "It's not about the Fourth of July as a holiday. It's about time I spend with my family. Just like I go home for Thanksgiving and Christmas. I'm disappointed you won't go with me."

Mathew knew her work schedule well, the fact that she'd been away from the city for a long time before that didn't bother him. But recently he didn't understand why he was in that mood, and what he hadn't expected was the deep worry on her face. "Listen to me, Smiling. It's not that I don't want to go with you. You know I do, but to be honest, business wears us out and we need to spend time together. Besides you also know we can't break those contracts, so please understand that I can't come with you this time."

Smiling nearly choked on the sandwich she just ate, so she drank the mineral water. That was the problem. She felt her heart sink, listening to him and seeing his decisiveness.

Ambition was the cause. She had almost everything to herself. Except for true love, that was the reason she looked for a man who cared and shared her feeling and emotions. Career orientation had created a barrier between them. She realized that when she observed the way parents loved each other. If he chose a long-term relationship with her, what he needed to focus on was caring and understanding her family first. If not, she had to fight about it, and wanted to verify Mathew's love towards her.

"If you want me to understand you, Mathew, then I want you understand me, too." She said coolly, and suddenly realized that she and Mathew seemed to have a long distance. Now, in everything they did, they must ask the other. He was a kind, decent, loving man, but perhaps work had unintentionally become a barrier separating their feelings. If so, the tow of them needed to fit it, improve this problem. "Everything has been arranged, we cannot change it." "You look strange." He commented.

"We haven't argued in a long time. In fact, I don't think we've ever actually done that." She said gently. "Look, Mathew. Why don't we just do what we have to do, and then we can spend some time together and enjoy a vacation?"

And Mathew felt his resolve weaken, finished chewing his sandwich, and tried to change the subject. "Then when are you leaving for Florida?"

"I'm leaving tonight. The flight will leave at two AM." She felt sad, so she put her soup-spoon down on the table, trying to hide her emotions and encouraged him. "You don't have to worry. Shirley knows how to solve the rest of my designs and she'll arrange and handle the job well until I return."

"I know," Mathew put his bottle down on the table. Understanding her sense of responsibility and always telling him to trust Shirley, she could fill her role during her absence. "I'm going to miss you."

This was not the first time they'd been apart since they'd known each other. He confessed that he fell in love with her a month after their first date. She loved him too, and a year later, they were engaged. But there was a part of her that always held back. Maybe because Mathew and her family were not on good terms as she expected or maybe it was because she didn't trust him. Not exactly like that, but she pushed that thought aside, refusing to deal with that issue now. "I'm going to miss you, too."

Mathew glanced at his watch. "I'll take you to the airport." He said, pushing his plate aside.

❋❋ ✻ ❋❋

From the restaurant, the driver took them to the Ritz Hotel where Mathew dropped her there, and as soon as he left, she packed her clothes and essentials into her carryon, then took a shower, washed her hair and rested for a few hours. But before she could do that, Shirley Thomson, her blonde-haired assistant arrived with some fabric samples that she had to review carefully before delivering them to the sewing factory, along with her airplane tickets. passport and some cash for her before she left. She had to leave the hotel at seven PM, in time to check in for a flight at Paris Airport at nine o'clock and would depart at one PM. She expected to arrive in New York in ten hours, which was five AM, local time, and from there she would catch another flight at seven AM to the Orlando Airport. If there's no delay. she would be home with her family before noon, and would have plenty of time with her parents until their dinner. She had called her sister, Gloomy last week, and they were coming home half an hour apart.

"Thank you, Shirley." Smiling said, after choosing the type of fabric to recommend to the client, signing off on some contact documents, and looking through some files, and an hour later Shirley left. She was confident that Shirley was fully capable of handling their clients while she took days off.

✿ ❊ ✱ ❧ ❦

Smiling smiled at Mathew two hours later, when he waited for her outside the hotel, watching her on the plush rear seat of limousine after the driver put her luggage in the trunk of the car. He drove with her to the airport as promised. It was going to be a long journey for her, but there was nothing for her to do, just put her head back against the seat and relax.

A VIP service was waiting right outside the airport when they got there. The greeter recognized her immediately. They had taken care of her before. Mathew arranged everything for her as always. They checked her luggage in for her, and they left them in front of the security gate.

"Take care of yourself, and have a good time in Florida," he said his final goodbye, and then kissed her long hard. "I'm going to miss you."

He seemed looked sad and abandoned. "Me too," She was also a bit emotion, remembering their passionate lovemaking last night, and he suggest they get married after she returned. "I'll call you often. I promise."

They always contacted each other via phone whenever they were apart, even for a few hours. Mathew liked to keep in touch with the woman he loved, as if she is always by his side. They had agreed not to get married for a couple more years, but their lives completely intertwined. She was thinking about his suggestion. She knew that was what he wanted too, and she was willing to consider it.

Mathew pulled her into his arms for a long embrace then gave her a quick kiss, and took one last look at the woman he loved before she made her way through the security gate.

After completing the procedure, she waved goodbye one last time to her tall, handsome man also waving at her with sad and regretful eyes.

Home. How funny she thought. London was where she decided to settle and grow with her career, but Melbourne would always hold her heart. The first place where she understood what family, and love, and affection were. After settling into her spacious, luxurious and surprisingly comfortable seat in British Airways first class for the flight to New York City, and the flight departed on time. She knew the flight time would pass faster if she could read a book or sleep during the flight. She decided to do both. But first of all, she had to get some sleep, so she lowered her seat as low as a bed and determined to drift off to sleep.

Chapter 3

The love of family is one of greatest blessings in life.

Jennies sipped her tea from the cup that her Spanish housekeeper brought to her in the living-room after hanging up the phone with Bush Jr, and continued to sit on the sofa, thinking about him who she was lucky to have. Her son was the most affectionate of all her children. He loved everyone in his family, and never gave her a moment of worry. In addition to his superior abilities, he was a combination of the best elements of the Tu and Nguyen families, plus Jefferson's. Yes, Bush. Jr had inherited many of her good genes. He was handsome, intelligent, and courageous. But it's easy to trust people, easy to be taken advantage of, especially women. She didn't care about those issues or his business, but his love life was her top priority, and she frequently worried. At the age of over thirty years old, her son was still unmarried, or at least had brought his girlfriend home to introduce to the family. In addition, she also cared about her other children and grandchildren. They were good people who in the world of Jennies Jefferson had been a legendary victory for more than three decades. She was the founder, guiding light, principal designer, and CEO of the most important men's and women's ready-to-wear lines throughout the United State, and rapidly reaching international markets. With the set of Bush Jr, Justin and Gloomy and along with her team, she had a businessman, a lawyer, and a doctor on her hand. Her pride in them was as great as her love, even though, she still had to think about their comfort, as well as their tastes and feelings. She believed that she was a good mother, an easy-going, reasonable, generous-spirited mother-in-law, and an affectionate, adoring, devoted grandmother. Those factors had given her a sense of satisfaction after many years since she joined Jefferson's family and always reminded family members of their responsibilities when bearing the surname Jefferson. She lived exactly as she was taught, getting what she wanted in life. Proving that she had done exactly what she wanted and what she'd promised. She accompanied her children from childhood until they became adults, and she didn't mind the sacrifices she'd had to make at all. At the age of sixty-two, although she had tiny wrinkles and lines around her eyes and mouth, it was still possible to judge that she was still a beautiful woman, with an illustrious career, and a golden life.

Jennies looked back on the past thirty-two years of her life, despite there were many ups and downs, but she was successful in every way which brought money, status, a home which gave her great pleasure, a job she enjoyed and had a tenderhearted husband who loved her and with whom she was still in love after thirty years of marriage.

She was a rich woman, not only in dollars and possessions and property, but also had a large family. But family was always her top concern. Always and always would be a part of her life. But she never expected that they would disperse and live separately like that. The house felt silently, a far cry from the old days when they were young and lived here. There were no toys or clothes left on the floor or lying around in the living room. TV didn't turn on, the music didn't play, the fridge was full, the phone didn't ring often, their friends didn't come and the house became empty, neat, and clean, and she wasn't used to it, even during the years they left to go to college, and then lived for their own lives with their own families. She knew that it would be right for them to leave when they grew up, but she hated it anyway, even they fulfill their duty as children, remembering her birthday and sending birthday cards for her. On the contrary, Jennies also kept endless lists of their birthdays and always remembered to send birthday cards or their favorite toys. They were married to nice women and men, had happy, stable marriages and children, and in cities where they liked, lived and worked and the worlds they had there. Even though they visited both of them during the holidays such as Christmas, Thanksgiving and others occasions, but nothing made her happier than when they came home, even complacent knowing that her whole family would be gathering tonight and tomorrow.

At that very moment, she could hear the front door opening and closing, causing her to abandon her memories and returned to the present. She rushed to greet Brian with his briefcase in his hand and Steady at his side. As usual, she said. "You're home." Then went to hug Steady and kiss her husband on the cheek.

He felt the stress of today's busyness slowly disappear when he got home and was happy to see his wife. "Hi, honey."

He always greeted that way, and following routine, he loosened his tie, placed his briefcase on the chair in the hall, and glanced at the pile of mails on the table.

"You look tired. Was today a difficult day?" She asked as she took off his vest then handed to their butler already standing in the hall way and apparently to greet them enthusiastically, and Steady went straight to the kitchen to find something to drink.

He smiled at her beautiful face. "Yes. There are a few snags in the contract that I'm reviewing."

It was the same smile that had made her heart ache for so many years. "Can you talk to me?"

"Why not," he slipped his arm around her and they went into the living room where he could sit comfortably and relaxing on the couch. He loved every time came home, telling her about his working day, even though they still called each other during the day. "But you know, I don't want to bring troubles home, honey. What about yours?" "Good," she said.

Should be at the age of sixty-five, the old age would bring havoc, but he was still in good shape, still attractive in a cute, manly way. Diligent physical training and jogging had made his body lean and toned and his head had streaks of gray hair around his temples, small wrinkles around his eyes. Even those small traces of time only made up in a gentle attractiveness. And just looking at him still made how much she was in love with him, and tingle. He was kinder, gentler, more considerate, in fact he was more sophisticated and seasoned, and even better looking than he had been when they got married, and all of that was in build and coloring, he was similar to his son. It was like seeing the same person thirty-one years later. They loved their home, their children, their careers, and each other. There was nothing more than either of them would have added, except maybe had any more children. She'd been thirty-seven when Bush Jr was born, and at the time that had almost seemed too old to her, so she stopped. And now she regretted not having at least one more child. However, her six adopted children were enough to bring them great joy. Realizing that she smiled warmly at him, stood went to the kitchen, enthusiastically pouring him a glass of wine without asking, and then brought it and gave it to him. He looked like his pressure dropped when he realized that. At this age, he shouldn't drink alcohol, but at times like this, it would help him relieve the stresses of the day.

"Thanks," he said, sipped the wine as she happily sat down, snuggled up close to him, and he put an arm around her shoulders.

She could see how tense he was as he finished the wine in the glass and placed it on the table. He didn't seem to change much, but on the contrary, he only seemed to get better as he got older. But lately, she saw it differently, perhaps because she worried about him. He had to work hard on two important tests for heart disease and high blood pressure in his old age when complications could happen at any time. He would have to have regular health check-ups that she always reminded him of, otherwise his health condition would get worse. He was her love, her life, that why she wanted to take good care of him. She wanted to live with him for another forty years. Over the past thirty-one years, she had gone through a bittersweet life with him, and didn't want to change anything. However, her only wish now was to spend the rest of her life with him. But it's time for them to enjoy their old age. "I think it's time for us to think about retirement. We have worked hard over the years. Let our children run the business. Let's spend time together like our first time living together in the past, honey."

Her scent had been the same for many years. He took her hand, brought it to his lips and kissed it. The ring he'd given her so many years before was cool against his skin. Ngân Nguyễn although was over sixty, but she was not like other women who fade away as they got older, because she knew how to take care of herself. To him, she always looked beautiful and sexy to him. She was still look good in shape and beautiful with minimal makeup, her long hair, her charming lips, her beautiful appearance and beautiful voice, just like in those days when everything had felt magical. He recalled the first time he took her to his room in the hotel. Her face was red with the kind of wine they'd love to drink then they'd spent hours in their room making love. That's a lifetime ago, and they had shared it thirty years later, they still as loved as ever. They respected each other, and loved each other passionately. She was everything precious to him, and he's secretly grateful to fate for giving them everything they desire. "Good idea, honey. I thought about it, and I also remembered our happy past."

She looked at him lovingly, because he knew how much it meant to her. He tilted his head, kissed her lips softly, lingeringly as the passion like before came to them again. "Why don't we go away for couple weeks next month when time allows. You have every right to decide and let me know."

Steady returned to the living room, holding a glass of orange juice, and saw her parents kissed each other which made her smile at the way they showed affection for each other everywhere. After nearly thirty-three years of marriage, they were still very much in love, and it showed as they sat on the sofa and cuddle like a couple of teenagers. They had been arguments over the years, although they had never been serious. Their marriage had been stable since the day they married. She couldn't imagine being lucky enough to have a marriage like theirs, just wanted more not less. The men she met in business were not the kind of men she wanted to be involved with. Because she had no patience for bullshit, lies or narcissism, and the most of which had turned out badly or been disappointing for one reason or another after she had been set up on the blind dates. Putting the glass down on the coffee table, she sat across them and smiled.

"Is Brother Bush Jr coming to dinner by any chance?" She asked them, even though she didn't like it. Her younger brother was coming to dinner with the family as usual on Thursday, and the question made her mother looked straight in the eye.

Steady worked for her after graduation, and she quickly determined that her designs were prosaic and tended to lean more toward past styles that had been reliable and solid, but she had little of the forward vision toward the future that she looked for a design assistant position. But she had the strengths and usefulness of skillful marketing, had a great mind and arranged details that could make people pay attention. She quickly separated Steady from her design team and put her to work as her assistant. Her responsibilities increased rapidly during the past thirteen years with her. At the age of thirty-seven, Steady became vice president in charge of marketing, and they reviewed all of their advertising and promotion campaigns. Together they discussed and give each other feedback on advertising images until they gleamed. Steady was brilliant at what she done.

"Not tonight. What makes you ask?" Her mother asked with her face open and concerned, because she did ask her more than twice already.

"No, particular reason," her voice sounded foolish, naive even to her own ears. "I just need him to confirm some things that I'm doing."

"What's thing?" Her dad interjected curiously, looking at her with searching eyes. "I might be help."

Steady knew he wasn't a fighter. He was a loving person. Because of this, she tried to divert him away from his question. "Thank you, Dad. Don't worry. I..."

"I'm not worry, but the look on your face says it, Steady." He interrupted, staring at her intently. "That's why I'm concerned."

"Honey, why don't you go upstairs and take a shower?" Jennies cut in, forcing her husband to stop. "Leave it to me. I can handle this."

"Okay." He agreed, kissing her on the cheek for reminding that it was tactful and much wiser for him to leave this to mother dealing with daughter. "I'll leave you two alone to talk." And then he got up, and left.

As soon as her father left, her mother asked. "Is something wrong, Steady? You should tell me."

"Wrong? Why?" She forced a laugh. "What makes you suspicious?"

Normally she didn't know what her daughter was thinking, but today something bothered her, and because it's bothering Steady, it's bothering her too. "Steady, I feel like you have been acting a little strangely lately. It seems like you're worried about something, I guess."

Steady knew nothing good ever came of arguing with either of her parents, though her dad was really easier to talk to. But her mother's perceptiveness never ceased to amaze, and her words stung a little. They were as tuned in to each other as any mother and daughter had ever been. And she was a woman who knew how to size people up and subtly manipulate them into telling the truth. What a marvel she was, but it annoyed her.

Wincing at that tone, she met her mother's eyes. "Don't be too skeptical, Mom!" Steady shook her head to explain. "In the guest list that Dad gave me, I just want to ask if Bush Jr invites anyone else at the last-minute, especially people who are not family members?"

"I thought about that too. You see, Steady. Bush Jr hasn't really had many friends, I mean close friends. He'd been caught up with business most of the time, and the family. Oh, wait a minute, I suddenly remembered a couple who used to be the owners of a hotel that your brother bought it, and they were also your grandfather's friends. Their names are Angela and Danny Stanley. I'm sure he will invite them, but..."

"He did," Steady cut in. "They're on the list."

"Then I can't think of anyone else."

At that moment the doorbell rang, making the whole thing off nicely. Steady stood up. "I'll get it."

She hurried to the front door and opened it. *What in the world?* Her eyes widened, her breathing became more rapid and her chest felt heavy when she saw him outside the door. And she felt like she was going to pass out from his appearance, greeting her with a floral bouquet, and flashed her one of his most charming smiles. "You look thrilled to see me."

They stood where they were, on either side of threshold, and he saw the lack of response on her face, so he added hopefully. "Are you going to invite me in?" "Steady. Who's that?" said Jennies.

She was too shocked to respond or what else to do, just out of panic, but she told herself and tried to force herself to remain outwardly calm. *Don't let him see you frightened. Don't let your mother and family get angry, even though they can help you solve this problem for you.* "My friend, mom," she replied and stood aside, letting him enter.

He walked in on the wide squares of rose-veined tiles in the foyer, and gave her a bouquet flowers, trying to appease and please her in the only way he knew how.

It made her heart soften even though she knew what she was doing was stupid. He didn't care for her, possibly never had.

The man behind Steady looked handsome with sandy blond hair and bright eyes, a well-proportioned muscular figure in a suit without tie, and he brought flower for Steady that she had never seen anyone in her group of friends doing it, but he looked familiar. Jennies walked over and extended her hand in greeting.

Finding her charming, he took her offering hand and brought it to his lips, kissing her wrist. "Nice to meet you, Mam. I'm Paul Sicilians, how do you do?"

He much more polite and poised than Steady's usual friends and introduced himself with impeccable manners. But she was also sensitive to her mood so that she could read the tension, doubt, and anger on Steady's face as she placed the bouquet of roses on the hall table and was trying to give a forced smile.

"It's even better than pleasant to see you, Paul." She said and, in an effort, to make him feel welcome by giving him a hug and offered a glass of wine, but in turning, he smiled and said he would prefer a cup of tea.

It was a welcome unusual gesture compared to the amount of cans of beer that Steady's friends always consumed every time they visited. "Come into the living room and sit down. We'll have tea." She invited and asked the mandarin to bring them tea.

"It'll be brought up in a few minutes, ma'am." Margaret said, flashed a quick smile and hustled toward the kitchen.

They made their way into a high-ceiling living room. Jennies sat down on the sofa while Paul sat next to Steady in a matching one opposite her. She observed Paul through objective eyes, endeavoring to see him as clearly as possible. If this man had intention toward her daughter, and she was certain he did, she meant to find out everything there was to find out about him. "So, Paul, tell me, how are the things in your business?"

He understood that it wasn't a question, but an interrogation. "As a photographer, I capture the beauty of any genre I see. That's what I do for a living."

Margaret returned, placed the silver tray with a teapot and three porcelain cups on the glass-top coffee table, then stood still, waiting to see if her master needed anything else.

Looking up at her, Jennies said. "Thank you, Margaret. I'll take it from here."

Margaret nodded her understanding, Jennies waited until she left before she dropped a piece of lemon in the China cup, then picked up the pot to pour the tea into it. "Being a photographer must be very interesting. Had to create many poses to get a vivid image. You must have artistic talent which I think requires a creative mind to be able to do it."

"You can say that way. But my field of expertise draws inspiration from people for my photography. I mean pieces of life and that's the art that I follow. Their reality often reflects their inner self on the outside, so it will reflect a different image at different angles on the camera. I know how to capture those moments, because those are important memories that need to be preserved." He answered, smiling as he silently took the delicate cup she offered, and then said politely. "Thanks, ma'am."

Jennies nodded, amused at his interpretation and watching he sipped his tea. "You know, Paul, I admire your work. I've seen your gallery photos. But those artistic photos always make me think and wonder." She watched his reaction, her gaze never leaving his face as she took a swallow of her tea.

"Will you?" He wondered if she was being sarcastic, and the fact the tea was hot tea was the only thing that would do the trick. "I usually don't discuss this aspect, but since you seemed interested, I think we will comfortably go deeper into this field."

Actually, she knew him well and recognized him right away when he walked in. She smiled. "Did I offend you by saying that?"

"No, ma'am." He put the cup down on the low antique table between them and leaned back against the Venetian velvet cushions on the cream sofa, ready to answer all the questions she might have.

She noticed that he was smart, and they looked very sweet together, but she also sensed that he's hiding something and saw something unusual in her daughter's eyes which made her face was tense, scared, losing her beautiful features.

They chatted for few more minutes, but Steady couldn't hold on to her suppressed mood, so she asked her mother for permission to take Paul to her room, because she had something private to discuss, even though she knew her mother would never allow that.

Just like her, Jennies couldn't bear to see her daughter seriously unhappy, and it hurt her heart to see misery etched on her face. However, she reluctantly agreed, not wanting to delve into the private aspect between the two of them, and thought that they needed private space to resolve the issue. On the other hand, she sometimes didn't understand this daughter's feelings. Of course, Steady had always been a sweet, lovable person, but she herself simply lack the depth when it came to doing something other than choosing material for an outfit or meal from the menu. Steady, with her stubbornness, composure, and unshakable ambitions, was completely beyond her scope. Still, Jennies wasn't a fool to not see the way Paul looked at her daughter and understood many things. With a strange mixture of anxiety and leery as she watched them quietly ascend the stairs.

As soon as they stepped into her bedroom, and the door closed behind them, Paul was be full of admiration as looking around. There was a huge array of pillow atop the modern four-poster bed, was covered with a lacy white spread and plumped with thick quilt. Antique perfume bottles and cosmetics on the dressing table that he could know exactly how it would smell. It would smell the way her skin did. Her closet was full of designer made especially for her, her shoes were the best in Rome, in Florence, in Paris. Another closet contained all kinds of handbags with famous brand such as Hermès in every color and type of leather, from python to alligator to calf. Bookshelves were displayed many trophies. Weigh bench shoved into a corner, big flat television mounted on the wall near the gauzy white curtains that fluttered outside the open sliding doors and windows, and the private bath. Truly this was the room of rick girl. But somehow, he thought that this was also a welcoming place for a man like him who longed for an hour, a night in the comfort of cuddling her in a thin white sexy nightgown on the bed where her hair was spread out and the candles lit around the room. He wore a tight little smile, burying his self-disgust then went straight to the thing he needed. "Have you got what I ask for?"

His words made she go cold inside, and her temper began to tick like a bomb. How had she ever thought him handsome? How had she ever fantasized about him? How had she ever considered making love to him? What a messy, confusing she had created, how many mistakes, and how many broken hopes. Their relationship ended when he used her nude photos as blackmail.

"I thought that fifty grand I paid you last month bought me the last copies."

"I know," he said, having the good sense to look guilty. "That's a lie. But this time is different, I swear to you I'll give all the originals."

She wanted to slap him, to deny what had to so obviously been the truth, but she had to put all her anger into her hands and clench them into fists. What a bastard he was, what a hypocrite. God, why did she trust him? He always brought copies, always promised they were the last copies in existence as he sold them to her for large amounts of cash, always insisted on closing the deal with a glass of champagne. And a month later, he showed up again with other requests. She shot him a look of contempt. "Save it for someone who'll believe it."

They each knew that they were still at war with each other. But Paul flirted with her condescendingly as if she were being ridiculous. "Go ahead, cursing me all you want." Then he moved quickly without giving her time to react, grabbing around her waist and pulled her against his body, then kissed her on the lips, before she could do anything more than get upset. "But cursing won't help."

Panicked and irritating, she raised her hands against his chest, trying to push him away and said in an angry voice. "Let go of me!"

"If I only could," he said. Then, as if her words had finally registered, he dropped his hands and backed off a step. "You really want me to?"

Steady gave him a sardonic glance. "Yes!"

She didn't expect that he was that kind of person. In fact, she was afraid and angry in equal measure, and that the only thing she knew for sure. Her mouth went dry as a sudden memory surfaced, reminding her of how she'd met him many times at the company's charity events, even once at a Christmas party her parents threw. After all, the only time she'd any direct personal contact with him was agreeing to be a model to pose for the photos shoot taken at his studio for an interesting article on People's magazine, and asked for her phone number. From then on, she started dating him, and they'd gone out. That was a quick, amicable date when he'd pick her up in his luxury Audi and took her to dinner at the Italian Restaurant where everyone seemed to know him. He pulled out a chair for her and complimented her on her beauty her. He said that several times throughout dinner, using it as filler for a conversation that faltered more than it flowed.

"Then I advise you to comply with my request."

Naive fool, this lying bastard had never loved her while she quickly fell in love with him. The problem was that she didn't see his true nature clearly, because he hid his past as best he could and often made-up stories about his life. She disgusted him now, the man seemed to have no regard for her, no love, no kindness, no respect, and no warmth, and had only been after her money. What he cared about was the world around him, and she was a convenient ATM machine.

"This is never going to end, is it, Paul? You keep on bleeding me until there's nothing left. You're such a bastard. Why are you treating me this way?"

The Jennies Foundation business would definitely bring him celebrities. Over the past years, he had received invitations to the most importable places, parties, and charity events, full of millionaires. They were actually pretty nice people, contributing millions and millions of dollars to worthwhile charities every year. Where he was greeted with air kisses from all sorts of people, he had hardly shaken hands with before. He knew he was reasonably good looking, but he had never considered himself exceptionally attractive. But he thought he knew how he could get women interested in him, and going to bed with him without threatening or complicated. On the contrary, it's erotically enjoyable.

Women had always been his problem. He liked them, liked everything about them, and didn't discriminate. The color of their hair or their eyes or their skin color, he loved them all, whether they were tall, short, thin, fat. It didn't matter to him. They were all wonderful, and to him, each one showed their uniqueness. Because they liked him too. Plain and simple. His stupid libido had always been his downfall. But he only changed his promiscuous ways with women he knew well, especially wealthy women with whom he could use them for sex, found a way to seduce first, of course, then later came the deeper pleasures. He'd never been one to shy was from danger, especially if it involved a slightly over the top woman like the sly, gorgeous and stunning Jeremy Jefferson as she performed in the show. She was dressed for the occasion in silky dress that must have been very expensive and the diamonds that sparkled around her wrists and neck. He always recognized her and knew she was Mr. Brian's pampered daughter. She was truly his guardian and would be the perfect solution for him. So, he wouldn't give up this delicious bait easily. *Hello, sweetheart, you'll wait to see. You won't be able to get rid of my hand.* He had been successful. It wasn't that hard as he knew how to distract her with charm to approach. At first, they simply chatted, then brought her into his love trap.

"Come on, you know I wouldn't do that. You know that, right babe?" He said without emotion, reaching out to touch and squeeze her butt. "I know how much you hate me, but the problem is that with my great career, I can't admit I've failed, and I'm in financial trouble, so when things get really bad. Especially borrowing money from gangsters at high interest rates, and they threaten to break my legs if I don't pay back the amount of money I owed them. If you love me, please help me one last time, otherwise they will do it."

No matter which angle she considered, it still didn't make sense to her. He still believed he'd possessed her. Her heart no longer had any feeling for him nor was she, his possession. which made her see even more clearly the depth of his depravity and cruelty. She used all her strength to push him away. "Fuck off. That's your problem. Not mine."

That's where the problem was. His charm began to disappear, replaced by anger and heat. However, he didn't think he could threaten her with physical harm, or at least not to make her notice it, because he had to move forward further than he intend to accomplish, at least to her. He was the one who held the key, the person who could ask her to meet his requirements and accept all the risks, because he couldn't ignore a loan shark. "Look, that amount of money is small number compares to the prestige of the Jefferson family."

She shook her head in disbelief and remembered it a second times at a cocktail party for his friends who were painters at the Artemis Gallery in Miami, where the vibrant music from the seven-members band seemed never to get tired. Laughter and water splashed from a pool, surrounded by hot, sexy and seductive Spanish girls in tiny two-pieces bathing suits. That night, they started experimenting with drugs, getting high on coke and marijuana, those were the first time she willed herself shared it with him. Smoking and using illegal substances were absolutely taboo in the family and was not good for her health. But in order to not be a coward, she was brave, and passionate to enjoy that moment with him, and then had sex with him indiscriminately and unconsciously. Now it had become her nightmare. After that night when she woke up naked in bed with him in his studio, she remembered nothing. It was obvious she had drunk too much alcohol. Or because of the effected of stimulants? Therefore, after leaving, she didn't consider coming back to see him. But few days later she ran into him again in the fashion show and realized that he was pleasant company.

Instant love, she thought Paul could became a regular part of her life. She'd slept with him again, and he'd told her he loved her. But he'd proved himself to be her worst nightmare. Because the next they were strangers when it was impossible to imagine how someone who was her lover, could bury his pride and asked her for a loan to pay for his debt from the loan shark.

Because she was blindly in love, she was weak-heart and helped him to wire him fifty thousand dollars, but it didn't stop there. He'd kept asking her to borrow more money. This time he wanted her to give him cash. This wretched nature of his made her hurt and began to doubt him. A man who had spoiled her, loved her and slept with her, suddenly became a stranger who'd lied about or omitted nearly everything important about himself. Therefore, she quickly left him and ended her relationship with him. But she also wanted to know what kind of person he was, so she hired a private investigator who was willing to look into every aspect of Paul's life, and what she wanted to know.

According to her investigation, Paul was still single, but he often picked up any number of women to seek help for his sex addiction, who were easier to deal with as they looked no deeper than his expensive suits, flashy cars, famous friends and healthy bank account. In addition, his total drug intake since his teens consisted of half a dozen joints and one experiment with cocaine fifteen years earlier with his friend. As to alcohol, he was only ever seriously intoxicated at private dinners or parties. In a bar he would seldom have more than one large, strong beer. He also liked to drink cold martini. But the worst part was he had a gambling problem. That's why his business began to struggle a couple of years ago, and in his tax file and financial statement, she realized just how horribly in debt he was. Back taxes, credit-card bills, overdue lease payments made his credit rating was a disaster and his financial situation was so desperate that he declared bankruptcy.

It's no surprise that any liar would sooner or later overreach. True enough, he ended up blackmailed her to solve his problem, and no wonder, because by nature he was a bastard. She'd already paid him more than two hundred thousand dollars over the last six months. Her cash was drained, and she could withdraw money from her bank account. Now, he asked another $150,000 dollars in cash, and came all the way here to extort money. If not, not only her naked photos, but also her other depraved photos would spread quickly on the internet, and they would be the hottest topic. Her heart felt like it was breaking into a million pieces, causing her stomach to contract, and whenever she thought of that moment, it filled her heart with a renewed hatred and wondered how she could have ever given herself so cheaply to someone so undeserving. But that was the trouble with having millions stashed away in stocks, real estate, or the bank vault-someone like him was always after a piece of it. You could never be certain if they cared for you because they truly found you fascinating and really loved you, or if they were attracted to you because of the number of zeroes on your bank statement. She reminded herself and she should know him better since the night she went out with him, but he assured her that it would be the last time and go away. She wasn't that foolish anymore. She didn't trust him blindly. The battle really began since then and starting a nightmare when he rang the doorbell of her parents' house.

They hadn't known anything about this, and she had no intention of telling to them or of pretending none of this had ever happened. Of course, they would help and protect her to get out this mistaken she'd made. That was an option, but she also knew full well that they would not solve her problem with him with money, but with power so that he could disappear from this world for threatening Jefferson's daughter and family. That why she decided to clear the matter up quickly by herself and kept him out of their lives, and she couldn't. One hundred fifty thousand dollars wasn't hard for her to get. She would never have considered herself spoiled. She worked for what she wanted and fortunately she hadn't lived extravagantly over the past few years. And she did, indeed, have her mother's head for business, not for money. The trust fund from her grandfather could keep her comfortable enough so that she could drift from interest from interest as she chose, after she turned it over to her father to invest. Big problem was how she could withdraw that cash amount out her bank account without her parents' notice, and didn't want her checks to record any of those payments, and confrontation wasn't her style. So, she sought help and planned to ask her younger brother to handle it instead. She trusted him implicitly, and trusted his handle. He had two characteristics she put great store in. Honor and integrity, but beside that, the men like Bush Jr always found the right weapon to help her out of this matter better than her parents. But now, for the first time in her life, she was truly scared of this man.

"Because you want to pay off your gambling debts, you blackmailed me?" She screamed at him. "Christ! I think there's something wrong with your brain."

"Do you? Well, dear, it doesn't bother me what you think. You'd better imagine it's the biggest scandal for you, and I can't imagine that your family will be terribly pleased with the news, if I'll send your pictures to them. That's a warning."

They stood there for a moment, equal in their antagonism. "Is this how you treat your women with threats?"

"I'm not doing that. I'm giving you facts and think, Steady. Does your family like threats? So what do you want to choose, honey?" His smile was cruel, dangerous, and not at all humor.

Tears threatened to flow, but she blinked them away. She wouldn't give him the satisfaction of seeing her like that. In addition, she had to restrain herself from slapping him on the face because of the vision he had drawn. She knew how vindictive he could be, and she didn't to start a war with him. She knew what he was capable of. So, she pretended to give up. "Since its cash. I'm working on that and you will get it soon, to settle things between us and leave me alone."

His eyes glinted with victory. "I try my level best, Steady. Do it one more time for me, I will go away, for good this time. I promise."

What a hypocrite! Who could believe the promises of a deceiver? But she'd do what he said, because there's no other option. She gave him a smug smile for his words didn't mean a thing. What kind of fool would take comfort in the word of a criminal? "How touching. But what I know about you is that you're a liar who took advantage of me, Paul. If I recall."

He couldn't refute that and knew she had lost trust in him. "Whatever, but I can wait any longer. Time is money, babe. You've got a couple of days to decide how you want to play it. Get rid of your pictures, or pay the consequences. You know where to reach me."

The pain came again. He always did what he said. She shut her eyes then opened them again as there was a knock on the door outside, and they all turned to pay attention to her father's voice. "Steady! Dinner is ready. Please come down to eat."

She wanted to say she wasn't hungry, but otherwise it would only make her parents more suspicious. "I'll be right down Dad." She said, taking a deep breath as she looked at Paul.

"I would like to have dinner with your family." He said as she opened the door and stuck her head out, making sure nobody nearby, and then glancing back to him.

"I don't think that's a good idea. If you want to get money from me, it's better not to let them doubt you."

She had a point, and they went back downstairs, into the kitchen where Steady found her mother placing a bowl of salad on the dining table and her father was sitting and reading the newspaper with a glass of wine next to him on the table. His head turned, looked up at her with a smile, and recognized Paul's presence.

Paul stepped forward with his hand reaching out and introduced himself. "I'm Paul. It's great honor to meet you, sir."

With careful consideration, Brian put the newspaper he was reading down next to the glass and stood up. "Thanks, I know exactly who you are, same goes." He took his hand and shook firmly, and then offered. "You're just in time for dinner, Paul, are you staying to join us, aren't you?"

"That's a nice invitation, sir." He glanced at Steady who had an expression of displeasure at all. Therefore, he forced the polite smile on his face. "I'd love to, but thanks. I actually have an evening appointment and it's a long drive."

"In that case, I won't stop you. See you next time then."

"I hope so." He replied, shook hand to goodbye, and turned to Steady who was standing very quietly nearby. "And I think Steady has an important work to do."

He said goodbye to them, and in an instant, Steady pulled him to the front door, opened the door and pushed him out.

"Good night, Steady. Remember what I said." A crooked smile tugged at the corner of his mouth. "There's nothing I can't do. Remember that."

That expression contained an implicit warning. "Bastard!" She tried to keep her voice low, watched him get into his car and drove away so fast that the tires rubbed against the road surface and screeching in protest. She found that she was shaking violently when she shut the door. For the first time in her life, she had actually wanted to kill someone. She immediately imagined a way to kill him, envisioning him crawling at her feet and begging her for mercy. But she would be merciless, plucked his eyes from their sockets and the heart from his chest. She wanted to ease him from the earth.

Paradoxically, it was at this same moment that she felt as though she had begun to function again, and she discovered in herself a surprising emotional balance. She was obsessed with a man and he was on her mind every waking minute. But she had begun to think rationally again. If she was going to find a way of destroying him, she must keep her mind clear and find a good method to deal with this situation.

What was she going to do? First, she must give up the idea of killing him and began planning for it. Her first instinct was to think of her brother as she walking up back to her bedroom.

"Steady," her mom called her, and she stopped at the landing, held the staircase, looking down to her mother's face. "Supper's almost on the table."

She saw the worry settling there, and could feel her dad's eyes on her, assessing her. Her worries were getting bigger, but she decided she had no option. She wanted them to understand... everything. Also, she couldn't bear to tell her Paul's story. It was so painful, so harrowing. And she hated feeling vulnerable, not knowing what to do. She fixed a bright smile on her face. "I'm not hungry, Mom. I'll eat later."

Watching Steady acutely, Brian could see her eyes darken with a secret as he sat back in his chair. She's hiding something, he sensed, just liked the emotion crisis that she kept locked inside her and wouldn't share with anyone, especially not her parents. He looked up to his wife. "Did something happen between them, honey?"

"Good question, I sensed that, too, whatever happened, she didn't want us to know." Jennies was beginning to panic, wondering if it had anything at all to do with Paul Si. And that's what she wanted to know was how big, and why? "And that was getting me really worry about her."

He could tell that. He'd been picking up the same feelings that Steady was in some kind of trouble. He had to know what the hell his daughter was trying to hide. But he decided not to probe now. Better to wait for his daughter to tell him what she wanted to tell him in her own time. "Let's have dinner, honey. I'd prefer to drop that for the moment. I have something to do, and I'll talk to her later."

Yes, Steady wasn't hungry when she's back in her room and knew two things for certain. One, she was being blackmail, and two, she wanted this nightmare over for herself and for her family. She needed advice and help. The only person would tell her what to do, or could handle that for her was her brother. She had never asked a favor of him before, but she was in way over her head now. A quick glance at the time told her that Bush Jr would be home, so she picked up her cell phone and dialed his phone number. The call went right to voice mail. It was the same at his home. The house keeper was out, the answering machine was on. All she could do was, leaving a message for him, and asking Bush Jr to return the call as soon as he could. *"Please call me any time, no matter how late. It's important."*

She hung up, hoping he'd call her back, told herself to remain calm and collect her thoughts, so she's pouring a glass of wine.

Chapter 4
Let love guide your heart, let God lead the way.

Tiffany Stanley stood in the kitchen, lost in thought, and couldn't help wondering what the rest of her life was going to be like. What was her destiny to be? She couldn't find the answer, but for once in her life, she did what her heart told her to do, and it felt great to be somewhere with someone who changed her life. She was satisfied with her personal life, having been challenged in her profession before. Perhaps she would be happier if she had never met him. But it happened, and it completely changed her life when she couldn't resist playing the role of a professional stylish motorcyclist. Miami was where she lived, had a house, her work, her routine, but she'd discovered a lot interesting things in the past few months. Here, somehow, she wasn't only satisfied, but also excited. With grim determination, she would choose her fate rather have it handed to her.

She was a woman with a mission and couldn't believe she was inherited a fortune. Right after she'd have to deal with the lawyers through all the proper legal channels about her dad's life insurance and discovered her true identity, as well as her exact family history. All she'd learned about him was that he and her mom had been involved in very short, very hot affair, and guess what? Her mom had ended up pregnant. There was nothing she could do to change it now, but at least she had right to discover everything there to know about them. Not the information on her files, but that's the way for her to find out.

Rules, they existed everywhere. She believed in them absolutely. And after the initial shock had worn off, they would welcome her with open arms. But What rules did the Jefferson's live by? She wondered. What type of glue had fashion them into a family? How could she fit in? And why it became more and more important that she needed to find out? So, she's drawn to those things and finding out discreetly was a priority. She searched through all information of Jefferson family.

But the end, she'd followed her heart and instincts by moving from Miami, settling in this pleasant city of Melbourne with a series of purpose, outlines carefully in her mind toward about how to get to know them. Yet Jefferson Bush Jr was the one member of Jefferson family she instinctive turned to, after she'd read all the information about him that had told her he was an interesting man, and why was he her nephew, for crying out loud- so attractive? If in order to be able to approach each other, how should they meet each other? She wondered, over this emotional relationship or over something more personal? In either case she could hardly wait to meet his face-to face, and acquaint herself with him. It wasn't easily done, and took quick thinking or careful planning. Zealously, she began to make plans, good plans, no rush, no hurry, but solid plans. First, she just needed to dig deeper, synthesizing all the details to get a complete picture, and before she had gone to those plans, she had done quite of research on him. For the first time in her life, Tiffany wanted to know this man completely. She needed to understand where he was and what he was doing. So she carefully looked up his background, and decided how to approach a man like Bush Jr.

And according to everything information she could find on him and from the moment she met him, Tiffany understood why Bush Jr was pure alpha man at thirty years old, never married, of course, women would go crazy, wanting him because they found him irresistible. He dated some of them, but it only lasted a few weeks, because it didn't seem to get seriously involved. He was a highly respected businessman who ran a great company with a talent that had made it what it was today, and was the controlling force behind one of Florida's fastest growing, most successful companies. In a recessionary economic, Jefferson Global Web of Money was the largest American Investment Bank in Orlando, and had been for years, that shone a light of prosperity. In addition, wealthy, independent and powerful, he was also very kind, generous, virtuous, and of good character. All the qualities in a man like that attracted her. Still, she hadn't prepared for the utter beauty of the man when they finally met face to face. Her feeling was quite different, and something else that she didn't recognize. *It was odd, really, to think you knew someone and discover there was more to learn. And the more you learned the more you want to know.* Therefore, she had to know how she actually felt about him, and needed to see how things developed.

There was no reason for the Jefferson's family to know about her identity, to suspect her connection. It would be better for all parties if no one knew. Otherwise, they could very well attempt, and possibly succeed in blocking her from Bush Jr altogether. She needed more time to observe, to study, to consider. Then she would act.

Up to now, what she'd done had shown no signs of suspicion. Her mind was awash with so many diverse thoughts, but the most prominent focused on Bush Jr. Thinking about it brought her back to that time in the past when she happily went to The French Café, after she read his text message on her cell phone earlier. *Meet me at The French Café at six, just a couple of blocks down from convention.* And she parked her motorbike on a side street and made her way inside.

It's one of her favorite cafés and bakery, a place that was attracted with many works of art on the wall, offered tables, couches, and free wireless, and was now open for dinner, did a bustling business. The smell of roasting coffee and the putter of the espresso machines hit her in warm, welcome in wave. The table inside started to fill up and several patrons had their laptops open, taking advantage of the free Wi-Fi connection, and she had been surrounded by the gentle buzz of conversation. It didn't take long to reach the counter to order and paid the croissants and coffee to tide her over until diner, but as she waited, she carried her number, decided to take the place outside to the empty table and sat under an umbrella in order to enjoy a cup of coffee where she could get a more complete view of Orlando's attractions while she was waiting for Bush Jr, rather than inside.

She sat back in the metal chair, thinking how wonderful it was to be here, and remembering when her mother had told the truth about her father and Jefferson's family. All she needed to do was convince Bush Jr. Even though she didn't know what to do, she suddenly started driving her motorbike to follow him from place to place. She and Bush Jr had never met each other until the day that the plan went into motion, and then, the first time they'd looked eye-to-eye. That was her final and the most vital mission.

A pot of coffee and a jug of steaming hot milk were placed in front of her along with a basket of breads. The aroma was enticing enough to make her gain weight without taking a bite. And to her surprise and delight, the waiter spoke in French. "Voilà, mademoiselle!" He exclaimed with a nod, brought more items to her table swiftly.

Tiffany had smiled. "Merci," she said back in French.

"That's French. Are you French?"

"No, but I can speak French."

"I see. Anything else you may need?"

"Not right now, thanks," she said and he grin intact, took her number. *"Bon appétit."*

He stepped back, turned around then went inside, leaving her with a few minutes of heaven as she picked up the pot, poured coffee into the large cup, added the frothy milk, a generous spoon of sugar, and stirring before she inhaled the scent of it.

The first sip was delicious. "Mm," she couldn't help sighing then she eyed the basket of different breads. She could smell the fresh croissants which had also miraculously appeared on the table, along with small slabs of cream-looking butter on a plate, plus a dish of dark raspberry jam.

Without waiting any longer and unable to resist, she took a croissant, broke a piece off, added a touch of butter and a generous blob of the jam. It seemed to melt in her mouth, as she enjoyed people watching, realized that said a lot about her and her personality. But they seemed friendly, relaxing and patient. Life was slow to reflect the pace by people who made their living here.

Her enjoyment was interrupted when her cell phone beeped to let her know someone was calling. She immediately pressed the answer button and smiled as soon as she heard the familiar voice. "Hi." Bush Jr's voice came over the line as clear as if he was sitting directly across from her.

"Hi, yourself," she said cheerfully. "How's everything going?"

"Huh?"

"How was your marketing project coming along?"

"It's good, busy and nuts."

"Really?" She heard his laughing. "Something was funny?"

"I was supposed to be paying attention and listening to an important financial report, but unfortunately all I could do was wonder how much longer the thing would take so I could go to see you."

"Oh." That was the most intelligent way of conversation Bush Jr used to flirt with her. "Are you tired? Do you need some time to relax?"

"I was, but now, after hearing your voice and seeing you, I feel a thousand times better..."

She paused, because her heart seemed to melt and at the same time, she heard the voice of someone else distracting her. "Do you mind if I can sit at the table with you?" He saw surprise quickly flicker in her eyes when she glanced up. "Or is this table just for motorcyclists?"

Recognizing that was him with a smile as their eyes met. She smiled back, hung up and slipped the phone back into her leather pocket, and then stood up. "Sure, be my guest."

"Thank you." He said appreciatively, gave her a hug, and kissed her cheek. "I'm sorry I'm late."

She shook her head. "But you're not late, and even if you were, you're certainly worth waiting for."

"Thank you for your sweet words," he complimented, pulled out a chair and sat across from her.

"It's my pleasure, sincerely. Do you want coffee, or anything else to drink, Bush Jr?"

"No, but can I have a sip of your coffee, Tiffany?"

She looked at her coffee cup and hesitated, thinking that he was trying to learn about her preferences through her coffee cup. "Sure, if you don't mind."

He picked the cup up from her, took a sip of coffee and made a face. "Do you always drink it too sweet?" He asked then set it down back on its saucer.

"That's my bad habit." She laughed.

"Now I know. Do you want to find a quiet place and have a dinner with me, Tiffany?"

"That's exactly what I mean. Where are we going?"

"I'll let you decide that." He requested, regardless of all the possibilities, what he wanted was to be with her, and he didn't want to appear overly eager, because the truth was, he could hardly believe his luck. "My tastes may surprise you."

"Everything about you surprises me."

"Mm." The sound might have been agreement, or it might have been something else. She was beginning to enjoy this, giving some thought to his tastes and asked. "Do you like Thai food?"

And he nodded. "Love it."

She sincerely doubted that, but managed to hide her knowing grin. "Great, I know a small restaurant a couple of blocks over. The food's great."

This was certainly an interesting development, so he didn't object, because he just never expected a female motorcyclist like Tiffany to be interested in him. "The choice is yours. Let's go there then."

With a wide grin, she left ten dollars bill under her cup. "Ready?"

"Of course," Bush Jr stood, walked around and offered her his hand as she got out of her chair. This was gallantry for which she was grateful.

Knowing the place was only a short distance, she left her motorbike parked from The French Café, and dust had settled over the city as they move onto the sidewalk. Streetlights were beginning to flicker around them with other pedestrians busting in and out of the shops and restaurants facing the streets, turning to look at them walking side by side, and right away Tiffany noticed their curious eyes. Normally she didn't give a damn what other people thought, and didn't worry about anything, but why she felt nervous now? They did make an odd couple. She was in her motorcycle gear and he looked like an elegant and stylish businessman. Bush Jr felt that, too, but it seemed not bother him. For now, at least, they had time ambled slowly on the street.

She pointed straight ahead a few minutes later. It was a restaurant she had gone there many times. "That's the restaurant I recommend."

When Tiffany said the restaurant was small, she wasn't kidding, but inside, it didn't look small at all, even it had a garden, and the scent of spices and basil once again made him ask himself how long it'd been since he had eaten Thai food again.

It smelled of jasmine, tea, ginger, curry and the aroma of spices and the sizzle of cooking meat from the kitchen where the sound of rattling pans and voices speaking in some Asian tongue came to greet them as they walked in the door. The owner was delighted to see them and Tiffany spoke briefly to him who led them to the table in an intimate setting in the back that required them to remove their shoes and climb into the low seats.

The room allowed for private conversation, quiet to enjoy culinary dishes. This was perfect. "Do you eat here often?" Bush Jr asked, gave Tiffany his hand, and helped her taking her seat before he slid into the opposite side of the booth. "Every once in a while."

The waitress came immediately who was a petite Asian woman dressed in traditional Thai grab with a welcoming warmth smile and long black hair wound onto her head. "Hi, I'm Crystal," she said as she handed them each a plastic-covered menu. "The specials tonight are Thai fish cake, spicy beef salad, and spicy shrimp soup. I'll give you a few minutes to look over the menu, then I'll be back for your order."

But before she left, Tiffany called her name, "Crystal." And she surprised him by announcing that they were ready to order when he just glanced down the menu.

"If so, I'm going to take your orders?" Her order pad at the ready and she glanced at Tiffany.

"We'd like to have two glasses of Rombauer Chardonnay, a bottle of mineral water," Tiffany ordered. "And instead of Thai food, we want the restaurant to cook for us the following dishes."

"Yes, we're very pleased to serve you," Crystal said, eager to please.

"Medium rare on the steak with Cobb salad, Crystal?"

Crystal wrote it down. "Dessert?"

"Not for me," Tiffany replied, glancing at Bush Jr. "And you?"

"I'll wait until after my meal."

Crystal glanced at Bush Jr. "Will that be all, sir?"

He looked at Tiffany, thinking. Red wine wasn't his favorite, but since it was Tiffany's choice. He folded up the menu and glanced back to Crystal. "Yes, we will call more if needed ma'am."

Before she left, Tiffany pressed the focus. "Crystal, we'd appreciate it if you'd snag a basket of rolls from the kitchen when you bring the drinks by. This gentleman had a rough day, and he's tired. You'd know how tiring a long rough day goes?"

He wasn't like that, but there was no point in arguing, just keeping quiet, analyzing the situation. *This gentleman had a rough day...* This woman was very interesting. He liked the sweet, caring way she expressed it to him.

"I'll say I do. Sure, I'll take care of that for you right away." Crystal collected the menus and left.

Once the waitress was gone, Bush Jr leaned back against the booth. "Forgive me, Tiffany. Would it embarrass you if I told you this? You're always the one in charge?"

She should have known better, and realized that tone. He was a boss who didn't like others exceeding his authority. "No, and why did you say that?"

"Because you just ordered for me without consulting me."

To highlight the good reason, she smiled. "It won't become a habit. It doesn't embarrass me, either." She said easily, patting his hand. "Your brain is tired and it's too overworked to be asked to make decisions. You need relaxation, could use some red meat, and time to recharge. So I ordered them for you, and to prove what I did was right. Next time, if we have a chance, I'll let you order food for me."

Her explanation made sense, even logical. Nothing made him more annoying than using his own style of maneuvering to fight back, and that was a lovely idea. He admired a woman who dared to speak her mind to a point.

"That's interesting," he said, smiling, not expecting her to mention it next time. Could this be considered a promise? "So what do you think about the restaurant where you'll notice once we're seated that there isn't any silverware?" She grimaced. "That's Indian Restaurant or finger food?"

"Good guess, but not exactly. With the meal, we'll each be given a wooden board and mallet."

"A mallet? You mean a hammer?"

"Of sorts, that's so we can crack open the crabs ourselves. We'll get plastic bibs, too, but everyone wears them, so you won't look silly or feel out of place."

In the culinary field, she already knew about these types of restaurants, but she'd never actually been to one. This was sure to be an experience.

"Sound like fun crab restaurant."

"Something like that, but don't feel you need order the crab." Bush Jr assured her. "Next time you'll find out when you're going to have dinner at my beach house. It's private and quiet. You'd be comfortable."

"Your beach house?" She lifted a brow. Such an intimate dinner needed to be considered seriously. She mused, this was a good opportunity to take, especially a Jefferson businessman. "How can I refuse such an offer like that? Hooked pinky finger to promise."

He crinkled his brow. Her naive remark fascinated him. "Pinky promise?"

"You know a better way?"

No answer he couldn't say. She made him feel young, foolishly young and irresponsible. Bush Jr couldn't remember feeling that way about anyone on the first time meet in his entire lifetime. He reached his hand out tentatively. Their pinkies twisted and locked. "Promise honors."

Pure energy rushed between them, but it was like a nice, heady buzz that made her feel good in her tummy. "Promise honors." She repeated. And Crystal interrupted them when she returned to set their drink and food in front of them.

The impressive piece of Angus beef was rare, crusted with a peppercorn brandy, and placed over fried oysters. They forgot their serious conversations for a moment with the smile expectantly. "Can I get you anything else?"

"This should do it," Tiffany said then glanced at Bush Jr, "unless there's something more for you."

Looking at his plate, where the huge steak was hot and juicy, Bush Jr shook his head. "I think this is enough."

"Just holler if you change your mind." Crystal said.

"We'll do and thank you." Tiffany replied.

And after she left, Tiffany took a roll out of the basket, broke it in two and buttered it before passing that half to him. "So, you will let me know when, right?" She was already intrigued by him.

He took the piece of roll she offered. "I will. But I mean it's not a normal dinner like this. I'd like you to go out with me like a date." Bush Jr said, nibbled the half of roll, and he caught her starting with a tinge of red flushed her cheeks while she chewed thoughtfully.

"What? Date?" This was the best part of all happened. She swallowed bread, and took a sip of wine to chase away her worries.

The need and suspicion mingled in those gorgeous blue eyes. "Yes, like a date. You know better word?" He replied with a grin and touched his glass to hers.

For the first time since they'd met, her heart lifted and filled up with joy. There's no other word for it. She took a sip of wine from the glass. "No, I suppose it would."

Savoring the taste of wine, Bush Jr satisfied the flavor he'd nearly forgotten, then set his glass down because the scent of the steak was too good to resist. He cut off a small piece, tested the first bite of it, and realized it was the best thing he'd eaten in a week. It was tender and perfect. "Unless …"

He watched her take the first bite of her salad. "Unless what?"

"You have a man in your life. A serious one, I mean." This was a good start so he could learn more about her without having to put himself at risk, and was she willing to share any of her personal information?

Whatever came, would come. That's definitely personal question that she didn't expect, and he unintentionally made her lose interest, but if she tried to avoid answering now, she would also be questioned later. She stabbed her fork into the salad, and decided that giving him tidbits of information would do no real harm.

"I'm not married, but had a boyfriend." She admitted.

"I was afraid of that. I'm not really surprised, only regretful." He had no reaction to retreat.

"How's your relationship? Are you happy with him?" Bush Jr asked very gently, anxious to know if there was still a chance for him, and those were important questions. If she was happy, he would automatically retreat. He was willing to fight for what he wanted, but he wasn't stupid or crazy, or anxious to get hurt. And he held his breath waiting for her reply.

With the fork half way to her mouth, Tiffany stopped, hesitated, not completely sure what to say with the man she'd only just met. He had a right to know. Or did he? They had only talked each other for a short time, but they were clearly powerfully attracted to each other, and she knew she ought to tell him the truth. "It didn't work out well." She said fairly.

He reached for the wine, and anxiously to know. "And why is that?"

"When I figured it out, he was a real jerk." She said sadly, pushed away her salad. She didn't know why she told Bush Jr that, but it was part of the story.

There was a look in her eyes that said I've been hurt. Bush Jr knew he was making her uncomfortable, but he couldn't figure out why. He took a drink. "Oh, forgive me. I have a habit of poking into secrets."

Actually, she didn't want to talk about this at all, with him or anyone else. Because it was too personal and too painful to relive. Especially not wanting to reopen her own pain. When she knew Jack, she'd intended to spend the rest of her life with him. But she didn't expect him to be a cheating bastard. Then suddenly, senselessly, he was gone, she'd promised herself never to become emotionally attached to a man again. Therefore, every time a man had intentions and showed his feeling for her, she always found a way to back off. But now, as she cast a look at the man who was barely knew her, but also break through the emotional barrier she'd so carefully built. He was surely curious about her past, and sooner or later, he'd start pressing her for answers. She finished what was left of her wine. "It's not your fault."

Guessing how awkward she must feel, instead of pressing her further about it, he avoided it by gesturing with his fork and looking for an apology. "Look, I didn't mean to pry. Hell, yes, I did, because it's a specific reason that might help me understand, and not take it personally. I'm sorry if I upset you."

"It's all right." She reassured him and recognized she had lost her joy. The food was delicious, and the second glass of wine was poured for them, Tiffany thought. Now would be the time to bring up some personal matters. She was as curious as he was. But she had to remind herself. Don't rush right into talking about what you want. Let him relaxed and absorb first. Actually, Bush Jr was already relaxed, enjoyed his food, by cutting off another piece of meat and stuffed it in his mouth and silently blessing his meal. And so was she. She took a bite of the salad again, and found it as good as advertised. "Let's change the subject to something more appealing."

Bush Jr took another bite of beef. "Oh." He's pausing to chew and swallow then added. "With what topic?"

When she looked at him, she knew there was an important question she hadn't asked him. At first, she had told herself she didn't want to know, but she realized now that she should ask him. "About you." She said, turning the table on him. "Who is there in your life?"

This conversation was getting personal, too personal, he thought. He was going to keep his private life from her for now, but getting this woman's attention had been too problematic. "My mother, my sisters, my cleaning lady, my dentist, my secretary," he said, and never heard her laugh like that before. Easy, feminine, and fresh.

"They sound like good ladies for you." She admitted, amused by his evasive response. "But I meant a lovely Mrs. Jefferson."

He shook his head. "No, I'm not the marrying kind."

That, she believed. She reached and tasted the wine again. The wine she'd drunk so far made her a little braver than she normally was, and helped her imagine how he lived in his own house, so she dug deeper. "Then tell me about your private house in Melbourne."

His expression didn't change, but she sensed that she had surprised him as he stopped chewing.

It didn't feel question, he realized. It felt like being interrogated. "How?" He couldn't help being curious. "I didn't mention my home's in Melbourne."

And when he set down his knife and fork, and wiped his mouth with the red cloth towel, she explained. "Your phone number tells everything about you on Google. And because I'm so curious to know about you."

"I see." Bush Jr smiled, took a sip of wine, pleased that she already checked his background, which sort of blew his mind. Usually when he took dates to dinner, he didn't let anyone have time to get to know him well, so he usually played a certain role that he could get away with if he revealed too much. But for her, he found himself comfortable doing it without knowing why. "Do you want to know where I live?"

She took another swallow of wine, and their eyes met over their glasses. "Yes. Am I allowed to know that?"

He set his glass down. "I have a house in Sherwood Hill." It was the first time he had ever been so frank with her, but she had opened the door for him to say it to her. "It's on the beach-side, and got a great view."

"I thought so."

"Did you?" He looked at her in amusement. "How? Don't tell me you also Google that?"

Those beautiful blue eyes darkened while a ghost of a smile played around her mouth. "No, I didn't. But you did mention that. Do you like it?"

He nodded slowly. "Of course. I enjoy my time there."

"I think it must be a comfortable and relaxing place." And because she was afraid to ask directly about what she wanted to know, but then she got brave and asked for more. "Or maybe your relatives also live there?"

"Actually, I live by myself. But I never feel lonely."

"Because you have a big family."

"Yes. I have two brothers, three sisters, assorted cousins, brothers and sisters in law, nephews, nieces. When we gather together it's an asylum."

The way he described it made her laugh. "Do you want to change that for the world?"

"No, because that's my world." Bush Jr was happy to answer her questions, but it was too much about him already, so he decided to change the subject to her. "That's enough information about me, it's time for your turn."

Tiffany grinned, didn't argue, knowing that was a delicate line and he's probably right. "Fair enough," she said enjoyably, and amused by his reaction. "If we're attracted each other, I don't see any reason why we shouldn't. What do you want to know?"

"Tell me about your family. Is there anyone grow up around here?"

For an instant they had become such close friends that they felt brave enough to ask about each other's personal lives. "No, my family lives in Miami."

"Beautiful city." He wiped his mouth with his napkin, stared at her, and leaned back in his seat. "Do you still live there?"

She smiled at him in answer. "Yes, but because of my business, I often move to many places, and I'm currently in Orlando. It's been a little over a year so far." "So, you travel a lot, don't you?" He asked, and she shook her head.

"I used to. I was supposed to follow family tradition and studied law. But I ended up becoming a chef."

"Is that so?" Tilting his head, Bush Jr observed her more closely. "I can't imagine it, that's why I must ask. Motorcycles are usually a man's hobby and best friend, so how can a nice girl like you be passionate and drive it?"

"It began when I was six my father took me a ride with his metal horse. I was hooked."

"Were you nervous or scared at that time?"

"Yes, I was, but after a while, I was fascinated, then I find myself liking the feeling of speed and being attracted to the craftsmanship of the Harley which it had both. That's why I love riding Harley." She stopped, surprised that had been the answer out of her mouth. He would think she was crazy.

"It's difficult not to notice. You're the only motorist I've known that look sexy in motorbike." He smiled more deeply. "And you're very font of him, aren't you? Your father I mean. Tell me about him."

Bush Jr had a beautiful smile. She thought he might be flattering with her now, but she couldn't sure. It was peculiar as she'd been thinking how nice it would be to have dinner with him every day. "For fathers, I have the greatest respect. I have one myself. But he passed away six years ago."

A brief silence fell, filled with unspoken emotion. Shit, why would he talk about a subject without seeing what was coming? And he also saw the pain in her eyes and how quickly she disguised it. So, he broke this silence.

"I'm so sorry that happened. Besides, I never meant to imply, but then I did it again."

She saw the change in his expression at this moment, both regretful and sympathetic. Usually, she hated that. It only reminded her how heartbreaking it was. But somehow Bush Jr's concern, instead, comforted her. She didn't like feeling vulnerable in front of him, but at the same time, knowing he cared meant something to her. "No need to apologize. I'm not offended."

Bush Jr wanted to press her to share more, and he also kind of wanted to give her a hug or said something comforting. But he didn't do any those things. Because he knew it would be smarter if he got rid of the problem, and just in time the waitress came to clear the table, and placed two cups of coffee in front of them. He smiled because the distraction was just what helping him in this moment.

Tiffany found herself more charmed again with each passing minute and they talked freely and easily about more of topics. Bush Jr told her that it was a blessing for him to be born into such a large family, and she laughed as he recounted a story about his trip to Vietnam. In return, she told the stories about her summers in Thai Lan where how she was trying to eat fried scorpions. And by the time she and Bush Jr finished their coffees, the waitress came by and asked if they wanted to refill their coffee, he shook his head in reply, and asked for the bill.

He was such good company, and so easy to be with, someone worth spending more time with. The waitress returned with the bill tucked inside a black leather folder. "Here, sir."

They tussled briefly over the bill, and she offered to split the payment in half. "Um, no," he looked at her with disapproving eyes, then lifting his butt up to take out his wallet. "That is simply not how things are done. I invited you, Tiffany. Let me do what I should do."

Noticing that the waitress was smiling with satisfaction, she silently agreed, watching him pull out some large bills from his wallet. Enough to make her eyebrow lift, then he placed them inside the folder, and handed it to her. "Keep the change."

"Thank you," she said, smiling broadly. "Hope you both have a wonderful evening."

"We will." He replied, smiling at her as he tucked his wallet back in his pants pocket.

That was a generous tip, Tiffany noticed as she slid out the booth, and he helped her put her shoes on her feet. She liked that about him. Automatically, he took her hand rather than her arm as she'd expected. Before she could make any counter move, he was leading her out of the restaurant, guided her down the sidewalk toward her parked motorbike. She felt the warmth of his fingers, the pressure of his palm and did the best to lace hers to his.

It was a beautiful January evening. Above them, the darkened sky was twinkled with stars. Crowds of people flocked the streets to enjoy the warm night air. But the wind teased her hair and anticipation flowed through her veins as sweet as the wine she'd drunk. Oh, how badly she wanted to take a wild leap and do something crazy.

Bush Jr suddenly realized how much he was liking being with her. Damn, everything about her appealed to him. Whatever perfume she was wearing was a real turn-on. It was so feminine and sexy. "I really enjoyed dinner, Tiffany," he confessed as they stopped before they reached her Harley Davidson motorcycle nearby. "It's been a long time since I've had a lovely time like tonight. Thank you."

Tiffany loved the way he spoke and didn't want the evening to end. Within a short span of time, she felt as if Bush Jr and she had always been the closet of friends. True, they didn't share a lot of common interests, but there was a bound between them that was beyond explanation. The knowledge stunned her, and she didn't notice that she'd placed her hand in the crook of his arm. "I feel the same. One I shall never forget. And perhaps we should continue the conversation if I walk you to your car."

He gave a soft laugh and took her hands, forcing her to stopped walking. "I don't drive. That's the problem. Remember?" That's not true. He could call his driver, picking him up.

She nearly laughed at herself. "That's right," but she shoved the problem fast, and didn't want to lose this opportunity. "Then I'll bring you home if you like." Why not? She found him attractive and she would be delighted to take things to the next level.

He found he liked that idea very much, and pleasing himself. "That would be lovely." Bush Jr said, leaned in and kissed her cheek. "Once I got to know you, I realized you're a good person."

There was something so comfortable, so right about the gesture, whispering in her ear. But once again reminding her of what she had those things and they hadn't brought her happiness. "Thanks."

His gaze settled on her full lips and wondered what it would be like to kiss her. He had only to lower his head a little and he could kiss them.

They were so close that her body was touching his, caused her skin to hum and spellbound, she held his gaze and knew in an instant that he was going to kiss her. Her heart squeezed. Unwanted desire, wicked and wanton crept stealthily through her blood. "What are you thinking?"

Maybe that part was sheer ego, he smiled in thought. Tiffany was the type of person who made life interesting for a man like him. Her response had been so cool and control. It made him wonder what it would be like to peel that intellect away, layer by layer, and find the woman beneath, and worked his way down to pure emotion and instinct. Hardly aware of what he did, Bush Jr gently brushed the hair away from her cheek in a sweet, intimate and natural gesture.

"I was hoping you'd say that. But the problem is…" He paused as seeing her moist lips part and offer themselves to him. Now I have to kiss you.

"What's problem?" She asked with eager anticipation at the expression in his eyes, and waiting the answer.

"You, and this."

The next thing she knew, he had moves, smooth, unexpected, incredible moves. It wasn't fast, but it was deliberate, she had no time to react and think, as he drew her into his arms. His breath was warm against her face, his eyes as dark as the night, and his strong hands yanked her closer, pressing her breasts, already full, were crushed against his vest jacket. For the first time in years a hot, yawning desire uncoiled deep within her while one of his hands glided down her back, gripped her thigh, and hooked it to his waist. The erotic position aroused desire inside her as her clitoris rubbed against his thigh that she could feel him, and his muscle. Thanks God she wore jeans, otherwise, with friction like this he would have felt how damp she was. In response, her arms encircled his back without any reason or logic, she felt safe and secure in his embrace, and she faced her tumultuous emotions with directness and truth. She couldn't help it, she wanted this man. She remained still, watching him, waiting.

That silent space brought them into private space. Then lips touched softly. Eyes remain opened widely and unblinking in the moonlight and aware. Pulses throbbed. Desire tugged with the unexpected action and the moment he covered his lips, bringing the cold on hers. His numbness and his sweetness intoxicating her. She couldn't deny it, couldn't pretend it away, couldn't think or to stop him even though she knew they were standing on the public street in the night traffic. Because two souls seemed to merge into one.

As soon as she wound her arms around his neck, he stopped entwined and transferred on the lips, and thrust his tongue past her teeth into her mouth, stirring, conquering, demanding, and felt her open to him, easily, willingly, and trustingly. Her tongue mated anxiously with his, touching, exploring, twisting, wrestling then entwining forever.

She wallowed in it and let his mouth was doing magical things to her and every nerve in her body reacted. It was the most erotic kiss she'd ever experienced, lips and tongue draw in the sweetness, and absorbed.

It, of course, wasn't the first time she'd been kissed. But it was the first time in a while. And either she'd forgotten just how amazing a good kiss was or this one was more than good. In fact, she thought it was perhaps the most erotic kiss she'd ever experienced, and she never wanted it to end. Because he was making love to her with his tongue as if they'd done this before, as if they already knew how each other kissed. And if she'd thought the mere touch of his hand was moving through her veins, his kiss traveled somewhere even deeper within. To her panties, yes definitely. But it was even more than that, more than sex. She'd never felt so connected to a guy just from a mere meeting of their mouths.

There were many people walking on the sidewalk, cars pass back and forth on the street, but Bush Jr and Tiffany were unwary of everything. All they could do were concerned with the fire of love burning within them. And thankfully no honking and anyone was whistling or telling them to get a room. They were going their own business as if nothing had happened.

Instinctively, wanting to give, she pressed her soft figure to his long length, clinging to him for support. Everything around them faded. No longer did she hear any sound, accept the fain sound of stunning pleasure that hummed in her throat. Her lips parted in welcoming, demanding more.

He kissed her like he sucked it as a candy cane and deserved the most delicate tenderness. Good God, how could a woman take him so far with only a kiss? And he still couldn't believe he'd kissed her that way. It hadn't been just a casual kiss. It had been a damn long time since he hadn't been able to hold back with a girl. Causing his groin now was uncomfortably tight, and his skin literally itched with wanting her. He tried to hold her like that in these glorious moments because he was trembling, until he found his own balance again.

This attack of his was like a tidal wave, she was almost unable to hold on before he raised his head and gently drew her away. "I bet you didn't think I kiss you, did you, Tiffany?"

Her eyes narrowed more in surprise than annoyance, "uh."

Tiffany couldn't quite remember how to from words. *Not good.* She knew, in that endless moment, that somehow this man would have to belong to her, for however brief this time together would be, she had found him, a man who could make her feel like the woman she always knew she was. And she knew their relationship was beginning to improve. Rectify her mind, she said. "No, but I think we'll have to do this again sometime."

"Ah," the sound came out slowly. She wasn't a woman who was easily impressed, yet she was a woman who could be easily pleased. Deliberately, his fingers were gentle as they danced through her hair. "In your own odd way, you're a very practical woman."

Why should she want to indulge in something so foolish now when she never had before? "In every situation I'm always a practical woman. So, let me drive you home. We can talk more on the way there."

"Yes, all right, but listen … I might as well …"

"That would be lovely." Understanding, she said for him when she saw him hesitate. "So let's make this night last forever."

Hearing this satisfactory answer, he had a big smile on his face. From another woman it would have been an invitation. From her, Bush Jr reminded himself, it was a combination of wine and naivety. It was clearly that she was not simply taking him home but wanted to enjoy the whole night not just talking, but exchanging feelings and needs of the soul that go beyond the hunger and thirst of the body. And when they both naked, aroused with sex, and how wonderful it would feel to put inside of her. She knew it would happen, could ask him to talk in a sexy voice as his hands touched every part of her body.

What he was feeling was so new to him, he couldn't explain it. The only thing he knew for certain was that Tiffany Stanley was different from any other woman he had ever met, and the more time he spent with her, the more he desired her.

Indeed, that night, while the world should have been asleep, they were lying together in bed, naked, skin to skin, body on body, touching, caressing and kissing each other as the fires of their lust burned and the undeniably tight evidence of his desire was pressed deep between her legs, warming her cheeks and lips ruddy that she wished it would never end. And it had not. So she and Bush Jr both thanked God.

Of course that would continue, but what she couldn't have imagined was how strongly it would affect their relationship so that she could be close and intimate with Jefferson Bush Jr. They were like a picture and shadow, inseparable from each other now. In her plan, she just wanted to find out about Bush Jr, and didn't want to fall in love. But now she had failed in every aspect of the issue.

❉ ❊ ✱ ❅ ❆

Satisfaction over the memory, and brought her back to the reason for tonight. She was anxious to prepare a special, intimate dinner as a surprise for Bush Jr, and his gray hairs housekeeper Mrs. Palmer who seemed surprising that Bush Jr had brought a woman home and introduced her to her. Mrs. Palmer had always had Saturday and Sunday off, so she used his spare key and code to open the gate and doors to let herself in. Tiffany looked around the kitchen with its high-dollar and high-tech appliances made of stainless-steel and glass. When she moved in with him. She knew everything about the house. The kitchen was large, practically the size of her entire apartment with high ceilings, two double-size ovens, a microwave, an espresso maker, another coffeemaker that had so many buttons, a huge stove with eight gas burners, a restaurant sized refrigerator, two sinks and a dishwasher that could handle the aftermath of an embassy dinner, a few other electrical gadgets she had never seen before, and had all kind of ingredients she needed for in his modern house. On her first visit, she had taken an instant liking to it, and she felt at home there, as if she truly belonged. Aside from that, the house was lovely, full of charm, where they were holding hands took a long walk down the beach or in his big comfortable bed, they made love for hours which she had never made love so often in her life. It's very passionate, very romantic. They went back to their own lives as always, but on weekends, they'd been together, with him sharing her bed, or her sharing his. The rest of what happened in her life, she could handle herself. And when she was there, she felt enveloped in quiet luxury and comfort. It was peacefulness that she cherished.

All these points aside, Tiffany had always understood the social and even the physical risks she was taking, but not the emotional ones. Falling in love with Bush Jr was not part of her plan. But she had realized from beginning of their affair that she could be happy with him anywhere. She was deeply in love with him. Now she'd have to find a way to break the news of her identity without also breaking his heart.

Checking the roast chicken into the stove, she thought was his favorite. Food was almost secondary at this stage in her life, she wanted to prepare it in her own creative way, combined with a variety of green salads, beautiful presented, served with crusty fresh bread with fish sauce as a dipping sauce that she had prepared in the glass bowl a few minutes before. Moving to the refrigerator, she took out what she needed, and began to slice those items. Once she had done, so, she arranged them on the bowl and added basil leaves. Later she would drizzle oil and dressing on top.

As she worked, Tiffany sniffed the aromatic air to evaluate, and then glanced out the window, thinking *when one cooks in one's own kitchen for relative, lover; it can be a pleasure, not a profession.* She wondered if he knew how much it meant that he accepted her for what she was. She doubted it. *Only my work must be taken seriously.* He was forever telling her, and she understood exactly what he meant by that. But she was sure of Bush Jr, knew full well how much he loved her, just as she loved him with all her heart. She thought it was about right time to tell Bush Jr who and what she was in the hopes that he would understand why she had to do it. But deep down, she wasn't sure she'd done the right thing, and couldn't bring herself to broach the subject. Their journey from acquaintances to lovers had been smooth and natural, and she couldn't imagine being happier. Their personalities meshed perfectly, which added the sexual sparks. He left nothing to wish for, in any respect. Bush Jr was a gentleman who knew his way around, both in and out of bed. Especially in bed. Her relationship with Bush Jr was a happy one. They lived in their own house quite near to each other, and the most, they spent time together was at his house on the beach because it was much bigger. She cooked and he didn't.

And during these months they had grown closer, come to know each other most intimately on every level. This was truly a love affair for them, and they both knew it. Last weekend, he told her that they could arrange to be together in a more reasonable way, and when she asked, 'what sort of arrangement?' He reached for her hand, and carefully put the electronic key in it then said. "That's the key of this house, my darling. Why should we rotate where we spend our nights? My house, on the other hand, is convenient for getting away and relaxing. It seems a logical arrangement might be for us to live and work during the week and spend weekends at my place."

She was please and surprise, but she already made up her mind. "Do you want us to live together?"

"Yes. I want you to move in with me, be my love, and we will enjoy all the joys together."

Wow, that all sounded wonderful to her. Bush Jr was a good man. The type of man she was blessing to find. Honest and straightforward, he didn't play with love. If he wanted something, he went after it. Did he mean permanently? She opened her mouth, but with no idea what to say, she closed it again, and closed her hand around the key, just stared the man she'd been sleeping with for nearly six months who without any hesitation gave her his house key. It'd be a big step toward trust. And it made perfect sense for them. Every morning, they had business to run and were passionate about each other at night. Comfortable was the word that defined what they shared. And it was true that when you were in love, everything became so beautiful. The corner of her eyes was suddenly wet, her tears seemed to be suppressed and rushed out.

"What's this?" he lifted a fingertip and touched a tear that clung to her lashes.

"It's nothing. I feel foolish."

He brushed another tear away with his thumb. "No, I don't think I should." He'd seen her weep before, but that had been a torrent. There was something soft in these tears, something incredibly sweet that drew him. "Do you always cry when a man gives you a key and ask you move in?"

"No, of course not. It's just, I never expected you to do anything like this."

He brought her holding key hand in his lips and smiled as he kissed her wrist. "You deserve better, darling."

That's not what she meant. It was more a matter of convenience to him. But to her, it was like a form of commitment. She looked into his eyes then smiling down at her hands, she knew he cared and wanted her now. It had to be enough. "Bush Jr, you are the one makes me better."

"You know I love you."

"I do know that. It's more important than anything."

And so they indulged in the power of love, which only sex could express.

⁂

It made her feel foolish and light-headed. But her thoughts were her own, she reminded herself until she could do those things for others. It occurred her that, and her guilty conscience was getting the best of her, because he didn't know one important fact. She'd been lying to him about something since the very beginning. She needed to tell Bush Jr the truth about her. Get past it and stop hiding. But no, she'd been so taken aback by the speed of events between the two of them, at how fast things had gotten out of her control, and the truth was he was a good and ideal man who gave her the feeling of true love after a long time of being alone. And yes, it was selfish, wrong, and she hated herself for it. However, each time she thought about what to say, her mouth clamped shut and the right words couldn't come out. She'd promised herself she would confess to him. It wasn't right to start their love off with a lie hanging between them, but still didn't have the courage to say it. She wasn't doing anything to hurt him, after all, and she just hoped Bush Jr was a reasonable and understanding person.

And life ran smoother when everything was where it was meant to be. That's right, but. she had been foolish to think that everything would go smoothly. But life was not a dream when what she didn't expect, it came and troubled her, terrified, really. Her period had not occurred for more than three weeks. First, she thought her periods were so irregular. Maybe it was from too much work, plus she wasn't suffering nausea, wasn't tired, and wouldn't have had a clue that she was carrying a baby. *Don't think so, it would make you worry.* But she started to suspect it and she figured, better sure rather than uncertain.

Even though she hadn't been to the doctor yet, but her heart pounding as she sat on the lid of the toilet and glanced down at the pregnancy test stick in her hand. Not one but she'd taken the same test three different times, each kit made by a different manufacturer. Every one of them had the tiny results window turned out with its pink line still giving a positive reading, confirming that yes, indeed, she was pregnant. With Jefferson Bush

Jr's child. She instantly filled with dismay and just a little trepidation. That meant the soft spread of emotion was glowing inside her had blocked her ways. Oh God! That hadn't been part of her plans. He knew she wasn't on the pill. Though Bush Jr usually took care of birth control himself, there had been a few times he hadn't bothered with a condom, several instances where passion had overruled sanity. She had been somewhat aware of that, but she didn't want anything between them. She knew she'd made a mistake. And now...God, and now this-a baby-could change everything.

Damn. Now what? Tiffany let out a heavy sigh and sat down on the dinning chair. Oh, God, how far had she gone in such a short time? She'd always been so certain her emotion was perfectly safe. Mistake, she forced the word into her head even as her heart tried to block it. This, her heart told her as she rested a hand on her flat belly nervously even right now it didn't seem as if there is a baby at all, but a life was growing inside her. She should not be pressured, couldn't be distracted. She ordered herself. She must be strong and courageous, and hold positive thoughts, keep a cool demeanor. It should have been something wonderful. She would not be made to feel guilty or responsible if she loved him so much, and suddenly all she wanted was his baby.

Baby, the reality of a baby at this point in their relationship might be something else, and this was an enormous burden to put on a relationship that was barely six months old. What would Bush Jr say to all this when she told him? Tiffany wondered. Maybe God had other plans. It was amazing how that worked sometime.

Give me strength, Tiffany silently prayed. She also was a woman who appreciated the unexpected and was about to impact everybody's life. She would be having this child one way or another. And that meant Bush Jr would have to know about it. But however, she had worried so much about the strange encounter that after she told him about the news. She had to be intelligent about this and made the right decision. Hers, his, a baby was the most painful decision she had ever had to make. Bush Jr hadn't recognized her; she was certain of that. What would happen when he did, when he found out who she was? What if Bush Jr hadn't to be ready yet? He might not be pleased at all, and yes, he might be taken aback, even shocked. She had no idea what she felt. She was still too stunned to sort it out, although a part of her was thrill, and she told herself that was insane. They weren't married, and what if from here on in, things just got worse? She carried the child and planned for her future.

There were so many 'what ifs' to consider, and many questions bouncing around in her head today, but no answers were forthcoming. "God! I annoy myself." Finally, she reassured herself. Sometimes, unfortunately, it's necessary to take chances, to react. His surprise would turn to happiness. Bush Jr would eventually love the idea when she told him. And probably he would throw his arms around her and embrace her, tell her that she and a baby were all he ever wanted in the world and nothing else matter. The thoughts of that now filled her with a rush of happiness. "Everything will be fine."

Spurred by those ideals, and all she wanted was to create a beautiful, unique, effortless and memorable dinner to start her plan for a romantic night. Next, as she promised herself that she's going to quit being a wimp and tell Bush Jr the truth tonight what he needed to know her secret. As well as telling him that he was going to be a father. Nodding in approval, she glanced at her watch to warn her that time was running short. Now there was a happy thought. At least it would stop her thinking about the problem that was worrying her. The oven timer chimed, reminding her that the apple pie she had prepared from scratch was done. She domed a pair of oven mitts, opened the door, reached inside and removed the hot pie, then set it on a cooling rack atop the granite counter. Next, she sliced fruit, checked the supplies, and put them in the refrigerator. Everything had been prepared, she walked to, and knelt in front of the fireplace. She set up the low heat and the electrical flames leaping up the chimney. A fire was not necessary, but she liked the effect. It helped to bring a warm, roseate glow to the living room.

Pleasing, she rose to check the scene she'd so carefully set. The table for two was laid with a white cloth and vase of red roses in center. Though dining room had had possibilities, with its soaring ceiling and its huge fireplace, she thought the drawing room more than intimate, added to the China looked old and lovely, with little rosebuds hugging the edges of gleaming white plates. She'd arranged the heavy silverware and two crystal tulip glasses and folded the deep rose damask napkin into neat triangles.

Perfect, she thought so, but suddenly remembered.

Music, how could she have forgotten the music and the candlelight? She went to the stereo and selected several of her favorite compact discs through his wide selection of CDs. But finally, she decided Chopin though she was more in tune with the Rolling Stones than with classical music. She switched it on and slipped the disc into the player. As the music filled the room, she nodded in her approval. Then she went on a treasure hunt for candles.

Ten minutes later, she had over a dozen ranged throughout the room, glowing and wafting out the fragrances of vanilla and Jasmine. She'd set the stage carefully, wanting to give him the romance he made her capable of. Then she'd felt his cool fingertips on her skin and seen the flicker of desire in his eyes. She must have it all tonight.

She decided she was going upstairs to put on a nice, silk dress that she'd brought with her. Tonight, she would be a lovely and sexy woman. But crap, she'd barely had time to do that when she saw headlights of his car splash illumination on the lane outside of the windows. She thought, it much better this way. Bush Jr had seen every inch of her. She no longer had anything to hide. She would seduce him first with her body and then with her dinner. She giggled to herself as she untied her stained apron over her sexy lingerie, placed it on the handle of the stove, and then hurried to the doors to greet him.

Chapter 5

The smile stayed on his face, and satisfied with his strategy when Paul droves back in town. Drumming the tips of his fingers on the steering wheel when he stopped at a red light and saw Papa John Restaurant across the street. He could get takeout. And right next door was the ABC fine wine store. He also needed to buy a few bottles of good wine to throw a celebration party for himself and what he hoped would be repayment of some of the debt he owed. He believed firmly that opportunity knocked only once on a man's door and right now opportunity was trying to beat his damned door down. This was exactly the moment, the crucial moment that he had to resort to blackmail. Blackmail was such a sweet thing when you held all the cards. Maybe the right word should be restitution. Blackmail was an ugly word, but sweet at the same time. In fact, over the past few months, he had been infatuated with the beauty of her. She was really innocent, believed in love, believed in sweet words and happy future that he had drawn. But money had such a powerful attraction that it could crush love. And of course, he chose the taste of money through his life which was career. Girls could be found anywhere. Paul loved it when things worked in order, and after locking the door of his studio, he tossed his keys and placed the pizza box onto the table in the living room.

"Perfect!" He told himself that everything was going according to plan, and took off his vest, dropping it over the back of the sofa, then loosened the tie at the thought of the money he was going get. One hundred fifty thousand dollars was enough money to change the course of his life. God, he could use a drink and a woman. *Money is a powerful aphrodisiac.* Pleased himself, he rolled up his sleeves, walked into the kitchen, opened the refrigerator, and found an opened bottle of wine, pouring himself a drink.

Steady, he knew, she was now perspiring by his intentions. She's searching for a way out. Smiling, he glanced at a jar of olives, took out two and dropping them into the glass.

"Proud of me?" He asked them, then took a sip. "Um, delicious!"

He plucked one olive from the glass and sucked the sweet chili from it, enjoyed the cold juice mixed with the warm of Gin which reminded him that he should drink less. But he went to the liquor cabinet, where he poured one measure of vodka with lime juice, then took the glass to the table into the living room, where he dropped into his favorite chair, picking up the remote control to turn on the TV. Then as it started glowing, the volume low, he opened the box and pulled out a slice of pizza and took a bite. A sportscaster started rattling of the day's scores while highlights flashed in rapid-fire images the screen. He liked to eat while watching television. The truth was that he loved his private way of living and thinking. There was only one rule in his life, not to get attached to anything but money. Money could help him doing a lot of things.

Money that would soon be in his hand, he thought. Yes, the sooner, the better. So, Steady understood that his visit was not by chance, that she could make it happen quickly.

That's an intriguing thought, and it should work as planned. He took another bite of pizza, then took a long sip of cool wine, but he told himself, only this glass. Saving the drink for his next celebration.

Drank all the wine in the glass, savoring the last drop, put it down on the table, he needed to make a phone call. *Oh yeah, the fun is just beginning.*

Paul finished second slice of pizza and was on his third glass of vodka when his cell phone on the table took that moment to ring. Bringing him back from his thoughts, he picked it up, and glanced at the screen. It's a strange number, but he hit the button anyway to read the text message. *This time, I'm going to send somebody to deal with you, and I hope you'll keep your words.*

"Yes," his inside tensed a bit as he said himself, and the doorbell rang.

"What the hell?" He wasn't expecting anyone at the moment, but grinned when he heard the man's voice said. "Paul? Are you home?"

He knew who was ringing the doorbell and unable to wait. "Coming," he hurried to the door, unlocked the top and bottom one, pulling the safety chain lock and opened it without first looking through the peephole. The smile on his face disappeared. Not the one he expected. Instead, he was hit in the face by a powerful punch that he had no time to dodge, and the force of it made him dizzy and off balance, falling backward into the house without being able to recognize his attacker.

The pain welled inside his head, lights flickered and stars burst before his eyes, and the side of his face quickly swelled up and his ears buzzed in disbelief. But he tried to hang onto consciousness to fight, and dazed he looked up to see a figure approaching him, holding a stun gun in the hand, ready to attack him again. "Hey wait!" He demanded.

But it was too late, he squeezed the trigger. A hundred thousand volts of electricity jolted through his body. In heartbeat, he lost all control, felt pain explode as his body convulsed, and everything went black, taking that pain away from him.

Chapter 6

Family is not about blood ties, it's about concerning for the feelings of others.

F eeling happy to come home to his beautiful house and parked his car behind Harley Davidson, the gleaming black and chrome motorcycle with its vanity plates belonged to Tiffany. The kind of motor engine, he mused, that scream out, traffic police, one more speeding ticket, please. Obviously, his life had become much more interesting since he had met a woman who was teaching him how powerful the throttle at the fast speed of motorcycle was, and how erotic it was. He stepped out of the car, shook his head at it without being able to suppress the smile on his face as he crossed the driveway to the fancy glass of the entry door and held a bottle of wine in his hand. He was about to use his fingers to enter the code to open the door, but the door swung open from the inside. Light and warmth poured out, and she appeared in the doorway with a warm smile to greet him.

He loved to see her face smile up at him, her mirror blue eyes seeming to fill themselves only with him. "Hi, babe," he said, as he always did, returned a smile to her as she stared at him.

He was beautiful to look at, she mused, thinking. Physically, he was as close to male perfection as she could imagine, with chestnut, thick and full hair, and clear brown eyes. In particular, was his killer smile on the long, narrow face, expressing both sexy and angelic. His tall figure seemed to be suitable for Italian fashion suit, and the truth was, he had been on the cover of several magazines, to the absolute credibility of his family. Today he was wearing a black one and white shirt, matching his dark angel looks. Classy and expensive, everything about him was expensive, at the big time, in the noble period, and a life everyone dreamed of having. But from the moment she saw him naked, she knew there was no part of him was soft. Sophisticated, tough, erudite, shrewd, he was an interesting man.

"You're always on time. I just finished work and you brought wine." She said, stood on tiptoe, wrapped her arms around his neck, and gave him a long, passionate kiss. "This is the style of the man I like the most."

He held her tight for a moment, with the bottle stuck between their bodies, and then his face revealed a smile of pure gratitude as he stepped back, letting his eyes traveled down lazily her feet then upward to her head, then lingering on the high swell of her breasts with two pink nipples hidden behind a thin bra rose high before they looked up into her eyes.

"*Oh, sweet Jesus!*" Bush Jr exclaimed, shoving her quickly into foyer of the house, pushed the door closed with his shoe foot, and his eyes followed the line of her body again, from top to bottom, observing every detail. The blood in his head was starting to heat up as he realized she was mostly naked. On her skin only two tiny pieces of thin Victoria's lingerie that concealed nor let her body which looked damn seductive included with her musky perfume. He went right to the obvious question. "What mood is this you're in, Tiffany?"

She followed the direction of his gaze was lingering on her sensitive parts and looked down at herself. "Happiness," she replied in a low voice, removing his tie and tossed it aside on the floor. "Affectionate. What mood is this you're in, Bush Jr?"

He didn't feel awkward or embarrassed at all, for she was always walking around the house without clothes on, and he had no shame when it came to matters of nudity and physical intimacy. Instead, her fiery Venus-like figure always attracted him. It was a part of the feeling she gave him, because he was tied to her. While one part of him opposed the feeling, another part welcomed it. "Grateful, and in addition, you smell good."

She eased back and giggled. "You haven't seen anything yet."

"I've been seeing enough, and it's full of surprises." He said, handing the bottle to her, and looking at her lustfully.

Admittedly, she had a tall, bubbly and voluptuous figure, but mostly in her long legs. By his estimation, their smooth length, much more than the formation. Beautiful body with white, pink, fiery skin without a wrinkle, without a spot, with blond hair braided in a strange way, lying down the middle of her bare back, close to her waist where like begging to be held by a man's hands. And she was wearing her sexiest lingerie, with a black lacy bra had tiny polka dots, matching with tiny lace panties. They're sexy and had ever been his pleasure to observe. Her bra didn't fully cover her plump white breasts and slid down the curve of them, pressing against it so tightly that her nipples stood out in arrogant relief. Turning his gaze back to her face, he thought. High cheekbones that could cut glass, a mouth made for wild sex, and blue eyes of the sea of sin, diamond drops on her ears and a slim gold watch on her wrist, along with the glitter of diamond tennis bracelet. His lips cursed slowly.

She glanced at the label and inspected the wine admiringly. Her years of working at foods had taught her something about knowing the best vintage, and fine wines were one of his passions. It was an exquisite Dom Pérignon Vintage 2004.

He considered one of Tiffany's finest traits to be her appreciation for good wine. "Your favorite, isn't it?" He said with a broad grin.

Bush Jr was also the kindest, the gentlest, most caring person she'd ever met in her life. She also knew he was one of those rare people who would always be in her life because he knew. "Perfect, come along, Bush Jr, I've more surprises for you." She said, linked her arm through his and, with stars in her eyes, walked with him to drawing room.

Very close to perfect, with colorful items, candles flicking in the silver holders on the white tablecloth, the scent of good food, the gleam of fine crystal, and the music played low through the hidden speakers. Bush Jr might not realize he was being courted, but she thought she was doing an excellent job of it with the bottle of wine helping as she nestled it into the waiting silver icy bucket.

Puzzled, Bush Jr took his suit jacket off, hung it carefully on the back of a chair as noticing a dining table arranged with candles lit on the white tablecloth, a single rose spread from a slim vase while the tea lights flickered in the clear glass, adding the music was playing softly in the background that he could feel the romantic mood envelop him and had no idea what the hell she was up to. "Wow, it's quite romantic around here! What do we have for tonight?"

"Nothing, it's just a home-cooked meal, Asian-style. Why don't you open the bottle now? Let me put some clothes on. Dinner will be served."

The room smelled seductive, and so did she. Tiffany was one of those women who oozed sexuality. Her body was like a beautiful sculpted statue, and the way she moved as her round, firm buttocks swayed unconsciously and sensuously. The kind of female trick that Bush Jr knew it would draw his eyes to her exposed attractions that made him want to run over and touch them.

"No need." He caught her hands before she could turn away, and his own sliding around her waist, reaching down to her bare buttocks where he squeezed her curves, then pressing into his hips. "Please don't. Stay sexy. Like that."

She felt the bulge in his pants, silently telling her that he was aroused. "What you see is what you get."

Unable to contain his overflowing emotion, his hands reached up to cup one of her breasts. "And what you're doing is driving me crazy." He said, then covered her mouth with his own.

Not resisting as her mind swimming in his passionate kiss as his tongue slid past her teeth, explored, and increased pleasure when his hand was on belly crawled up one of her breasts and rubbed it. She felt her body go limp in his arms, the blood flowing up and down her body made her realized how much she loved this man.

Moaning, her hands stroking his hair and her arms around him returning her greedy satisfaction with him by kissing him deeply, passionately in the ways she knew he loved. Two tongues intertwined and it was the most passionate kiss they'd ever shared. She felt his arms enclosing her, his fingers easing into her hair to hold her head where he wanted it as he began to deepen the kiss. And what that mean? She had no idea, so when he finally lifted his head, a cocksure smile twisting his lips, she said. "Are you feeling alright? What happened?"

"Never better, why do you ask?"

"Because I'm able to tell a great deal from the way you kiss me today. What did you have in mind?"

He was thinking of stripping her naked so his fingertips started to tingle. "You," he said so simply. "I thought about you the whole time we were away. And now, you seemed a bit mysterious. No, you're astute, but the reason being was the outfit you're wearing. You know. I have a weakness for romance, love to be seduced and passionate."

How could be wearing the outfit so sensual, so erotic, and such a turn-on? "Indeed, I am, but that wasn't what I have for you tonight. In fact, there are many more else."

His smile was quicker this time and skimmed his hands down her sides to her hips. "It looks to me like you're doing it just fine, and so far, I like it."

His fingers were brushing the split between her buttocks, and erotic images filled her mind. "Oh, there are many other good things." She promised with a seductive smile teasing her lips that she would show her gratitude in the only way she knew how. And she did. "Would you be interested if I told you why we aren't rolling around on this fancy rug, finishing what we started?"

Sex, obviously and he liked what she meant, nearly been enough stimulate to practice. "I thought we should start dinner first."

Really, really, is that what you're trying to do?

Since she had decided to take him to bed tonight, Tiffany saw no reason why she shouldn't start the proceedings a little earlier than planned, so she moved her mouth, cruising seductively just under his ear, bit his lobe between her teeth, and her hand slid onto his crotch. "Sex now, food later, it's good for you." Her other hand slid into his shirt, caressing, teasing and inviting.

The fact was he was always hungry around Tiffany, but not hungry because of the delicious dishes she cooked, but because of the seductive smell emanating from her, making him want to bury his face all over her body and enjoyed. "Are you sure that's what you want?

If she'd been intending to set the stage for romance, she had succeeded expertly as she felt his hands reach behind her firm buttocks and squeeze, according to the order of the plan. And felt his naked, hard and hot penis pushing inside her, making her moan deep in her throat as she pressed hard to cut him off. "Don't ask me anything more, and make love to me, Bush Jr."

Her demand made him laugh. He liked her this way. Because that was probably an invitation of happiness. The kind of happiness in which sex and love had to be mixed. He could enjoy her in a hundred different ways, because every time he smelled the scent of sex coming from her, he was immediately affected. That scent had the power to drive him crazy, and it made him horny as hell. "All right," he answered as his cock stirred, his erection coming to life. He scooped an arm under her knee and lifted her in an easy movement. His lips nuzzled her ear. "Sometimes you're really bossy."

Simply giving in, she looped and tightened her arms around his neck, feeling his erection rubbing against her thigh and around the fragile barrier of her panties demanding entry. "I know. I can't help it, but you love what I do to you, right?"

She was right. His willpower had very specific limit, and he was fast approaching it as his erection harder and more painful against his trousers and wept for release. "I do. You're a lovely naughty woman."

It felt good when his warm lips found hers again. And when she tasted his hunger for her, felt his need for her as he toed off his shoes, and slowly walked and carrying her into the living room.

As he lowered her gently on the beautiful rug in front of fire, he stepped back, and she watched him quickly pulled off his shirt, removed his pants, revealed just how hard and muscled he was, and a lot more besides. His erection sprang free as he pulled his pair of black boxers' briefs and threw them impatiently to one side as a fire crackled, like accompaniment to the romance of Chopin and his beautiful naked body.

She sat up, touching the tip of his erection, and wrapped her fingers around then started to stroke, driven by the need to feel him in her hand.

She liked the way her touch, pleasuring him, made Bush Jr's body shuddered and reacted. "Oh, Tiffany..."

Each movement of her hand stroking his erect penis up and down continuously made him moan in pleasure, and when he couldn't stand this torture, he pushed her backward and gently lowered them both to the rug. Excitement filled him, he crawled up and his mouth fastened on hers as his hand caressed from her throat, down to her round breasts, cupping one of them, using his fingertips to circle her nipple over the lacy fabric of her bra, and felt in satisfaction as her nipple tightened to hard point. "Sweet," he whispered.

Before she could complain or ask anything else, he lay on top of her, chest to chest and between her parted thighs, his weight flush to her pelvis sent the heat spiraling deep in her innermost core where it was wet and hot and dark. Desire swirled through her blood, she bit her teeth into his shoulder, craving that wild taste of his flesh.

Enjoying the feeling of her smooth, warm skin under his body, but the thin lace straps of her bras made his palms feel entangled, as did the tiny lace panties covered the juncture of her thighs were blocked her from him, and abraded the skin of his groin, a gentle but cruel pleasure. Quickly his hands found the clasp in the center of the bra and surrendered to his magical fingers removing them from her, revealing her swaying breasts before he left them on the floor. His eyes worshiped her high, bare breasts. The more he looked, the more aroused he became. So he began tasting the scented sweetness from them. His tongue licked around the rim of the nipple, before sucking on its red-pink hard nipple, while his hands quickly removing the remaining tiny lace panties on her body, so that there was no longer a barrier between her flesh, and to satisfy his need for enjoyment.

There was no shame between them, not modestly, they had been through so much, and he knew her so well, knew exactly how and where to touch her, and ignored the way the part between her thighs was seductively tempting him.

But he had to taste more of her. His tongue left her breasts, then traced a path down the middle of her torso.

Her abdomen heaved up and down in response as his tongue circled her belly button, but he's still taking that slow journey her skin down to the center of her body to where her legs joined with his breathing hotter and faster, and then he blew on her pubic hair to make a small space for his tongue. So, he could smell the musk of her arousal from the welcoming place was wet already.

Desire pounded through her vein, her back bowed, her fingers tangled in his hair and she drew his head closer still, cradling him against him, feeling his mouth and tongue working magic, touching, flicking, sucking, and toying with her as if he knew exactly how to pleasure her. Her body arching, pushed her ass up, smacked him in the face with a desire she had never even dreamed, and hoping he never, ever stopped. On a cry of pleasure, she could only moan his name to relieve herself.

Her moaning along with tilting her pelvis up for more, unable to control the rush of her pleasure, made his hunger grow more and more intense while he tried to keep his tongue in place. But to increase the intensity give her to the climax, he inserted it slowly deep inside her and felt the contraction. Her lust overflowed, and he sipped like it was fine champagne, and he intended to make the drink last. He didn't stop. He consumed her so much that his face was soaked. It's from him and her.

Before she could absorb all the ecstasy feelings, a new feeling of excitement came as he inserted a finger inside of her, pushing in all the way then withdrawing, then circled her swollen center, finding the perfect steady rhythm. She nearly came right there, and at the same time, couldn't help but crying. "No more. Inside, I need you inside me, oh please …"

With her blue eyes fierce, he paused, knowing she near her climax as she tried to reach for something only, he could give her.

He crawled up her body, hands caress her breasts, lips skimming her nipples, and his dick paused at her entrance that was ready to open, to receive it. As if the first thrust of him inside would make her come. "Don't make me beg again," she whispered, and spread her legs.

As desperate as she, he drove in deep. She cried out as his piercing hit the magical spot. She tipped her head, her mouth opened wide. "Oh, God..."

She's so close. "Is this what you want?" He asked softly, repeating the question as he stroked her mindlessly, bringing her to the point of desperation then easing off again.

She was panting, her breath fast and shallow, her blood coursing hot through her veins, her mind spinning in images of lovemaking and desire. *No, no, she wanted more.* But she couldn't answer when the shock vibrated, wave after wave, and everything else went away. What they'd had was good sex. And more than that, it was Bush Jr. The way he made her felt with a look, with a word. He was maddening, bossy, unrelenting... and hers, for now.

He held her tight, strong hands gripping her waist, keeping their bodies pressed together as he jerked upward, thrusting in and out, faster and faster.

Fast and furious, they locked into their own rhythm, each driving the other growing more urgent. Pleasure surged up like waves crashing against each other.

The orgasm milked every muscle in her body, squeezing mercilessly so her hands found slippery purchase on his sweat slicked shoulder, and her fingers digging into the rug for stability.

Bush Jr tried to go slow, but there were too many sensations breaking over him to know anything, but the driving needs to claim her.

He groaned. "Tiffany ... It's too good. I'm going to lose it."

She felt him tense, but the climax ripped through her, shredding her system to tatters, and her hips jerked helplessly as the orgasm hit her, then the spasms after spasms kept going on and on. "Oooooh," she whispered as at last he lunged upward, thigh muscles straining and taut.

With a growl and one last, hard thrust, he spilled his seed inside her.

Wave after wave of it slammed into him until he collapsed atop her, his body as covered in perspiration as hers, and his own heart echoing the frantic beat of her.

She melted like candle wax onto the floor when he released her. They simply lay there, weak and sated as her head resting on the hard muscle of his chest, but she felt wonderful then managed a smile wondered what he was thinking.

The lovemaking had always been good between them, and Bush Jr knew it could easily become addictive, again.

He felt joy and happiness. Not only just the way she made love, not just her beauty, intelligence and sexiness, but he also grateful to her for cooking many of his favorite dishes. This was his Tiffany and there was no denying that he was in love with her. Bush Jr mused as he took a deep gulp of her favorite wine at the table where they sat together naked in satin robes, after they made love over and over again until they were exhausted. Now they were pleased they were chewed, swallowed and chased the delicious food down with the luxury of drink in silence when their bodies required energy. He looked at his lovely woman, and it's gratifying to see her devouring her food. She's as hungry as he was as her hair was still rumpled around her face. His hands had done that. Her cheeks were flushed as the satin robe threatened to slide off one shoulder and revealing one half-hidden, half-open breast as if to suggest teasing that had brought him on an erection again. His reactions were nature and healthy, and there was something reflecting through the candlelight in her eyes, as if she had a secret that she wasn't quite ready to share with him.

Tiffany returned his wistful eyes looking at her, and was pleased that he was enjoying the food she cooked, obviously enjoying the dinner she had worked so hard to prepare. No one had ever treated her like the way Bush Jr had treated her, and never in her life had she slept with a man she hadn't known for so long. To do so was reckless, potentially dangerous, and certainly irresponsible. But remaining a physical relationship was inevitable. She had no desire to worry about her mistakes with him, but convincing him that they belonged together was crystal clear. A goal she could achieve.

"Is something wrong with looking at me like that?" She asked with a frown. "Your expression looked very funny, Bush Jr."

"No, I'm fine. I was reminiscing about our lovemaking." He reassured her and raised his glass. "So, I toast for that."

Set her fork down on the spaghetti Bolognese, one of her specialties, and looked at him intently. His hair was a sexy mess, his eyes were languid with contentment, but he looked happily as he was smiling like a happy and relaxed child. His sexy and private part seemed to be acting back through the satin fabric, making her feel excited, her face burning as memories of enjoying carnal pleasures together appeared before her eyes, her nipples tightened pain-fully while her thighs squeezed together to relieve the pleasure. Not a simple combination, and simplicity wasn't always what she looked for. She reached for her glass of fine wine and touched it to his. "I love looking at your naked body."

They swallowed the rest of wine, and when they set their own glass down, he cupped her face gently in his hand and kissed her with such deep slow, such deep, concentration. "You're so beautiful, and you taste better than dinner."

He never told her she was beautiful, never cupped her face and kissed like that. Every emotion inside her swam to the surface, shimmered in her heart, in her eyes. "Do I?"

"Yes, and dinner was delicious. I enjoyed every bite, especially the wonderful chicken salad." He pointed at her with his fork before he stabbed more salad. "It's really been a while since I've eaten these foods. How did you know I like these dishes?"

Bush Jr always said good things about her cooking. "I observed and paid attention to know your interests, so I think these are your favorite, perfect with champagne."

He'd dined in the most exclusive restaurant, banquets of the richest and most powerful celebrities in the government, as well as delicious food all over the world. Logically, practically, and honestly, he couldn't say he'd ever tasted better than the dishes he was currently enjoying from her. "Absolutely perfect, they are delicious."

"That's the secret Vietnamese chicken recipe I use to prepare it," she told him exaggeratedly. "The lethal weapon is fish sauce." She liked to meticulously prepare dishes and liked to tell stories to him. Maybe it was because he so clearly didn't expect it and was so appreciative of the things, she tended to take for granted. And even though she'd never considered herself a nurturer, but it made her feel good to be needed. "Now I must kill you."

She made him smile. "Very nice," he lowered his head to touch his lips to hers. "I wouldn't do that if I was you. And we don't have any secrets to hide from each other, do we?"

"Yes." She held her glass out so he could pour wine into it for her. God. Should she tell him? He deserved to know. *Bush Jr, I'm your ...* was so strong that Tiffany bit the inside of her lips to keep from speaking, but instead. "We should tell each other the truth. Be honest."

Bush Jr removed a bottle of champagne from ice as his eyes never leaving her. "That's the most important thing. You're a chef, and I like to eat your cooking. Did you create Vietnamese food because of me?"

She watched he poured the rest of pale gold bubbling liquid into their glasses and crossed hers to her. "Yes. That's the idea," she took a sip of her favorite champagne. "But the question is, Bush Jr, do I make you happy?"

He lifted his hand and ran his index finger over her throat and down between her large, round breasts when emotions stripped away his control and all logic. He'd known so many kinds of women, young girls were smart but greedy, the wealthy aristocrat made him even more bored with both their wealth and traditional personalities. As for the women who were successful in their careers, which both of them were looking for they didn't want to get married. Tiffany Stanley with the cool blue eyes and quiet voice left him uncertain as to what pigeonhole she'd fit into. It seemed she had all and none of the feminine qualities he understood. The only thing he was certain of was that he wanted her to somehow integrate into his life. "Yes. You've pleased me so much tonight, Miss Tiffany. I love you."

Bush Jr said openly that he loved her, and anytime he said it, it touched her heart. But it wasn't something they often said to each other, nor did they talk about the future. They lived in the present, and each one was perfectly content living alone during the work week, and their weekends together were always relaxing and fun. They didn't argue and disagree about those things. Because it was the perfect arrangement for both of them. The blood ringing in her ears, she set the glass down precisely then stared at him. "What? What did you just say?"

"You heard what I said."

"You said... you said you loved me. Are you telling me the truth?"

"No, I'm lying."

"Don't try to be funny. I haven't knocked anyone down before, but I can do it to you."

It made him laughed. "Well, in that case, forget it."

Her smile disappeared. "I don't want to forget it. I need to hear the sweet words that every woman wants to hear. Please."

"Getting feisty, are we?" He didn't mean to say it that way, but he did. So he should end it and finally had the courage to admit it. He scooped her up and into his lap, his mouth touching her nose, her temple, and her chin. "My love is always quiet, because I didn't know how to say to be true to my feeling." He pulled her close, feeling her huge breasts pressed against his chest, just the way he loved it. "Hoping you feel it that I love you."

She'd have known without the words. It was all in his eyes, in the way he looked at her, touched and caressed her. It had been there for a very long time, and she'd never noticed. "I love you. There. Satisfied?"

She kissed him to answer and whispered back. "I love you, too. And Bush Jr?"

"Yes."

"We need to talk about everything that's been going on."

He looked curiously, may be a little bit serious. "It's about me, isn't it?"

"About you, but not because of you," Tiffany sighed. "I just … I just guess I'm afraid."

His eyes softened with sympathy and tried to reassure her. "I tell you this. The best part is what we already have... Loving each other, being together, making love each other... I love everything about you, Tiffany. Whatever comes now is just an added wonderful gift, but it's not the best part. You are. We can go from here, babe. I'll give you everything I have. That's my promise."

Tiffany squirmed on his lap, looked at his face was serious, and his eyes fastened on hers, were filled with love. "What are you planning to do? And why are you looking at me like that?"

He kept his eyes on hers. "Like what?"

"Like you knew exactly what I was thinking and was trying not to think."

"Really?" Bush Jr relaxed his features and took both of her hands. He didn't just love her, he realized. He very nearly adored her. There were a great many things he found he wasn't certain of at that moment, but he knew without a doubt he couldn't live without her. "I want us to be together."

She noticed that he said us that meant she wasn't facing it alone this time. "Us?"

"Yes," he swore, and saw the shadow of concern in her eyes. There was no room for worries in their lives tonight. "And now is a good time to talk about the future, while we're both relaxed and happy."

A wave of raw emotion slammed into her as she looked at him. Why now? Why did he suddenly want, need, crave the idea of a future? "What lovely words. I want that very much. But it isn't only me that you'd be taking …"

"You mean my family, or your family?" he cut in, held her, kissed her forehead. "Babe, you're everything I want, and more. The fact that a woman I love is tough just adds some interest to the situation."

When she hadn't responded, so he continued. "Do you remember what I told you on the phone?" He asked, moved on to another topic.

She nodded her head. "Yes, I remember."

"My parents give a Fourth of July party every year. It's a command performance for me, my sisters and brothers."

Tiffany knew he was close to them, and if she remembered correctly, he was the youngest. He talked about his family a lot.

"Speaking of party, we will have a family dinner tomorrow night at their house. And because I realize you expressed an exciting interest in meeting my family. So, I'd like you join with us."

"Are you mentally prepared to introduce me to them?" She looked somewhat cautious. Tiffany was crazy about him, but she didn't want to push things. She knew how close he was to his family, and she was afraid that her appearance with him might be viewed as an intrusion. Additionally, she felt anxious about receiving their approval. Meeting his parents and family had never been one of her favorite pastimes, and at her age, it made her feel a little foolish. "This is big step forward for me."

This seemed like the perfect opportunity, and he said. "Yes, it is. You're the initiator, so you will have to accept. And I believe everyone will love to meeting you."

She startled by his offer. Her blue eyes shone with happiness, and she gaped at him speechlessly. Finally, she answered. "That's a nice invitation, Bush Jr. I'm grateful, really, I am. But that's not what I want to tell you. Something else actually I want to talk with you about."

His face went blank, holding her close. "Is it something I should know about?"

"I, um, oh Christ, this is hard." Sighing loudly, she avoided his eyes. "This is part of my past that would affect our present and our future."

"Nothing could do that. Or because you think I won't love you anymore, once you tell me."

Well, he gave good reason. She inhaled a deep breath. "No, I just think you'll be very angry, because I didn't tell you much of the truth earlier."

"It's okay, I can handle it, babe. I promise."

"I know you can," she said, trying to believe that. But wondering if she had guts to tell him her darkest secret. Linking her finger together, she silently prayed for strength. "I've been hiding a truth from you, and everyone else."

"Hiding, hiding what?" He demanded. "You know I hate secrets." Though he still spoke quietly, but there was some wariness to his tone, and waiting to hear whatever she had to say.

✿❋ ＊ ❋✿

A minute ago, from that time, Steady sat on the edge of the bed in her bedroom, swallowed the rest of wine in her second glass to calm herself after getting Bush Jr's secretary on the line and had the information what she wanted to know. But her patience ran out as she glanced at the clock on the wall. It's a little past eight. She set the glass on nightstand, picking up her cell phone and checked her messages, but Bush Jr still hadn't called her back. So, she called him again.

✿❋ ＊ ❋✿

Tiffany smiled at his puzzled expression, but she told herself. Now is the time or there will be no other time. and could hear a drum roll in her head. The moment you've been waiting for. A horrid rational little voice inside her head advised her. Don't dig yourself into a deeper grave. He deserves to know the truth. Let him know who you are and you're going to have a baby. Even though you love him with all your heart, you can't live a lie if you are together, and this will always be an obstacle between you. To avoid being judged, you must tell him. Therefore, she reached out and took his hand for a squeeze. "Bush Jr." she paused and took a deep breath.

"Good God, whatever it is, just say it."

Tell him, Tiffany. Get it out. But before she could answer, his cell phone in his suit jacket was so inappropriately, ringing at this very moment, distracting them both. It interrupted her answer, and took away all her courage to let him know that he was going to be a father later next year. Irritated, she ordered. "Ignore it. Let them leave a message."

Bush Jr looked at the vest hung on the chair, thought that he had shut it off, and he debated if he should answer it, still hesitant, the phone rang again. He was one of those people who could not ignore a ringing phone.

103

Because in his position, he should have answered the call immediately. He blew out a sigh. "I'm sorry, babe. Can we talk about that later? And if you don't mind let me check the call. I just make sure something hasn't hit a snag with my meeting today."

Business phone calls often came when the two of them were together, and he never shied away from it. Even though her mood and opportunity were ruined, but she tried to smile. "Sure, go ahead, babe. I'll go make you some coffee."

"Thanks, babe. That would be great." Bush Jr said, brushed a sweet kiss to her lips, and then came to his feet, setting her aside.

She cleared the empty plates from the table and then carried them to the sink while Bush Jr pulled it out. At first, he smiled when he saw who was calling onto the screen, and then the smile turned to a frown. He debated whether to answer. He couldn't deal with her right now, at least not personally. If she needed to talk to him about business, she could leave a message, then he might call her back but decided if he didn't, she would just keep calling. His sister, Steady was pretty, tall and six years older than him, and always striving to get what she wanted. If she was calling at eight in the night, it wasn't just saying hello. She had to be on some damned mission.

He clicked on the phone to answer. "Hello, Steady."

"Thanks God." Her voice seemed happily. "I've been trying to reach you for hours. You didn't return any call. Glad I finally caught you."

She never called anyone unless she wanted or needed something. She was always like that. And her operative sounded tense, upset. "I'm sorry, sister. I had it turned the silence mode all day while I was dealing with the meetings, and I don't work by the clock, you know that." Bush Jr explained. "But anyway, I'm at dinner with my friend now."

"Oh, looks like I interrupted your dinner."

"It's alright, we're just finishing up. So what's up?"

"I didn't want to bother you, but I really don't know what else to do."

That's not Steady's character, a determined woman who knew her own mind and wasn't afraid to show you how to run your life and anyone else. "No, it's fine. We've finished dinner, just waiting to have coffee. Is there something wrong?"

"It's too complicated to explain on the phone, but let's just say this... It's one of my personal matters."

"Steady, quit hedging and tell me what's going on?" Bush Jr demanded a bit impatiently. He was alarmed more than curious. "Well, brother, I'm... I'm in trouble." She had admitted.

The panic in her voice came through the phone loud and clear. "What kind of trouble?" he asked suspiciously. "I have trouble with Paul Si."

"Who's Paul Si?"

"The photographer I've been seeing off and on for the past few months."

"Tell me about him and what actually is it about?" He sat back in his chair, looked at Tiffany returned, and set a mug of coffee in front of him.

Tiffany heard his exclamation and saw his face change. She wondered, but just cleaned up the rest on the table as he stayed on the phone, listening intently.

"So those were the lies I discovered on my own. He had some problem with the law." Steady went on. "He told me that time, too, he was ashamed to tell me the truth. But he's a phony and a bullshitter. He has some money, and preys on models."

Bush Jr couldn't believe his ears. Though he'd never much liked Paul Si, but he was wanting to kill him, for the ugly things he did to his sister. He pretended to stay calm but sighed into the phone. "When did he ask you for the money?"

"Two weeks ago, he just came right out and asked for a lump sum payment for another business venture."

"How much did he want?"

"Not much, a hundred fifty thousand for last one and he'd walk away."

"Then why didn't pay for him?"

"Because I said no for, I had nerve to be angry at what he was suggesting. Then he explained that if I didn't cooperate, he would simply blackmail me. We've been fighting ever since, and he just showed up at our parents' house at dinner time. He gave me twenty-four hours to deal with it. Brother, it isn't often I can't handle things or find myself so scared that I called you for help."

Steady said in a heartbroken. It broke his heart, too, to hear her sounding so worried. "He's just trying to mentally terrorize you, and he succeeded."

"Not really, I think he's the type of person with a personality disorder and lack of conscience. And others who knew him also said he's a pathological liar."

"Without a doubt," he felt deeply sorry for her, and understood better than most people were very distraught and frightened when they find themselves in such a situation. "So what do you want me to do for you, sister?"

"I think, just giving him what he's asked for." She admitted.

"Then why don't you write a check to sort out the situation and solve the problem?"

"That's not easy just what you think, brother. He only wants to transact in cash."

"Cash?" His voice startled Tiffany. Her expression was intense not understanding what was going on as she was watching him and tried to listen.

"That's right. It must be small, unmarked, untraceable bills."

"Steady, leave it all to me, and I'll be paying him a visit." He said reassuringly, and willing to do that for her and their family.

Steady had felt extremely depressed about her relationship with Paul. He had in his possession a video or pictures of her naked body which he had recorded or took with a hidden camera. He had made her watch them which she now believed was doomed to failure. The end was coming, of that she was sure, she could only hope it would not be too messy. "I appreciate, brother. But be careful, he is a criminal. Who knows what further trouble he might cause for us? I mean I can't afford more problems right now. No nonsense, no scandal to taint our family reputation. I also wouldn't want anything to happen to you."

He realized that Steady was genuinely afraid, and he tried to reassure her. "Those won't happen, sister and don't worry, I'm always careful," he said, trying sound as if he had some control over anything. "No matter how smart he is, but the best weapon we ever have is power of money, and I'll let him have it right between the eyes."

Money was no object, but also Bush Jr was capable of anything, even murder. She was convinced of that. "Money is power, but it doesn't mean you can do whatever you want."

"We're a Jefferson, aren't we? But leave it to me." Bush Jr said, overwhelmed with concern for her. "Believe me, I know how to handle him in my way, and I'll safely arrange and settle this matter for you."

"And what way is that?"

"I have a friend who used to serve in the Special Forces and is currently a detective, but also is my secret bodyguard. He owes me a big favor. I think this is an opportunity for me to ask him for solving this matter for you."

Is it necessary? Needed to contact the police? Thinking with certainty, but she knew how Bush Jr's brain worked, and had seen how he handled the business. When he had made up his mind, he wasn't going to budge. He also was a sociopath who would stop at nothing to do them harm. Her mother had always said that. She sighed in relieve. "All right, brother. You do what you think is best, and sorry I dragged you into this mess of mine."

"There's no need, and that's what family does. I'll call Nick, and you call to let him know I'm coming."

❀❀★❀❀

Silent and thoughtful, he stared at his mug of coffee, after they hung up, and the worried light and anger in his eyes told her it was bad. Tiffany placed her hand on his shoulder, couldn't help herself from asking. "Bush Jr, you've got a peculiar expression on your face. Bad news?"

This was serious. He looked up at her thoughtfully, realizing once again that how well she knew him. "I'm sorry. It's Steady, my sister." The words sounded like a reproach, and she sat down next to him. "Okay. So, what's happened?"

With great effort, he told her the main part. "She was blackmailed."

"Oh, God!" Tiffany exclaimed, looked stunned. "What are you going to do? Need my help?"

He smiled at her. "Don't look so concerned, babe, but thank you for your asking."

And because he still looked worried, so she kept on asking. "How do you plan to handle about it?"

"Drive to his studio. It's risky to negotiate over the phone call or an email. It must face each other directly. I can be there within a few hours."

Tiffany grabbed his arm. "You should not go alone. I'll come with you." That was the only decent thing to do.

Bush Jr stared at her. "You don't have to come with me. This isn't your problem. I can solve it myself."

Steady was his sister. On top of that, she wanted to help Bush Jr. She'd thought he understood that. His problems had become her problems, too. "I know. But why should I sit at home and worrying about you and what sort of trouble you'd get into, when I could be there with you to protect you?"

Bush Jr bent his head and very softly kissed her for the notion of Tiffany with her soft heart doing what it took to protect anyone in the kind of situations they might encounter. "I can handle trouble." He reassured her. "I don't do it alone."

"I know. But let me go with you, just in case you need my backup. I won't hinder you. If stay home, I worry a lot."

Bush Jr considered the offer then noted that she was stubborn as a mule. "Fine," he finally agreed. "And get this started, I'm going to call my friend, then taking some cash."

She took both his hands, held tight. "You take whatever you think you need."

Bush Jr picked his cell phone up, got his feet and immediately dialed Nick's number. He didn't have any particular reason for doing so, but he was in need of his helping, and hoped the whole matter would be resolved as soon as possible.

"This is Nick." He answered.

"Hello, Nick. It is Bush, Jr."

"It's nice to hear your voice, Mr. Bush Jr."

"Sorry for calling you at this time. This is kind of a begging call. I'm hoping you can help me."

"No problem. Tell me what's going on."

"Can we get together this evening, Nick? Are you in the vicinity?" "Yes, I'm. And is everything okay?" he asked, alert as always.

"I need to ask a favor. It's kind of a tough one."

Difficult or not, it didn't matter. Bush Jr had been there through thick and thin for him, and he would do anything he could to help him. "You name it. I'll do it," he said. "Take your time."

"The thing is, this problem isn't the kind you usually deal with and it isn't mine. It's my sister, Steady." Speaking in a low voice, Bush Jr explained the reason and what happening. He went over everything to him. "Can you help me out on this? And I'd like to deal with him tonight."

"I see. I'm at work, but I think I can help you. However, first I need some information." Nick meant well. He wanted to help. "What do you want to know?"

Nick asked a series of questions about Paul, and Bush Jr filled him in as best he could.

"Good," Nick stopped him. "Just one last thing."

"Shoot."

"Does he own any guns?"

"That's what we need to find out."

"It doesn't matter, Bush Jr. I'll run his name and pull his record out from my database to see what I can come up with. But I want to know where we can meet?"

"I appreciate it, and I'll get back to you soon along with the location where we will meet. But I just said that I like to deal with him tonight."

"Don't worry about it," Nick said into his phone to calm him. "I'll be finish and set everything up here in about an hour, so I could meet you there around ten-thirty. What do you think?"

"It's great. And thank you so much. I'll give you a call or text when I'm leaving the house."

"You'll do that and try not worry. We'll resolve everything just fine."

Once he had hung up, Bush Jr asked Tiffany used his laptop in his office, went online and Googled Paul Si for his address. If he's not there, they turned around, come to his studio. That's a plan, and then he walked upstairs to his bedroom. He pressed a button and a panel of bookshelves swung away from the wall. Behind it was a safe, he opened it with a fingerprint lock. Inside it, he drew out some cash, and after placing them separately into two envelopes, he wanted to carry his gun, but he decided it was better not to, and closed everything before he went down to meet Tiffany in the living room.

"It said: Paul Si. 539 Mill Street, Orlando." Tiffany said as soon as she saw him and turned the screen so Bush Jr could read it.

His smile spread. "Good job, babe. Let's set it on GPS."

They left the house and as soon as they got into the luxury sport car, Bush Jr used his cell phone to call Nick again with the information he requited, but the call went directly to voice mail this time, so he apologized for calling at such a late hour, and also text-messaged the address to him, asking him to meet them there. Afterward he planned on heading to Paul's studio, just to make sure if he was there.

"Let's do this." Bush Jr said then he hit the freeway heading North.

Chapter 7

P aul blinked open his heavy eyelids as his head spinning, his body hurt all over and he realized he was breathing through his nose. Something tacky, some kind of tape, had been fastened across his mouth. He tried to move, but his limbs were useless, couldn't move or do what he wanted as his arms were bent behind his back and his hands were tied firmly together and immovable with duct tape, more duct tape bound his ankles to the legs of the chair. Fear buckled through him. Jesus God what was happening? He blinked and memory rushed back, his mind quickly put together the pieces of what had happen since he was attacked by a tall, muscular man. he'd used some kind of stun gun or Taser on him. But he tried to control himself by looking around. The lights in the room were on and the curtains were closed and a rustling sound could be heard coming from inside his office. Sitting still, he heard the drawer being opened and closed. *A robbery?* He forced himself to push aside the question. He had to focus. There it was again. The sound of rustling papers and someone rummaging through the drawers.

Calm down, Paul, he told himself. Concentrate and find a way to escape. If he could only get of the tape around his hands and legs.

Since his eyes scanned the room with all the spy tools lying around, he was impressed, knowing that some of these tools were professional and complicated to use, and this guy was setting up to do some real serious business. A parabolic microphone which lets you hear conversation at least three hundred yards away, and it's got a built-in tape recorder and an output jack. He picked up a pair binocular and knew it had an amplifier attached. Pretty high tech. And with all these devices, he could watch, listen, record, film or take pictures from long distance. It was his job to help him blackmail. However, he guessed Paul stored everything in his computer, and his computer and laptop were both new modern and were connected to his digital camera. But that didn't make it difficult for him to crack the code, because he'd learned from the best and trained in military intelligence, where he became a computer wizard, and knew a way to put his skills to go through everything, every inch of this studio without leaving a trace. When the screen was glowing, he typed in the access code and within a few minutes. A folder was opened and he sent commands to open private files. Information about Paul's business services in the past few months, names, addresses and phone numbers of the people he suspected where the ones Paul was confiscating money from, even information about the project Paul was working on. He deleted all the pictures on Paul's laptop and realized Paul had regained consciousness, but was still scare. Kicking open the door, he approached Paul and picked up the rope he had left on the floor earlier.

With his efforts, he put all his strength to run his wrists back and forth, trying to loosen or tear off the tape that was struck to his hands, but ineffective and suddenly a loop of thick cotton rope was slipped over his head. A noose was tightened around his neck. *Oh, God.* Panic flooded through him. He looked up and saw the rope run up to a block that was fastened to a hook where the ceiling lamp usually hung. Fear and outrage begin to show as he realized this maniac was going to torture him. *Fight, Paul, fight!* He tried to tug, to flail his head, wriggling and trying to find some way to free himself.

But the captor who had assaulted him came into view.

"I don't do that if I was you," his captor muttered as he observed his pathetic attempts at escape.

The first thing Paul saw was a pair of black boots, then a black ski mask that covered his entire head who was massively build, also wearing all in black-jeans, T-shirt, cotton jacket, and gloves. He wondered who the psycho was and why did he have to do this to him?

He thought about torturing Paul to find out where and what he needed. It would be simple enough as he read the expression into his eyes. So, he grasped the end of the rope, pulled and said. "I'm your worst nightmare."

Paul rolled his eyes in terror, and felt the rope cut into his neck and for a few seconds he couldn't breathe. He wiggled his head, trying to tell him stop. It's going to kill him and why? But nothing and the captor understood.

Leaning close, his captor's hot breath against his ear and uttered. "Good, Paul? Do you want to know what's going on?"

He knew who he was. Of course, he did. He had all his belongs, his laptop, his cell phone, probably his name on the poster or magazines. Oh, no, he'd come to realize that Steady sent him. He shouldn't underestimate her. He nodded as furiously as he could with the rope around his neck, and the captor ripped the tape off one side his mouth. It made an awful sound, but he didn't yell, just gasped for air and swallowed back his fear. He had to help himself or had to figure out a way to save himself.

"Listen," Trying to stay calm and not to think about how dire his situation was, he said. "I don't know who you are or why you're doing this, but if you let me go right now and no one would have to know anything. I promise to keep my mouth shut."

The captors seemed to read his utter dependency, his silly, stupid and pathetic desire to please him. "Oh, yeah, right. I believe that. After all the hard work. Do you really think I'm just going to release you? Give me a break. You're smarter than that."

He glanced up at his captor and swore he saw the mockery in the eyes looking down at him through the slits in his mask. And all his hope failed. "Then please tell me what you want from me?"

The captor looped the rope a few times around a radiator pipe. "This is my general idea and I'm going to kill you." He said, tied it with a clove hitch. What the hell was this sick bastard talking about? "You can't murder me."

"Just watch me," he replied, put the tape covered his mouth again. "Better than you deserve for what you did to a woman who trusted you." And then vanished from his field of vision.

Oh God, not only was he going to kill him, but he was going to do it slowly, and painfully, torturing him and somehow satisfying his own fantasies. Therefore, he must try everything to survive. Throwing himself forward in to the chair, knocking it over, struggling to slide to whatever doorway there was, yanking at the tape at his wrists until his arms ached, kicking his feet so hard that pain screamed up his legs to his lower back.

But it was all in vain and his captor returned, pulling up a chair and sat in front of him. Paul tried to avoid looking at his black mask face, but he could not help it. The captor laid a pistol and the living-room table. His pistol, he had found it in the shoe-box in the wardrobe. It was a colt 45.

His heart beating rapidly, felt as if it would explode as he saw his captor, took out the magazine on the table, rolled it up, attached it to the muzzle of the gun. Was this his punishment? "Please, please don't do it." He begged.

"Look at me," his attacker said sternly, slowly ran the muzzle of the gun up to his skull.

Fear turned his blood to ice, but he forced himself to meet his blue eyes were studying him without mercy. "Do you think I'm kidding?"

Paul shook his head to answer, but the captor pulled the trigger anyway. Bam, Paul jerked back, and he screamed in his throat with the panic surging through his blood caused his heart to thunder and he was about to pee his pants in sheer. But he heard this maniac laughed softly in his ear. "Not quite yet. No bullets. Let me show you everything else."

He held up the photograph that he must have printed it out from his hard drive. For god's sake he's a human computer or what? It's encrypted. How could he decode passwords, break through firewalls, get into and browsed through his files? "I assume that this is Steady Jefferson. Did you have fun with her?"

The question was a psychological impact. Paul had no way of answering. His mouth was taped shut and his brain was incapable of formulating a response. The photograph showed… *Good God, he wished he didn't take that.*

"You know who I'm talking about, right? Nod."

Paul nodded, and suddenly he had tears in his eyes. Dear God, help me. He prayed again.

"Let's get the rules of engagement 100 percent clear," he said. "As far as I'm concerned, you should be put to death at once. Whether you survive the night or not makes no difference to me at all. Understand?" More nodding.

"It has probably not escaped your attention that I'm a hit man who likes killing people, especially you."

He pointed at the others photographs that he had left on the living-room table. "I'm going to remove the tape from your mouth. If you scream or raise your voice, I will zap you with this." He held up a stun gun. "This horrific device puts out 100,000 volts. About 50,000 volts next time, since I've used it once and haven't recharged it, understand?" Paul looked doubtful.

"That means that your muscles will stop functioning. That was what you experienced when you opened the door."

He smiled at Paul. "And it means that your legs will not hold you up and you'll end up hanging yourself. After I've zapped you, all I must do is get up and out of here. Everyone will think you committed suicide."

Paul didn't like that option, so he nodded. Good God, he's a fucking crazy killer. And he could not help it. Tears of fear suddenly flowed and he sniffled.

He got up and pulled off the tape off his mouth. His mask face was only an inch from his.

"Don't say a word," he said. "If you talk without permission, I'll zap you."

He waited until Paul stopped snuffling and met his eyes. "You have one chance to survive the night," he said. "One chance-not two and this is how it works. I'm going to ask you a few questions. If you answer them, I'll let you live. Nod if you understand." Paul nodded.

"If you refuse to answer a question, I'll have to zap you. Understand?" He nodded.

"If you lie to me or give an evasive answer, I'll zap you." He nodded.

"There will be not second chance. You answer my questions immediately or you die. If you answer satisfactorily, then you'll survive. It's that simple."

Paul nodded, he believed him. He had no choice. "Please," he said. "I don't want to die, please! ... For the love of God."

"Interesting that you bring up God's love as an argument, and you just broke his first rule you do not talk without his permission."

Paul pressed his lips together, but his fear turned to sheer terror as he recognized the voice and the appearing of the second captor. "Want to know why? Because your dumb luck that you mess up with my daughter."

Impossible, oh, God, oh, God, oh, God! He knew.

Paul sent him a pleading look. "Don't do this!" he cried. "Please!" Yes, he was beginning to understand, and beg for his life.

As far as Brian could tell after taking a bath and stepped out onto the private balcony for a beautiful view of the lake as the June sun slipped low on the horizon. But the words floated in the hot summer air about the repetitive argument over money in the voice that itched his eardrum. They were careless, and he had not been able to contain his curiosity, so he leaned over the railing and pricked up his ears through the open sliding doors. For more than ten minutes, he had listened in astonishment to this rancorous bickering. It seemed became more intense as the man threatened his family and his daughter called him a son of a bitch that made him seethe with anger, and he would have taken measures to combat. If he came to know directly or indirectly, he thought he ought to take some sort of action. His daughter needed to be protected and resolved at all costs. He would do whatever he had to. Back to his bedroom, he picked up his cell phone, called his driver, telling him set the GPS tracking device under the bumper of Paul's car while he's still inside the house. Then calmly he went to her room, knocking on the door. *"Steady, dinner is ready."* And then as soon as the screen came to life, the indicator light starting to blink that given him an opportunity to do a casual business service with Paul.

Now he would pay, and he was going to have to punish him. "That's depending on your cooperative attitude." Brian said as his driver handed a thick manila mailing envelope.

Mixed emotions and thoughts were probably swirling in his head. He was shocked that he was her dad, and he could not have imagined that.

"This is all quite simple," Brian continued and answered for him. "I assume we met, and I know who you are. It would be easier for you if you answer my questions now. I don't want to hurt you any more than I must. The quick, neat way or the painful prolongation depends on which way you choose. So what's it going to be?"

It wasn't a suggestion, it was a command. "I swear. I'll answer anything you ask. I won't lie."

"Good, and answer calmly," Brian said, broke the seal, dumped the contents and began to spread them across on the living room table. There must be at least a hundred pictures, he thought. A few looked like the posed shots, but most of them were obviously taken without the subjects' knowledge and printed off a computer. His stomach turned over as he stared at the shot of Steady, his beautiful daughter, and pulled it out, then carried on. "I'm not going to kill you, because you need time to collect your thoughts. But the minute I get the idea you're trying to dodge a question then it'll cost you."

Paul swallowed. His mouth was dry as a bone, and he could feel the rope tightening around his neck as his killer was laced the restraining rope tighter.

"You like to secretly take photos when people aren't looking." Brian gestured to all the photographs strewn around his studio. Even at superficial glance, he could tell that most were taken with long-distance lenses, their subjects unwariness of the stranger watching them.

"It's my style of art." Paul replied. "People love having their picture taken."

"Even my daughter?" He said, held up the photograph. "She didn't seem happy with your art." Brian paused, glanced up at the ceiling to the light fixture, smoke alarm, and slow-moving fan as if pushing the hot air around where there might had been a tiny camera inside that Paul took and filmed, then watched his daughter as she'd writhed and moaned, and then used them to black mail. He looked back at him, the went on. "With the angle taken in these photos, Steady was here in your studio. How did happen to her?"

Paul did not know how to answer. He could hardly make sense of it himself, how it had begun or why he did that.

Brian raised the stun gun as a reminder.

Fear showed when Paul looked at the photo. "She was so beautiful."

"Of course, she's beautiful. But why I don't see her beauty in your pictures." The picture showed undeniable effect, and Steady would have had no idea she was being photographed.

His head suddenly hurt like a hammer hit it. This was one mistake in his career and his screw up, and it was all he could do was to beg and plead. "Oh, please forgive me."

"I'm not the one you ask for forgiveness. Did she protest?" Paul shook his head.

"So, she thought it was cool that you tied her up and fucked her."

That statement had transported him back the night he had taken Steady to his place and after they had supper, and then sat on the living room sofa. They began kissing and undressing to make love. But he wanted to take naked pictures of her. His idea had turned into an incredible stroke of luck with another camera was hidden in what looked like a smoke detector in the hall ceiling, and it took a low-res photograph every second. Now, it was gone.

"She was drunk. She didn't care."

"Did she?" His voice contained such contempt that Paul closed his eyes.

Lucky as shit, he considered himself too smart to disregard her family, and these pictures were proof that it made clear his role. Now, his every secret lay open to her daddy prying eyes.

"No, I drugged her." He had never told anyone before. He felt the rope tightened his neck as Brian sat down. "That's not art. That was sick."

"Yes," Paul admitted, the words torn from his throat. His jaw slid to side and his eyes narrowed in regret. "God, I'm sorry."

"Sorry means nothing to me." Brian didn't trust Paul, still suspected he might have more copies kept somewhere. "Show your honesty by telling me exactly which video or pictures of her you still have."

"What's it worth to you?" Paul asked, tried to offer to do anything he wanted if he would just not hurt him.

"What's what worth?"

"If I rid of all my images of her. Would you let me go and not prosecute me again?"

Brian could almost read the thoughts in Paul's head. "You're truly the most horrible perverts I've ever met. What you did to my daughter deserves the death penalty. But I told you would live if you answered my questions. I keep my promises. Let's deal it."

"I swear to God, honest. I don't dare keep any of her photos or video records anywhere else. They all are in my computer, in sand dish of my camera and my cell phone which I believe you got them all."

"Good, but I don't trust you. Because a deceitful like you always has a reserve as insurance for the future. But if there were any video or any of pictures somehow will make public or you ever touch her again, I swear, Paul, you'll wish you'd never been born."

He believed what he said. "Yes sir. I keep that in mind."

The killer slowly loosened the knot. Paul collapsed in a slobbering heap on the floor. He saw him put a stool on his coffee table and claim up and unhook the block and tackle. He coiled the rope and stuffed it in his bag while Mr. Brain dropped a kitchen knife behind him.

"You can cut yourself free."

As soon as they disappeared before him and he heard the front door open and close, Paul thought the ghost had paid him a visit. And he tried to cut away the tape on his ankle, and stood up to slice through the tape binding his wrists, then sank down on the sofa. But he staggered to his feet as he saw the chaos on his studio. A desk chair had been kicked over, the computer monitor had been knocked to the floor and the screen had cracked, the drawers hung open, closet and his darkroom had been turned out, and "Fuck." His gun was gone, his laptop as well. His hands shook as he reached for his camera. The lens was shattered, with spider-web cracks spreading over the surface. The back was broken, hanging drunkenly on one hinge, and no scan-disk.

At that instant, Paul was so angry that he picked up the bottle of wine and brought it to his mouth and drank it like water. The liquor burned a hot, angry trail down his throat and his fingers clenched hard over the bottle. In a sudden burst of fury, he threw the bottle of wine against the wall and watched it shatter. "Damn it all to hell," he muttered and fell back into the chair, holding his hurting hand.

✿⁂✲⁂✿

"You have reached your destination," said his GPS, and Bush Jr spotted a parking space, pulled into it across the quiet Mill Street from Paul's studio after they stopped at Paul's house, found he wasn't home. He turned off the engine, took what he needed from the glove compartment.

Nick was waiting for Bush Jr, and he emerged from his vehicle, then walked toward to Bush Jr's car parked on the street.

They stepped out of the car when she saw a man walked to them. That was Nick, she guessed.

"Bush Jr." Nick called out, as they approached. "He's inside."

Nick was forty-eight years old and had joined the Marines when he was twenty-one. He had spent six years in the military and after he was honorably discharged with the rank of lieutenant, he continued to serve in the police in both the weapons and the anti-theft division before he took additional courses and advanced to the crime and violence division of the criminal police. According to reports, he had been involved in thirty-three murder or manslaughter investigations in the past ten years. Fourteen of these investigations were supervised by him. Ten cases had been resolved and four cases had been closed. But he got into with the huge gambling debts that had to be paid off and back taxes due, and eventually got himself into a mess with the IRS and debtors. "Hello, Nick."

Nick was dressing in a dark waist length jacket over jeans, the kind cops wore to conceal their weapons. He was a powerfully built man in excellent shape, military haircut. He glanced from Bush Jr to her and back again with an outstretched hand.

"Thanks for coming over here so quick." Bush Jr shook his hand, flashing a happy smile, and then quickly made the introduction, waving between them. "This is Tiffany, my girlfriend. And Tiffany this is detective

118

Nick Keating, Florida State Police." "It's nice to meet you." Tiffany greeted Nick and offered her hand.

He smiled warmly and shook it in both of his, "the same here."

No one could spend four hundred thousand dollars to help someone without asking for anything in return. Bush Jr did it for him. He signed the checks to pay off his debts and save his family from brokenness and separation. He would never be able to repay this debt of gratitude to Bush Jr. He had not only saved him and his family's lives, but also saved his career. He felt he needed to be absolutely loyal to him, and willing to help him solve everything whenever he needed his help. He had never met Steady, he only knew about her through her images on magazine covers and in the media. If he remembered right, Steady was spoiled, but beautiful with coffee brown hair framed a face that would make a man look twice, high cheekbones, suborn chin, arched eyebrows, hazel eyes, and blessed with the Jefferson and feminine to boot. But she had enough confidence to win people's respect and make friends easily.

Except she needed help, and Bush Jr wouldn't have asked unless he was desperate. So whenever Bush Jr asked him for something, he was going to do everything he could to help him out. Beside he owned him a favor, a big one. It was time for him to return this favor, and he got down to business. "I pulled Paul's files as you requested."

"Thanks. Tell me what's in the file."

He told Bush Jr that through searching for Paul Si's personal background which wasn't hard for him to do. "Paul liked to shoot and was a member of shooting club. According to the public weapon registry, he had a license for a Colt.45 Magnum. But that's about it."

"More than I'd expect. And is it safe to just walk up and knock on the door?" Bush Jr asked.

"We don't really know how dangerous he may be. So, for now, we'll take all the precautions we can, and in case, we'll need the back up." Nick gave a warning, but he offered some helpful suggestions that he would do everything within the limits of law to put an end to the problem before they reached the door. So, Bush Jr told her wait here, stayed inside the car, and kept the doors locked.

"Okay," she agreed and understood. He wanted her someplace where he wouldn't have to worry about her. Still, sometimes there were unexpected surprise, some not the good kind. "Be careful."

His nod indicated he'd heard her, and Nick assured her. "While I'm around, we're fine. Let's go pay a visit to photographer Paul."

Bush Jr smiled, kissed her cheek, and with Nick at his side headed to Paul's studio.

With experience and training, Nick rang the doorbell, pulled him aside, reached his hand inside his jacket to where he kept his gun in shoulder holster, waiting for Paul to open. Bush Jr noticed that was a Sig-Sauer pistol that police were often distributed. There was no noise, no sound of footsteps, he didn't ring the doorbell, but instead he knocked hard, pounded his knuckles against the door.

"Open up. Detective!" Nick ordered.

⁂ ✳ ⁂

Paul nearly jumped out of his skin and cursed himself when the doorbell rang again, following by immediate pounding on the door like an explosion. *What's going on now?* Everything became more troublesome. One disaster had followed another. Stop it! He ordered himself. *He didn't sound like a detective. Detectives usually identified themselves. At least that's what they did in the movies.* He remembered the lesson he just did. He approached the door and keeping to the side.

Nick knocked hard again, this time there were footsteps and he heard a man's voice asked. "Is this some kind of joke?" "Of course not," Nick replied.

The calmness of his own voice brought him relief. He was hanging on. "I want to see your badge."

To his surprise Nick dig into the jacket pocket, took out a small case, flipped it open, and held up his badge in front of peephole. "Okay. Take a closer look. I am a detective with the Florida State Police. So, do you want to let us in, or do you want us to haul you downtown?"

Paul stepped up to the peephole, look through it. "Oh, fuck. Give me a sec."

The sound of two locks being turned, and the door opened slightly, a chain still securing it from the inside as a slice of a man's face peered through the crack. "Listen, detective." He looked nervous. "What are you doing here?"

And Nick got into his character. "I said open the door. I have a search warrant." Bush Jr's eye grew wide as he stared at him. Maybe that was going a little far.

120

"For what?" it was Paul, and he sounded annoyance.

"We believe you are dealing drugs from this address."

"That's ridiculous," he said, closed the door for a second, the chain rattling as it was being released, then the door swung open. "And where is the warrant?"

It was obvious that he knew, but on instinct and immediately, Nick had his own hand on his service weapon as he recognized Paul from his data photo. He stepped into, pointed the gun at his face so he couldn't close the door on, and looked at his hand and clothing to see if he might be armed. His hands were empty, and his clothes he was wearing, not ideal for concealing a weapon. So, Nick yelled. "Lie down on the floor!"

"What's going on?" Paul exclaimed, got down on his knees instead, and gave him a peculiar look. He didn't understand what was happening to him on this strange night when everything seemed to be going wrong.

"You don't need to know. You just need to do what you're told. Now hands behind your back," Nick commanded. "And stay calm. I won't have to hurt you."

There was no end to the tribulations Paul having to suffer that night. He did what he told him and let him locked a pair of handcuffs on his wrists while watched the other followed into and closed the door. And he stared puzzlement at one who he recognized at once. "Are you Jefferson Bush Jr?"

Bush Jr could see that he was astonished. "Good, you know who I am, and why I am here."

Nick replaced his gun in the holster then kicked out a chair. "Get up and sit."

And when Paul got up, falling into the chair, Bush Jr continued. "I repeat. Do as you're tell. And if you cooperate, you'll be treated well. This experience doesn't have to be unpleasant. What I need to have from you is something you're hiding in here. So, where are they?"

"I don't have anything to hide!" Paul said angrily. "But if you come for Steady, you're late. Your dad already took care of it. Take a good look around and look what he'd done to me."

Bush Jr's gaze moved past Paul and around. Despite his living room looked like some dated idea of playboy's love nest. Black leather furniture, white shag carpet, wall mounted stereo system, mixing bar, but his studio was a wreck. Drawers were pulled out, his computers, monitor, video equipment, cameras and printers were scattered in random places. And everywhere Bush Jr looked, there were file folders, papers, magazines, photographs had been dropped on the floor, left in disorder on the table, some of them were pinned to the walls. "Yeah, it's quite chaos, and you look like shit. Tell me what happened?"

Paul told him all chapters of the story, and Bush Jr couldn't hide his surprise. "How did you know that's my father?"

"Everyone who's anyone knows who your father is," he replied. "I know people who have invested in your father's Jennies Fund and have made a handsome profit."

Bush Jr took a moment to consider. Yes, his dad had always been a tough man, and no one played the market like his father does, but he had never thought he would be in action like this before. So, he pulled out his cell phone and punched in a number.

⁂ * ⁂

"Thank you. I'll transfer money directly into your account, Tommy." Brian was in the back of the Mercedes SUV, said to his driver, also his secret bodyguard when he pulled the car into the driveway and cut the ignition.

Tommy remembered when he was ill, and tragedy struck him hard. Lydia who was his wife, killed in car accident. With no one able to care for him, his son Jason was sent to live with his mother. Life as he had known it was over and there was nothing left for him to look forward to. And just when all seem lost, he met Mr. Brian who said the words of sympathy 'sorry about your loss' when he sat strapped into a wheelchair at his wife's funeral. And when it was over at last, he called him late that night which he never forgot when he sat alone in his office, the lights out, the only illumination coming from the one-bulb lamp on the desk, and unlocked a drawer, quietly slipped the gun he kept there out of its case and held the weapon in his hand. It was loaded, and he sat holding it, letting his fingers get to feel its cold, steel edges.

He hoped tonight he would see his wife again. His life was completely useless and exiting now would be a mercy for him. Nothing in his life mattered to him now. He was ready. He cocked the trigger and slowly raised the gun to his head. And then, as if had an invisible miracle from God, the phone took that moment to ring and distracted him. It's almost midnight, and the number came up on his phone was unfamiliar to him. Probably a wrong number, no one ever called him at that hour. Except when his mother called, but he knew her phone number.

The phone on the desk continued ringing, and then both annoyed and curious, he set the gun down. He was in no hurry, and he didn't want to lose his nerve, but just for this time, he answered the phone.

"Hello?" His voice sounded ghostly. He hadn't spoken to anyone all day, and he had had three stiff scotches that night to strengthen his nerve.

"Tommy? It's Brian. I'm sorry to call so late. How are you and Jason?"

Mr. Brian sounded sympathetic and concerned, but it took him let out a long slow sight, and staring the gun on the desk, in the light of the streetlamps outside.

"What can I do for you, Mr. Brian?" That was all Tommy could think of to say at first, responding with the question instead answering Mr. Brian's inquiry about him and his son.

He could hear the discouragement in Tommy's voice and went straight to the point. "Look, I know this is hard and it's probably not my place to say this, but I'll do what I can for you if you ever need anything. You can count on me, because I understand how you feel, son."

"No. How could you possible understand?" Tears spilled from his eyes, and his fingers ran gently along the barrel, planning to pick up again and use it at the end of the call. "And I'm not your son."

Grief and loss were feelings that he had received and experienced in life. It's not easy to come to terms with that feeling. "Fine, I know that sounds silly, but I'm serious when I consider that feeling. Because, I lost my first wife in the car accident when I was at your age now and lived alone with my father-in-law."

Tommy felt a soul-deep regret and startled by what Mr. Brian just said. He hated this, hated disappointing Mr. Brian, and had no idea how to respond, but he managed. "Did you?"

"I just wished that the accident had never happened. It was no one's fault, which had already been determined. It was just a fluke, but a cruel turn of fate."

"I'm sorry. I didn't know."

"It was a terrible thing, son."

Mr. Brian's voice was full of emotion and compassion when he kept calling him son, and his emotion overwhelmed then as he added. "Her death made me lose my motivation to live so much that I wanted to end my life because of that loss." "Oh God!" Tommy said, unconsciously pushing the gun away from him. "You did."

"Yes, I was so desperate that I no longer appreciated my valuable life. But somehow faith and her spiritual connection helped me overcome this pain, get up and move forward." Mr. Brian admitted then shared with him his own experience with the trials he had undergone. "No one is free from adversity in life, Tommy. Always listen to yourself, be brave to face your own emotions, and you just need to be patience and have faith in a kind and merciful God by comparing with Job's chapter in the Bible."

What an encouragement, but he had no idea how to respond to that when he wasn't sure he believes in a loving, benevolent, and hadn't read the God's word anymore. Tommy sighed. "I'm not sure what I believe anymore."

Brian believed in God. He believed in heaven and hell and that a man would be punished if he rejected God. He'd held fast to the faith that had been with him since he married his wife, Ngân. In his lifetime from there, he never questioned the word of God anymore. Never doubted his faith. Never wondered why he was being tested. It was just the way it was.

"Anything can be lost, but Faith and Hope is our dignity that we cannot lose, no matter what the circumstances," he advised him. "People live in despair are mostly living in the past, just like me before. Grief and loss are feeling only felt by those who know how to love. But because we don't accept reality, we no longer have hope for anything. Therefore, if we still have faith, believe that even the most painful things come into our lives. God could be used for something much better. You will have a more amazing life. Rearing your son, help him go to college, marry and have more children."

If God could take away a devout woman such as Lydia in his moment of need, how could he hope for understanding? "How can I do that when I'm a maimed person?"

"Don't think that way. Get rid of the negative thoughts. No one is useless in this world, Tommy. Simply, we don't have extraordinary bravery to overcome adversity. This time, you're enduring all the difficulties, but in fact, it's the foundation for you to excel in the future. Only the energy that comes from desperate situation can bring into play the visceral strength hidden in each of us. To do that, we need to strengthen our faith in God. And He will help you cope with difficulties."

Possibly, Mr. Brian did not realize the good results with his advice and encouragement that he should not succumb to his condition would have a major impact not only on his life but also on his son's future. Even if he could not bring himself to pray for grand things, he could trust Mr. Brian's faith, depend on his belief that how he finally got the message. "What do you want me to do, Mr. Brian?"

"I'd love to see you tomorrow, though, if you'd like to join us at home for dinner."

Tommy wondered if it was a good idea, but he felt as though something were pushing him to do it. "I'd love to see you, too. I'll be there." He knew he had to do it. "What time?"

"Why don't you come at six o'clock so we can offer you the measures should go far forwards solving your problem?" He suggested.

"I'll be there," Tommy assured him. Never thought words could save lives. When one was in a desperate state, looking around in disorder and dark. Then a good intention with a few comforting words was a lamp that could help overcome the dark fog and out of misery. "And Mr. Brian thanks for calling. You'll never know how much it meant."

"I feel the same way. I look forward to seeing you tomorrow."

"So do I." Tommy assured him, sounded a whole lot happier by the time they hung up, and he sat and stared the gun on his desk and felt as though he had just woken up from a night-mare. He felt guilty and self-indulgent as he picked it up, removed the bullets, and put it back in his desk. He locked the drawer, with shudder, thinking about what he had almost done for his son, and the person who found him.

The blessing in the death of his wife had just come clear that made him almost believe that he had her was watching over him, and like Mr. Brian said 'misfortune is the root of happiness and Faith is the acknowledge from God'. Then as he had promised, Tommy came and stayed for dinner, and thanked to everyone's encouragement, after returning home, for the first time since he had suffered physical pain, grief from loss and hopeless despair, he felt his spirit had become stable. *Yes, when you have God's words in your heart, all things around us change and worry ends when faith begins believe good things will happen.* Mr. Brian had been incredibly supportive and expressed his love for him. He not only provided practical help him recover and brought his fractured family back together, paid all his debt, his mortgage, but also spoke consolingly, and offered him a job that his dad, Smith Anderson used to be a driver for Bush Jefferson. He owed him more than he could ever repay, even his life and swore he'd pay him back one day.

His eyes dart to his boss in the rear-view mirror and thought Mr. Brian's call that night had been providential and had saved his life. "You don't have to, Sir. I'm just doing my job."

Tommy Anderson was six-foot-two, good looking. He had been a marine with raw talent, lots of potential and served in the military for five years when the war in the Middle East started. He'd survived his first tour with Taliban and Al-Qaeda in Afghanistan, and after that he'd weathered several tours of duty in Iraq, one of which included the destruction of his Humvee while he was still inside. That bomb explosion had nearly killed him and from that injury had won him a Purple Heart, but he was honorably discharged and sent home. He was a real hero with all kinds of commendation. But when Brian and his wife came to the funeral, lining up to show their sympathy and offer their condolences, he almost burst into tears, watching him with a sorrowful expression, Tommy was sitting in the wheelchair, looking like he died with her, and his son and mother were crying in front pew. Seeing him that way was huge shock and grief tore at his soul. He tried not to let it show, but he couldn't hold that emotion. It was the most depressing and harrowing funeral he had ever been to, and after they told him how sorry they were for his loss, he and his wife Jennies were quiet when they went home afterward. But having clearly learned the situation of Tommy and his family, and being moved by his compassion, he thought he needed to talk to Tommy, to soothe, to encourage, and offering a consolation of love, tender affection and compassion to encourage Tommy, or any assistance he may need. He decided to call him late that night.

Misfortunes never come alone. Tommy was wounded in the war, losing his good health, and the worst thing had happened to him was the death of his wife. But Brian had admired Tommy was a brave, persevering person, with a positive attitude about life. He completed his treatment, did well physical therapy to get the functional parts of his body strong and healthy again. And everyone who knew him was impressed at how well he had come through it. *Sufferings arise not to destroy people's mind, trampling on our dignity or dissolving our belief. On the contrary, looking directly at all the suffering, can face them courageously. This only way to achieve healing and move forward.* That was one of the reasons why he had hired him as a driver and a secret bodyguard as well. He had faith in Tommy's business sense, his ability and his loyalty. "You're not just like a son to me. You are a son to me, to us. You can buy bonds, using that money for your son in the future, college or whatever."

Tragedy and affliction not only let us down, but it's also an opportunity to start all over again. And yes. Positive words can help to change a person. The job as his personal driver wasn't real. It was merely a cover, a way to explain his presence at his home. Tommy had been hired to look into concerns Mr. Brian had about his personal and his family safety. If his or anyone in his family safety was in jeopardy, he would find the person or persons who posed the threat then solved it smoothly. He had never served other gentlemen in his life, but he thought never had anyone as unconventional or as generous as Mr. Brian got. Beside he had a gift for talking to people, with understanding and compassion, and made them feel that he cared, and it pleased him to work for Mr. Brian and knew he loved him and his son, and Mr. Brian had been like a second father to him. However, if he had known that his son had been on the verge of suicide, he would have been shocked. Moreover, he didn't want to overstep his authority and role. "You already gave us more than enough, Sir."

Brian waved off his concern. "Don't be silly, son."

Knowing that his boss' decision could not be change, Tommy could only nod in acceptance, exited the car and walked around to open the door.

As he was climbing out the car, his cell phone rang. He was about to ignored it while Tommy escorted him to the front doors, but he took it out from his vest pocket as habit, and when he saw the glowing screen of Bush Jr's phone number, he changed his mind. "Yes."

"Hello Dad," said Bush Jr. "Sorry to bother you this time."

"It's okay." He said, noting that Bush Jr sounded serious, the way he always did when he called to tell him something. "What's happening?"

"Nothing to worry, Dad," he tried to reassure him. "But I just want to confirm one thing from you."

"Sure, what's about?" Brian wondered.

"Is there anything else, Mr. Brian?" Tommy asked.

"Hold on a moment, son." Brian talked on the phone, but he turned to Tommy. "No. Thanks. Get some rest."

Tommy nodded. "Good night, sir."

"Good night."

Tommy opened and closed the door behind him after he stepped inside the house, Bush Jr asked. "Who are you talking to?"

"Tommy Anderson, but let's get back to the matter you asked." He said, walking to his office, and listened as Bush Jr went on and on about coming to Paul's house to take care Steady's problem.

"Do you think I should tell Steady?"

He removed his suit jacket and tie and left them on the couch, then unbuttoned the collar shirt and rolled up his sleeves as he poured himself a glass of whiskey. "No. She doesn't even know about it. Neither your mom. This is all my decision," Brian offered a simple solution. "Just saying that you do, and keep this is a secret between you and me."

❦ ✦ ❧

When Bush Jr finished his call, he slipped the phone into his suit jacket and gave Paul his full attention, but the way he was staring at him quickly made him more uncomfortable, and suddenly roughly grabbed him by the collar, hauled him up to his tiptoes. "Hey!" Paul yelped before he saw his fist slamming into his jaw to shut him up. His head whipped to the side, and his teeth cut into his gums and blood trickled onto his tongue.

"Dammit, let me go. You're hurting me." Paul said in disbelief at the direct hit.

"Alright," Bush Jr said, dropped him hard back on the chair, and then asking Nick to unlock a pair of handcuffs around Paul's wrists. And when he did, Bush Jr leaned closer to him. "Even though my dad just did, but I am still quite involved in this case, and if I hear you or hear of you saying thing against my sister, I will hunt you down. I'll find you wherever you hide, and this time, you're going to disappear without trace."

Paul Si looked into his eyes, rubbing his wrist. He believed him. The determination in his eyes told him that. But surprising, Bush Jr pulled out a manila envelope from inside pocket of his suit, tossing it on his laps.

"What's this?" Paul asked.

"See yourself."

And when he opened it, Bush Jr carried on. "That's the money you asked for." He answered. And Paul's eyes widened in delight. "Don't think that we're afraid of you. It's only to save your face."

Indeed, Paul thought he was about to die, but he was as happy as when the rain comes after a long drought that Bush Jr could see by the glint of his eyes. This was his wisdom. Threatened him, but still gave the ransom just like bestowed a favor.

"Just so that we are perfectly clear, and furthermore, if you don't stop and still try to blackmail my sister again. I swear, I shall personally make you vanished into the thin air."

Paul swallowed so hard that his Adam's apple dipped almost to his waist. Bush Jefferson Jr was into power, control and very power. "I believe you."

❦ ❧ ✴ ❦ ❧

When they walked outside and Bush Jr followed Nick to his car, Tiffany breathed a sigh of relief. Everything was fine, and two men stood there talking.

Bush Jr handed Nick an envelope contained twenty thousand dollars for his job. "Thanks, for everything."

"Like I said, no problem," Nick replied. "It's nice to work for you. If you need anything else, just give me a call."

"I will and thanks again." Bush Jr said, then headed back to his car where Tiffany's waiting. He pulled out his iPhone from the back pocket of his jeans, to call his sister, and when she answered it. He told her. "It's done."

Steady smiled herself and experienced a wave of relief that she finally didn't have to deal with Paul Si, and glad it's over. "Thank you, brother. Maybe I can pay you back someday."

"You owe me nothing, Steady." Bush Jr told her. "We're Jefferson's family." "Yes, we're." She admitted and felt the relief all the way down to her toes.

Now that his sister was safe and out of trouble, he could concentrate on other things. As soon as he shut the phone off, shoving it into his pocket, Tiffany unlocked the car door for him. "Let go home, babe. It's long day." He said as he slid into the driver's seat and pulled the car door closed.

Chapter 8
Love makes life beautiful.

As soon as he hung up on Bush Jr, Brian took an intemperate swallow, and after he set the glass down, he walked over to the grand piano and lowered the top board to cover the strings as quietly as he could. He didn't want to wake his wife. But as stared at the keys and sat down, and he hadn't played for a long time. He decided, placed his fingers on the keys and started to play the first thing that came into his mind. As Chopin's nocturne in B-flat minor quietly filled the room. He's alone with the melancholy music and it soothed his soul.

A moment in his peripheral vision distracted him. He turned and saw Jennies was standing in the shadows of hallway, regarding him with amusement, and immediately, she stepped into the lights, walking to him. Although no longer young, firm, or slender, her body still looked damn good to him. Her eyes glinted, her hair tumbling over pale pink silk robe, smooth skin against pink lace and the silk nicely outlined her curves, looking so desirable. She was a giver, not a taker. Looking back over thirty years, he wasn't sure he would have survived without her. He stopped, taking his hands off the keys.

After many years of cohabitation. She knew him better than ever. He always played the piano to relieve the pressure after solving a problem that she could recognize his nervous anxiety when Tommy came to remind him while he's having dinner with her. She ran her fingers through his hair. "Why did you stop? That was lovely."

He placed a loving hand on her waist, feeling her flesh through the nightgown beneath. Then squeezed. Not too hard. Just enough to gain her attention. "Because of you. Do you have any idea how desirable you look at this moment?"

The scent of whiskey filling her nose. "Then come to bed with me," she said bluntly, kissing him invitingly.

It was as much demand as offer. And right now, he needed to lose himself in this beautiful, loving woman. He pulled her into his lap and embraced her, kissing her exposed neck and tracing his lips at her throat, felt her pulse jump up to meet him, fluttering wildly. "I love the taste of your skin."

With those loving gestures, awakened the small stream that was sleeping deep in her body. As if receiving a signal, the wetness quickly came.

She trembled in his arms and responded passionately with a moan in pleasure. Automatically, his hips arched, and his cock hardened. "But we're not going to make it upstairs yet."

"Mm …" She let him know it's a good idea as she skimmed her fingers through the silver wings of his hair, lingered there. "Why don't we just take it from here?"

"Okay, I'm going to give a try." He untied the sash on her robe, and it fell open, revealing the gown beneath. It clung to her body, showing every curve, every dip, every hollow, and his hand skimmed from her face to her breast. Plump, soft and her nipples harden, crowning against the silk when he circled them with his fingers, and then moved down to her hip.

"You feel so fine under this material." He said as his fingers tugged at the buttons of his shirt, not stopping until it was all the way down the front over his broad chest. With a sensuous smile he drew her to him.

Another moan as her firm and high breasts against the warmth of his bare chest, and her fingers curl around his face, stroking his hair. "There's nothing under it."

"You're trying to distract me."

"Of course, I am." Her smile was slow, seductive and sure. "Is it working?"

"It always has." He lifted her nightgown, enjoying the feel of rick, soft silk as it inches up her beautiful body. His hands found her ass, cupped her, then moved and ran his thumbnail down the length of her inner thigh. "Always will."

Surprising her, he stood abruptly and lifted her onto the piano so she's sitting on the front of on top board, her feet on the keys. And standing between her legs, he took her hands. "Lie back." He eased her down onto the piano. The silk spilled like fluid over the edge of the gleaming black wood and onto the keys.

Once she's on her back, he let go, stripped off his shirt, and push her legs apart, and kissed the inside of her right knee and trail kissed and soft nips up her leg to her thigh. Her nightgown inched up, revealing more and more of his wife's sexy features. She groaned, knowing what he had in mind. Spread her legs wider, giving him all the access he needed. To achieve his goal, he gently bent down and kissed her clitoris, relishing the jolt that shot through her body. "I love...love when you do that."

Her whole body trembled as he slowly started circling his tongue around her sensitive sweet spot, continued over and over again, causing her moaning endlessly, she could only hold his hair tightly and writhe in pleasure, lifting her pelvis, bending her body according to the ecstatic feelings of sensuality.

"Yes, right there. Don't stop." She cried out in pleasure.

Her moans were like a stimulant, making him even more intoxicated, creating a feeling of pleasure for each other that made his face wet. It was both from his and hers. Her legs began to tremble, but she didn't want him to stop. "Oh, honey, please."

"Oh, baby, you are on fire." But not yet, he still didn't want her to come. Wanting to prolong this feeling of pleasure. His hands traveled up her thighs, caressing, gently squeezing and teasing while his tongue circuited her navel and his hand reached the junction between her thighs.

"Ah!" she moans softly as his finger slowly entered inside her while his thumb teased circle around the stimulated spot of her clitoris, causing her to arch up in pleasure over the piano. "Honey, I need you," she cried. "Please, oh please inside me."

He took off his fly, and let his pants fall on the floor. "I need you just as much," he whispered, lifted her feet off the keys and pulled them forward, so she slid gently closer so that their sexes fit snugly together. The need to rock her hips and rub against him was so strong that his erect penis was irresistible, he slipped it into her sensitive part so that their bodies could merge together. The soft, hot, moist flesh inside of her wrapped around and squeezed tightly, followed by a gentle rhythm, slowly causing pleasure.

Holding himself back, he watched she clutched his biceps, tipped her head and her mouth opened wide. She's so close, he realized. That was what he wanted to do, to make her feel everything she could. When she arched her body, moaning and painting, seeming unable to hold back any longer, he increased his speed and her legs flex beneath him and she let out a strangled cry as she came and each wave of contractions made him unable to restrain himself anymore, he erupted after the woman he loved.

Chapter 9

With love, you must experience first then lean the lesson.

When Smiling arrived at Kennedy Airport on Thursday morning, Mathew called her on her cell phone now after she checked in her luggage again and turned it on.

"Hi! How are you, Mathew? I didn't expect you call me so soon."

"I know, but I miss you already," he said mournfully. "Come back to me, Smiling. What am I going to do without you for two weeks?"

It was unlike him to be that clingy, and it touched her that he was. They were always together, so every time one of them went on a long trip, it became difficult for both of them. This told her that they were inseparable.

"You'll have my designs for the new trade show and have fun in Paris." She reassured him.

"How can I be fun without you?"

"Too bad. But I'll be back as soon as I can." She promised. This was a subject she and him had still argued and she said a quick goodbye, didn't want to make any abrupt changes in her summer vacation plan.

The Delta Airline flight left New York on time as the plane took off. And although she missed Mathew, but the thought of seeing her family again made her even more anxious to get home. She sat back in her seat with a smile, and closed her eyes, thinking of them. They had so much to catch up on, and always so much to talk about. Even better than seeing her sisters and brothers, she couldn't wait to hug her mom and kiss her dad.

***

At the airport lounge, Tommy checked his watch and wondered again why his boss always told him to pick up Jennifer Jefferson every time she came home, since he worked for him without using any car? But when his assignment he'd received from Mr. Brian. It was clearly answered. That he trusted him, and his daughter was needed a professional bodyguard, and her safety came first. Besides he had no other choice. He had a job to do. Nothing more. He couldn't forget his objective for a second with a personal code of ethics one he'd never yet broken. He drew the line at working for people he cared about.

He took a seat, waited patiently, and watching passengers waited for their flights by napping in the black plastic chairs or reading books. Until he heard the flight announced. He was up and pacing, and his mouth curved into a smile when he saw her the moment she stepped out from custom checking into the terminal in Orlando. For a second, he lost his focus, staring at the woman he was picking up. Dear Lord, Jennifer Jefferson was beautiful and seductive and sexy without even trying to be. She walked with a sense of purpose, pulling Louis Vuitton handbag. Happy to see her, he took a quick assessment of the well dress as she walked through the gate. There was nothing flirtation about the walk, but a man would notice it. Long, limber strides, a subtle swing at the hip, head up, eyes ahead, and swayed slightly in three-inches black heels that did amazing for those already pretty impressive legs.

Yeah, she was the kind of woman who could turn a man's head around. "Miss Jennifer!"

Smiling turned away from the traveling companions on the long flight from New York as she spotted him, and thankfully, Dad had arranged everything for her. Tommy. She'd been expecting him, and her first look at him brought a quick smile. He was wearing a black suit; his shirt was also black without tie. He exuded a very special aura, calm, orderly and always kept his cool as ice. It must have been his job as a bodyguard that made him look like that. Tommy wasn't exact Hollywood handsome. He was good looking and sexy, and there was something about him that hinted at danger. But his voice was sympathetic and the flash of humor that lit those piercing pale blue eyes when she turned and caught him watching her.

She was the prettiest among the sisters in the family. Tommy couldn't deny that, in addition, she was a lovely woman. Of course, her personality was like that, although she looked a bit tired after a long trip. Her pale features made her look fragile, but the wide, strong cheek bones undid the air of fragility and giving her face an attractive oval shape. Her eyes were round and large with the color of good cognac, the eyelashes were long and artfully accented with the smoky shadow that only made the cool green shade of the irises seem cooler. Her nose was small and straight, her mouth was wide and full, only lightly touched a peach-colored gloss. Her skin looked sun kissed, her hair was colored blonde from the natural brown. She wore it long enough in the back to be pinned up in a chignon when she wished, and short enough on the top and sides so that she could style it from fussy to practical as the occasion, her whim and her creativity. At moment, it was loose and casual, but not wind-blown. And he knew too well that it felt like silk against man's hands. She was gorgeous, rich, talented and outrageously sexy, also strong and independent, but all of those had not made her bitter. Even without a trace of makeup, it would also cause a man to stare. Which was exactly what he was doing.

She liked him because he was a good man. Kind, sharp, tough and invariably made her behavior easier as if they were friends. Also, she found him fascinating at a very basic and dangerous level. She looked up at him and smile after she could feel his eyes on her long enough. "Tommy. How wonderful to see you again."

He caught himself, just blinked and realized she was a woman that a man had to keep an emotional distance from. Get too close and you'd be sucked right in and she caught him staring. "Excuse me," he said distractedly, giving his short shake. "You look lovely as always, Miss Jennifer."

She couldn't help the smile that took over her face. She liked to accept compliments whenever she got them, but his flattery was a kind of apology. She decided to accept it. "You're gushing as always, Tommy. And please call me, Smiling. Why's nature so formal? It's so much nicer than the other names you're been using in your mind."

The smile that blossomed across her features made his breath come in hard, hot, heavy. "I have to, but if you say so, I'll do my best." He promised, and held out his hand.

Friendly in returning, she dropped her bags and took his hand offered, but instead shook it. She pulled him over and gave him a hug greeting in the way more than casually friendly.

With his face buried against Jennifer's throat, the scent of her sweet perfume entered his nose. The scent is light, but very special, making people pleasant but hard to forget. But a woman like Jennifer would have respect, and he had to remind himself that he was on a mission; he couldn't be distracted. He drew himself back. "Welcome home, Miss Smiling."

"It's always good to be back in Florida. You look great."

Professional training had helped him keep his nerves just at the border where they could be controlled and concealed. Still, under the training, there was a man. Smiling was a nature, lovely and self-confident. He didn't consider his affection for beautiful women a weakness. He was grateful that Smiling didn't find the need to play down or turn her nature beauty into severity, nor did she exploit it until it was artificial. She'd found a pleasing balance. He could admire that. It was bound to make his job easier. But from this point, he'd better keep their relationship strictly professional until he dropped her off on the front porch of the Jefferson's house. He couldn't prevent the smile. "Thanks, Smiling. I hope you had a decent flight."

She found her mood lifting automatically. "As far as I'm concerned. It's long, but pleasant."

"And tiring," he said remembering his position.

He reached for the handle of her wheeled carry-on bag, but she gestured her bag. "This is something I always carry myself."

Woman things, he understood. "Whatever you say, Smiling. Limo's waiting for you out front. We need to get your luggage and get going. The baggage claim is off to your right."

With her nod, he indicated the way, and walked along beside her toward the terminal instead in the front. And again, he admired her catwalk, moving in long, unhurried strides the made the side-pleated skirt she wore shift over her hips. "I think they should be in now."

She sent him a quick sidelong look. "I knew I could depend on you, Tommy. How's Jason?"

Once his wife died, he only had him, which was easier for him to manage, but he wished that he had a daughter who looked like his late wife. She had been the light of his like and she was gone. He still couldn't believe it, four years later. "Mean as ever," he said proudly of his son. "With his mom gone, he's always got me to order around."

"You're worried about him."

"Him and a lot of things. But, yes, he's at the top of the list. Raising a kid, especially a boy his age-alone isn't exactly a piece of cake. Fortunately, moms always helped out."

She knew the most important woman in Tommy's life was Lydia, and he lost her. For a while there, he'd been about as miserable as any human could be while still functioning and most of time, he was busy with his son, so he had little interest in anyone else. She admired his strength, the way he'd pushed forward instead of giving in to grief. She nodded in agreement, watching his face as he told her. He looked sad, and like he still missed her a lot. "Do you still miss her, Tommy?"

"Yes, sometimes," he answered, moved closer to her side. "But anyway, it happened a long time ago I don't like talking about it or thinking about it."

Noticing Tommy's change, she was also a bit confused, didn't want to ask any more for fear of digging into his pain. "I'm sorry."

"So, you said," he said, didn't want to discuss more his Lydia; not with Smiling who spoke little but asked questions that delved far too deep. Changing the subject was simple. "Smiling, let's get back to what's happening here and now. You have your tickets?"

An organized man, she thought as she reached into her bag then handed them to him as they stopped at the conveyor belt. "I like that."

"Just point them out and I'll haul them in."

He collected her LV bags, and knew for sure the taste of her. He handed the stubs to a skycap and waited while her luggage was loaded onto the pushcart. "I think your family will be pleased to see you."

"So, will I Tommy." She said as they walked through the double automatic glass doors, and a highly polished black Lincoln limo was waiting for them at the curb of the airport, with the driver standing tall and dignified beside it.

Tommy tipped the skycap as she flashed a smile at the driver who stored her luggage inside and closed the trunk of limo.

She was impressed with Tommy's generosity. Many people leaving the airport often didn't tip the skycap. "You are a meticulous man, Tommy." She complimented him as he opened the door, stepped back and offered her his hand to help her climb inside.

He liked her compliment. "That's what I have to do, Smiling." Tommy replied cheerfully as he took the spacious backseat facing her, and on either side of television set and the bar. But suddenly his attention shifted, and he let his gaze run up the long slender length of her stretching legs as they drove away. Really pretty legs. The legs when he heard her mother had once said that had refused to stop growing long after it were necessary.

Jesus! What was wrong with him? Couldn't a normal man not admire her beauty, sexy body and long legs? However, his thoughts, though fleeting, had been totally unprofessional in this moment. Completely out of the line. She was Jennifer Jefferson after all. No way, he was going to forget that, even in hell. And if he cared about her, it was only in his way, in his work time, and in the meantime, he had to remember his manners and where he belonged. Had she caught him staring?

She'd ridden in limos countless times, but she never took such cushy comfort for granted. As she let herself enjoy, Smiling watched Tommy reached over, switched on the stereo so that Mozart poured out, quiet but vibrant.

If he'd been driving himself, it would've been rock, loud and rambunctious. Adding, the plush laziness of the limo was the next best thing for his job to have a calm, serious discussion with her. "It's still a long way to go home. So, you just relax, and I recommend a glass of wine to go along with it then," he said, opened up a small built-in cabinet to reveal the bar. "Also, your feet probably hurt, I guess. So, you can take your shoes off."

It was as if he had read her thoughts after burning out from traveling, ready for a drink and freed her feet. And there was something so comfortable, so right about the tenderness and care. She'd adored this side of his that she enjoyed the feel of his charmed order. It made her relax, and she doubted he was a man that was wise to relax around. She slipped out of her shoes. "I'd never argue with the expert."

"Cognac," he decided and poured the yellow liquid in the small bottle into a glass, instead of the chilled champagne without asking. It's always a shock to the system to travel from one climate to another, and he handed it to her.

"Thanks," she said, taking a sip of cognac, closed her eyes. Warm, potent and smooth. Frowning a bit, and hum her appreciation for her drink, she sipped again, and then lay her head back against the seat. Yeah, it'd been a long flight, and time changed, include the sound soft and mellow made she feel so relax. She closed her eyes again, emptied her mind and enjoyed. This was also a habit when she was in the car.

Chapter 10
Family is moments to love and cherish forever.

The limousine pulled to stop in front of the elegant two-story brick house in Grant Haven and the driver said after he pulled her luggage out of the trunk.

"Here we are, Miss. Want me to carry those bags to the door?" "No, thanks, I can handle them." Gloomy said and gave him a tip.

It felt good to be home, and she felt surround by the warmth and generosity of her family and the house she had lived in for the past seventeen years with her parents and siblings, and to her mind, it was the perfect place to live, rambling noisy, full of music and voice. She had started life there, then, after an eight-year residence at another Los Angeles address, and had ties there, as well, but she always missed the familiar-her own room, tucked into the second story of the house, the love and companionship of her siblings, her father's music, her mother's laugh.

She could remember even now the warm rush of pride she'd felt when she saw her father man the desk in the Oval Office, or when she watched her mother rise to a thunder of applause at her fashion show.

Her parents had done their best to provide areas of normalcy for Bush Jr and her brothers and sisters. But Gloomy had always known she came from greatness. And such miracles had a price.

She remembered the day they had moved to stay into the home of her early childhood, how her grandfather had hugged them all, then grinned and told them that they were all going out for pizza and movie.

It had been one of the sweetest nights of her life. This was the house she had lived in as a child, and she could never quite return without feeling somehow as though she weren't a woman but was once more that small child.

Now she stood with her daughter on the walkway as her limo drove off. The house hadn't changed much, but it still drew her, still felt comfortable.

Love needed a home to shelter it, and she had been so fortunate in hers. And coming home and being with them was always fun and relaxing.

She hefted her garment bag, and suitcase as her daughter's hand held hers. They walked up the few brick steps in front of the house. The flowers were fading, but the pink, purple and red wild chrysanthemums were just coming into bloom as June edged toward July. Their summer hotness dulling as autumn blew close. Memories like being welcomed back.

At the top, they kept going across the porch to the beautiful doors with its stained-glass oval and its lion-headed knocker. The crowned lion eyed her fiercely and made her think of her grandfather. She knocked, using the brass crest of the Jefferson to thump on the door, rather than ring the bell.

The front door opened, and a trim middle-aged woman hurried onto porch to greet them. Her blue eyes lighting up with surprise as she was grinning broadly. "Oh, Miss Gloomy! Welcome home, Miss Gloomy."

"Dora." Gloomy would have hugged their longtime housekeeper if her arms had been free. Instead, she was greeted back with warmth and friendly smile and bent down to her five feet two of sturdy joy to kiss her cheek. "Hello, Dora, you don't ever change."

"You, too," she was happy to see her, happy to have someone in the house again. "I didn't think you were coming until tomorrow."

"I like surprises." Gloomy said, throwing her arms around the older woman in a warm hug. Dora had served a multitude of functions for the Jefferson over a fifteen-year period. Her mother's effective administrative assistant who had been her title during the JEN Foundation era. But what she did was manage everything that why she had been part of this family. "Have my parents been giving you any trouble?"

"Not a bit." Dora said, drew back, and even though pleasure sparkled in her eyes, she placed her hand on the chest as she looked down to see the bright-eyes pretty little girl. "Well, hello, a little doll."

Cathy greeted her with a smile. "Hi, ma'am."

With a laugh, Dora ducked down to kiss Cathy's cheek. "Don't call me Mam. I'm Dora. Come in, come in. Let me have your suitcases."

Gloomy made her way into the house, and Mrs. Dora followed her inside, carrying their suitcases. And when they were inside, she took time to appreciate the musty vanilla scent of the house, the aroma familiar and comforting.

"Miss Dora, I want to see my grandpa and grandma. They are home, aren't they?" Cathy asked, couldn't wait to see them.

"Yes, they are." The house manager confirmed as she shut the door. "He's upstairs in his office on an overseas call, and your grandma is back in her work room."

Gloomy nodded pleasantly at her. "I'll interrupt Mom first, then we'll go to see Dad. Don't carry suitcases up, Dora," she asked her for as she started down the hall. "I'll take it myself in a few minutes."

Dora nodded, and set her luggage on the foyer. "I'm going to fix you some tea."

Gloomy said thanks to her and looked around. Here things had stayed the same. Fresh flowers stood on the table, pillows sat fluffed and welcoming on the three sofas ranged around the living room, and the wide planed chestnut floor gleamed like mirror. She picked up the suitcase, walked slowly up the stairs with Cathy to along the hallway, which was really a gallery that cut in a semicircle above the foyer. Each of three doors opened to the gallery: her parents' master suite which considered of their bedroom, a library on one side, a music room on the other, and two offices they each used when they had to work at home which was often. And farther down on each curved wing was the other bedrooms.

She'd taken the room she'd always used on visits, and the door was ajar, so she pushed it opened. She stepped into the cozy bedroom where had been hers as a girl. Her room was still as it had been when she left for college thirteen years before. She could tell that housekeepers were keeping her place up: the floors and woodwork gleamed; the smell of pine and lemon was heavy in the air. Feeling warmly welcome even she wasn't a teenager anymore, but a woman, a married woman. In most ways her life had been blessed. She had loving parents and wonderful sisters and brothers; she was a mother and an aunt to two boys and two girls who were a source of constant joy and surprise to her. Those thoughts made her frown as she put her suitcase in the closet, took off her jacket, and turned back to the hallway starting for her mom's office.

Jennies Jefferson's workroom was fit for a couture company, with velvet furniture, black and white fashion photos lining the walls. It also completely offered space for her manikins, sewing machine, her worktable and supplies.

Soft music, a somewhat piano and violent concerto played from hidden speakers in the background. Gloomy leaned on the door jamb and wait as she watched her mother sat at the desk, worked through a few sketches for her fall collection. Focus and concentration were her two qualities, plus her unique talent, that helped to make her such a great success in the world of fashion.

That's it, Jennies thought, instantly filling with excitement. A fall collection of clothes based on those two colors red and blue, interspersed with other tones from these color spectrums. What a change from layer concept solid inner or outer with transparent or translucent outer or inner, made for nice look of her spring season.

She rose, went over to the other fabric sample and searched through them quickly, looking for the colors she now wanted to use. She found a few of them and carried them back to her desk, where she spread them out. Then she began to match the color samples to the sketches with her beautiful and clever hands, the nails perfectly manicured, a French manicure. As always, no color there, either, that she had already done for the fall line, envisioning a suit, or dress in one of reds, purples, or blue.

Her mom was still energetic, lively, and beautiful at her age. She was blessing with a youthful look and spirit. It was easy to see why her husband had been in love with her till the end. "Great creativity. I love it."

Jennies so concentrated and focused on her designs that she almost jumped out of her skin when she heard the voice said from the doorway. But her face lighting up, as she glanced at the door, and took her a moment to find her voice. "Gloomy!"

"Sorry to intrude, Mom."

"It's all right," Jennies said, popped up, and was halfway to her daughter before Cathy ran to and wrapped her legs. She looked up. "Grandma," Jennies felt the world spin backward.

She was the image of her mother. The sable hair peeked out of her cap and felt untidily to her shoulders. The small, triangular face was dominated by big brown eyes that seemed to hold jokes all their own. But it was the smile, the one that always seemed to cheer her up.

She scooped Cathy off the ground. "There's my little princess!" she said and pressed her lips to her cheeks. "How grandma missed you."

And Cathy kissed on her cheeks in turn. "You're growing like an angel, but heavy, grandma have to put you down."

"How was the trip?" Jennies asked as she placed Cathy back on the ground. "Are you tired? Do you want some time to relax?"

"Thanks Mom. I think I'm all right. How are you?"

"I'm fine. It's good to have you home, sweetie."

"It's good to be home, Mom."

"Have you sent your father yet?"

"No, Dora said he was on the phone, so I came here to interrupt you first."

"Well, he needs a break, so we'll double team him." She threw her arms around Gloomy and took Cathy's hand. "Oh, I've missed you. You'll have to tell me everything that's new and wonderful. How is your school? Are you hungry? Answer any or all of the questions in the order of your choice."

Smiling, they walked arm in arm, hand in hand with her up the back stairs. "The school is fine. I've got straight A's in report card for first quarter. I can read Vietnamese chapter book, and I eat some food on the airplane."

"Really?" Jennies found herself laughing. "I'm proud of you." And then she turned toward and led them to her husband's office.

They paused at the doorway and her mother gave a knock and opened the door.

Brian sat behind the desk, holding a cell phone to his ear and looked up. His hair had gone rich silver, and the sunlight that poured through the window glinted off it. As always, Jennies thought him handsomest man in the world, and she watched as those lines of care around his brown eyes turned to lines of joy.

Her dad, a tall man with gray hair and brown eyes, studied his computer and was saying into the phone. "I'll consider it. Yes, serious consider it." He held up one finger, indicating that he was about through with his call, then waved them in with a smile, as they let go of their hands, and Cathy rushed toward him.

He wrapped his arm around his granddaughter, brought her close to his side, and tried ending his call. "I'm sorry, Mr. Alan. I'll have to get back to you. Something comes up here. Yes, I'll be there... okay. Sure... I'll call... Thanks, I'll talk to you later." He promised the person on the phone, then he disconnected and placed the phone on the desk.

"Gloomy," he stood up with a warm smile and held out his arms.

Gloomy greeted her father with a kiss on the cheek before she hugged him. "Good morning, Dad, how do you do?"

"Good." And with a hoot of laughter, he hoisted her off the ground as if she weighted no more than a favored rag doll. "Still as lovely as ever," he said, kissing her on the way down. "How's my wonderful daughter?"

For as long as she could remember, no matter the situation, her dad had always been there for her. He'd loved her, just as he had others. To him they all were his wonderful girls. "I'm a little older, little wiser, and I'm happy to be here to see you."

And someone tapped on his leg, he looked down. "Oh, my sweetie," he murmured then leaned down, caught Cathy's face in both of his big hands and gave her a loud, smacking kiss on the forehead. "Pretty as a picture, we'd have some tea, don't you think?"

Amused, Cathy tilted her head. "Grandpa, I'm eight years old, I prefer ice cream."

The three of them laughed, and he stroked her hair. "I'm old and doting. My little Cathy is now grown up."

Chapter 11
Love has reasons that no one can explain.

Tommy had trouble concentrating after he took the empty glass out of her hand and saw the way she relaxed. He'd been thinking about Smiling a lot. Too much. He tried to push thoughts of her from his head. But no matter how hard he tried, he couldn't get over it when he'd found himself fantasizing about her, wanting her, thinking about touching her and kissing her so hard neither one of them would be able to think straight. His imagination ran wild as he saw he was stripping off her clothes, his thumbs skimming those breasts he'd only caught a glimpse of, kissing her throat, then tangling his fingers in her hair as he ran his tongue downward.

"Shit," he muttered, so caught in the fantasy that the crotch of his pants suddenly uncomfortable and tight. He regretted not drinking wine instead of soft drinks.

He wondered what it would feel like when he thrust into her, not giving one good goddamn what anyone thought? Goodness! Silently cursing the lust that continued teased the corners of his mind. He'd never considered himself a fool, nor had he ever had any kind of death wish. He'd always thought clearly and known what he wanted. Until he'd met this woman. Whatever he was around her, his senses were on overload and his normally clear mind became muddied. Or rather, his brain was infected with a virus. So, nothing could drive away the feeling except one thing, sex with Smiling.

For the love of Christ, what were you thinking? He muttered under his breath, disgusted at the direction of his thoughts. He couldn't have sex with this woman, especially she was the boss's daughter who had everything good in life. It was just too damned dangerous.

That was the bottom line, because he didn't think about those things, just saw her as a smart. Pretty and sexy woman. That was fact, and he knew it was wrong, knew it could lead to nothing but trouble and big problem. A thousand warnings flashed through his head, but he'd found it impossible to stay away from her. On the contrary, part of fear, part of sense of morality discouraged. He should force the desire that had already started burning in his blood to cool, but he quickly realized that this way couldn't be more stupid as he touched her arm, felt her warm skin beneath his fingers and the prickle of desire that came with it. "Smiling," he whispered.

Half asleep, half awake, Smiling opened her eyes and looked at him. "I'm sorry. I wasn't paying attention." But before she could hear whatever he was about to say, he reached out, pulled her onto his lap, and his hands landed on the waists.

Tommy's sudden action made her a bit panicked Her eyes opened wide in shock surprised, so she immediately brought her hands to her chest, clearly needing to push him away. But in that instant, she was hypnotized by his magical blue eyes that she didn't know how to react. Just stared at him blankly and silently assessed in her heart. Was that the response of acceptance or cautiousness? "What nonsense are you doing, Tommy?"

It had been impulse, unplanned, and he was no longer a solemn bodyguard when his mind shut off like a shattered lamp, and he regretted it. It was done, he thought, and he'd expected her to push away in refusal. God knew he was deplorable and considering that later. But what he realized was Smiling merely didn't protest, didn't attempt to escape him, as if stunned by the most basic contact of man to woman. That sent his thoughts reeling into different scenarios, and the sulky, defiant look she sent him began convincing him to take the risk.

"I want..." He inhaled, maybe taking in a dose of courage, before he went on. "Want to do what I've always wanted to do. That's my confession." "Confession?" She was wary, disbelief obvious in her eyes. "Why?"

His breath warm on her neck. "Because I can't get you out of my head, thinking of you night and day, and..." He tried to say something, but stopped as if he seemed to reconsider. The slide of his eyes down to her mouth that she knew he was imagining to kiss her. "I'd tried not to touch you, but I couldn't since I find you're the most fascinating woman I've ever met."

Her eyes widened even more. He didn't talk that way. Not to Smiling. Not to anyone. But he defined the meaning of every word in his words. For she was the fire in his blood, a need deep within his soul that seemed unquenchable.

The statement so direct and scary that she looked at him in disbelief, not moving, not speaking, just thinking. Should she feel sorry for his vulnerable? She thought, she should harden her heart, get up out of his arms to stop this madness before it went any further, and demanded to be taken home. But she didn't want hurt his feeling, and everything she felt deep inside her began to stir with a trembling need that banished all her doubts, and destroyed all rational thoughts. Instead, her palms pressed helplessly against the warm front of his suit jacket, and saw his gaze flicker to her mouth. Without conscious thought, she licked her lips and saw he lowered his head, trying to mold his mouth to hers. She knew she was in trouble, so she turned her face, searching for some shred of her sanity. *What am I doing?*

Feeling the taste on her cheek so sweet, he wondered if that was good or bad? Instead of stopping and releasing her, he brushed his lips over her cheek gently, patiently again, and then he kissed the length of her neck and rimmed the circle of her throat with his tongue. "I should be shot for this."

Oh my God! It never crossed her mind that Tommy would one day do that to her. His lips already touched her too. She tried to fight him. This was no way to start any kind of relationship, but she couldn't help but yield to emotions that were tearing her apart. Love or hate, she couldn't tell, but deep inside, she started to tingle and ache, her head lolled backward as passion she'd kept firmly controlled, strictly in bounds strained free to make a mockery out of everything she had once she believed of herself. But this was wrong, wasn't it? "Yes, Tommy, so please have some self-respect," she whispered. "I don't think this is..."

Thought he would stop, but he leaned closer, his nose pressed against her hair, his lips touching the shell of her ear interrupting her words and whispered. "Smiling, don't think."

She knew she should stop him. "Listen, Tommy, why is it you're always telling me to do what you need or want?"

"I can't do that. It's just an advice."

"I don't remember ever asking for any."

He couldn't find any reason to respond. But he could sense the constant flare of desire he saw on her face, smell her fear that was his undoing. Instead, he gently bit her ear lobe with his teeth.

Don't do this, she silently pleaded, and willed herself to remain impassive. But she began to tremble, confused and unable to control herself. Both, anger and passion sizzled through her blood. She tried not to respond, to push him away, but her hands were useless against his broad chest, as well as her unconscious mind and body had already begun to be lured into the trance.

Her half-lidded eyes and rapid breathing told him they were signals of desire, not fear. So he refused to listen what she had to say and allowed his hands to move to her back, down to her hips to pull her closer, drawing her into the man's rising desire.

"Tommy," she whispered, hoping to convince him what they were doing was insane, but she caught his blue eyes delved deep into hers, so deep she was sure he could see her soul. "I'm right here, Smiling."

Stop this madness, Smiling, stop it now. While you still can. She must maintain her self-respect. But once again, she didn't do any of those things. Because she was lost and seduced by the pleasure he brought. He was a demon who sent to curse and irritate her as he slid his fingers down her side, under her shirt, then moved in gentle circles, making her lose track of what was real and what was fantasy when the soft satin of her skirt gradual moved up, and moaning softly, seeing his eyes slid down to her smooth white thighs.

Take control of yourself. His inner personality advised. You have the good sense to know that this was the wrong time or place to do this. But desires were overflowing, and sex had muddled his mind so that he's having trouble getting over it. So, he continued slowly, trying the best to tempt.

"Let me love you, Smiling," he whispered against the side of her face, his breath tickling her ear, her skin prickling with anticipation.

"No-"

"Shh, Smiling, it's true, and I hate it." His hands at once gentle and confident found her ass and cupped her, then moved to her spine and forcing her breasts against to his solid chest.

She knew in an instant that she wouldn't stop him. She told herself not to panic as the feeling of desire, heat, and wantonness was burning inside her. God! What a sin. And through the fabric, she could feel his erection underneath, connecting with the juncture between her thighs, creating a hot pool of lustful desire. But her brain kicked back in. She caught his hand and held it still, half out of fear, half out of self-consciousness. "Tommy, please!" She said, but it wasn't the protest she was intending, but more a plea. "I can't... I just can't do it."

He had never touched her this way before. Never had he wanted this woman so desperately. Controlling his physical needs had never been a problem for him before. Especially in dangerous situation. But with Smiling, as if he'd had no will and making him crazy. She affected him in a way that bothered him, a complicated way he'd rather avoid. He knew deeply in his gut, if they ever made love, the course of his life would change forever.

But it could serve as a reminder that with love the chance of headache came.

Not that he was in love with Jennifer Jefferson, and far from it. But she'd gotten to him. No doubt about it. This woman had burrowed her way under his skin, and he had no other way to tell her how big his heart was right now, swollen to bursting with need for her as his body was aflame with long banked desire. It's the antidote to him instead of the cause.

Still, he perused her, his hands shifting to the warmth between her legs. "Tommy, please, no!"

"When I see the same heat in your eyes, I know you wanted me. So, don't expect me not to act on it," he said, groaning as he tried to make himself stop, but for just a moment more, he couldn't. "Why don't we stop fighting and do what we really want to do, Smiling?"

The words should have cleared her mind and her anger, her hatred for her own stupidity, her lack of sophistication, and his mysterious gaze. And he was right. What existed between them was raw passion that she should have let go of. But sensation layered over sensation, wrapping her in a cocoon of pleasure that made her let him keep going with his lips swept softly over hers, or wherever he searched for hers, the warm, drugging taste of it, and the feel of his hands, the strength of them as they stroked over her skin from her face to one of her breasts, then surrounding it. His thumb stroked gently across her blouse, causing her nipples harden and protrude against the lacy confines of her bra. While the other one to her waist, then to her hip. In the numb feeling, there was also an indescribable pleasure. But this was wrong. She managed to say no, though it was a whisper, and her lips barely moved.

Any guilt or worry about the consequences of his actions flew from his thoughts as he tightened his arms around her, crushed her breasts against his chest. There was only thought circled in his mind that he'd been waiting all his life to find his mouth pressed to hers in a kiss that was questioned and demanded, that was fragile, yet firm, and cut her off any further protest.

Every instinct told her to stop this madness, to pull away, but another part of her, that silly, romantic, feminine part of her, wanted more. So, finally she allowed, and this time she wound her arms around his neck, and returned his fever by inertia. It wasn't an issue of desire. It was one of trust. Without that, she couldn't muster the desire.

Again, stop this, Smiling, while you still can. But she knew somewhere in the deepest recesses of her brain that she was about to step over a line that could never be recrossed, that going any further was more than dangerous, it was playing with fire. But the feeling of his lips and tongue slid between her teeth, and she welcomed its touch. All thoughts of denying him vanished. Instead, she kissed him with all of the fever in her blood, with the vital and primitive need that was building deep in the most private parts of her.

He fought to keep himself from grabbing what he longed for. His hands found her breasts under the soft fabric, and tenderly lifting them upward until both erected nipples peeked over the lace.

Her inside to melt when he found them. An ache, deep and primal, swirled deep between her legs, and she closed her mind to anything, just wanted for more that made she felt cheap, but she had no strength to demand, no will to take control.

No, it was the conflict between her morality and her desires. But he was taking her beyond the expected, beyond the anticipated, and into what her mind was imaging. She wanted this, the fusion of their bodies, the blending of their souls.

"Don't think," he whispered. "Just let me give you pleasure."

She whimpered at the thought as her body went fluid, and the hard ridge of his erection pressing harder against the cradle of her pelvis. She recognized it. This was beauty, also was danger, but she accepted it, and because her remaining rationality was completely broken, she let him guide her. Control no longer seemed essential. Ambitions became unimportant. Need was only one now. And for the first time in her life, she instinctively let go, responding unbearably, her body aflame, her desire, allowing a man whose mystery and irreverence had touched her soul, started making intimate gestures like any lover would dare to do.

When she had stopped being herself and become the amazingly sexy woman. No longer made him hesitant at first. On the contrary, he also felt interested in attracting a beautiful, famous and rich woman in the sex he longed for. And in order to keep her in his arms for long term, he needed to make her achieve many climaxes of pleasure. With an oath, he lifted her abruptly and swapped the position onto the seat, and when her butt was resting on the edge of the leather seat, he dropped his knees in front of her, pushing her legs apart, slid his warm hands up under her skirt, skimming across her thighs, until they slipped beneath the waistband of her panties and surround a firm buttock. She lifted without hesitation, let the delicious slide of elastic and lace down over her hips, lower, and all the way off.

Their gazes touched, locked, ignited. Even with her skirt still on, and her panties gone, she felt no shame.

Once the panties had been stripped off, he pushed her thighs apart, exposing the very essence of her to him, and found he wanted to give her in the way he'd never given to any woman after his wife died, to take her to heights never before reached. He kissed the inside of her right knee and trail kissed and soft nips up her leg to her thigh. Her skirt inched up, revealing more and more of her goodies. She moaned, knowing what he had in mind. Her feet flexed, and he reached his goal to the current center of her universe then kissed her once.

"Tommy, oh! You really can be a bastard," she cried as waves of desire shot through her at the first intimate contact of his kiss, and his tongue found that special spot that only lovers discover.

"Just for you," he replied, then his hot breath blew her pubic hair to make small space for his tongue and pushed her knees wider to hold in place for starting to use his tongue to explore her from every angle.

His wet and slick mouth, which was just as hot and clever as his fingers, and filled with promise as his tongue was smooth like velvet wantonly teasing her. Top to bottom, side to side, and then circled around her clit, the sensitive sweet spot. Slowly at first, then faster and faster and she let out another sound, this time darker. The tendrils of pleasure radiated out from her core. Her toes curled, her thighs tighten and she gripped the edge of the seat on either side of her, head tipped back, and her hips thrusting upward from the seat, anticipating, inviting more of his touch, of his kisses, and of him.

He didn't want to stop, just give her as much pleasure as he could. So, he replaced his teasing tongue with his fingers traveled slowly up her thighs, luring her into relaxing again, until his thumbs reached the junction of her thighs.

She almost screamed as he slipped a finger inside her and pushed in and up finding what she would swear was the back of her clit. At the same moment, his thumb circling her clitoris, around and around and around.

No time for slow, he used everything he had to make it quick, rough, the pad of his thumb and the side of one finger going fast and furious. And the faster he did, the more she moved.

He made love to her now in a way she hadn't known existed. In a way she would never forget when her mouth unconsciously moaning non-stop. But if he continued to torment her like this would bring her to a climax. So, she clamped both hands to his wrist, held his hand in place. "Stop, stop, no stop."

"You need me to stop?"

Confused, moved to aching, her eyes flew to his. "No. This will be over, Tommy. Right now, I want you inside me."

Her response made it impossible to wait any longer. He knew she was ready, and he wanted to be inside her more than he wanted to see another sunrise. He let go of her long enough to undo his fly quickly, stripped off his pants.

He wasn't wearing any underwear, and she saw a most impressive erection sprang free in front of her, and he tugged at his pocket, pulling open his wallet. What on earth was he doing with his wallet? She tried to slap it away from him, but he kept on, pulled a foil square out. A condom. How strange and serendipitous. "Good, I was just wondering about that."

That made him chuckled softly, delightedly, then ripped it open with his teeth, and pull it out before slipping the ring over the tip of his cock. She felt him shift as he rolled the latex over his length and incredibly hard. She swallowed hard, letting her eyes met his. Waiting.

"I've never wanted anyone the way I want you," he admitted.

Shamelessly, she commanded. "Then take me. Now."

Christ, he loved how direct she was. Taking her order, he scooped her from the seat and lowered her over the top of him.

A little sound came from her throat as he began to kiss her again, lifted and settled her astride him. She wanted him so badly that shifting a little in impatience and in total control, she took his and guided herself slowly from the head of his cock, buried deep inside her, until her pubic bone met his. She loved the feeling of fullness, the intimacy of having him as close as two people could get and biting her lip to hold back a moan.

Feeling hot, soft, tight, and wet, God damn, it's so good. He wanted more. "Lift up," he whispered hotly in her ear, and then rather than wait for her to comply, he grasped her ass in his two big hands and roughly showing her how to raise up on her knees until he nearly slipped out of her, and then to sink back down, once again taking him fully inside her.

Their groans of pleasure mingled, his low, her high, urging them on as she grabbed his arms and he paused to stare into her beautiful eyes, eyes that shine with her love and desire. "Tommy?"

His dark blue eyes locked hers. "Yeah?"

"You're ruining me for everyone else," she said, but stop it. Enjoy this moment. And she began to move like that, urged on by his hands.

He was glad, closed his eyes, but shaken more than he wanted to admit by the admission. He thought he heard her say, but it might have been the whisper of his wild beating heart. His world had changed today, forever. Her, too, because they both melt into it, bodies arching into each other in a slow, tender, gentle rhythm, relishing every treasured inch of her.

Opening his eyes, his mouths came here again, fused to answer her, kissing hot and deep, until they ran out of air, he wound his fist in her hair and forced her head back, sucking on her exposed throat, and asked hotly against her ear. "Tell me you want me."

"Just don't stop. Please don't stop." She answered him with this way, didn't care that she was begging. She was so close, need more, would do anything for completion. The weakness should have embarrassed her, but it didn't. This was right.

He didn't, and slid a hand around the back of her neck, pulled her mouth down to his for a slow, deep, and wet kiss, then gripping her hips and held her in place to accept his thrusts, driving exactly the rhythm she needed that he built up speed for either of them, and stirring the hunger.

"Tommy... oh, no... oh, God... Tommy..."

The first spasm hit, her nails digging into his back as her release came fast and furious.

Overjoyed, he exclaimed. "I can't hold back..." And then, moving rapidly to give her every last bit of pleasure he could, then buried his face in her neck, his fingers gripping her ass, he unleashed the essence of his sensuality.

He was still, feeling the ecstasy of passion and the agony of despair. For this was the first time they would ever come together as a man and woman. He knew it and she did, as well.

When she caught her breath and her world stopped spinning out of control, she wasn't sure what to say afterward, or even how to act. She felt afraid of how easy it had happened. The man had turned her into a blithering idiot. He started to pull out of her, grabbed his pants and gazed down at her so harshly. "I'm just a damn fool, Smiling," he said, disgust tainting his words as he put on his pants. "Hell, what a mistake!"

That's what she didn't expect after he seduced and made love to her. "Mistake?" she said, reeling, afterglow fading and humiliation burning through her brain. "You don't have to try and mix up a mess sex and guilty when both of..." But she couldn't finish her saying, when her breath and voice were suddenly lost, and he was breathing faster now, harder, or was the anger and shame surging through her veins?

She swallowed hard and thought that might be coming from another source. And yet, there was something more, someone else in the car with them. A chill ran down her spine as she realized Mathew was sitting on the other seat, and watching them, a look on his face that told her he'd seen everything. "Oh, God, what was I getting myself into?" She asked, disgusted with herself, regretting what had happened. *Yes, people become miserable because they allow desire freely.* At the same time, there was the other one calmed herself. It's just illusion.

But the only thing she could do was hearing the command in the tone called her name and was yanking on her hand.

❦ ✳ ❦

Seeing that Smiling slept well, Tommy didn't want to wake her up, just gently took the empty glass from her hands, set it aside, and he let his gaze to her long legs, exposed from toe to thigh, then looked at her sleeping position with her head lay on the chair. How had he never noticed that her delicate features looked so cute, how the curve of neck and shoulder made elegant contrast?

He didn't know anyone who could've slept at all in that passion. Maybe he hadn't looked, he admitted. He liked looking at her now when he waited. She was asleep on the seat like a child beside him. Her face seemed a bit pale, and without makeup, the faintest of shadows could be seen under her eyes. But thin lips were very soft and naturally red. She looked like a treasure that a man should protect, cherish. Unconsciously, he was about to raise his hand to touch her face, but he shook his head, telling him not to be rude. However, after a while, he took her arm and shook it gently. "Wake up, Smiling."

The voice was clearer now and more insistent, accompanied by hands-shaking. Startled, she blinked herself awake, and saw the man was sitting next to her, his big hand clasped over her with his blue eyes with concern was Tommy. For a second, she didn't know where she was, but couldn't erase the image of a man she'd just made mental love.

"Are you all right?" Tommy asked.

It had just been a dream. But why did it have to be so real? The turbulent, churning sensation through her system hadn't faded. And why had she dreamed of making love Tommy? Just thinking about it made her feel like blushing.

"I'm fine ... well, kind of." She mumbled, shaking her head at oddity, but she noticed that his hand was still holding hers, his big, calloused fingers wrapped around hers.

As if he, too, recognized that he was touching her, he slowly released her hand. "We're home, Smiling."

She sat up straight, jerked her gaze to see the limo turned through the electronic wrought-iron gates opened, then looked back at him. "Wow! Sorry, Tommy. I slept the whole way."

Who knew how sexy she looked when she slept? He did now and could watch her sleep forever. "No need to apologize. You need it."

Embarrassment washed over her. Dear God, had Tommy heard her moaning? Calling his name? Heaven only knew what else she might have said. "Did I talk nonsense as I sleep?"

"No," he reassured her, but he tossed her a mischievous smile.

Chapter 12
Home is where Love resides.

Within fifteen minutes, they all sat around the table in the living room and after Mrs. Dora served their teas on the table then she took Cathy into the kitchen to get ice cream for her to eat. Gloomy sipped her tea, enjoying its delicious aroma and feeling more relaxed than she had in weeks. "This is wonderful." She placed her tea cup on the saucer and rested her head against the back of the couch.

"How's Bill doing?" Her mother asked after sipping of her tea.

"My husband is very respected by everyone."

"We're all proud of him.'" Her father interjected.

"So how's everybody and where are they all, mom?"

"Everybody's fine." Jennies told her. "Justine's family was the first to arrive from yesterday and they are staying at your brother James. They'll all coming for dinner tonight. Smiling will arrive soon." "Where's Steady? I didn't see her."

"Probably into the home gym doing yoga or intimidate her with Tai Chi."

"Did I hear somebody talking about me?"

Everyone turned and Gloomy saw Steady was in gym suits fitness, exposing with sweat between her breasts with a delighted grin, walked toward them, gave a kiss on her cheek then hugged her before she sat down next to her to chat with them. "Good to see you."

❊❊✳❊❊

It was best not thinking of that, of what had happened or nearly happened. Smiling glanced out through the privacy glass of the limo when it pulled up in the circular driveway in front of the house. She put her shoes back on, gathered her bag, and before she could scoot toward the door, Tommy quickly got out the limo, walked around to open the car door and automatically offering a hand to assist her out. She realized it was a move that was a more polite, respectful gesture than usual. That expressed their positions. Man to woman. But the moment she stood on the driveway, he let go of his hand.

Smiling, he thought, was anxious to see her family after the long, very long flight from London. So he didn't want to keep her. "I believe your parents are expecting you, Miss Smiling. I'll bring the luggage in later." Cleverly, he turned his back to pay the driver and tipped him handsomely after he'd taken the luggage out of the trunk.

She gazed at the house she loved, the one constant in her life that didn't change. It didn't matter where she lived or where the job took her. This was truly her family home. Even though the curtains were closed, but she knew her mother, father and even her siblings were sitting inside, chatting, laughing like a family. That's what she thought of when feeling overwhelmed. It brought her comfort and gave her strength. Without wasting any second, she was dashing up the steps, reached for the door handle, and ringing the bell.

The doorbell rang interrupted their conversation. "Ah, this must be your sister here?" Jennies said, walked to the window and peered through the slats of the blinds in time to see Smiling standing in the front door. "Stay, I'll get it."

She strode across the main entrance foyer before Dora was also making her way to the front door, intending to greet her daughter on the steps.

Smiling was relieved and delighted when the door opened, and her mother cheered. "Smiling, my daughter."

Jennies ran into her outstretched arms and hugged her with intense affection. "Goodness, you look great. I missed you so much."

Her throat seemed to constrict with emotion, but her eyes gleamed in relief and Smiling kissed her on the temple. "Me, too. I miss you so much."

"Come on in, your sister Gloomy just arrived and I'm sure we can get some more tea and food. You must be hungry."

"Not really, mom. But I can have some tea." Smiling said, following her mom into the living room while behind Tommy carried her luggage inside.

Brian glance up and caught sight of Smiling, he stood. "Well, look who's home." He gave her a bear hug. "We've missed you around here." She kissed her father on the cheek. "Glad to be home."

Her father smiled as he glanced in Tommy direction. "Thank you for bringing my girl home, Tommy."

"This is my job, sir." Tommy said and he didn't want to break into the family reunion, he "Excuse me. I need to move the car into the garage." He left after his boss nodded.

"Tommy is a very interesting and attractive man, isn't he?"

Smiling frowned at him. It was just so strange. What had he been thinking to bring up this topic? "What do you mean dad? Are you going to hook me up with him?"

Such a suggestion confused him, he just wanted to compliment Tommy on his own terms, but he didn't want anything sidetracking everyone from the job role at hand. Besides, he didn't expect Smiling to have such a thought, but he didn't let that happen, because she was engaged.

He gave her a reluctant laugh. "I don't know what you're thinking, but no, I can't do that."

Smiling grinned. "I know, just joking with you."

"Hello, sister." Gloomy cut in, and they were in each other's arms, hugging, laughing and talking all at once. "Do you realize it's been seven months since we've seen you? I've missed you."

"I've missed you, too." Smiling looked at her older sister with deep affection. "And you look wonderful."

"I thought maybe there was something we could cheer up then." Gloomy offered. "Always is." Her mother said, pointed to the couch. "Set yourselves down."

Within minutes, Jennies handed Smiling a glass of lemonade. "Do you think you'll ever move back?" She asked, looked thrilled to have two of her girls at home. This was what she loved the best, her entire family in one place.

Smiling smiled. Her mom still made comments about her moving so far from family, and she knew it still painted her to have even one daughter far away, because she's thinking that she might choose to live there permanently. Have kids there. Grow old there. "Eventually, but not yet," she said honestly. "I love what I'm working there. It's a wonderful place for a fashion designer."

"So is Melbourne," her mother said, trying not to pushy about it. "I just hope you don't stay there forever. I hate having you so far away."

It was a comfort to know she was surrounded by people who loved her, especial her mother. She was proud of all her children, and in their own way, each of them was doing well. More important, all of them were happy, and had found their niche. She never compared them each other, even as children, and saw each of them as individuals, with different talents and needs. It made their relationship that much better with her now. And each in her own way was crazy about their mom. She was like a best friend, only better. They had her unconditional love and approval, and she never lost sight of the fact that she was their mother, and not a friend. "I don't think we have to worry about that, Mom. I can fly home within a day, if you ever need me."

"It's not about the distance. Your father and I are fine. It's just three times a year when you come home for holidays. That never seems like enough. I don't mean sound ungrateful, and I'm glad you come home. I wish you live near us or in the city like your brother, Bush Jr."

She couldn't have counted the number of cities she'd been in or stayed, but her favorite remained London. Yet she'd chosen to live for long lengths of time in the states where she liked the contrast of people and cultures and attitudes. She liked the enthusiasm of Americans, which she saw typified in her parents. "I know, Mom. You and Dad should come to see me. Melbourne had been great, but London is such a beautiful and interesting city. It will be hard to leave when I final decide to." She didn't tell her that she was thinking about it.

Knowing that her mind could not be change, she changed the subject. "So, tell me about Mathew then," Jennies insisted as she was always worried that Mathew was so independent about everything, and he seemed so unaware of her needs and feelings. Jennies had done her best to like him in the past three years, but she just didn't. "How serious is it? When are you two getting married?

Oh, sure, she thought about getting married, but she'd never thought about family and the future and having babies and all that kind of stuff, yet. "He's great man, but marriage was a big step."

"Look at Mom and dad," Gloomy pointed out, and Smiling's eyes turned to hers. "It must be wonderful to still be that much in love after all these years."

"Yeah, they're perfect together," Steady added. "Our parents are proof that there really is such a thing as happily-ever-after. How could we ever find something like that? It only happens once. Mom used to say that too. She always said how lucky they were. You should count yourself lucky."

She had always wanted to have a happy relationship like her parents, both till madly in love. Smiling studied the gold band on her father's finger. Thirty years, she thought, and it still fit. That was a kind of miracle.

"I wish we would be like that." She said, feeling her luck wasn't getting any better. They were her role models for the perfect marriage. She still wanted one of those, if she ever found a man like their dad. The man was easygoing, kind, good-nature, and loving. There was nothing wrong with her future husband. Mathew wasn't a cheater, a liar, or a drunk, and it was hard not to love him. For both, the arrangement between the two worked very well, even when they couldn't be together. But the reason she just didn't want to be married to him yet was because both of them wanted their careers to be more prominent, more successful, or maybe it's because she's so arrogant, to be afraid her career would stop after getting married. So many times, couples told her that everything had been great while they were living together, sometimes for years and years, and then it all fell apart when they got married. One or both turned into monsters. She wasn't afraid that Mathew would do that, or even that she would. But why take the chance when things were perfect as they were? However, her family, they seemed determined. "We're considering it. We understand each other perfectly. We're both busy, we both have major careers. And I don't want to rush him."

"Three years is not a rush. That's a long time," her father cut in, looking disapproving, but giving her options. "Been engaged for a long time, and you haven't gotten married, there will be many problems. It's time for him to make some changes. Unless you're happy with the way it is. And if this is what you want, then we have no complains, do we? Is it?"

"We'd really like to see you married, sister." Steady said.

They were all concerned that Mathew had engaged to her for three years, but they still hadn't married yet. That's why everyone always so disagreeable about him. Her mother had been indifferent to him, but her father had really disliked him. She had seen right through him. And why did she always have to stick up for him and answer people's questions about his behavior? "Of course, it would be. I meant that I've waited for three years, and I can wait little longer if I must. You'll have to see about that." Smiling promised and threw that topic to her sister. "Now Steady, it's your turn. How's your love life?"

"A man in my life? No, I don't have one." "A pretty girl like you? I don't believe it."

"I meant, I haven't found the right man in my life. I've dated, sometimes seriously, been asked a couple of them, but I never felt that I wanted to throw away my independence on some man."

"Why was that?"

"I guess I'm picky. Choosing the wrong mate is more frightening that being alone for lifetime."

Everyone laughed. "She's waiting for a man as handsome as her father." Her mother said for her.

"They don't grow on the trees, mom." Gloomy pointed out.

Steady smirked at her sister. "The important things are sometimes coming late whether it's in love or in life. And although waiting for long time, I believe in the end, the man of fate will cross the great sea and find me." "How confident is that!" Smiling said.

She flashed her sister a grin. "Of course. Everything in this world is arranged by the Creator. Have you heard someone say this? I'd rather get married late than married the wrong man."

"Right," Brian interjected. "We always want you to find a good and worthy man. He doesn't need to be rich, very too smart or very handsome. But he must be sincere, kind, hardworking, and most at all, they are willing to change themselves for you."

Jennies was content to listen to them chatting, but want to change the subject. "Anyway, Smiling, I'd like you to go Miami event for my behalf."

Smiling racked her brain but drew a blank. "What event?"

"The charity fashion show at Golden Sun Resort will be an art auction."

She knew her family donated heavily to charity, especially organizations for children like St. Jude Children's Research Hospital. "It sounds interesting," she suddenly anxious. "Okay, mom, I'll go."

"Good, your brother Bush Jr had kept the penthouse suites at East Air for you."

That wasn't surprising, but peace, quiet, and sounded very nice. She could use that so she would relax, eat great food, and getting beautiful tan at the beach. "But I'll need a nice gown for that."

"Yes, I already prepare and the jewelry that go with them."

It was happy when Brain listens their conversation, but it was time for him to retire and leave them alone and gave them some girl time. "I have to go back my office," he said, stood up. "I'll see you around." "See, you Dad," they all said.

And after he left, Steady invited them "Swimming?"

Smiling looked out to the pool. "A swim sounds good."

They went up their room to put their bathing suit on. Everything was there, everything in place. Their home had been unusual in that each of the girls had her own room as a kid. They all commented on how strange it felt at times to be back here, and in their beds, where they had grown up. It made them feel like children again and brought back so many memories. They had so much to talk about, and share, and whatever tensions had existed between them over the years had vanished when they met as adults. They helped themselves to a bottle of wine to join in the pool. It was a hot balmy day, and the cool water felt wonderful.

Steady was the youngest sister, classically striving to be better. She loved her sisters with a deep, solid affection, and jet she always felt she had to do something more than they did. Not that they had set such impossible standards. Her oldest sister, Gloomy had been set on going to medical school and became doctor. She met her husband two years later and married him that July. At twenty-nine she had an adorable little girl, Cathy of her own. She was happily married, and she and her husband were planning to have one more child. For her the world of careers held absolutely no appeal, unlike her younger sisters.

In some way, Steady had more in common with Smiling, her younger sister. Smiling was ambitious, competitive, excited about being out in the world. But in Steady's eyes, her sister's lives seemed so settled. As far as she could see that they seemed to have everything they wanted. Smiling was happy and at ease in the world of fashion and modeling business, Gloomy was equally so as a doctor.

When they were sitting at the table and toweled dry, Steady filled their glass with wine then raising her glass in a toast, "to a new and better future for our girl here." "To a new and better future," they all echoed and drank.

"I keep hoping you will find the right man soon." Smiling smiled at Steady. "They say there's someone for everyone. But I guess you know that."

"I used to believe that," Steady said. "I'm not sure I do anymore. We say that all the time. But why are we waiting? Is real life going to start when some guy arrives? Or shouldn't we concentrate on enjoying our lives now?" She added, thinking of her ex-lover.

"Not always. And you shouldn't stop finding for Mr. Right," her mom said, patting her arm.

Obviously, she was about as qualified to find her own Mr. Right as a surgeon was to operate on himself. "What's that supposed to mean?"

"Mr. Right exists. It is just because, you haven't found the right man for you."

Her mother had said the same words to her when she was going through her rebellious phase, only much more sternly. "Seems to me I've heard those words before in the mind of poets." Steady teased.

"They're still true." Her mom learned back and regarded her. "God always arranged for us. That's why I think He'll get the perfect man for you somewhere right here in Melbourne."

Chapter 13

Keeping the promise, Smiling had decided to take Atlantic Coast Highway by limo instead private jet to Miami next day. Although the time would be longer but she could see many beautiful scenes. Adding to that, she was in no hurry when Tommy was her companionship, sitting across her in tuxedo which contrasted with his blue eyes and blond hair. He looked handsome and dangerous, not mention sexy. What's the harm in having an attractive bodyguard who would obviously escort her wherever she wanted to go? And the city of Miami was not like the city of Melbourne that she understood and loved. Even she had been there many times before. The ocean stretched on forever. There were nude beaches where the sky was clear, the temperature warm where was stylish and extremely modern with spiraling high-rise hotels, crowded together and gleaming in tropical sunlight. It was also swimming pools and trendy shops, countless restaurants and night clubs, but she preferred the quietly rural atmosphere of her own family's hotel.

Five stars East Air Resort was the one of place that attracted the most tourists in the area. It was a place people loved to visit every time they came to Miami, and where there's enough nature to be beautiful, also shopping malls and lots of luxury restaurants that had everything from five-star dining to fast food, lined the busy and noisy streets, exciting in their own way. The sidewalks were packed with the usual summer crowd. It occurred to her that she'd seen more tourists who's hanging cameras from their necks in the hour since she stepped out of the limo, and stared at the familiar landscape Sunrise Beach, and then wondered if she'd had time to get to the beach, swimming, relax and enjoy the weekend, or checked out anything else.

It was lovely resort, luxuriously expensive, just Jefferson's style, Tommy noted. The villas overlooked the Atlantic Ocean and were built directly into the mountainside. And after they got into the private elevator with the executive manager who was tall in a beautifully tailored dark suit and a bellman immaculately white uniformed hotel carried up all their stuff, then opened the door for them to check on. When they stepped in massive foyer,

Tommy realized the penthouse was huge as the manager snatched up a remote and began punching buttons. The shimmering blue drape over the floor to ceiling windows opened then all the drapes.

The floors were marble, and the chandelier looked as if it was Italian. There was an open living room with multiple seating areas. Choosing another button, he opened a wall panel that revealed a 78-inch curved Samsung television with Boss Sound Touch audio system over the arched fireplace. A grand piano of showy white was placing to giant dining room that could easily seat twenty, and he had the impression of expensive artwork, but what really caught him attention was the view.

The entire west wall was floor to ceiling windows. He could see down the beach and the ocean beyond as Smiling led the way and he followed. The next one was more living space, and the restaurant size kitchen, complicated electronics filled a glass front cabinet, and he found out few bottles of fine champagne inside the refrigerator. Again, the view dominated everything. Light spilled into the house, and he knew if he opened a sliding glass door, he would hear the sound of the ocean, along with the cries of seagulls.

They went to the nice size guest room and master bedroom where had a big with a fireplace, a huge bed with a silky cover, with a luxury bathroom had the tub was large enough for five, as was a separate rippled glass shower stall offered crisscrossing sprays, and lovely clear jars were arranged on glass shelves and held bath salts, oils and creams. There was a huge patio with a pool and seating right outside. It was good to be rich.

And because this was a major social event, and held at noon instead of evening, Tommy glanced at his watch, checking the time after he saw his room was next to hers with the connecting door, and their suitcases were placed in a walk-in closet. "We'll unpack later, but now we should keep going, if the auction is important to you."

She loved how he handled the business, and when she was around him, she felt better about herself. As if she could do anything. "Follow the procedure." She said, smiling and following him.

When the elevator door opened and Smiling walked ahead of him out onto the street to the limo was waiting for them. Instead of taking a quick step to catch up to her, Tommy enjoyed the view from behind. This had become a habit and besides, she had a sexy way of distracting him. Her long wavy hair, covering her bare back. One side of her hair was lifted up by a hairpin with diamonds, matching with a pair of glittering starlight on her ears. Her hot figure in a long chic black silk evening gown with a low V-neck slit. The hem of the dress was split high on both sides to the hip that showed off her legendary legs and every inch of her flawless figure. And hitting the ground were black Chanel heels. In her hand, she was holding a not-so-cheap diamond handbag. Every perfect part of her, including there appeared to be almost not back to the dress that he could see her creamy skin all the way to her sharply bottom, moving with every step she took, exuding luxury and aura of the upper class. Realizing he was distracted, he shifted his gaze away. This wasn't the time for this. He had to conduct everything according to his role, including her looking incredibly sexy. He had to do his job duties without thinking anything for himself. Forcing himself back to his duty, he gave the driver their destination and sat across her silently and solemn.

Until the limo stopped at the curb, he stepped out of the limo and quickly his eyes darted around. His senses were all active to be able detect any danger lurking, to promptly protect Smiling. Blended in well with the Cadillac, Jaguars and Mercedes being valet-parked in the lot half a black from the main entrance where there were throngs of people crowded into the roped off section. Cameras were clicking, flashes popping, and onlookers waited for a glimpse of their favorite celebrities. He opened the door for her, and she stayed close to him as he'd instructed and didn't do anything to draw attention their way, other than the little of attention he wanted. He'd never been to the Golden Sun before, and this wasn't his thing. Not really, but it was fun to observe the celebrities, actors, models, singers mingle and powerful people. Men in dark tuxedos, women in jewels, furs and high-end evening gowns by famous designer. But Tommy noticed that Smiling was cheered and applauded, so he was careful to keep the distance between them. However, she stepped closer to him and casually placed a hand on his arm. "I want you be a guest with me, Tommy."

He snatched his hand away, took a step back instinctive defense, and stared at her with his big blue eyes unblinking, stunned probably. It was obvious that they had recognized her.

And before he could protest, she reached to his arm and led him toward the arched white double doors at the entrance to join the reception line. They looked like a staggeringly handsome couple arm in arm. The intimate movements of the two of them immediately many curious glances cast in their direction, especially noticed by newspaper reporters. So their cameras flashed a continuous light took these pictures before their eyes. And according to response of his profession, Tommy quickly pulled her arm to stand behind him and covered her. "Stay away!"

Smiling tapped Tommy on the shoulder, but he didn't turn around until they were out of the way. "Yes?"

"You didn't need to do that."

He didn't want to see his and her names and photos in a newspaper. Her fiancé would probably see it. Include the stares from the crowd made him uneasy. Whispering to one another and they never took their eyes off them. Who knew what they could be saying? "My job can't involve with yours in any other way, Ms. Jennifer," he added, trying to reason with her. "People will go wild gossiping. They travel fast, and it won't be good for you." Smiling was quietly aware of it, and there was simply no way of avoiding the press here. She knew that being with Tommy meant that they would be constantly hounded by the press. They would want to know who he was, and whether to start a flood of new rumors about her love life. And sure, enough as she glanced around and saw half dozen photographers kept snapping their picture, few of guests and all the employees made note of them holding arms. She turned away from them and cameras. "Amazing how rude some people can be, isn't it?" She told him. "But I don't give a damn about that. Let them be curious and wonder. That's common sense. What I do in my personal life is nobody's business. Be my guest first, a bodyguard second."

Not sure how to take it, he handed the computer-generated tickets to the ticket collector behind the table, and the woman smiled. "Welcome to the Golden Sun's Ball." She glanced down at their tickets. "Oh, I see you're one of our VIPs. You'll find a table right in front of the podium reserved for our most special patrons."

"Thank you." He said and naturally, Smiling latched on to his arm and led him in.

The minute they stepped through the doors, Tommy glanced suspiciously over his shoulder as they walked toward to the main ballroom with its polished floors and was already filled with people.

The two of them immediately became the focus of all curious eyes on them. She nodded to people who waved her, smiling at those who didn't. Most of the faces were familiar and knew her. That was one of problems with these parties. The same people, the same conversations. The band-an orchestra, a good old-fashioned set of musicians with saxophones, trumpets, violins, flute and piano discreet in black dinner jackets, had taken their places on the wooden platform near the dance floor where massive chandeliers, dripping with teardrops of crystal and lit by dozens of lights were suspended an intricately carved ceiling. The fact was the entire ballroom seemed to glitter from chandeliers to the crystal glasses on the table, to the peals and sparkle of diamonds were decorating and glowing on hairs and ears, throats and hands to the long sweeping dresses in pastels contrasted with dark evening suits. Everything glittered, and everywhere the feminine scent of perfume.

Smiling stifled a sigh. She was so damn tired of glitter, so bored with these endless charity functions even when they were for a good cause. Why couldn't she just write a check and be done with it?

Even if she'd enjoyed the social aspect of these things, wine tasting, followed by an expensive dinner, which was then followed by an auction for overvalued objects she didn't want or need wasn't her idea of fun, and yet here she was again.

It was the family business, of course. Jennies' Foundation was the only real line of business in Florida that they attended these things to give it support, and her attendance was mandatory. She wished she could just write a check to the children's hospital and call it done, she had to endure these events, and she'd still end up writing a check.

A waiter stopped to offered them each drink and she took a glass from the silver tray. Tommy shook his head and the waiter disappeared through the crowd. She enjoyed drinking wine, but not the heavy red wine that she supposed was an indication of her very red blood. She could ask server get margarita for her instead. But she had to manage to keep from shuddering at each sip until the lunch she'd be able to get her favorite drink which was a delicious blend of half champagne and half sparkling green apple juice. She couldn't stand champagne on its own but mixed with apple juice it was great. All the servers and bartenders at these events, maybe knew what she drank, without having to ask. But she was trying to make the best of it.

Sipping from her drink, then shaking the glass with her hand, she looked at the crimson liquid when a woman's voice called from behind, interrupting her. "Jennifer!"

They turned to find a woman strolled over to kiss Smiling's cheek. "How delightful to see you, darling."

"Hello," Smiling said and smiling, because she was her mom's friend, and because she was well-known for her generosity; she gave to all the important charities that would be reported in the media. "How nice to see you, too."

"Why didn't you tell me you were back in town?"

Beside Smiling, Tommy looked at a tall woman with beautiful white hair and big hazel eyes who hugged Smiling fiercely. She glittered from head to foot, from the diamonds that hung at her ears to the glint of a diamond on her ring with poppy-pink fingernails. She was into her sixty, he guessed, but had a noble appearance, and the long black dress sparkled under the light, highlighting the curves of her body. All of them were specially designed products, compared to the famous brands, they're much more valuable. Somehow, he managed a smile for her curious eyes.

Smiling kissed her cheek in returning. "Quick trip, Miss Charity, for family time and little business. You look divine."

"Thank you," she said, made herself looked at Tommy up and down as he stood behind Smiling. He was handsome. Like the hero in the novel, in a tailored dark suit that draped elegance over tough and ready muscle. His eyes were blue, and his smile was charming. "You aren't alone?"

With the case of experience, and with the confidence he carried everywhere, Tommy offered his hand. "How do you do ma'am?" He greeted her. "Since I'm her bodyguard, I have to do it myself. I'm Tommy."

The man who identified himself as Jennifer's bodyguard had a warm smile and somewhat sincere, and an easy way about him, even though he looked her directly in the eyes with his own eyes cool and cautions. Miss Charity discovered that as she accepted a quick handshake, and said in half-joking, half-truth voice. "I remember that. And are you protecting her from me?"

His hand felt warm when he shook hers. "I'm trying to decide if I should. But I'm pleased to meet you, Mam."

She laughed at his formality and wondered how she could have one like him for herself. "I like you, Tommy. Please call me Charity. I'd like to think we are at least shall become friends."

Warning signal just flashed, and made him narrow his eyes, but politely, he said. "Of course, if you allow me. By the way, you look lovely, Miss Charity."

He sounded as though he meant it. What impressed Smiling most was the fact that his voice carried none of the patronizing tone that so many people used when speaking with the old. Something flashed in Miss Charity's eyes. It was both gratitude and pride.

"Wasn't it nice of your young man to tell me that, Smiling? I want to have a man like this. Would you be willing to let him work for me?"

Smiling understood her metaphor, so she curled her lips in a smile, but inside she wasn't happy at all. Was there anyone in this world who wouldn't be interested in a man who exudes masculinity and charm like Tommy? "I can't decide on this, because he's my father's bodyguard. And with as famous as you, just open your mouth then a lot of people will come to work for you."

Tommy realized that he should not cause any more attention, especial one he knew very important business associate with Smiling. In so a casual a manner, to give himself distance, he stepped back behind Smiling.

"I know, just joking with you. By the way, I'll be happy if you could come to my dinner party next week?"

They had met few years ago when she'd attended her cocktail party that Miss Charity was giving to raise funds for the survivors of some global disaster, a party which would give her plenty of media coverage, praising her work for charity and her generosity. "It's so nice of you to invite me. I will if I'm still in town, Miss Charity."

"So much traveling. It must be important to your business." Miss Charity said when the organizers announced everyone to take their seats at the elegantly decorated banquet tables, each seating eight.

"For now, I don't intent to spend my time away from my family."

"I'm glad to hear that. Would you join the table with me, so we'll get better acquainted?"

"We'd love to," Smiling said quickly, before Tommy had a chance to come up with an excuse. He could've begged off and let the women talked, but of course he didn't. He wasn't going to leave her on her own even with the perfectly harmless older woman. Smiling thought she had trust issues, but as a bodyguard, he couldn't. "And see you there."

"Wonderful." Delighted, Miss Charity tipped Tommy a wink, and be led the way into the dining area.

Smiling saw the look of playful longing in Miss Charity's eyes and the easy response of Tommy's grin, she finished the unwanted drink, and gave the empty glass to Tommy with an angry smile.

Seeing her sulky expression, he asked. "Something wrong?"

"She's lovely," she replied. "But I should warn you about Miss Charity. I'm told she had quite a reputation in her day, and she still has an eye for an attractive man."

"I'll watch my step, and thanks for the warning."

Despite Tommy was her bodyguard, but she had to admit he was the most elegant man she'd ever known. Tall, athletic, outgoing, handsome, he was a man's man and a woman's fantasy and by far the most masculine. He attracted female eyes without even trying. "I get the impression you usually do. I don't want you mixing in and trying to start something here." She said dismissing the sudden pang of jealous she felt as ridiculous.

He pretended to be mad at her. "I know. I'm sorry. I swear it won't happen anymore."

She knew he wasn't that kind of person, so she scanned around the room. By her count, there were fifty tables, which mean four hundred people were in attendance. An orchestra began softly playing Mozart, providing a pleasing background without being so loud to intrude on the conversation below.

Tommy wondered if he should follow in or wait out here. He was still thinking, then Smiling told him to follow.

They were interrupted another time before they found their table where Miss Charity already sat, and as Tommy pulled out a chair for her to sit and stood behind her. Smiling found herself seated at a table of seven honorees who were millionaires, billionaires, and big headed of economic and political stature. She knew the most of them. There also were five forks on the table. What was she supposed to do with five forks? Use fresh one for each bite? Defend her from the others at the table?

Strange how much she'd changed since then, Smiling thought, and yet one thing hadn't changed that she didn't truly fit in here. She liked her own personality, not the one had attended a hundred or more of these charity events, gone to cocktail parties, simple parties or any other parties. She would never be one of them, no matter how casually friendly they were to her like Steven Hall who was one of her father's oldest friend. He hugged, kissed her cheeks before, and she thanked him after he commented. "You' look lovely as always."

Now he sat across from her that she had to exchange a nod to him and the others around the table. They were truly philanthropists. They gave millions and millions to worthwhile charities every year, and that wasn't for their corporate tax deduction. She liked the most of them as they liked her, but she didn't want to be too friendly with any of them. Because it was somewhat reassuring to note that they were looking at her with open admiration. And in some ways, she could hold her own, also avoided any scandal might be happening by the media.

A few minutes later they were served lunch. And as soon as coffee and apple pie were served, the auction for charity had begun. She and Tommy went into the adjoining room and walked among the tables where the donated items were on display. Nothing there called to her, though she supposed she'd do her part and bid on at least a couple, whether she wanted or not. There were small white envelopes and thick, rich paper for the attendees to use to place their silent bids. After a quick perusal of the items, she bid on a pair of unexciting pearl earring. If she got them, she would donate them to center for abused women, but another woman was bidding against her.

There was another hour of biding after that, and finally the auction was over, she didn't win, but she wrote generous checks to donate, and as she watched the elegant couples sway and twirl on the dancing floor. She didn't want to bother not one, but many men would ask her to dance. She turned to Tommy and gestured to him. It was time to go. "Let's get back to hotel."

Tommy smiled, understood and nodded his head, took out his phone and called for the limo.

❊❊＊❊❊

Back to the penthouse, Tommy brought her favorite drink at the table and the first thing that provoked his eyes was to see Smiling swimming gracefully through the water in the pool with long smooth movements, and her body was gleaming in the sunlight. The second thing was her string bikini but topless that he could easily see her rosy hued nipples against her white skin of her breasts in the water. So seductive, making his face hot, and his heart seemed to fall to the ground. If the world was filled with hot women and Jennifer Jefferson was the definition of fiery. Not only because she was a fashion model, but combine that with that she had curves, lots of them, and in the middle of her busty buttocks was covered by a tiny piece of bathing suit, so how could men see it without lusting after it and supposed to ignore a situation like that? Neither a saint or a blind man could resist, let alone him.

She wouldn't notice, so his eyes kept roving over her body, enjoying the sight of her long legs propelled her forward, and her slim arms cut through the water in quick, smooth strokes until she stopped. He wondered how many laps she'd completed before he'd come. It seemed to him as if she swam to drain herself of some tension.

Waiting and watching until her tip her head back in the water so that her hair slicked back, and as she stood, water skimmed her abdomen without any excess fat, and caught his eyes were looking at her passionately. "Are you studying me, Tommy?"

Being asked, he was startled and quickly looked away as shame overtook him by his fascination with the sight of her. "I'm sorry. I didn't mean to stare."

Tommy's innocent expression was lovely, wishing he would feel comfortable enough with her to simple enjoy himself like that. It was okay for him to stare at her. "I don't mind, Tommy." But even as she said the words, she could see his muscles tense.

Changing the topic, he asked. "Ready to get out?"

She glanced up sharply. There was the weariness around his eyes, she realized, but gorgeous. He hadn't changed his clothes, except the vest suit and the bow tie. His pants weren't tight, but they did fit his tight butt and muscular thighs. His shirt was unbuttoned, revealing a strong, muscular, six pack body, and the sleeves rolled up. "Yes," she answered.

He bent down, and with his iron-strong arms wrapped around her body, lifting her out of the water as water sluicing off her body, and stood her on the edge of the pool with his hands went to her hips while her fingers curled into his shirt. His rock-solid abs right against her stomach and one of his legs wedged between hers. Their other parts were aligned with each other. But that unusual strength of his made her aghast. She was skinny, yeah, but she wasn't bony skinny, and she weighted more than it looked like she did because all her activities gave her muscle. For him to so easily lift her like that it excited her left her speechless and couldn't look at him, she couldn't bear to. If she did, she might never look away. She had knowing her own mind, making her own choices. A man like Tommy would have little respect for a woman's wishes. But she aware he was no more comfortable than her as he had released her with his face suddenly red. The man with a cold, stern expression like him sometimes blushed like that. But his blush was lovely to her. She enjoyed embarrassing him because that's when he showed another side of himself, the side that was vulnerable and sweet and innocent. "It's an interesting thing for a man like you to blush, you know?"

He was a man who's very good at hiding his emotions, until the appearance of Smiling. The blush was unexpected, and it seemed to fascinate her. He had seen her top naked on many magazines and she didn't need to bother with a bra. But the reality was quite a surprise, included the touch lightly of the hard, pink peak of her breasts, and her damned bikini barely covered and exposed enough delectable skin to send his blood pressure up to fifty points. He nodded. "I... that is." He shifted away from her, hoping to control the arousal it wasn't the right time to feel.

It would be better, much better, for them to keep their relationship on a purely business level; friendly but careful. She chuckled at his repressed and used her fingers to arrange her hair as they went to the table and towels dry. "I'm not embarrassed, why should you be?" She asked. "And I've already told you, I don't mind, Tommy."

The breeze would make her hair dry quickly. She liked that way, but Tommy picked the towel, gently dried her face then rubbed her hair dry in the gesture that would have been mere gentleman. And without moving, she seemed to let him. But his concentration shifted from what he was doing, his gaze cutting to hers, he draped the towel around her shoulders and brought her drink instead.

Tommy was good company, a man of many talents, and she'd always thought she was immune to his charm, but she was becoming worried that she wasn't. There's something sweet but uncomfortable crowded her chest, making her heart ache in an odd way. The emotion was unfamiliar, unwanted as banishing an image of them naked together. Suddenly in panic, she warned herself. Dear God, what was wrong with me? And quickly she turned around and sat on the bench and stretched her legs.

She was a woman who relaxed easily with her legs stretched out and her bare feet were crossed at the ankle on the chair and a glass in her hand. She was so sexy. He sensed that he could be easily aroused by her, that he was being aroused by her. But he forced himself to look away and distracted by his changing body, he turned his chair slightly, so he was looking more at the ocean than he was at Smiling. If he kept looking at her, she might guess what he had been thinking, and nothing would be more embarrassing. Sunlight didn't normally bother his eyes, even living in north Florida and his job, so he often had to remind himself to wear sunglasses. Now was one of those times, and he gratefully seized his from where he tossed in his shirt pocket. Hiding his eyes was a damn good idea.

Smiling gulped down some more of her drink as they sat there, not speaking much and tried to control their own feeling. Her swimsuit stopped dripping and her hair dry enough that it began to lift in the breeze, adding the peace and quiet atmosphere began to make her sleepy, and she thought how nice it would be to stretch out on the chair and take a nap, but on the other hand, she wanted to spend more time in the sun. "Will you take me on the jet ski?"

"Sure," he said without hesitation, and his blood pressure returned to normal.

The two of them went down to the wooden dock that stretched out into the crystal clear, aquamarine water, and when Tommy took the jet ski out of the boathouse, he handed her a life jacket. She put it on, and little while later when she's sitting behind him, she could see that he was being cautious, didn't go at full speed to be careful with her. Grateful for that, but she wanted to have some fun with it. So, she told him speed up and spin, because she wanted to enjoy it thoroughly. She liked having Tommy around to do things with and had had too little of it in her lifetime, since Mathew romances were always brief. It seemed unfair to compare about him to Tommy, and she didn't want to encourage Tommy unfairly, by sounding not having like this with Mathew. And by the following weeks, she would be back in London, she wouldn't be able to be with him for the day like this. Maybe he could enjoy have dinner with her family. She already given it a lot of thought, and knew her family love him. They went swimming together after that. She didn't want to question herself why she felt so at ease and relaxed with him. She wasn't a woman who had legions of friends, but, rather, acquaintances, people who came and went in her life. Where she gave friendship, she gave herself with it completely, with no limitations, and therefore she gave it carefully. Though trust wasn't fully in place, she felt friendship for him, and despite her reservations was pleased to have him with her. She had a great time, and they were laughing and teasing like old friends by a gorgeous sunset on the beach.

"I can't remember when I've had so much fun," she told him when finally, they went up to the house.

"Same to me. I'd forgotten how much fun this is." He said happily. "You'd better get out of that wet suit. We'll have dinner."

"Then where are we going for dinner?" Smiling asked.

"I had the impression you enjoyed being around a lot of people," Tommy said. "But I don't want a bunch of them staring at you or us while we eat. So, I suggest we're having dinner at here."

She smiled at that. Damn it, the longer she knew him, the more endearing he became. "I'd love your idea, Tommy. I'm tired of the restaurants and tired of crowds."

"So, why don't you take a hot bath, try to relax. I'll order you some food and set it up."

He felt comfortable with her, enjoyed being with her. Today had been ordinary to her, but to him it was a rarity, and it had been a true pleasure. he didn't want it to end. Not yet. He needed to figure out a reason to find a way to make her more interested and impressed with him. He buzzed room service right the minute he was alone. And instead ordering, Tommy asked the head chef prepared chicken, steaks, potatoes, corn and condiment for him cook. "Will that be all?"

"Yes, that would be fine."

"We'll have that up to you within ten minutes. Thank you, Mr. Tommy."

"You're welcome and thank you."

And few minutes later after he took a quick shower, put on jeans and white T shirts. They brought them to him. "I hope everything is satisfactory, Mr. Tommy."

"I'm, it will be." Tommy said, signed on the paper and gave him a large bill.

Yes, Tommy was satisfied enough to switch the stereo on jazz, bluesy and mellow before he forked the meats onto the grill, the meats sizzled on the hot rack, and began drizzling barbecue sauce over the meats, adding some freshly ground pepper, then prepared a tray of the meats for dinner. Tonight was beautiful with full moon, cool winds, suitable for dining outside, but in the end, he didn't make such a decision, and lighting some candles.

When Smiling put on the comfortable nightgown, the smell of food was so delicious that entered the room and straight into her nose, making her stomach groaned. Then she hurried out of the room. At the doorway, she stopped and gasped in amazement, couldn't believe her eyes. Image of the man wearing an apron in the kitchen that was Tommy. Plus, dozens of candles lit, and the moonlight spilling in through the window made the room glow. Melodiously music played softly from the hidden speakers, the recessed lighting offered soothing tones, and the most impressive was the smell of sizzling meat on the grill he was cooking. Her heart suddenly skipped a beat. Because her weakness was romance. If she didn't know what kind of person Tommy was, she would be skeptical at these moments, but this man truly made her admire.

She walked into the room. "You're just full of surprises, Tommy." And noting the meal had been set up on the dining table and a bottle of fine champagne was on ice in an elegant silver bucket. And at the voice of her, their eyes met. "I never would have guessed." "Guessed what?"

"You're a romantic and you can cook."

Seeing her expression, Tommy felt please and satisfied. He wiped his hands on a dish towel, laid it aside and removed the apron. "Nothing wrong with being romantic, and of course I cook. I'm known throughout the civilized world for my barbecues," he teased her. "Next time is fishing if you like, I promise. But now, sit down and have a taste, see how my cooking skills are."

When she did, he pulled the bottle of champagne into the iced bucket, eased the cork expertly out, and then poured it into the glass for her. "Do you cook a lot?"

He'd seated himself and offered her a platter, then poured himself a glass of wine. "Only when I entertain a beautiful woman."

Her eyes jerked up. She wasn't sure if he was teasing or telling the truth.

No one could lie to eyes like that. He had done it to impress her and had damn pleased with the idea. "Smiling," he toasted her. "The main idea was to impress you, but I also wanted to do something a little special for you, since you're here."

"Oh." She felt embarrassed at letting him see how much it had matter, but comforted by the easy warmth between them. Her lips curved and she sipped from her glass appreciated. "I can see why." She said, looking down at the plate of rustic food beautiful decorated with grilled beef and chicken, go with baked potatoes and corn on the cob salad, she then picked up her utensils and eagerly began to try a piece of beef. Enjoying the sweet and sour taste, just cooked, and immediately raised her index finger to praise. "Tastes great. So where did you learn to cook?"

He smiled slightly please. For someone as difficult to eat as Smiling. This was a compliment. It gave him a quiet sort of pleasure to watch her enjoy his food. "Honestly, in the military. During I was training, one of the tasks assigned to me was cook for more than one hundred soldiers. It became a challenge to prove that I could do it. So, I learned quickly and I found that I rather enjoyed cooking. When I got home, I cook when I'm tired of eating out. So you should eat more."

She nodded in agreement, then ate voraciously. And had to admit that anything Tommy cooked was delicious. "Thank you. It's been a while since

I've eaten these. My father used to make these for us." "What about your own cooking?"

"Cooking? It doesn't exist." Studying him, she took the last bite. "Naturally, you find it odd that I, as a woman don't know how. Because I don't suppose to cook, even though, I try to learn my way around a kitchen, and would like to experiment with recipes, with herbs, and sauces."

And then they ate in silence, and he pleased to see Smiling clearing her plate, then thought better of it. "I didn't mean any disrespect. More apple pies?"

Tommy's kindness was magnetic, and she supposed it was the reason for this anticipation she felt every time he was around her. She learned back in her chair and rubbed her stomach. "I don't know where I'll put it. I'm stuffed." She said, seeing him stood, trying to clean up. Rising herself, too and helped him carry the dirty dishes to the sink. Then her next move surprised him and threw him off guard. She moved to face him and then she lightly touched his lips with her fingertip in a gesture that was both friendly and intimate. "Thank you for everything, Tommy. Dinner was delicious, I enjoyed every bite and appreciate all the hard work you did preparing the meal."

The way she said it made him think she didn't get that kind of reaction from people very often. That wasn't surprising. "You're welcome, Smiling. Glad to be of service," he whispered, looking at her with a slow smile.

Her gaze skimmed over his face, over his mouth, and then to his surprise, Smiling wrapped her arms around his neck, pressing her body against his, and had gone up on her toes to reach his mouth.

He blinked when her soft lips pressed against his. The act was so unexpected, so quick, and he'd intended to control the situation like an experiment. But intentions changed as mouth met mouth, and his body automatically went from comfort and protect mode to something primal. Something that had him taking hold of her and dragging her to him.

It was just a fleeting kiss as a simple act of gratitude. But the moment their mouths met, the instant heat rushed between the two of them. And as if attracted by an inextricable attraction.

Since it was going to be a major mistake, Tommy decided to make the most of it. Something they'd both regret. And maybe that would stop them from doing it again. So he took far more than he should have as her lips parted and her small tongue pressed between his lips, as if she was asking for permission.

By the way, he hooked his arm around her, just at the top of her butt, drew her closer so that not only to deepen the kiss and their chests were touching. But also let their bodies came together, and the fit was even better than his fantasies, and letting her feel how hard she made him.

The soft sound Smiling made was from a silky feminine moan of pleasure. A signal that she not only wanted this but wanted more. She wrapped her arms around him and gently ground her sex against his. It was sweet torture.

She started this and he had no problem finishing it. The kiss was already hot and deep. He deepened it even more. Because he was stupid. And because his stupidity knew no boundaries, he followed her lead. The brainless part of him was already begging him to strip off her clothes. Sex would follow immediately. Great hot sex. But his self-esteem rose, too. It wasn't right. It couldn't be right. Smiling kissed him with ulterior motives. Granted, but she was forbidden fruit that he knew he couldn't have passionate sex with. He needed to regain his thought process and keeping his own body under control he would. Because he considered himself a disciplined man who knew how to control his baser instincts and resist temptation. He would prove that a man like him could be trusted to put her first, to expect nothing from her. He would prove that he was someone she could trust and not expect something from her. Cause God knew, if a woman could trust a man not easily to be tempted, then that woman would trust that man in all thing.

He forced himself to stop, and when he stepped back from her, both of them were gasping for breath. "I think we should stop." He pleaded distractedly.

"I'm sorry. I let your attraction draw me in and cloud my judgment." She said, touching her lips with her fingers. She hadn't meant for things to go so far. She hadn't wanted to feel so much, and thankful that he'd managed to keep a clear head. "I didn't plan for that to happen. I hope you know that."

The attraction he felt for her could really complicate everything. "It was my fault as much as yours." Tommy said, looking her face flushed with arousal, and now tousled hair made such a hot picture that wouldn't to be easy if he continues to see her like this. Therefore, he forced himself to create more distance, and suffering pain in his groin. Calming down wasn't easy but saying goodnight would do the trick and prevent any more mistakes. "Good night, go to bed, Smiling."

"Night," she whispered back, turned, and left the room as mysteriously as she started it.

✻ ✻ ✻

"Damn it. What's wrong with you?" Angry with herself and her lustful female on the way to her bedroom, and mentally kicking herself as she lied down on the bed and began to feel foolish. "You're an idiot!" Why had she kissed him? Why? That was a dumb move. It wasn't wise to think of Tommy in connection with any of her business. It probably wasn't wise to think of think at all. But she couldn't seem to stop thinking about him. Almost from the first moment she'd felt something. Attraction was one thing. He was, after all, an attraction man in a tough, dangerous kind of way which was a first impression mistake she'd fallen into. But one fiery, soul-melting kiss hadn't changed anything. You thought so? Bang her fist on the mattress as she wondered if she had been unfaithful to Mathew, just being with Tommy in this situation, even though they were meant to be friends? She wouldn't have like it if Mathew went out with another woman which seemed like a reminder of real life. In some way, she felt she owned it to him to tell him what had happened. She had to stay focused. They both did. Sense of intimate needed to have limit. Storing her thoughts away, Smiling decided to call Mathew, and hesitated because of the hour as she looked at her watch. It passed midnight over there. She couldn't imagine what Mathew was doing at that hour in London, though she was certain he was not sleeping. She dialed him finally, and the phone rang four times before he answered, and sounded pleased to hear from her. He told her he'd been working nonstop for the show, and he'd been just about to call her, let her know the show was great success.

"You should go home and get some sleep at a decent hour." She reminded him.

"That's what I'm doing now, I'm going straight from the show," he said simply then asked her suddenly. "What are you doing?"

Missing you, but instead, she blurted out. "I'm at East Air."

"With whom?"

"With Tommy."

"Tommy Anderson?" He sounded shocked. He had expected her to go alone or with her parents. "I thought you'd go with your brother and your parents, or something like that."

She smiled at his naive. "Yes, with Tommy. Any problem?"

"No, I'm just curious."

"Or suspicious," she challenged.

This was new. "I guess I'm a little of both."

The Miami auction sale was one of the most sophisticated events of the year, it was not the kind of place she would have to go by herself even with her parents. "I need a bodyguard. Tommy's fine about it though."

"I know, but I didn't expect that," he scowled and was jealous anyway. "And I just don't like the idea of you spending time with him."

She laughed, enjoying the edge of jealousy and peevishness in his voice. Maybe it was good for him. "God, Mathew, you make it sound like we went out for an intimate date. His job is to protect me."

"That doesn't mean you have to hang out with him in your off-time." Mathew argued. "You know well you can hire someone else."

She knew, only too well. But she only used trusted people. Mathew clearly didn't feel that way. And if she so much as mentioned Tommy, it would only piss him off even more. "It's too bad you couldn't be here. But just for the record, I'd rather be with you than Tommy any day."

He wished they could do that, and the tension eased. "That's one hell of a compliment, Smiling. I'll try to make it next year. I promise."

"I'll hold you to that." But where would they be next year? Would they be married by then? They were questions that still had no answer. "Have a good night, sweetheart." "The same to you. Talk to you tomorrow." He promised again. "I love you, Smiling." "I love you too," she said, squeezing her eyes shut. "Take care of yourself two weeks."

"I will. You too," he said, sounding as though he was really going to miss her. It made her smile and felt better as she hung up, tossed her phone on the bed. And then minutes later, she drifted off to sleep.

After hanging up, Mathew reached for the front door, and noticed that it stood partially ajar. The door had not been jimmied, and the glass panes had not been broken. That meant only one thing, someone had unlocked the door. Only that person knew where his spare key was hidden. Smiling with anticipation, he eased open the door and walked into his house. After closing and locking the door, he made his way to the poor, then smiled as he saw a woman who was naked and waiting for him in the water. Well, wasn't this a beautiful sight? "What are you doing here?"

"What does it look like?" She showed off her breasts. "I figured after a long stressful day for the show, you might need a good fucking. And that's one thing I'm good at."

Without saying another word, Mathew kicked off his socks and shoes, stepped out his vest, and tossed it on the floor, and then pulling his shirt, pants and box.

He had an amazing body and made good use of it. "Come on in," she said invitingly, thoroughly enjoyed the warm water and the prospect of night with him. They had been having an affair for a long time, in the process of doing shows. No promises love had been exchanged and wouldn't give affection to each other. Nights like this they spent together just for sex, wanted nothing more.

He dove into the pool, swimming crossing between her legs, then came up to embrace her. "I'm actually very fond of you at this point, you know."

She laughed. "Honey, you're fond this." She grabbed his penis and rubbed it up and down between her feminine lips, and when it's hard, she inserted his erection into her body. "Make love to me."

She was an incredible woman, and he had a great time with her. The one thing she could never do with him was say anything bad about Smiling and offered the best sex. "It would be my pleasure."

⁂ ✻ ✻

While he cleaned up, Tommy put the dirty dishes and bowls in the dishwasher and told himself that she kissed him just to thank him. That's the whole meaning. But he wondered why that kiss moved him equally as much as the passion had yet somehow differently when he slammed the door shut, turned on the autopilot, wiping his hands on a towel, then went back to his room. He needed time to gain control of his head and his hands. So, he turned down the volume on his phone and set it on the nightstand then sat on the edge of the bed, unsnapped and unzipped his pants. He liked to lose his pants, but yeah, probably not a good idea.

But no matter how firmly he ordered his mind to stay calm and blank, it just kept opening to one single thought as he lay on the bed.

Smiling kissed him. That's a very serious error, but what did it mean? Why should he even think about it? A kiss was just that. It had just been a product of the moment, nothing more. But it was hard to describe it as nothing more. Was it the kiss that had changed things between them?

Damn her for stirring up all this need that he'd managed to live very contentedly without until now. It annoyed him. Just remembering his helpless response to her infuriated him. So, he forced himself to critically dissect what had happened. If he was attracted to what she seemed to be, that was reasonable enough. He'd lived a solitary and often turbulent life. Though he had chosen to live that way, and certainly preferred it, it wasn't unusual that at some point he would find himself pulled toward a woman who represented everything he had never had. He reminded himself as he lies there in the dark, knowing he'd never be able to sleep, and trying to come up with a solution. Something else was what it was, he admitted. Would being with her become an addiction, the more time he spent with her, the more he would crave? And he didn't know what to do about it.

Cursing, he didn't want to think about it or her. He wasn't going to overthink the situation, he promised himself. He'd made mistake, obviously, but it wasn't earthshattering. He'd kissed the girl, that's all, but it's a hell of a kiss. Damn it, he had to get her out of his head. A man like him wasn't a willing victim to his emotions, especially emotions that Jennifer Jefferson wouldn't welcome ever again. He was simply going to go on with his life, and a few more days to let the reverberation die down and things could get back to normal.

She wasn't the type of woman to hold it against him. But because of his care and charming.

Stop it! He dragged his hand through his hair. *Enough!* He had to quit thinking of her as a woman, she was his boss' daughter. That's being the case they'd both to deal with it. And all he had to do was remember the reasons he had come over here and she was part of an assignment, nothing less, nothing more. Yes, don't let sexual attraction for her get in the way of doing what's smart. He needed something to take his mind off her, and all he had to do was get through tonight, and bring her home tomorrow. He closed his eyes, controlled himself remarkably well, and soon he was sound asleep and dreaming about what he wanted to get rid of.

Chapter 14

When it rains, looking for rainbows, when it's dark, looking for stars.

Tiffany needed to change her dressing style, because dressing in elegant clothes would be lovely to be with him, and of course, she'd admit that visiting and meeting his family had influenced her decision to purchase few of new outfits. She hadn't worn anything so blatantly feminine and flowing in years. But since she met Bush Jr, she started to pay attention to the fashion through fashion models, learning how to dress and match their colors. She spent so much money to own such some special fashion and some colors she'd never tried to arouse her interest. Half dressed in her lacy bras and panties, she had tried on and changed three different outfits in front of the mirror. It was completely unlike her to worry about her wardrobe before. She felt she needed to dress appropriately that the outcome of this time would determine their future. And finally, the dress she had chosen was a designer-made dress that was luxurious and dignified and it had cost a fortune that she dared to buy in her lifetime. The dress fit her perfectly. It had been constructed from carefully selected white and blue bandannas, it featured a knee-length zigzag hemline and tended to cling to every curve and draw every eye that she'd rarely worn and only paid too much in a weak moment.

Before, because of her job and she dressed according to her own taste and pleasure, from leather jeans to silks. But she perceived being beautiful was not an outward appearance, but needed a change in self-perception, insisting she looked phenomenal, and everything must be perfect and fit for Bush Jr, and didn't want to leave a bad impression on his family. She also taught herself how to do makeup, and today, she considered her makeup was flawless, and looked dewy and healthy. She had taken special care on her luxurious, honey-colored hair today, was swirled with stray tendrils curling by her ears. She reached for a can of sparkle and sprayed it, and just one quick press of the pressurized button and her hair glistened. Besides, she slipped into the black satin high heeled pumps that lifted her to a height equaling Bush Jr's. A pair of pear and diamond earrings that her mother had given to her, and pulled it all together into a style both respectable and elegant. This meeting was so important, and she longed to make a good impression so as not to embarrass Bush Jr. She dabbed the new, exotic perfume she hadn't used yet behind each ear and into the deep V of her breasts and then stood back, giving herself a critical study the results, by looking at her once more from every angle in the elaborate, gilt-framed mirror over the Georgian chest. The effect was stunning, and she's satisfied the way she'd changed into. It never eased to amaze her how different she looked since moving here. The result was part eccentric, part exotic. Just as she knew it transmitted a primal sexuality. But until Bush Jr scanned her from head to toe, and greeting her with admiring whistles when he came to her house at exactly six o'clock. She was perversely satisfied.

This wasn't the woman who drove a Harley motorbike. "My Lord, what a transformation!" he said approvingly, feeling a disproportionate sense of pride as he took a step back to view her again. Jesus, she was gorgeous. Not like the Tiffany he knew. On the few occasions he realized that Tiffany was not interested in fashion. So, her way of dressing was very bad. But tonight, she looked quite stylish like the one who had graced the covers of magazines and modeled silks and sables. For God's sake, she never wore makeup. But today, her makeup was artfully applied to accent clear blue eyes, lashes were darkened, the lids lightly touched with sparkle shadow, and some color over her cheeks but not her lips. She'd wound her hair up, swept it dramatically back, so that only a few wheat-colored curls escaped to tease her temples, adding with the silk wrap thrown easily around her shoulders, one nearly bare shoulder peeked through, and the lace dress draped across her breasts, nipped in at her waist and fared again over her hips, making her look both sexy and manipulative. Even her perfume was different.

Even though he was drawn to her, but he still felt as if he's looking at a stranger. However, to be fair, this was indeed an improvement that she had tried for him, or so it appeared, and in a word stunning.

"Don't look so surprised," Tiffany said, offered a responding smile, but she recognized all the doubts peaked into self-disgust and mortification as Bush Jr stared at her. "It's wrong. I have makeup on. I thought it was appropriate." "Not that." He kissed her hair.

"My hair then?" Tiffany said, lifted a hand to her hair. "I don't know what I was thinking. I only wanted to try..." "Not that, either. Is that a new dress?"

"Yes." She smiled. "Don't you like it?"

"You look way too good in that dress and good enough to eat. Oh my God, Tiffany, since when are you interested in fashion? And who did the dress?"

He had never said anything like that to her, and she laughed. But things were different now. She thought he knew anything about dress designers, and they had the important of time, visiting his family. "You did say it was a casual evening, and..."

"Yes, I did. And wait, don't answer that. Let me guess." He stopped her. Over the years he had learned how to recognize designer clothing from his family. He snapped his fingers as it came to him. "That was a Chanel dress, wasn't it?"

He looked proud of himself, and she laughed at him again. "I'm very impressed. I'll have to be careful what I wear from now on, and I only hope I'm not a disappointment."

"I don't think you need to worry. You look lovely in many ways, Tiffany," he said warmly.

She smiled, her heart singing. When you were in harmony with yourself, it would be easier to see in the eyes of others and when you became better and loved yourself, a positive energy would be formed around you, and attracted others to approach you.

She kissed him on the lips for his sweet talk.

Chapter 15
Home is where love gathers.

He took the key from her and locked the dead bold on their way out. Neither said another word until they were in his car, and thirty minutes later to his parents' house. His home or James' in Merritt Island maybe more convenient to organize, but no one ever considered changing the tradition from Brian's and Jennies' overflowing home. Because this was where the family began, and Friday dinner at the Jefferson household was never a quiet, dignified affair with the sounds of children shouting, adults arguing. Then there were always the scents of something wonderful streaming through the kitchen doorway. This, no matter where any of them lived or worked or moved to, was home.

The family's member sat around what they called the family parlor, with its familiar mix of antiques and family photos, red roses in the slim vase on the piano, as they might have sat, talked, and sipped wine on any evening.

The prospect vanished as Bush Jr stopped in front of a closed wrought-iron gate and used an app on his iPhone to open the gates. He drove through it up the long Jefferson mansion, and reached to parking space behind a dark sedan sat parked near the steps that led to the main doors. "Ready to face my family?" He asked, switched off ignition.

She knew that showing up tonight would be the best way to capture every member of the Jefferson family's attentions. "Yes. Are you going to tell them?"

"Of course, I'm looking forward to seeing their reactions." Exciting, he pressed the button and the doors slid up, and then stepped out of the car, walked around.

She took a deep breath as he helped her out of the car.

She looked nervous; Bush Jr realized. "Don't be so nervous," he said warmly, slipping his arm over her shoulder and squeezed. "They're going to love you."

She smiled before saying "I hope so" seemed mean and saying "I don't know" wasn't exactly true. She forced herself to relax, disguising any uneasiness, but the prospect of meeting his family had completely unnerved her. What if they objected, or didn't like her?

"Mom and Dad have been waiting long time enough to meet you."

"I only hope I'm not a disappointment."

"You won't be, Tiffany, I promise."

She knew he was worried about their reaction too, not hers, and let him lead the way.

The Jefferson House was elegant, style, discretion, and bigger than his. It had been built on five pristine, manicured acres, which had a six-car garage, another building where their live-in housekeeper and gardener resided, two big bay windows and wide front porch where they walked over and Bush Jr was smiling with a little girl, who was sitting on the swing, rocking slowly as she played on her iPad.

"Hey, Angel Baby."

Angel Baby looked up, grinned as she watched a man drop his beautiful woman's hand. "Ah, Uncle Bush Jr!" She shouted happily, slipped off the swing, placed her iPad on it and hurried to grab him by both arms. "Up."

"You bet." He scooped her up, whirled her around and smacking kiss on her cheek. She'd inherited his father's dark hair and eyes. She was a good kid, smart, caring, generous and easy going. "When are you going to grow up and marry me, Cathy?"

"Tomorrow!"

Her laugh was musical. "That's what you told me last time."

Tiffany wasn't sure what her feelings were at finding this family, but what she was certain of was that they seemed happy, at ease with each other, and very affectionate. If she hadn't seen it for herself, she wouldn't have to believe it. The girl smiled and her curious eyes met hers.

"Good evening. Miss, I've never seen you before." she said innocently then turned to her uncle with a spate of Vietnamese. "Who is she?"

With a laugh, Bush Jr answered for her. "Cathy, this is Tiffany, my girlfriend."

Surprising, Cathy gave her a quick and easy smile after. "Aren't you?"

"Yes, I am." Tiffany said simply and watched Bush Jr dropped her down.

"Nice to meet you, Miss."

She looked down into the pretty face of his niece. Even though it's the first time they met, she knew how to talk so cleverly. Wanting to give her a kiss, but she trailed a finger over her cheek. One day, she thought, she would kiss her own child just that way. They're hers and Bush Jr's. "Nice to meet you, too, Cathy." "She's pretty," Cathy stated and flashed her dimples to Bush Jr.

Filled with the emotion of the moment, she crouched down to hug her. "Thank you. So, are you"

And it's terrific as Bush Jr pulled open the heavy door and letting Cathy pull them along, as well as their hands, but Tiffany found herself dealing with fear, as she took a quick scan around, and filling impressions. "I'm nervous."

Bush Jr knew quite well what she was experiencing. He remembered it well, and the sights, sounds and smells always hit him hard every time he came to visit. "Just smile and leave the rest to me."

But when she stepped inside, she realized that she was foolish to be nervous about meeting his family, and her nervousness became amusement. Her first clear thought was, Wow. In front of her, inside of the palatial house was just as spectacular as the outside, but in a different way. It was all home heart. And why was there so many people? It's like his whole family in an enormous living room that could serve as a conference area, and had its three long, cushion sofas, several upholstered chairs near a huge modern stone fireplace took up an entire wall by a floor-to the ceiling, and the pair of wide arched windows that dominated the far wall looked over the ocean. The comfortable furniture where appetizers were already out and bottles of red and white were breathing. It was homey, smelled wonderful, and crammed with Jefferson's body. They were dressed casually, expensive and classically cut, in evening suits and cocktail dresses, standing, and sipping wine. They looked sophisticated and fashionable, made noise, laughter and lots of it. Music blasted from the stereo in the music room down the long hall. Children tumble over the floor or were welcomed into laps. Finding them like that, overwhelmed her, and made her feel even more nervous. However, it was as if Bush Jr had read her thoughts anyway, because before she could get her bearings, Bush Jr reassured her. "They're going to love you. Trust me."

And Cathy brought attention to everyone else by introducing her without hesitation. "Everybody says hello to Miss Tiffany."

Everyone stopped what they're doing and their heads turned in unison, caught the surprise as they saw an extremely attractive couple were led by Cathy, that made people greeted them with a warm, welcoming smile, and seeing her, there was joy and excitement in their eyes.

By natural reflex, Brian turned his head to look, caught a girl in a chic modern dress, with a graceful, beautiful figure, hand in hand intimately with his son. His lips lightly traced the curve of his face, stood up and spoke. "There you are we just talked about you." While Bush Jr's brother James, who set his daughter from his lap on the couch, and one of them whistled and hurry over to meet them before they made their way to them.

Her heart clenched as he threw himself into his dad's arms with open enthusiasm, and she enjoyed the scene.

He hugged his son tightly and cheered him even more as he stared at the visitor. It came like a bolt from the blue. His son never presented any woman to the family. Brian carefully hid his surprise, but he was obviously curious about Bush Jr's companion and dying to ask him about her. "Well, I see you've brought a guest with you."

Bush Jr almost laughed at the fierce strength of his embrace. "Sorry Dad, I took so long. I had a little business to deal with." He apologized as his dad turned his attention to Tiffany and silently surveyed her from head to toe.

"This is a business you're talking about, and I don't know who is this lovely woman next to you?"

Satisfied that for the moment his father would remain on good behave and Bush Jr saw the gleam light his father's eyes was on Tiffany had hung next to him, clearly not wanting to interrupt their greeting.

Although she recognized him from the pictures she had seen before, but her heart was beating so fast all of a sudden, she's also nervous, Bush Jr slipped an arm around her shoulders, squeezed gently, implied to reassure her and told her to stay calm, before making the introduction proudly. "Dad, I finally brought Tiffany Stanley, my girlfriend. Tiffany, this is my dad, Brian Tu."

Hearing his son's own mouth introduce, making him unable to help but exclaim in surprise. "No way, I can't believe it. When did that happen?"

"Recently," Bush Jr said proudly. "But I've been keeping her to myself for a while."

"Whoa." Brian took stock of the woman facing him but smiling and mused in a delicate way. Big blue eyes, a doll's mouth, and blonde. Not the type his son usually looked at twice. He knew very well his taste generally ran to Asian woman who was as beautiful, charming and honest as his mother. She looked very elegant, but no less sharp, tough, determined, bright five senses and delicate face. Looked like this girl's personality was not bad.

Hearing this direct introduction, her heart unconsciously pounded. A sweet feeling like warm water crept straight into her heart. Her lips curled up in a smile in response to the tall, healthy and attractive man like Bush Jr. His hair was black, streaked with silver, his eyes were brown, sharp and deep in a weathered face. He seemed to be sizing her up with his hand extended, and added before she could speak. "What an interesting surprise!"

She took his soft hand and smiled when he clasped hers tenderly.

His dad said to Tiffany and despite his eyes kept fixing on her face, he inclined his head to his ear and whispered. "She's beautiful."

He liked her, and he was pleased, too. A good sign, "I think so."

Bush Jr's father grabbed her hand, even though Bush Jr still had his arm wrapped around her. "Well, this is an unexpected pleasure to meet you. How are you, Tiffany Stanley?"

Tiffany recognized a similarity. Power, both sexual and intellectual that made her cheeks going warm and at the way he studied her, measured and judged. Especially, he glanced at the black ink of her tattoo crawling up her shoulder like a sleeve. It was conspicuous and it made her to wonder if he'd misjudged and disliked her? However, deep inside, she was very glad and happy that Bush Jr made her relationship public. If it was before, their relationship scared her. But now, she's confident enough to do the way women do in times like these. She shrugged out of Bush Jr's hold, politely embraced him. "I'm fine, and how do you do, Sir?"

"Well enough." He hugged her back, but he thought that physical contact wasn't good enough to welcome her, so he leaned into her, kissed her on her cheek, making the gesture tender and intimate. "You can ditch the sir', call me Brian by the way."

That's a surprise greeting, making her cheeks blushed even redder and her heartbeat, too, accelerated. But there was something familiar about the gesture. It was Bush Jr's. She realized the same casual intimacy. She knew this feeling was mutual. They had made her feel welcome and been loving that she kept the polite smile in place as he looked into her eyes and said. "And welcome to the family."

This never happened. Bush Jr watched the two with amusement. And Tiffany broke the greeting contest, giving a quick look, "family?"

He knew that meant his dad had approved and decided Tiffany was a good girl. It reminded him that he'd always bragged he was a good judge of character that he could tell quickly what he thought of someone. Bush Jr tried to explain but thankfully they both saved by his brother James. "Dad, Take it easy from them."

Bush Jr let his gaze slide to him. "Well, you little sneak, Bush Jr. I did not see this coming, and I have to pay Justine 50 bucks for my bet, but I'm happy for you man." He pumped Bush Jr's hand.

And he turned to her with a hand out-stretched in greeting. "Hello, Tiffany. I'm James Jefferson."

Her smile came again, shook his hand with a firm grip, and murmured quietly, "I'm pleased to meet you."

"We consider anyone associated with Jefferson part of the family, Tiffany." He answered for Bush Jr, returned the smile at her and volunteered to turn an introduction to the other members of family, who waited close by. "Here is my brother Justine Jefferson and sister Jennifer Jefferson."

"I'm delighted to meet the woman who has finally captured Bush Jr's heart." Justine said warmly to Tiffany.

She recognized most of them, greeted them with a warm smile by her special brand charm and graciousness. "Thank you," she replied. But she paused a moment as their hands met, and focused on the face looked oddly familiar, and trying to recognize her. It's very beautiful, almost unbelievably so. It's an oval face, very classic. She had her bright brown hair clipped short for summer, with the addition of flirty bangs over her wide eyes with heavy lidded and thickly lashed. The nose is short and straight. She had seen her somewhere before; she knew she had. Where? "Jennifer, you are familiar to me. In a magazine. Yes!"

She couldn't continue before Smiling could speak. "Yes. You may have seen my photo in some magazines. But I'm designer and model for Vogue's now with the nick name's Smiling."

As soon as smiling told her what she did, she realized why it had been familiar, even more impressive she was Bush Jr's sister. "That was it. Oh, God, I have got the honor of knowing you, Jennifer."

"Thank you. The pleasure is mine, Tiffany."

From there, Smiling's attention switched to Bush Jr, and asked. "Well, bro, the bars fully stocked and I'm playing bartender today. What can I fix you?"

"I think we'll join you in a glass of champagne, please."

And when Smiling response, his dad looked over to them then invited them all to the living room. "We're going to sit down, and you're going to fill us in on all the gossip." "It's fine, Dad," Bush Jr replied.

He led the way, and when they sat on the large overstuffed sofa across him, and the other lowered themselves onto around. She smoothed her dress and cross her legs next to Bush Jr, reached for her hand. His dad saw the gesture and grinned proudly, as though he were personally responsible for bringing the tow of them together.

A moment later, Smiling came back, carrying two flutes of champagne to the table near them. Each of the two of them took a flute and thanked Smiling, who smiled in return as she sat down next to her dad.

And after clinking the flute with Tiffany's and took a sip of champagne, Bush Jr asked. "Where is everybody else?"

At this moment Steady walked in, a smiled spread across her face by hearing their conversation. "They're in the kitchen, preparing the dinner." She answered for him, as set down the plates of salted almonds and cashew nut that her mom had showed in her hands from the kitchen on the table, in front of them, and then moved to greet Tiffany warmly. "Hello, Tiffany. It's good to see you." Putting down her glass, Tiffany replied. "Me, too."

And after the hugging, Steady looked at Bush Jr was popping two nuts into his mouth and bit down with relish, so she continued. "Linda brought over a monster chocolate cake, and sweet-talked Spencer into making lasagna."

"God bless him. My sister in law's lasagna is work of art." Bush Jr told Tiffany.

"Speaking of which, hang along with dad, brother." Steady said, stood, and held out her hand. "And lady and gentleman, if you'll excuse us, Tiffany and I need to meet the others, say hi and we can get acquainted."

They seemed very happy, seemed like friends as well as relative, Tiffany thought. "I look forward to it." She said, looked at Bush Jr and kissed him in full view of everyone.

Bush Jr smiled and then noticed that everybody was staring at them. Yes, people. I have a girlfriend. Get used to it. And before he could say anything, Steady grabbed Tiffany's hand.

"She's bossy, too," Bush Jr warned her, gave her a hard, firm and reassuring kiss on the mouth. "Just yell if you need help, and I'll rescue you."

Justine gave a long, interested hum while his family took the lead and shooed them away. "Go ahead and tell them we're waiting for supper."

"I'll do that." Steady said as Tiffany gave Bush Jr an apologetic shrug and followed Steady out of the living room.

And when they left, his dad commanded. "Let's have some these, Bush Jr and tell us your story."

"She's delightful." Brother James said to him.

"I know."

"You look happy, son."

"Do I?" Bush Jr thought he was sulking at a missed opportunity.

"I don't think I've ever seen you so relaxed."

Yes, because she made happy. It's a new feeling. He'd never described himself in those terms. He smiled at his dad. "I think you're right, dad."

* ❋ ✱ ❋ *

They walked into the family kitchen where the luscious scents that greeted them. With her cooking experience, Tiffany could smell delicately roasted meats, spicy sauces, the baking chicken, cakes fresh from the oven, but she looked at the woman who was putting the finishing touches, and satisfied that the massive, polished mahogany dining table was properly set for dinner with the loveliest porcelain utensils she had ever seen.

"The salad looks very nice." Steady said to her mom.

Three pairs of female eyes turned and smiling at two women walked into the room, but Jennies instantly focused on the blond young pretty woman who she had never seen before.

After she waved in greeting and said hi two others were helping to bake, and they waved and said hi back, Tiffany stared back the one who was looking her up and down in affectionate way. "I didn't realize you were bringing a guest, Steady."

Rapidly, Tiffany took everything in and for some reason she felt in love with her at first sight. Bush Jr's mother! Dear God! She was lovely. Despite her age, she was beautiful with finely wrought feature, her skin was naturally white and smooth, full of life, her body exuded the elegance of a lady and Bush Jr inherited his mother's beauty more. With her hair was a lush sable brown with hints of golden highlight in a neat bun at the back of her head, lightly accented with a gem clip, and in perfect, elegant French fashion black dress, equally luxurious and noble, discreet but without losing the inherent charm. Emphasizing the face with light makeup made the five senses more

194

sophisticated. Her large, dark brown and direct eyes, nose was narrow and straight, and sulky mouth. There were emeralds at her ears and at her throat were square-cut and big as woman's thumb. And the faintest hint of dimples fluttered in her cheek as the welcoming smile curving her lips that had earned her instant admiration. Before she could decide what to do, his mom extended arms and smiling.

"Hello, there! I'm Jennies Jefferson." She quickly introduced herself in greeting as she kissed Tiffany on both cheeks. "I'm so glad you could join us tonight, Miss... I'm sorry, I don't know your name."

Taken by surprise, both the statement and the lush and outrageous beauty of Jennies Jefferson, she went with nerves and fumbled, but she like her immediately because of her charming smile and warmth. "Tiffany Stanley. It sure is great to meet you, ma'am."

"Call me Jennies. It was nice of you to join with us, and what a beauty you are," she remarked, standing back to view the dress with pride. This was the latest design of a famous fashion designer. A few days ago, she saw it in a magazine. Exchanged a look with Steady, she said. "Your new friend has a great dress."

"She's not my new friend. Take a guess, mom."

"I don't know. Who?" She asked in confusion, her eyes narrowing as she searched Steady's face.

Steady smiled. Clearly, she was trying to decide who Tiffany was. "You're not going to believe this."

Tiffany, notice her curious asking, she volunteered without wavering. "Actually, I'm Bush Jr's girlfriend."

"Girlfriend!" Jennies exclaimed in surprise, her eyes widening in disbelief that she had met the woman who had finally stolen her son's heart. "Are you kidding?"

"No, it's true. And I appreciate you tolerating a Friday evening intrusion."

Jennies stared at Tiffany, stunned. In many years, she'd known her son. This was the first woman he'd brought home to Friday dinner who admitted his girlfriend, and she liked this woman instantly. "No,. It's no intrusion. We're delighted instead, My son's beautiful girlfriend is here to dine with us today is truly a precious gift."

She sounded happily and tugging her in for a fierce hug that rivaled her mother's. Her words and action made her immediately sympathetic with happy, and hugged her back for her easy-going and very open-mindedness.

It's not like she was worried because she found out that his parents were Asian. They always paid attention to meek, gentle girl. "Thank you, the pleasure is all of mine." She said politely, and cast a longing glance around, and offered hurriedly. "Is there anything I can do to help?"

Jennies' grin widened. "Heavens, no, Tiffany, but thanks for asking. Food's going to be ready in a few minutes. Let me get you a glass of wine, instead."

It wasn't so difficult, she realized as Jennies steered her way. Tiffany smiled and tried relaxing. Bush Jr's parents were exactly as she'd expected warm and sincere. And she and Steady walked and talked with the rest of Bush Jr's family, answered excited question.

Ten minutes later, the entire Jefferson family was seated around the huge dining-room table, abundant with the food, and the conversation went on in a rattling mixture of Vietnamese and English, sometimes simultaneously. Brian and Jennies sat in their usual seats at the head of the table, James and Linda and their children Maggie and John, Justin and Spencer were with Jimmy and Dorothy, Smiling was with Steady, Gloomy was with Cathy, leaving Bush Jr and Tiffany seated next to each other, as if they were a couple, another part of this big family. The focus, the attention shifted away from her. She felt more at ease and relaxed further when she sipped from her glass of champagne and realized that they'd been charming person, friendly, witty and very polite.

She thought this Friday night dinner highlighted the meaning of family. A cozy scene filled with chrysanthemum plants and white orchids, the softly shaded lamps giving off a warm glow, a variety of food prepared by variety of hands, it was a kind of ritual, she realized how welcoming it was. And in fascination at the humble act of honoring the food, she did the same when she bent her head and close her eyes, saying grace with them before adults helping to serve or feed or tend to their own children and those belonging to others. They chatted over dinner like one of the simple joys of life. And sitting around them she'd thought as family that she could be laughing and talking with them as if she'd known them all her life.

"Yum, this food is indescribably delicious," Tiffany said in all sincerely as she glanced over to see Bush Jr break off a large chunk of crusty, piping-hot Italian bread. "Thank you for bringing me."

"Don't thank me," Bush Jr said as he glanced at his mom.

"I want to hear everything from you." Bush Jr's mom said, smiling as she looked across the table at her.

Conversation and the ever-present sound of flatware scraping against plates seemed to stop, and then so many voices speaking at once.

"So, Tiffany was your girlfriend, how come you didn't mention her before now?"

"How did you two meet?"

"Why did you not tell us?"

"Are you in love?"

"What you are up to?"

"Do you have any plan for the future?"

Tiffany felt as if her entire life was on display for everyone in Bush's family to see, but despite they asked a lot of very pointed questions, as though she were interviewing, but she felt relaxing as his hand slide over to touch her thigh and joined the conversation to increase everyone's attraction.

"I can't believe this is happening to me after all these years of being so sensitive to women. With Tiffany, everything's different." He paused and then continued. "It would be better if I just told you what happened." It was easier that way, like telling a story, then he told his whole family about his beginning, how he met Tiffany Stanley, and in that case, she helped him everything and drove him to convention.

And from that point, she got involved. Taking turns, he was surprised when she admitted he'd got trouble on the highway and she had met him. He let her talk, filled in the rest, and loving the way she gave herself so genuinely, not realizing it was a gift.

They listened and Steady teased them nonstop after that and laughed with the others.

And the food was delicious, so she focused on that while Smiling spoke proudly of her modeling career in rescuing them. And she made only few comments, spoke only when questioned and smiled demurred at all the appropriate times.

Tonight, this room looked as wonderful as it had in his grandfather's day. It was a most cordial and convivial atmosphere. Most of those present tonight, especially his Tiffany made him happy. His parent would be proud, and noted Tiffany was comfortable with everyone, a little bit quiet for the rest of meal, but smiled more often, and her gaze consistently darted around the table, as if studying everyone's mood. By the time dessert was served. He asked her. "Are you having a good time so far?"

Tiffany tilted her head, and her eyes and his met. The quiet words and knowing look gave her an approval she couldn't have asked for but received anyway. "How could I not? I'm with you and your family's so beautiful. I've been fed, spoiled and pampered. Your mother was very kind to me and your father…"

"What about my father? Don't tell me he made you nervous," he teased her.

He kissed me, she wanted to say, but she didn't believe Bush Jr could possibly understand how much that had affected her. "Nervous? Don't be ridiculous," she grumbled. "He's so much like you. I'll try not to disappoint them, or you."

"That's because he was impressed with you." Bush Jr explained honestly. During dinner, his family had been giving him signals that showed him wholehearted approval of Tiffany. "Hold that thought." He leaned in to kiss her and waited for a lull in the conversation. But moments of silent and rapt attention were hard to come by, so he clinks a glass with his knife. "Everyone," he called out, and looked at both his parents.

Everyone presents knew that he had something special to say to them. All family announcements were made from this day was a tradition which had begun with their grandfather, Jefferson. "I think you'll all be interested," he began, without raising his voice, but said in an excited tone. "I know you love me deeply, and my love to you deeply the same. But there have been changes in my life now. So, I'm especially glad to be here today to share with all of you my very good news." He reached for Tiffany's hand, drawing her closer to him. "Tiffany Stanley has consented, moving to live with me."

His announcement was met with a few gasps, a cheer, and another spontaneous round of applause. He turned to Tiffany, who looked flushed and beautiful, and he gave her a swift, chaste kiss.

That seemed to hit them straight. Jennies heard it first, and her face went brilliant with a smile. A step like that was a form of commitment. Bush Jr was obviously crazy about and in love with her, and she liked her too. Things seemed to be talking a serious turn. "This is just wonderful!" Jennies grabbed her husband's hand, squeezed it. "I believe he's so seriously smitten with her."

"Smitten?" The word made him smile, then his smile faded into unexpected anxiety. "Define seriously."

"Honey," she patted his cheek. "He's over thirty. This will happen sooner or later."

"She's not his type."

"Exactly. She's nothing like his type. But she's perfect for him."

He gave her a nod of approval, even though they all saw the tattoo on her arm.

"That means you two living together and getting married later?" The question came from several of them at once, to Bush Jr, to her, and to each other that she didn't know who to answer or what to say. And her heartbeat thickened again as his family stared, waiting for an answer. She didn't have one.

Tiffany looked at him confused.

"It's possible, but it'll take time. We need more time." Bush Jr answered, glanced at his sister, Steady who came up with that question. Sometime she was very annoying.

"Oh, don't look at me like that, brother!" Steady scoffed. "I'm so thrilled for you."

And he turned to his mother for help. "Mom, this is just an announcement."

Understanding, Jennies nodded, sighed and stood up, walking around the table to where he stood and wrapping her arms around him. "It's great to see you two loving each other." She murmured, and looked directly at Tiffany, held out a hand.

Not knowing what to do, Tiffany got her feet. "Mrs.-"

Jennies just shook her head, held Tiffany's hand tightly, pull her into her arms, then kissed her cheek. "My Bush Jr has a hard time falling in love, but falling in love with you, just because of this, proves that you're very talented. I heartily approve and welcome to the family, Tiffany," she told her. "So, Mrs. – is far too formal. You do keep telling you that, and you must call me Jennies."

Oh, how nice that sounded. "You know I can't," she replied. "That's not respectful."

To Tiffany surprise, she took her face in her hand, and laid her lips on each of her cheek, and then suggested. "You shouldn't be so polite. Because sooner or later we will become a family."

Her cheeks suddenly became rosier when she heard those words come out of his mother's mouth. She shyly nodded. "Yes, if you give me permission, I will listen."

Both of women looked pleased, as though closing an important deal, then his mother turned to him, she smiled lovingly, held tight, and slowly eased back to kiss his cheek. "I've been saving a cask of exceptional champagnes and excellent wines bottles," she said casually. "This seems like an occasion to enjoy them."

"She needs a minute." Brian stood as his wife made way out of the dining room and walked to Bush Jr. "She's happy."

He embraced his son then turned to embrace Tiffany. "This is a lovely dinner I ever have with the guest like you, and I'd like to welcome you, welcome you to Jefferson family."

"Thank you." She had an urge to hug him back, to just throw her arms around his neck and a breath in that nice, spicy after shave she'd caught on his throat. Feeling foolish, she folded her hands instead. "I hope both of you could come to Bush Jr's house, maybe next week for dinner, when I've had a chance to cook and serve."

"You know how to cook?" He pinched her cheek. "Nice work, Son."

"She's a chef." Bush Jr corrected. "A wonderful one."

"We have a big Sunday in remembrance of grandpa coming up," Steady cut in. "I have a proposal to make for party at dinner." "What's that?" her dad asked.

"Instead, we hired a ball, or a hotel ballroom like we used to. I thought it would be more fun, and truer to us, if we kept it simpler. You and I can handle the music." She paused, turned her eyes to meet Tiffany's, and then she asked her a question she didn't expect. "If we do that, would you handle the food for us, Tiffany?"

"It's a great idea." Bush Jr agreed. "What do you think?"

Tiffany was full of surprises, she looked at Bush Jr with wide eyes. Jefferson's family was a very famous one, with a great many equally famous friend. She had envisioned a party with family, friends and neighbors, something would traditional, something befitting for them.

"Tiffany!" Bush Jr said. "Come back to earth, honey!"

Tiffany tried to refocus, but she still couldn't speak properly. "I... I can't..." "Don't be quick to say what you can't, Tiffany." Bush Jr said.

She shot him a cautious look. "But I think you need a professional at this."

"Nonsense!" Bush said. "Tiffany, honey. Don't put yourself down. We believe in you."

"I will try my best." Tiffany couldn't refuse. "But I want to know how your family wants to organize a party?"

"I'll leave that to you. You're clever, so come up with a theme. We'd help you. So, think of something and we're sure love it."

"I do cook for living, and helping you is my privilege. So, I'll create a party that must be memorable."

Everyone talked at once again, and Tiffany found herself whirled between hugs, stumbling over the answer to question again. And she heard the pop of the champagne cork over the question, the laughter, as the housekeeper poured the best wine into the flutes around. She let herself lean against Bush Jr, looked up, meet his eyes. Family, she thought. She could have family her own, and understood, now that she could touch it, that she'd do anything, everything, to keep it.

It's a pleasure to watch them together and to witness the whole family embrace her. Even his dad had concluded that Tiffany made him happy. He's not wrong.

"Everyone," his dad gave an attention. "As I said earlier, I welcome you to our family, Tiffany, and I don't mind telling you, it feels good." He raised his glass to his family, lingered his smile on her then went to Bush Jr. "If your grandpa were still with us, he'd be proud of you."

The mention of this loss would normally have made her heart clutch because of their family's part in her loss too.

"We miss him every single day," Bush Jr said. "So, raise your glasses." He concluded, lifting his, and cried merrily. "Cheers to family."

Amid the general round of amusement, Tiffany raised her own glass. "Cheers to family," she repeated, as did everyone.

"Down to the hatch," his dad added, and they all drank each other's health, and agreed vociferously.

Chapter 16
The best thing about memories is making them.

Against one wall from the hall, there was a giant pegboard covered with photos of Jefferson Bush at different ages. Brian and Jennies were greeting their friends and guests who knew Jefferson Bush and beside them was a long table, also covered in white linen, decorated with more flowers and a guestbook for everyone to sign.

With a quick look around the crowded auditorium of Faith Fellowship Church, Steady located her family was seated front and center pew and scanned the crowd. She could spot only few people she recognized. Every now and then she'd spot a familiar face, but couldn't remember that person's name. She thought everything would be arranged according to expectations.

It seemed as if everyone was inside the church. The priest took to the pulpit and opened the pray, and when the choir finished the spirited hymn, her father and mom approached the podium and made the introduction.

While up on there, Jennies didn't say a word to fight a losing battle with tears, a tissue wadded in her fist. Brian offered up some anecdotes about Jefferson Bush the man and the father. "He was the most generous man and dear soul I ever met." Brian intoned in a voice shaking with emotions as he admitted he was a lucky man not only when he became his son in law, but also his own son.

They were applauding his speech of gratitude to his father-in-law, and tears of happiness suddenly flowed from their eyelids with emotion. Then a few of them went to the podium to praise the good, odd, wonderful things about Bush Jefferson and prayers from families and friends. To close the ceremony there was a solo of 'Amazing Grace' by her mother, Jennies, and her father played piano. Her singing voice was still clear and beautiful soprano when hitting high notes. "Amazing Grace, how sweet the sound that saved a wretch like me! I once was lost, but now I'm found; was blind, but now I see ..."

Once again, Jennies felt emotion and tears welled up as she caught Brian's eye just before singing the last word out and he gave her an encouraging smile and a quick wink that somehow made her heart flutter even in this emotion state. Her throat clogged as she suddenly felt grateful to God who had arranged their fate for them. With the back of one finger, she swiped away her tears.

And before Steady could continue her friendly conversation, a long string of microphone tapping sounds were heard, and her father's voice rang out. "Hello, everyone!" He said to the attendees. "Our family is certainly delight ours be here today to remember Sir Jefferson Bush and to gather together had been our tradition over the years. Thank you to everyone who came to join our family. Thank you for bringing so many of his cherished memories to life. It means a lot to us. So, everyone enjoys yourself and have a good time at the party with us."

After that message, Brian left the podium, glanced down the first row of seats and saw his dad's friend and lawyer who were sitting next and talking to Bush Jr. He hadn't changed all that much, Brain noted when they walked straight toward them. He still had the same arrogant polish, the same evidence of expensive taste he'd had way back in the old time. Only the leather briefcase was next to him "Grandpa had spoken well of you." Bush Jr said.

A hint of a smile just the merest suggestion touch Mr. Roth-well, giving him the impression that he didn't smile often. "Your grandfather had one of the keenest business minds in the country."

"He's incredible, wasn't he?"

Mr. Roth-well's nod betrayed no hesitation, and there was a polite sound made them all turned. There was an elderly woman with the black hat, Bush Jr noticed her. There had been something vaguely familiar about her. Perhaps she was an old neighbor who'd moved away, or some acquaintance of the family. She had on just a touch of makeup, and she was rather attractive even for her age. She was nervous, too, twisting a handkerchief out of shape in her slender hands.

His dad both hands extended in greeting as she came toward. "Hello, Mrs. Stanley." He gave her a kiss on her cheek then hugged. "I appreciate having you here."

"Your father was a great man, Mr. Brian. I was honored to know him."

The name brought Bush Jr back the memories. No wonder the woman had seemed so familiar. She gave him a hug and shook hands with Mr. Roth-well.

And as soon as she left, Mr. Roth-well reached for his briefcase, and said. "Is there somewhere I could talk with both of you and Mr. Bush Jr in private?"

He was an old school friend and had been the Jefferson's attorney for thirty years. He was tall and thin with a straight nose and sparse gray hair, he was in his mid-sixties, the same age as he had been. But he oozed confidence and charm, his manners were as polished as alabaster. Neither his designer suit nor his starched pinstriped shirt had a wrinkle anywhere.

"Of course, you can, Mr. Roth-well." Mr. Brian responded, thought about suggesting onto the limo, but quickly changed his mind, and he gave him a curious look. "Is something up?"

He nodded his head answered and watched Mr. Brian turned to the pastor who walked over to them and shook their hands. "Pastor Steven, you don't mind if we can use your church office for a while?"

The pastor Steven had a lovely smile. "That's not a problem for me, Mr. Brian," he said. "You know where it is."

And after he left, giving them his permission, Brian turned and indicated James, Justine and Jennifer who stood around. "You please handle and greet the guests for us? We'll be home after this." "We will do, Dad." James replied.

"Mr. Roth-well, let's go in the church office." Mr. Brian said, and they followed his leading way.

The pastor's office was neat, with hardbound books on philosophy and religions of the world were arranged in an orderly manner on the shelves. Pictures of Lord and beautiful spots on earth were decorating on the walls, as well as his framed degrees and awards. And when they gathered and took a seat all around the desk.

"I guess you all wonder why I'm here today," Mr. Roth-well began. "And I hope I didn't disturb you?"

"Not at all," but Brian looked at him, and felt a knot forming in his stomach. "What's it about?"

"All right," he took a deep breath, and went straight to the point. "I was wondering ... have you ever made the acquaintance of Ms. Tiffany Stanley?"

It changed the air, and the room went quiet as they heard the name, and Bush Jr watched his parents exchange a look.

"Tiffany Stanley?" His dad repeated, and his expression guarded suspicion visible in his eyes.

"The name rings the bell, but not really. Why?" Bush Jr answered for them. "Would you like to explain?"

"That's the name of the woman who is your grandpa's daughter, and she also was the beneficiary on his life insurance policy. That's the reason why I came over here today, to get this all out in the open. It's been a secret too long."

The statement was like a spear piercing the shield of his heart and buried deep. "What?" Bush Jr said, his mind started to spin.

Bush Jr exclaimed, his eyes were wide in astonishment, and his words were unintelligible as he gave him a skeptical look. "Mr. Roth-well, are you sure about you just saying?"

They appeared surprised by the assertion. He looked from one face to another. It was obvious that they knew nothing about this, and Mr. Bush Jr had been startled and shocked by his words, he realized when he looked in astonishment from him to his dad and back. Therefore, without a word and taking the lead in the discussion, he reached to then set his briefcase down on the desk, and then flipped the combination. From one of his neatly ordered files, he withdrew a copy of the document.

Bush Jr's heart dropped a little as he rose, bent toward, and passed them over the desk into his hands. And when he sat back on the chair, he said. "I hope I could be wrong, but I don't think I am. Please, look of this, Mr. Bush Jr."

"What the hell is this?" he asked in the barest of whispers.

"Just something we've been waiting years for. Didn't know if it would happen," Mr. Roth-well explained.

"Why?"

"So, you can see it for yourself."

The 'it' was a couple sheet of papers, and with obvious reluctance, Bush Jr's gaze fell on the grainy picture on the copy of the DNA PARENTAGE TEST REPORT, completed with dates, which told him a few things about her. Blood type was O positive. The same as his grandpa's that he'd already known. He felt his heartbeat thudded through his brain. *"Jesus … it can't be possible."* He whispered, and it sounded like a prayer.

Bush Jr was starting to believe. Mr. Roth-well could see it in his eyes. He watched him go through the pages.

The longer Bush Jr stared at it the more terrible he became and made his fingers tremble. He had trouble breathing for a second as his eyes settled on the name of Jefferson Bush and Tiffany Stanley was the two parties are confirmed to be parent and child. A sick sensation curled in his stomach. His gaze flicked back up at Mr. Rothwell. He tried to gather his thoughts, unsure where the whole dialogue was going. "This woman is Tiffany Stanley?"

He noticed that Bush Jr's expression change as his face turned a violent red, his eyes expressing his thoughts. Puzzlement, doubt, disbelief, reluctant acceptance, and the papers on his hands began to tremble. "I think so. Got a problem, Mr. Bush Jr?"

There's a family resemblance that went on for generation and paternity test were good enough for him really believed it. He had an aunt, the most improbable aunt he could have imagined.

"Bush Jr, what's the matter?" His dad asked in concern, leaning in, peeked at what he had seen. "Oh, dear God…" He was startled at once as he had carefully studied the photograph of the woman, too, then looking at him, he said. "Was she your girlfriend?"

There was a ringing in his ears and his head was going to explode as he stared at his father as if he couldn't believe what he was hearing, and it would be a godsend.

"*What?*" Mr. Roth-well couldn't believe his ears, his eyebrows raised. "Well, that certainly interesting," he exclaimed. "Are you telling me that you all know her… and Mr. Bush Jr's girlfriend?"

Brian swore pungently through clenched teeth.

Mr. Roth-well felt something snapped in his brain, as he looked at his dad. "Don't you know that your father-in-law had another child, a daughter, who was born a few years before your son was born?"

His dad shook his head, and his eyes suddenly clouded over. "For Christ's sake, no. But what are you saying? I have a step sibling?"

"This is a shock, Mr. Brian. I must admit it." Mr. Roth-well exclaimed coldly, hoping his words had penetrated. "But once I've documented my finding, all her records at Miami Hospital, that before Angela Stone was married, she was pregnant. I'd contacted your dad, and he had changed the will."

Nervous, even fear, he was hardly able to take this in. but he accepted, as he investigated Mr. Roth-well's, now blazing with anger, that man spoke the truth. He was aghast. How could he have been with his father-in-law and not know any of these things?

When Mr. Brian remained silent, his eyes turned to Bush Jr's. "Would you recognize your grandfather's handwriting?"

"I suppose I might," he said, trying to sound lighthearted when deep inside he ached.

"I have a copy of the letter of Mr. Jefferson sent to us."

He took it out of the file and handed it to him.

Bush Jr recognized the handwriting on the letter at once. Words and phrases jumped out in his eyes, burning his mind as he read them.

Dear Jefferson's, especially to you Bush Jr.

I know you probably didn't expect this letter and I must admit that I never thought I'd be writing to you, but I feel as if I have no choice because I found out a few years back, and because my daughter's future, her life and all of you deserve to know. Tiffany. She's older than you a few years. The result of an affair I had before with her mom.

His grandpa had known all along without telling him about the report. The one bound to change his destiny.

It's best that she remained unaware of that, until and should carry into effect when the paternity test was done and proclaimed.

Jesus, he could barely believe it. He had an aunt, and she was Tiffany damned Stanley. For a few seconds, he couldn't breathe, couldn't think, couldn't allow himself to accept the impossible possibility. "No way!" He blurted out, stunned. "No, it can't be."

Bush Jr sounded disapproving and shocking on both counts by those unexpected revelation as he looked at him. "I mean... We would have known. Someone would have told me. Grandpa would have...." His expression changed from denial to something darker, as if the muscles of his face were drawn by the fingers of fear. "And why's now? Why's not sooner?"

And Bush Jr would have crumpled them into a ball if he hadn't rescued it and slipped it back into its file and took his seat again. "Because I wanted to be sure, and I must apologize if my work has brought a bad news and upset greatly you and you and everyone else today. I just wanted to make a surprise for everyone in Jefferson's family, but it didn't go well, and I'd no idea you were in any way involved with her, and I should have realized you weren't aware of all the facts. I suppose I assumed your grandfather had told you about of it."

"He didn't have a chance." His father cut in. "I remember now. He told me that he was waiting for some information, that he'd explain everything once he found out the truth."

"And why was that?" Bush Jr gave him a keen, penetrating look.

"When he heard that she was leaving, he used his connections to find her whereabout. Finally, he found out that she was in Miami and pregnant, most at all, he also knew why she left. So later, when he found out where she and her daughter were and married to Martin Stanley." His dad replied him. "He would have wanted to speak with her, to know."

"I simply don't know." Mr. Roth-well cried in and informed them. "I can tell you what I know or representing Mr. Jefferson's file all requests that if there is a legal battle in the future, it's the best to approach the matter with facts rather than raw emotion. So straight out," he concluded. "You have a step aunt, Tiffany. She's a daughter of Jefferson Bush."

Undone by these unexpected announcements, Bush Jr was also now convinced that Mr. Roth-well was telling him the truth, and his Tiffany was his step aunt, and she was also his girlfriend. *Oh, please God, please tell me this isn't happening. I'm dreaming this. I'm having a nightmare.* But it wasn't. It happened. Oh my God! Why did You put me in this situation? Why not someone else, but her. The person I love. Now is my aunt? God, why is it so cruel? Me and her are already in an incestuous relationship. His already battered heart sank even deeper, and it had hurt like hell. All good things were beginning when he drowned in happiness, then the big storm swept it all away. It also plunged him into darkness. How can he bear the crime of incest? Despair, anger, hurt, and disappointment coalesced into a hard ball inside him. Unable to speak, tears built. His stomach soured and knotted. Bile rose in his throat and burned his nostrils. He felt sick.

"Are you all right, Mr. Bush Jr?" Mr. Roth-well asked when he saw the look on his face.

Suddenly Bush Jr was having trouble taking in air and all he could hear was his own labored breathing. His mind suddenly whirled, everything in front of his eyes rotated and then faded away. His whole body felt powerlessly, and his head smashed against something hard. For a second, everything went dark like the night covered him, but still heard Mr. Roth-well said. Then there was a light show of stars in front of his eyes, white noise in his brain, and something hot and wet trickled down his face. The smell of blood hit his nose, and in his ear, he could hear the panicked sound of his mother, calling his name, and then feel into the void and lost consciousness.

Chapter 17

Home is where memories are created.

It was traditional for Jefferson's family to hold every Fourth of July Day. The guests invited to attend the party were mostly family members, but there were a few friends and neighbors, and would be offering wine, food by the servers, dressed in the local costumes of the area stood around smiling in the large formal dining room. All the antique furniture had been removed from the room to accommodate with circular skirted table, interact with chairs dressed in gold.

And from the entrance foyer with its tables set with gigantic spilling vase of all kind flowers that their fragrance spreading into the huge main room, as large as a basketball court, with wooden floors and high ceiling hung with bur-gees and banners. At one end of the room, a band would perform music, and dancing wouldn't start until after the buffet. All around the edge of floor, tables and chairs were set up with flowers and candle centerpiece on blazing white linen tablecloths. At the far end, there was the reception room, with a bar set up at one end and buffet table just being organized at the other. Stewards and caterer in white jackets hurried to and from the kitchen, bearing great wooden bowls of salad and heavy stainless-steel tray getting ready for party.

Tiffany had accepted the offer, not because Bush Jr but also for her own. Therefore, she wanted to prepare a properly impressive menu, and the party would get started until one. She spent the morning to set up everything. Now she looked around the kitchen, clean, shiny, and warm with cook helpers. She'd already sliced fruit, checked the supplies restocked the refrigerator. So, everything set ready for the guests. She made her rounds checking for dishes, or anything else out of place. Duties done, she told herself then poured an indulgent glass of sparking juice for helping plan a party, and through the window, July flowers right there in the courtyard, just as Jefferson's had been this past summer. Thinking of that, she wasn't just content, but happy. Tiffany smiled, sipping her drink.

"Lovely day," she told herself in an easy family way. "I was just thinking how different my life is now, and all things considered, how glad I am it is."

Family, to Tiffany's mind was where your heart always feels at home. And with a smile, she lifted her glass. "To you, Dad," she toasted and sipped again. But her spiritual thought was broken by her cell phone rang. She set the glass down on the counter then picked it up. "Tiffany here," she said, leaning against the table.

"It's Steady, Tiffany."

"Hello! I was going to give you a ring later, tell you that everything is set."

"Oh, that is good, Tiffany, but listen to me," Steady rushed on. "I rang you about something else. I'm afraid Bush Jr had an accident a short while ago."

Tiffany's smile faded, she went cold, and her own heart nearly stopped as she held the phone with an expression of horror and felt completely disoriented. She couldn't bear what Steady had just said. It couldn't true, and she lost for words. "What? Jesus." That's best she could come up with and wanted to know the rest of it quickly. "How did it happen? Is he all right?"

"I wasn't in the room, Tiffany," Steady answered, reacting to the fury in Tiffany's voice. "I had no idea what had happened and any detail, but Gloomy told me he banged his head and was conscious when he was taken to the hospital. That's all I know."

Her heart pounded so hard and so fast that she pressed a hand to her chest. She had never been as shaken by anything in her life. "How badly was he hurt?" "Again, I don't know, but the ambulance took him to Wuesthoff Hospital."

Tiffany was trembling violently by then. She wanted to cry, but there was no way she could give in, she told herself. She had to stay strong. Who knew what was going to happen or what she would have to deal with?

"I appreciate you calling to let me know, Steady. But I want to be there."

Without thinking and didn't bother saying good-bye. Tiffany just clicked off, took a deep breath, moving her tremble body, headed directly for her jacket and collected her purse before returning to the kitchen. Why today? She muttered under her breath. Why did it happen today and not another day? They're all happy together, and she wanted everything to go right. Attempting to rein her frustration, Tiffany had to go to the hospital to find out the damn answers to those things. To find out the cause of the incident.

She went to where the head chef was working. "Sorry, Bush Jr was in an accident," she told him. "I don't know how bad it is, but I need to run to the hospital and be with him. Would you take over and carry on with Linda and Spencer for me?"

"Sure, no problem," he said in understanding then with an express concern, he asked. "How is he? And you?"

"I don't know. I'm having a little trouble breathing, but that should pass." She told him and appreciated. "Thanks so much. I owe you."

He hugged her. "Don't worry, dear. Just leave it to me and go there with him."

But before leaving, she showed him what she'd put in the fridge for the guest then hurried to explain the situation to Linda and Spencer, before she dug in her purse for her keys, didn't care how she looked in night dress and high heels, pushed the swinging door, and walked crisply out of the kitchen, leading into the enormous marble floor, chandelier dining room, down the hall toward the doors heading to the parking lot. Nothing else mattered, but her last thought before leaving was thank God someone else had to handle for her. She sat in her car and drove away. Now, she didn't care about anything but him. The car rolled at a terrifying speed, holding the steering wheel tightly, stepping on the accelerator more and more strongly, and maneuvered her car through the traffic.

Although the drive to the hospital was a relatively short, but each minute seemed to be three times as long, and thanked God, she finally arrived without being pulled over by the police as she found a parking lot close to the emergency room entrance, pulled in and cut the engine. There were people coming and going. The ambulance was next to the automatic doors. Wuesthoff Hospital was one of the city's finest, or so she'd been told, and immediately she rushed straight into as the glass doors opened automatically ahead of her. And when inside at the lobby, she realized that the hospital was a huge medical complex with many physicians and nurses in white uniforms and rubber soled shoes, moving from area to area, but no one paid her any attention. She'd never liked the feeling of a hospital, any hospital. The odors of antiseptic, talc from the latex gloves, and disinfectant burned in her nostrils. But she had no problem making herself dealt to this situation. She was good at things like that, and then walked straight to the information counter, where she could ask for Bush's room number.

Behind the counter, a gray-haired receptionist with reading glasses perched on his nose looked up, and immediately gave her a smile. "Can I help you?"

Tiffany gave him her sweetest smile and asked for information. "I want to find a man named Jefferson Bush, Jr who was just brought in here by ambulance."

He dragged his eyes from her face then scanned and checked the name on his computer screen without any hesitation. "The patient is in intensive care. Take the elevator up to the second floor. Check in at the nursing station. Someone there will tell you where to go."

"I'm so grateful for your help." Be aware of the effect of her attraction towards men, Tiffany wasn't afraid to use it to her advantage when it suited her. "Is that left, or right?"

"Left through the double doors," he said, pointing to his left at the end of hallway.

Flashing him a smile, she said. "Thank you." Then she strode through the doors, and the elevator opened as soon as she pushed the button. She rode alone up to the second floor, and the moments she stepped off the elevator, she looked at an arrow on the wall indicated to the nursing station. She turned the corner and stopped to speak to a nurse in green scrubs with short auburn hair at the desk.

"I'm here to see a patient named Bush Jr. They said he was on this floor."

"He's here. The doctor is in with him now. What's your relationship to the patient?"

"I'm..." a friend didn't sound right. Bush Jr was way more than that. They might not let her see him if she was only a friend, and she sure as hell wasn't going to pretend to be his sister. "I'm his fiancé," she said. "Can you tell me his condition?"

"He's listed as stable. That's all I know. As I said the doctor is in with him now. He'll talk to you as soon as he comes out. There's a waiting room down the hall." She thanked her and headed in that direction.

∗ ∗ ∗

Jennies sat in the waiting room, feeling like she was living a nightmare while Brian took Steady back home so he could manage his regret to all guests for what's happened, and Gloomy was somewhere in the hospital, maybe get the paperwork drawn up or gave a medical history on him.

She was even more shaken the moment she saw him just right after they put him in the private room. All she could do was watch him as gently touch one side of his face with her finger and stood there crying quietly. Because she had no illusion about how dire his situation was, she sat down on the chair against the wall, closed her eyes, and started to pray.

⁂ ✻ ⁎

Tiffany stopped in track before she reached to the waiting room when she saw Gloomy went out the exam room with a doctor who was checking the charts that she didn't know her present.

"As you see, it's the head injury and he's still unconscious. We have to keep an eye on." He explained.

The name tag on his white coat identified him as Dr. Brandon. He's looking at the medical record of Bush Jr. She was lucky enough to meet Dr. Brandon in the case of Bush Jr. He was in the same class as her, older than her, and his gentle, sympathetic and helpful personality reminded her of her role. How many times had she been the operating room, fighting to save a life? She'd struggled and studied to be a doctor to ease pain, to heal, to somehow in some way make a difference. Now, when her brother was hurt, she could no more than worry and wait. She willed herself to be calm. "I understand, but he's going to be okay?"

"He should be. We've done preliminary X-rays, several brain scans, and CT scan." The doctor clicked his pen, jammed it into his pocket and described to her the effect an injury at that location would have on his head. "They're clear conclusion. There is no hemorrhaging. So, it's not causing blood seepage between the skull and membrane covering the brain. But because of the strong impact, he lost consciousness and his fever got me concerned."

"Those symptoms can occur after an accident, or from the head injury." Gloomy pointed out. "His brain regulates his temperature and body heat, and it's deregulated right now."

"That's right," the doctor said. "However, just to be on the side of caution, we still need to keep an eye on his condition, in case I missed something."

"Thanks." Gloomy was relieved, but wanted to know. "So, when can we take him home?"

"There's no reason to be rush." He suggested, put his hands on her shoulders. She wasn't just a doctor as he knew and respected. She was a sister of a patient. "We'll keep him overnight to monitor the concussion. If he won't have nausea and headache have subsided by morning, chances are he may go home. But he must have bed rest for the remainder of couple days. No harm's been done, and I do think he should scan his head again before to leave. And I'll give him a prescription for the first couple days."

"I couldn't agree more," Gloomy responded.

The doctor thought of something then. "We know Bush Jr is important person. That's why I'm afraid word will get out. Someone will leak it to the media. They always do. But we'd like to keep the press out of here," he said firmly. "I'm sure you would do, too. I'll put a warning on his chart. We don't want photographers showing up, upsetting everyone, and violating the privacy rights of other patients."

Gloomy knew the protecting a patient's right to privacy was vitally important in hospitals, and reporters showing up would violate those rights for other patients as well as Bush Jr. And the medical staff didn't want the disruption, nor did Gloomy. She hadn't thought of that until now. "Neither do I," Gloomy said with a grim expression. She didn't want anything putting pressure on Bush Jr now or jeopardizing his recovery when he woke up.

"Good, then I'd like you come to my office that we can agree upon principle."

"Yes, thanks for all you've done Dr. Branson. I'm going to talk to my family. Then I'll come up."

Doctor Branson extended his hand, and Gloomy shook it.

"Your brother is going to be okay." He said, then turned to leave.

✿❋ ✳ ❋✿

When she heard that Bush Jr was out of danger, Tiffany was a little less anxious and as soon as the doctor pushed his way through the swinging doors, she called. "Gloomy."

To her surprise with the voice speaking her name, Gloomy turned, and saw Tiffany with the looked of panic in her eyes, walking straight to her.

"How bad is he?" She asked in a worry voice.

Gloomy was a doctor and could tell Tiffany precisely, the concussion and the internal bleeding, which the doctor were finding out. She was also a sister. "The doctor gave him a thorough examination when I arrived and came to tell us that he has a fever that why he wanted to make sure the concussion isn't worse than it appears. No swelling on the brain, nothing like that. He's getting the care he needs. Might need to stay another day or two, but if he seems okay in the morning, there's a chance they'll release him."

"Thank God," Tiffany replied, a surge of relief rushing through her. "I've been insane with worry all the way here. And where is he now?" "They just moved him out of ICU, into a private room." "Is he awake? Can I see him now?" Tiffany demanded.

"Of course, you do. But not now." Gloomy reached for Tiffany's hand, holding it in hers before she rushed to there. "He has a fever, but he's okay." She assured her, indicating a small niche a bank of windows. It was a small area, mostly unoccupied at that hour. Complete with a square of carpet, a coffee table had time-worn copies of People magazine, Golf Digest, and Good Housekeeping were littered on it, and two side chairs, the spot offered little privacy for chat. "I think we'd better sit down."

It wasn't exactly the answer she wanted, but grudgingly Tiffany accepted it, holding her silence when Gloomy led her to the orange leather chairs, and the moment Gloomy sat next to her, she confirmed to her what she already knew, more or less.

"Did you know?" Her tone was firm. She was in charge now and being in charge was what she did the best.

"Know what?"

"About the will?"

Tiffany inhaled, bracing herself. "Yes. And it was the blessing I'd never prayed for."

"But you didn't tell him or us."

"I suppose. I should have told your family this before, but for reason, selfish reason, I kept my secret." She could explain, but right now, it wouldn't matter anyway. She hadn't told them. She covered her face with her hands and started to cry.

Gloomy put her arms around her. "I know you've been heartbroken. But..." Gloomy let her words trail off. Then, when Tiffany continued to wait patiently, she tried again. "But what you're feeling now, Tiffany, it won't help at all."

Gloomy made her acutely uncomfortable. This was not what she had expected to hear from her, and she realized she didn't like her look aimed at her. In fact, she hated it. "I can figure the damage was already done and damn the consequences. But I've been so worried for Bush Jr."

Gloomy could hear the disapproval in her voice. "I know this sounds callous," she said firmly with a soothing voice, but Tiffany was beyond that now. She was crazed with fear for her brother, so she sidestepped the question. "Why don't you take it easy, and it would really be better to wait until you can talk to Bush Jr in a better condition to solve your problems?"

Tiffany had an eerie feeling as she knew what Gloomy was talking about, and couldn't imagine what happened to Bush Jr, particularly on the day was traditional for Jefferson's family. The situation had been painful for everyone involved. The truth was now exposed. Probably through Mr. Roth-well who she suspected that he had kept track of her. She knew this would happen one day, but she'd never expected it happened on this day, even though she had intended to let Bush Jr know. He detested liars. When he found out the truth about her, he'll be furious. And now, they had to hate her. She doubted very much they could feel more contempt for her than she felt for herself, so she had left the subject slide away without further comment. But what truly disturbed her was she's impatient. It's so clearly etched in her mind. Although in pain, Tiffany blinked back her tears. "And when will that be?"

"I wish I knew, Tiffany." Gloomy said honestly and explained. "And life isn't that simple. Any effort you try to please him, or comfort him, or cares him would only have upset him more when he wakes up and sees you."

It seemed that from her expression. Whether she liked it or not, Tiffany had no choice, but understood the seriousness of the situation. Squeezing her eyes shut and forcing back her own dread, she nodded her head in silent and adjusted her emotion, telling herself that he must have been shocked, but it's not entirely true. There were some things to avoid him getting hurt, so she couldn't tell him, and was certain that it would work eventually. Even if not, she was prepared to accept whatever limitations they had, and determined not to let go of their love. Meeting him was planned, but falling in love with him was something she didn't anticipate. When she accepted and went this way, she promised herself not to let him get hurt. But at this moment, she couldn't do it. It changed nothing for her, but it changed Bush Jr's entire life. But what feared her now was not whatever happened in the future, but all she really worried about was Bush Jr's condition. "I guess you're right." She agreed with a look of anguish and stood up. "Can I see him for a moment before I leave?" Gloomy stood up, too, and nodded her head. "I don't see any problem with that."

They walked down the hall and when they reached to the door, and through the glasses, Where Gloomy heard Tiffany mutter "My God" as she saw his mom sat on the chair across the bed.

Tiffany had only been in a hospital few times. Once to visit her father just before he died. Two times when her mother was having her brothers. But those visits had been nothing like what she was now facing. Bush Jr was stretched out under white sheets in a regulation hospital gown with tubes and wires were attached to him, monitor beeped endlessly, and there was a huge bandage on his head as well.

Her intestines and liver hurt like hell that her hand clenched on the glass window like anger in her heart, only looking at him with helpless desperation, and tears ran slowly on her face. All she wanted was to approach the bed, touching and kissing him, but she didn't want to intrude, just stood there. Tears trickled down her arms, like acid eating away at every cell of her, and with guilt and regret eating away her heart. She quietly turned around, step by step away from there, silently with salty and bitter tears.

Seeing this scene, Gloomy bitterly shook her head, felt sorry for Tiffany and for herself. But she'd said enough. Whatever happened next was between Tiffany and Bush Jr. And next days and months would be difficult for all of them to accept and change the way they addressed each other. She let out a deep sign and went to see the doctor again.

🌿🌱 ✳ 🍂🌾

Bush Jr opened his eyes slowly, against soft lights that seemed impossibly bright, but he tried to fight it, wanting, needing to orient himself. And the first things he saw were an IV bottle, dripping liquid with pain medication through a needle into his arm, and could hear the soft beeping of the heart monitor. It took him a second to realize that it was his heart being monitored. Adding the scratchy, sterile-smelling sheets, hard mattress, and metal guardrail told him obviously that he was in a hospital. But how the devil had he gotten here? He thought there might have been an accident then he had no real idea of what had happened.

His head hurt like hell as if his brain was trying to escape his skull, and his eyelids weighted a thousand pounds, but he gathered enough strength, rolling his head to one side, and became aware of someone nearby in the room with him, but not a nurse. The presence was more restful and sitting in a chair by his bed. He'd recognized her anywhere. The strong, calm woman he'd first admired, then loved, then respected. He tried to reach out but couldn't as the wound on his head transmitted the pain, causing the muscles of his face to wrinkle, and the eyes to close with a painful groan.

Because that made Jennies wake up, opened her eyes to see Bush Jr moaned and opened his eyes, facing her. She exclaimed happily. "Thanks God." And on her feet instantly. "You woke up."

The first word out of his mouth was "Mom?" Then struggled to sit up, but the room spun, and his mom quickly held him back. "Hey, take it easy, son. I'd better call a nurse."

He felt back on the pillow and closed his eyes. "No nurse." His unmanageable head hardly seemed to belong to him. For a man who had always enjoyed unusually heath and agility, his weakness was maddening, but surprisingly his hand caught hers.

"Okay. I'll just sit here." Jennies said, trying to sooth. "How are you feeling?"

His head hurt so much that he groaned, reaching his shaky hands up to hold it where the bandage was wrapped. "Oh God, my head... hurts."

Her gentle hand reached for his forehead. "I bet it does." That was easy to believe.

"What happen? What are we doing here?"

"You scared the hell out of us. You passed out, and before anyone in the room could catch you, you hit your head on the desk. It gave you a nasty concussion and a lot of blood. We have to bring you to a hospital."

The final moments of the events of the day came back to him in rush. He'd been in the church, in the office with his parents and his family's lawyer who reported that he had an aunt. He didn't remember anything after that. But his mind went to Tiffany that he didn't want to know what hurting himself would be like. "Mom, what's going on?"

His mother sighed, sat heavily and rested her head on one hand. When she lifted her face to him again, he could see the she'd been crying. The sight of it frightens him. The face he'd always looked to for comfort was shattered. At that moment, the door to his room pushed open then and incoming his father. He always looked stronger than his mother, more reserved. His eyes were dry, and he wore a faint, sad smile on his face when he saw him awake. He didn't know how long he had been listening and he didn't know how much he knew. He came to stand by his bed and put a cool, dry hand to his forehead, as if instinct to check his temperature.

"Dad, it was truth?" He tried to sit up again but realized by the warbling of the room that it wasn't going to happen.

He drew a deep breath. "I don't know son, but the entire evident would say yes."

"You knew, didn't you? You knew what happened between Grandpa and her mother in the past?"

His parents exchanged a look. "Not really," His mother said, looking down her fingernails.

He managed to push himself upright with great difficulty. His father jumped up to help him. His head felt like a helium balloon; the room had a pleasant spin to it.

"Son, that's not how we know of."

"Then how?"

"I don't have a great many of the details, but what I do know indicates that there was always a parade of women through his life, and at first no one thought Angela Stone was any different, until he's been behaving like a teenager in love ever since."

Bush Jr heard the name before, but it didn't bring any bell for him now. "Who's Angela Stone?"

"She's Angela Stanley now. She was a pretty young woman who worked at the reception desk in his Orlando office nearly thirty-three years ago. I assume they were attracted to each other, physically at least. It was only a matter of time before he took notice of her and asked her out. And of course, she would say yes. No one could resist your grandpa, his charm, his money, the way he had of making a girl see stars."

He cleared his throat. "Truth be told, I never ever bothered to remember their names most of the time. I think Angela was the only girl like the other that he saw more than once. I knew she was different right away. There was a goodness to her that attracted him, decency. She wasn't like the others. They saw her first at a Christmas party then he brought her to dinner at his house. And we realized that they were lovers."

"She was quiet," he remembered, "clearly intimidated by the evening. I don't know; I liked that about her. She didn't take it for granted or have the usual air of pampered entitlement that so many of your grandpa's friends seemed to have."

"Anyway, they were a hot love affair. We thought. Well, maybe this is it. A real girlfriend: not one he's hired- literally or figuratively. But for some reason she left your grandfather and disappeared from here, after my previous wife passed away. We didn't see her again, I asked about her and he said they didn't share the same interests."

"A man like your grandpa," his dad said, "so broken and lonely inside from all those years, from the things he'd endured and seen, can't really love well. He was smart to know it. That's why he never married again."

"What are you telling Dad?" he asked then went right to the obvious question. "That grandpa knew Angela Stone, but didn't know she had a baby with him?"

His parents exchanged a look again. "I'm not sure. All I know is that they went their separate ways and eventually she left the office. I never saw her again, until now when she showed up today, and with all of information's in the documents."

Bush Jr looked at him and saw that he was telling the truth. He tried to process the information. Tiffany is his parents' stepsister. She is his aunt, too. God, how twisted was that. How cruel and bitter it was. His entire life had shattered. He slipped back down on the bed, the whole his body was numb. Maybe it was affected from the painkillers. He should ask them to give him more of this medicine. How good would it be if supplied for a lifetime.

The door opened softly and Gloomy walked in. She was washed with relief at seeing him. "Hey there, it's so good to see you awake, my little brother." She said as she approached the bed.

His father rose and kissed him on the head. "Get some rest, son. This will all seem less awful in the morning. And I'm going to tell the rest that you're feeling more like yourself. They've been worried about you."

His mother rose, clutched her purse to her side then kissed his head too. "I love you, son."

"I love you, too, Mom," he said, more from reflex than anything, and hold his mother's hand. "I'm sorry for making you, daddy and our family scared."

"We'll see you tomorrow," his father said, looking back at him from the door. "We'll talk everything out, Bush Jr. It'll all be okay."

Bush Jr took his advice, saying. "Okay." But he wasn't sure about what tomorrow held anymore.

When their parents left, Gloomy moved the chair beside the bed closer to the bed, sat down. "Don't you ever scare us like this again." "Don't scold, sister. How much damage did I do?"

Scanning quickly his face, she tried to ascertain how he was as she took hold of his free hand, the one that wasn't attached to tubes and wires to comfort him. "You were concussed, and..."

"Not to me," he said impatiently. "To the party."

Setting her teeth, she folded her arms. "You never change. I don't know why I bothered to worry. Dad must apologize to the guests."

"He did?"

She knew his tactics too well. "Of course. How are you feeling now?"

He tried for an empathetic smile and pulled himself together, but it made his head hurt. "I don't know what I feel. Awful, angry, hurt, relieved, humiliated. I'm not sure." He answered her honestly and told her all the things their parents had revealed.

"This wasn't how we were planning for the Fourth of July. I'm so sorry about the way this happens Bush Jr. I had no idea, especially with Tiffany. And no wonder why you were so distraught."

Hearing her name caused his head ached like crazy. "It's certainly interesting, isn't it?" Bush Jr said still sounding shocked. "I hate that kind of situation; one doesn't have a satisfactory explanation."

"I'm so sorry for all of this, all the mess, Bush Jr."

He refused to sorry about that now. What good would it do? "I'm not sorry."

She looked at him, confused, and he pointed out. "If we already knew the facts, then let's face them."

She couldn't help smiling, leaned in, and kissed him on the forehead. "I'm glad to hear it, brother. In the family we're always said the Jefferson's knew how to cope when things were tough. Well, at least one of us now is you.

Despite his bad mood, Bush Jr laughed little with her, because as sad and awful as the truth was. He was happiness that this woman whom he loved and who had been part of his life since his childhood. "Yes, I know." He said and sucked in pain-filled breath and pressed his hand against his head. He hadn't healed as much as he thought. "But I'm afraid I haven't taken in everything, I guess I'm still a bit out of it."

Like their father said they would talk everything out. And with her doctor's voice that put him on guard. "Not surprising when you think about it, Bush Jr. Well, anyway, Dr. Branson told me it wasn't life threatening, but he wants you to have follow-up CT scans tomorrow."

"Do you have any idea how long I'll be here?"

"Dr. Branson still concerns about the concussion. You took five stitches in the head. He wants to keep you for another day or two, or at least until the dizziness goes away. Additionally, you've had a shock today, so before you think about leaving the hospital, I suggest that you should rest, recuperate and sleep a lot, brother. The more you rest, the sooner you can come home, and letting these good people take care of you." She said jovially.

She sounded so reasonable, and confident. So, he managed a smile. "All right, sister."

But when she looked at his eyes, she saw another question in them, and she knew what it was, she could almost read his mind. Sighing to herself, she dove in. "Brother, I thought you should know that Tiffany was here."

"Should I be surprised?"

Gloomy smiled a little. "She's worried about you, but I said she'd come another day. I was afraid, facing the fact that couldn't be an invalid and easy for both of you now."

The point was well taken, Bush Jr nodded. Tiffany suddenly seemed like a stranger to him. "I understand, sister."

And his sister looked at her watch then, back at him, and decided she had stayed long enough. "I'll come to see you tomorrow," she promised him.

Her father was right, there was plenty of time to talk him further the next day. She hoped the situation wouldn't be too bad, and the last thing she wanted was for him not to grow agitated or upset. Rest and quiet was what he needed; the doctor had told her that. "I'll stop in tomorrow afternoon and again until I'm leaving. But if you need anything, the bell is there. Just ring for the nurse."

"I'd like that very much. And have I told you recently what a great sister you are."

"No, but you're right. I am. So why don't you close your eyes and try to sleep." "I thought you wanted me to wake up." He teased.

She laughed out loud, looking at him, because for the first time in the day, he knew how to joke. "Don't you know you're not supposed to argue with a doctor? Rest is the best medicine for healing."

Even though he was depressed about Tiffany, but he enjoyed being with his sister. Even now she made him feel better. "I'll work on it, doctor."

"I'm serious, you should rest." And with a last smile, she realized how much she was going to miss her brothers and sisters when she went back to San Francisco. Despite the sad occasion, she loved being with them, and whenever she was with her family, her life in California seemed so distant and without meaning. This was where she was happiest. It was hard to compare the two worlds and yet that was where she lived and worked, and what seemed so important when she was there, especially her job, she had saved a lot of lives. But it was nothing compared to all this. "I'm going to miss you when I go back. I always do." "Me too," Bush Jr said sadly.

She reached over and gave him the last kiss on the cheek then left him.

Alone, Bush Jr turned onto his side and closed his eyes, endeavored to relax. He knew how to be strong, and he would be. But right now, this was impossible. He was still filled with unease, and there was the depression how insidiously it had crept up on him, filling him with hatred for Tiffany and for him. A lot had happened in a few hours, and his entire life had changed in the blink of an eye. It was a great deal to absorb, and as he thought about it, his mind wandered to her. He was thinking of the time they had spent together earlier this week. It was hard to believe it was only five hours before. Five hours ago, he had been with her, been in love with her. But that feeling had passed and what was real love anyway? He didn't know anymore, and now, he was licking his wounds. His future had seemed so bright, but now it suddenly seemed coldly distant and lonely. He just wished it was a dream, but it was so harsh, he wanted to scream out loud why she was treating him like that? And the lethal combination paining and hurting brought the hot and silent tears that gathered in his eyes, and seeped steady down his cheeks. Embarrassed, he wiped away tears.

"Real men don't cry. Bullshit!" he whispered himself. He had always been an arrogant, cold person, never once showing his weakness. But this time he realized it just like everyone else. If you're a human, you'd got a lot of emotions, but not always strong, if so, it's just a perfect cover-up. He quickly wiped his tears again when he saw the female nurse walked in. Probably, his sister had let she know about him.

She noticed that he was crying, but she gave him a smile. Men's tears were not precious, just because men rarely showed their weakness. It was extremely rare to see them cry. But once men cried, it meant they had suffered so much that their bones and marrow were broken, there was no way to cure them. She put a hand on his forehead to check the temperature, then blood pressure, and pulse again. She pleased when the fever had broken and everything was in the normal range, right where it should be. She hung the blood pressure cuff on the wall and assumed that there's no better medicine for a man than his family. But she knew for sure that wasn't a reason for, because he looked like disheartened. So, she gently tried to cheer him up.

"How do you feel, Mr. Bush Jr?" she asked in a kindly tone, glancing from him to the monitors surrounding his bed, checking his vital.

Sondra Richard, according to the name tag that swung from lanyard at her neck. Forcing a small smile, he answered. "You don't want to know."

"Of course, I want to know." she said, offering him a sympathetic smile, then listened to his heartbeat with her stethoscope. "Because I'm a nurse in the intensive care."

All normal, but she didn't seem convinced and Bush Jr sighed, so she asked. "Your headache bothers you? Or are you still feeling dizzy?"

He hesitated just long enough for her to guess at the answer. "It's not bad," he told her. "But I would appreciate anything you can do for me to have a good sleeping, instead."

Lovesick and suffering because of love, she thought, and with a smile, pocketed the stethoscope. "The doctor didn't prescribe a narcotic, but I'll see what I can do."

He watched her check the infusion tube then quickly she typed some information into the keyboard positioned near his bed.

A quick smile as the nurse turned to leave. And through the windows of the room, he could see the fireworks exploding brightly in the night sky. "Thank you, grandpa for giving me a memorable day in my life.

Chapter 18

The measure of a man is the way he bears up under misfortune.

Plutarch

For the next three days, because the health condition was stable, Bush Jr was released from the hospital. His head was getting better, healing on its own, and his attempt at following the doctor's instruction to stay at home and rest. So, he called Gloomy from the car on the way came back at his own house, and she was happy for him. It felt good to be home, but it's going to be a big adjustment for him, so he needed to take some time off and think where home would be a different place now. Not like it did during his routine, flowed along, but as if something essential was missing and he wasn't sure he could rest.

Liar, Tiffany had been a liar, and she'd lied to him all along, hiding the things that were most important. Correction, the woman he'd thought was his aunt. Her deception made him feel numb with misery. The emptiness inside him was a big hole. It was hard to believe that it was only last week they'd been happy together-and now.

Now he felt nothing but sense of profound loss. All the happiness had been sucked out of him. He was in no mood to go back to work. He needed to be alone, away from servants, employees, also some fresh air to clear his head, and a drink to settle his nerves and distance, a great deal of distance. So, he had phoned his father and brother James, asked them to take charge for a while on business issues, department heads, managing consultants, advisers, and attorneys. They were probably the persons in the world who understood the mix of emotions he was feeling. He had told his office not to expect him at all that week and maybe not the following week as well. His instructions to them had been not to call him unless the building had burned down. They had answered that they had thought of it themselves and would be taken care of it, which reassured him. He also didn't answer his cell phone when Tiffany call called; by locking her number which he saw she did many times. He wanted to wait to see how he felt, and all he needed was just going to punch the shit out of a bag at his gym room then nursed the bottle of wine. Drank and drank nonstop. For the first time, he felt the joke of fate. It couldn't be grasped, nor could it be controlled. Bottle after bottle until it's intoxicated in the bone. It was an easy escape and would hurt only him. But he knew there was no hope of that.

The next two weeks ticked by interminably, and Bush Jr almost doubled over with pain as he sat on the couch, took a long swallow from his glass and felt the whiskey hit the back of his throat as he tried to figure out what had happened. *Loss of love can make a man desperate; desperate enough to do anything to bury the truth, to hide from its pain.* But the liquor didn't drive away his thoughts. He was wondering how it had come to this. Each day felt like a thousand years to him, and just as long to him. Oblivious to his agony, he felt as though he was trapped in recurring cycle. Where did Tiffany fit into this? He got through the night, though he didn't sleep. What kind of woman was she? Was she friend or enemy, lover or assassin? He didn't know. She had lied to him, yes. He believed that she knew who he was before she ever met him. And in thinking on it, he was sure that she had planted everything. However, he couldn't forget the way she had looked at him, the way she held and made love to him, made him vulnerable. For all lies, there was something real there, too. But for all he knew that all bets were off. She might be gone for good.

It would be good for him, Bush Jr thought. It was just his bad luck that the woman he tumbled for was a cold-blooded killer. Therefore, he learned his lesson. Suffering would make him stronger, he made a mistake in life. So didn't regret what happened, needing to use a strong mind and inner strength to overcome. He pushed back from the couch and prowled the house. Who the hell needed all that anyway? He told himself. But no matter how many demands there were on his time, his brain, his emotion, he still found odd moments, day and night, to think about Tiffany. The woman made him insane.

He'd been in too deep, and he'd nearly forgotten how it had all started because the whole picture was suddenly so appealing. He was so steeped in her, and what he need was Tiffany.

She'd been like a ghost, teasing his subconscious, playing tricks on him, coming to mind at the most unlikely of times. But damn it. Was he so stubborn, so pigheaded, that he would let the one small, insignificant fact that he and she had bond a related thing going?

You're a chicken. That irritating voice inside his head wouldn't leave him alone.

Insane maybe, he mused, but appealing. It wasn't just about money. It was about love. A family of his own, a woman who loved him was his aunt. However, as close to the surface as the idea was, it quickly submerged again.

Cursing under his breath, he jammed his hands in his jean pockets, walking barefoot into his kitchen and out onto the deck, designed to take advantage of the ocean view and where they like to eat breakfast together. Under the pale sun, the sea was gleaming brightly this morning. It was smooth, hardly a ripple on the surface. How many mornings such as this one had he been with her, taking long walks on the shore, collecting shells, and then they lay on the deck chairs, where he'd kissed her madly as both sweating. Her breasts beneath a thin blouse pressed up against him, and he'd hoisted her hands over her head, proceeded to strip her and make love to her, that he got aroused now just thinking of it. And then, in his mind's eye, her face, clear as day, came into view and he remember her playful smile, could smell her perfume in the air. It was the most perfect moment he could remember in a very long time, maybe in his entire life.

He wondered why he was trying so hard. Did he want them to get back together? Did he? He missed her, of course. But to let her back in his life, could he trust her? She's a liar. There was no forgiving that. That was what he'd always thought. But maybe, just maybe, he'd been wrong. And he was alone because he hadn't admitted to the woman, he loved that he wanted her even he was her nephew. He didn't want to be.

He sensed her everywhere, yet nowhere. One night he could have sworn he caught sight of her bike parked down the road by his house, but when he walked outside to investigate, the motorbike was gone.

Chapter 19
There's nothing more painful than crying.

Because the bad and sad thing happened to Bush Jr and her family, and all the insanity she'd gone through with Tommy for the past five days, Smiling just wanted was to go back home. So, she had called the airlines, and asked them changing the date on the flight back to London. Fortunately, they had a seat in first class for her, the only seat left on the plane. She grabbed it and was booked on a six o'clock morning flight. She'd be home by eight London time, and when Tommy drove with her to Orlando Airport, she had called Bush Jr to say good bye, before she took off.

And when she finally arrived, and the plane landed as a jolt with the first rays of morning were visible in the western sky. Her throat caught, and she realized she was back in London so soon, the city where it all started. The flight had been long, which wasn't unusual for a Monday morning. But her mind and exciting had been focused on Mathew, the man she'd loved. And in her mind's eyes she saw they had hot soup and fresh bread in front of the fireplace. Then they would make love and lie in each other's arms. They would talk about everything or nothing, have long, comfortable silences, and then make love again, until the fire died, and they crept into the bed to lay spoon fashion against one another. Soon.

Rather than contact him by phone and let him know she'd flown back. Of course, he'd be happy, but she planned to surprise him. It was worth it just to see how he would react rather than just waiting for her.

But for a second as the decelerating jet screeched down the runway, she thought of Tommy, and the good times they'd had, but she wouldn't let her wayward mind drew on him. Under the guise of the friendly, he'd burrowed his way into her heart. He brought out many indescribable emotions that no man, not even Mathew could.

"No," Smiling whispered though the thought wasn't unpleasant. She wasn't going to jeopardize her future with Mathew, and she was glad the things with Tommy had gone no further after the kiss, they'd both agreed to keep things purely professional. It would have been wrong of her, and she felt guilty enough about it now. But she had decided not to say anything to Mathew. It would only hurt him. She smiled to herself then, thinking how pleased he would be to see her, and how happy she would be to see him. She thought about leaving a message for him, to tell him that she had changed her plans, and then she decided that it would be more fun to surprise him.

The plane taxied at the gate, and she unbuckled her seat belt, grabbed her bag and emerged from the enclosed walkway into the terminal of London International Airport. Soon she'd go back everything that she had postponed.

She followed the stream of passengers toward the baggage area, and picked her single piece of carry-on luggage off the carousel. Her fingers tightened over the handle of her luggage, and with a sigh, she pulled it away the past to the present, walking outside the terminal and waited her turn in line for taxi. She watched her driver place her suitcase in the trunk, then got in the cab and waited for him to join her. When he was settled into his seat, she gave him an address of Mathew's house where they always liked to stay together.

It took twenty minutes to drive into town, and when she stopped by Mathew's house, felt little strange and out of place, as if she were trespassing. In a normal world Mathew would be standing on the doorstep, as impatient to see her as she was to see him. She pushed the bell.

Soft chimes responded in clear, dulcet tones, but didn't bring him to the door. No sounds stirring within. And she almost thought he wasn't home. But she gave it another try, pushing on the button and finally, she heard the familiar dulcet tones of the electronic chimes.

"Coming!" Mathew's voice preceded him.

Smiling braced herself as the door opened and she found herself standing face to face with him.

"Smiling!" he had said in surprise and shock at seeing her. "Oh my God, I thought you were coming back next week. Why are you back here so early?"

"Everything suddenly changed," she said, and her confidence lifted a full notch at his reaction. She assumed that Mathew had missed her just as much as she had missed him and expected he would kiss and take her into his hungry embrace, or said the words she needed to hear, but instead.

"Why don't give me a call?"

Romantic, she accused herself. Give him a break. It's obvious he's worn out. She was about to step into the house and giving a kiss to answer when she heard a female voice. "Mathew? Who's here?"

She appeared, wearing a red bikini and flimsy, see through cover-up. "Oh," her avid, pretty face clouded for a second as she recognized Smiling, then was masked with a perfectly set smile, but looked as if she wanted to disappear.

What the hell is she doing here? Dark clouds seemed to come, covering her head, and she guessed for sure that they were shady. Anger quickly followed. Smiling wanted to scream as she stared from her to Mathew. Her face was getting more and more unsightly, and she was uncomfortable. Mathew was at ease and concerned with her silence. It was a blow she hadn't expected, and it hit her like a wrecking ball. *What the hell is going on between them? And how long?* Whatever it was, she already knew it wasn't good. It was written all over their faces. The man she lived with and loved had been cheating on her. Why had he done this to her?

Suddenly, she felt pain in her heart, chest tightness, her body trembled, her mind was spinning as if she was going to faint, but she had to try to stay calm and fight back as she stepped in, passing into the hallway, and behind, he closed the door.

In silence, Mathew watched her, the anger on her face almost painful to see, but she's trying to control her emotions, and when she could speak, her voice was hard and cold. "Mathew, something going on here I don't know about?"

Smelling jealousy, he spoke up to explain. "I know this looks bad, but it's not what you think. Everything is just..."

She stared blankly at the man who was more than an hour ago, perfect in her eyes. Betrayal. This word was like a powerful punch that destroyed his image and indignation rose in her heart. "Just what, Mathew? You're going to tell me that you and she had nothing to do with each other. It was just a misunderstanding." She put her hands to his chest and gave a push, passing him.

His face dangerously bland, but Smiling stared hard at the woman who was her assistant in disbelief. "Hi, Shirley. Should I apologize for interrupting you?" she asked, politely, she hoped.

Shirley lived well and had a lot of fun being Jennifer's assistant. It had been a great blessing for her for thirteen years, had been her best and closest friend, and how the hell could she had had an affair with her fiancé for how long? she'd never known. They had both betrayed her totally. It was a terrible shock for her.

Had that really happened? Mathew had been cheating on her with this woman, had lied to her, and been sleeping with someone else. They looked happy in love.

Shirley could see how shaken Smiling was and had known she would be. She put her hand on the shoulder of Smiling and said. "Smiling sister, please calm down."

She quickly pushed her hand away and smirked. "Who are you acting for, Shirley? Am I too attached to you to tease me like that?"

Mathew heard that, quickly hugged Smiling tightly. "Smiling, calm down, listen to me. I and Shirley really have nothing to do each other. Yes, everything is just a misunderstanding."

She smiled bitterly and sadly. Oh God how she wanted to believe him. But the look of sheet terror in Shirley eyes convinced her otherwise. "Misunderstanding? Do you think an explanation like that will make me believe you, Mathew?"

"You've got it all wrong. I really don't have any feelings for Shirley. She and I were just hanging out today. That's all. Please, believe me, Smiling."

As soon as his words ended, Shirley's calm face gradually disappeared, replaced by a surge of anger. "You are such a bastard. You told me you didn't love her, promised to break up with her. How dare you trick me, Mathew."

Mathew glanced in disgust at Shirley. "What nonsense are you talking about? Just shut up."

But Shirley refused to leave it alone and obey him. She knew Smiling no longer had any trust in her, so she turned to look her straight in the face, no more trying to justify or cover up for herself, and said loudly. "He and I are in love. If you already knew, then I won't have to waste my time acting in front of you."

The relationship between her and Mathew had been attached for a long time, so she shouldn't rush to judge, waited to see how he would explain. However, listened to what she just said, verify that they had not only slept together, but also had been in a relationship for a long time. Smiling smirked with a look of contempt and extreme anger was thrown at Shirley. Her endurance seemed to have run out, and she really absorbed Shirley's flip.

Slap! Smiling's palm struck, then pointed at Shirley's face and yell. "You're as bad as he is. I really made a mistake in trusting you, Shirley."

The sudden slap caused Shirley's white cheek quickly turned red to stand dumbfounded, covered her face with her hands, couldn't believe Smiling dared to hit her, making her furious, and her eyes turned indignantly to Smiling. Once they'd turned their back, they would both turn their back. "Really! I've been patient with you for a long time. I've hinted at you many times, but you're stupid to not realize that," she admitted. She knew Mathew wanted her. Had always known. From the first time they'd met, never he said 'I love you'. But she knew he did, because Smiling always seemed to get in the way, and she could sense these things. "He didn't love you He loved me. He was just using you for his shows. He told me that many times. We used to laugh at you when we were in bed. I helped you around for all those years, while you were making great shows. You had his name, and without your name, no one is going to invest in his products, also I'm the one who's keeping your head on straight. Without the two of us you're nothing. And if he wasn't engaged to you, we have been married for a long time."

Mathew heard her say that, he yelled. "Shut the fuck up!"

The more Shirley spoke, the more she revealed herself to be a sour, out-of-control woman, despite her broken image. She wanted to get even because she'd been caught. The two of them had worked together for so long, how could she act so skillfully? Was there any other lie in this life? "The two of you are truly a pair, your dignity is equally rotten."

Though inside was so angry that Shirley clenched her fingers into fists, blue veins bulging on the backs of her hands, with a slight tremor, but she tried to suppress her anger and lowered her voice. "Will you fire me then?"

For God's sake, she really didn't expect her to be so brave, and her words brought her from one shock to another, was about to slap her again. But though her heart was breaking into a thousand pieces, it's best for her to act civilly now and she also made a painfully true point. "Of course, what do you think? But I haven't decided yet. Let's this trash settle down and see what happens. Now, if you have any self-respect, just leave. I'd would like to speak to Mathew alone."

Shirley was grateful that Smiling was talking some time to think about it. It was a terrible shock and an ugly story. She dared not look at Smiling anymore. The more she looked, the more she felt ashamed, only quietly leaved.

And the minute the door closed behind them. Smiling wanted to smash something. Hot, scorching anger engulfed her. She couldn't ever remember being so angry, angry at herself, angry Shirley even angry with Mathew.

"Please, don't listen to her, Smiling." Mathew said, stepped forward, his arms extended, as though he meant to pull her into them.

But Smiling took a step back, afraid of his touch, of his gaze, and of him. "Don't!"

Again, he stepped forward, and she nearly tripped as she scrambled away from him. "Don't you ever touch me again," she warned in a threatening voice. "You make me sick. Stay away from me."

So hurt, so upset, and so damned mad that she couldn't take it anymore, and didn't want to stay here any longer. She reached for her carry-on suitcase, and started to leave.

Dear God, how did I let this happen? "Smiling, wait. Just listen to me." Feeling a little agitated, Mathew ran after her, catching her arm just as she opened the door, and slammed it shut with the flat of his hand, then spinning her around. "I want you sit down, Smiling. I can explain."

She scolded, trying to pull herself away from him. But he was stronger than her, and she snapped her back was pressed hard against the door. "Let go of me, Mathew! I don't want to sit down."

He had no power against her pain. "Not until you hear me out," he said, the fingers on her shoulder firm but gentle. "Like I said, Shirley and I is not a thing. I wasn't hiding you, at least not like that."

"Then like what?" she asked, her heart shattering into a thousand pieces. "God, how can you go behind my back? With her? Why not someone else? Jesus, Mathew, why?"

Her voice was cold, but her gaze softened a bit. "You know, sometimes, I'm weak. I don't always act with my brain. I act with my heart, without thinking the consequences."

Fighting tears and shook her head, couldn't believe those shameless words came out from the mouth of her fiancé. This was a man she had trusted, believed in, made love with. She'd given him her heart. But now none of it made sense with his unfaithfulness and tears began to slide down her cheeks.

"I thought we had something special, something unique, something like no one else!" She stopped then, her eyes glistening, her misery palpable. "I was wrong. Just a fool."

"No, God no." But there it was. "I didn't mean... look, Smiling, I'm sorry," he tried to explain, but that was the truth, and he felt like the shit he was. He'd never intended to hurt her, but, of course, he had. "I should have told you."

"No need to explain further," she said, and her pain morphed once more into a fierce anger. "No matter how you explain it, you're still a traitor."

Yeah. It was. But he couldn't say that. He couldn't say anything. He'd already tried to apologize, and she was having none of it. He kept his silence.

"You don't love me. You never loved me." Pushing him away, she needed to be free. "It's over." And couldn't stay here a minute longer. She found the handle, yanked hard, and he made another reach for her arm, but she yanked it away, slipping through the narrow opening.

Smiling's previous childish tolerance had now been replaced by strength and determination. He knew she was agitated, so he let her go, waiting for her to calm down, he would prove his love for her. "This isn't finish, Smiling."

His voice whispered behind her, reverberated through her soul. Forcing herself to walk when her legs wanted to run, and she didn't dare to look back as she heard he call her name, or caught a glimpse of Mathew standing in the doorway and glazed at her, afraid that if she did, she might lose her heart all over again to a man who could change from warm to cold as quickly as the winter wind could change directions. "Fool," she whispered to herself, swallowing her tears, the same sadness swirled around as she waved to hail the cab, knowing full well, her love was far from hurt. It was dead. And through the window of the car, it was summer time, suddenly the rain came again. Maybe God's also sad for her.

❦ ✿ ★ ✾ ❦

Back home, she could only hide in her room, dropping onto the bed on the side of the windows, drawing her knees to her chest and let the tears that had been building up fill her eyes again. Outside, it's going darker and darker. It's just like her heart right now. A gloomy black. Adding the phone in her bag kept ringing, making her uncomfortable, then putting her hands

235

over her ears so she wouldn't hear it. But it wouldn't let her go. So she reached for her bag and opened it, then turned on the vibration mode on the phone. If it was true, and it probably was, Mathew had destroyed the last bit of faith she had. What kind of fool got her heart broken. What idiot thought he would love her forever. That he wouldn't cheat on her? And especially with her personal assistant. Stupid! She muttered under her breath as spied a framed picture on the nightstand. The picture of her and Mathew happily together. Not anymore. She set the picture face down on the table. Maybe she'd tossed it later. Permanently, and she considered giving him back the engagement ring, and then she'd have to figure out what to do about their work together. It was all so complicated and felt like such a mess to her.

Dropping her head to her arms, transparent tears kept flowing out of the corner of her eyes, and then down the cheeks, down the chin. She cried from the depths of her soul. Deep racking sobs convulsed her small frame, and she sat rocking alone in the dark room. Desperation ripped through her heart, and all her faith in love died as quickly as the flame of candle in the rain.

Smiling lay curled up, buried her face in the pillow and cried. Her tears soaked it, her body was still shaking. Until she was too tired, she slowly calmed down and fell asleep, and when she woke up on next morning day, feeling as though she'd been on a two-week drunk. And despite every inch of her body ached, her head hurt like hell, and she didn't even want to get out of bed all day, she dragged herself to the kitchen, thinking about what the rest of her life would be like without Mathew. She worried that she had been hasty in her decision or reaction, and as she sat huddled over a cup of tea, she realized again that she'd had no other choice. The promises he made, she received were just lies, and that she would never have trusted him again. There had never been a time when he had faithful or honest with her. How heartbroken she was when she saw the man she loved, betraying her so that she couldn't be forgiven. There had been no choice except for him to leave. But the emptiness she felt around her sucked the air out of her like a vacuum. Her life felt like a wasteland, and she knew that she would miss him. No matter how dishonest he had been, he had always been so sweet to her, and she had loved and living and working with him. She thought they were so happy.

He once said only love her, and that love was like fate. But now received a lot of bitterness. Why love only hurts you more? She didn't have the heart to tell her mom and dad yet that he was gone, but then the phone in the kitchen rang. She glanced at the caller ID and recognized her mother's cell phone displayed on the small screen. And because her heart was in turmoil and knowing that she couldn't have talked to her without sobbing. She needed sometime to absorb what had happened before she told them, and she hated worrying them. So, she let the call go to voice mail.

The following morning, at the crack of dawn, she woke up, feeling strangely empty and lonely. Naturally in her mind's eyes, she saw a glimpse of life as it had been. She used to awaken to Mathew stretched out beside her on the bed, one arm flung over her waist, his hair tousled, his breathing rhythmic and deep. She would stare at the curve of his spine and muscles of his back, his taut skin. God how she'd loved him.

"It's over," she reminded herself and cried again. But finally, when her tears had dried up and her bed room was flooded with the sunlight, she glanced at the clock near her bed. It was nearly ten, she told herself that lying in bed, hiding under the covers, was not going to solve any of her problems and, in fact, would only made them worse. Whether she liked it or not, she simply had to get a grip and deal with them one way or another. With that in mind, she had herself some toast, and cup of tea, trying to achieve normalcy. Then she was about to call her family, but thinking about what happened to her brother, she didn't want to upset them more. The whole situation was a disaster. She called her lawyer instead. He would handle mostly contracts for her, and then she was thinking of telling her clients that she was closing her business when she went back for Fashion Week in September, and then winding up her business in Florida by the end of the year. It was time. Her life had changed now. She had moved on. She had never thought that would happen, but it had. So, she'd have straighten that out and fast.

With strong thoughts, Smiling called her father finally after speaking to her lawyer. She told him she wanted to come back Florida after her fashion show in September and asked him to prepare the house in Miami for her to stay which her father said was fine. He didn't ask why and she didn't say anything about Mathew, but she would until after she packed all his belongings, include a picture of the two of them, their embracing each other during their love period, and handed him the two-carat diamond engagement ring he'd placed on her finger three years ago. Her personality was fair. Once he'd chosen to betray, she'd give it all back to him, and then decided just how to forward with her life without Mathew Neilson. Yes, that's what she'd do.

Chapter 20

Love never gives up, never loses faith, is always hopeful, and endures all things.

1 CORINTHIANS 13:7

Tiffany had seen him twice in the next few days when she left the hospital, but when she could not get hold of him on the text/phone call/visit, and right now, speaking to him was impossible. She knew there was a problem, but at any rate, she had to try. Since that fateful day, things between them became cold and deadlocked, and the last two weeks had almost killed her. Now it was time to settled things. So, she girded up her courage, drove to his house, parked her bike beneath a single oak tree near the front of his house, and pocketing her keys.

She spotted him inside his house again, couldn't wait to see the man who haunted her dream, but her stomach churned at the thought of facing him again. There was something powerful and potent about Bush Jr, something she could never ignore. Sure, she'd hurt him, but it was far better than watching him begin to hate her. She swallowed hard, and didn't waste any time, she marched briskly up the walkway to the front door. She'd keep light, polite, and just check on him. Surely, he'd let her inside and begin to forgive her? Surely, he'd understand why she had done it and realize things could be mended again between them?

The thoughts lifted her spirits. It was just the incentive she needed to propel her up the front steps. This was the first time she'd actually set foot back on the Bush Jr's property. It felt strange, somehow, and she couldn't decide whether she should ring the bell or simply walk inside. She still had the spare key. No, she'd ring the doorbell, which was the courteous thing to do. She waited there, crossing her arms under her breasts and wishing she knew what she was going to say to Bush Jr when she came face to face with him.

Fool, stop it! Forget and put Tiffany out of your mind. He ordered himself, but knew it was an impossible task.

Women had made him furious before. But hurt. That was something no woman had ever done to him before. He'd never considered the possibility like frustration, fury, passion, laughter, and shouting that no man who'd known so many women-mother, sisters, lovers-expected a relationship without them. But pain was a different matter.

Pain was an intimate emotion. It's more personal than passion, more elemental than anger. When it went deep, it found places inside you that should have been left alone. He should have bought a third ticket, he thought, gone along with his parents on the gift cruise he'd given them for holiday. He could have work on the ship and enjoyed a nice sail in the Greek Isles. That would have given him time and his distance. He was sure of that, had been sure. But he failed in any way.

Bringing his thoughts to the present, Bush Jr walked back into the kitchen, opened the fridge, looking for a bottled of beer. Cool air wafted from the barren interior as he peeked inside. The housekeeper hadn't stocked it, and he didn't care about that. He closed it when all he needed was a hot cup of coffee. It would soothe him and make him mentally clearer. He plopped the packet of fine roast into a basket, added a cup of water to the pot, and pressed the on button. He waited until the coffee machine gurgled and sputtered its last drop of fresh coffee dripped into the pot just about the same time the doorbell rang, irking him. He wasn't in the mood for anyone this time, if any, to be notified in advance, not to stop by like this. Whoever it was could go the hell away. Cursing, but he walked slowly to the doors. "What?" he demanded as he flung open the door. Then within seconds he stood there, felt the fresh wound stab through him as four eyes met, and no one spoke up.

"Tiffany." It was Bush Jr who broke the silence and spoke first. Her name came out in a rush of confusion and astonished.

He could have called or sent her a text, but he hadn't done either of those things. On the contrary, she had called him and texted a million times, left a thousand messages ever since. All it said was I'm sorry. He'd never responded. Not once. Because he was devastated by the fact of her, and he didn't want to resume the same relationship they'd had before. Originally, he thought he would never forgive her. But here she was, showing up to his house. It was difficult to believe that they hadn't seen each other in few weeks.

"Hi." Some of Tiffany's composure had returned. She was trying to get a chance to tell him the things she wanted to say. She had a lot of explanations and apologies for her own stupidity.

Awkward silence followed, and the air between them felt charged, adding to Bush Jr's discomfort.

Why hadn't he done that? He couldn't take his eyes off her, but said not a word, didn't come even to hug or kiss her, like they suddenly become opponents in the ring.

Bush Jr glanced at the woman who was related to his grandpa and happened to be his aunt. He couldn't see the slightest resemblance. In fact, she was his diametrical opposite, but that wasn't such a terrible thing. The strange thing was to see her again, standing in front of him, and despite being short-tempered and in a resentful mood. He became weak without wanting to blame her.

She hated his silence, but as she glanced at him, it nearly took her breath away. Not he dressed in black jeans, white Polo shirt button-down. It was the first time, seeing him like this, didn't look impeccable and businesslike, and because he looked tired and weary. His hair was uncombed. His face was pale from too much alcohol and the lines around his eyes hinted at a lack of sleep. He hadn't shaved in a couple of days. Stubble hugged his lips and jaw. Only his eyes were the same. Dark and intense, and she wished he would smile at her again, not at his aunt, not at the subject of their relationship. And since he wouldn't come to her, she reached for him, one slender hand turned upward beseechingly, but Bush Jr stepped back instinctively.

So much had changed now, everything had changed that he wanted to shrink away from the magnetism in her blue eyes, from the beautiful angles of her face. But Tiffany still looked as fresh and beautiful as the morning, as sultry and sexy as midnight. Her scent was there, as always, as if it was still clinging to his skin. And despite the pain, despite the anger, despite the fact that she'd wounded him shamelessly and he was still bleeding deep inside, he felt an overwhelming urge to run to her, to suffer any ridicule, to feel her arms wrap around him again as all of conflict died. His fingers itched for that. And God help him, he would crumble if she touched him. That was a problem. So, he curled them onto the knob, trying desperately to hang on his sanity, and done anything that might betray his true feeling.

Maybe because things had never been cleared up between them; maybe because there were too many things left unsaid. Maybe it was time to clear the air. And now the opportunity was here. "What do you want?"

You. I want you, Bush Jr, and I always have. I wish things were different between us, and God, I wish I never had hurt you.

Tiffany kept her hands in a pleading position. This wasn't like him. Bush Jr would never treat her like an unwelcome stranger, "to see you. It's been too long."

But she knew from the tense way he was standing and realized that he wanted to preserve the distance between them, and she couldn't stand it when he looked at her like a bug size considered squashing. Her temper reared. For God's sake, this wasn't what was supposed to happen. But if she lost her temper, he'd shut the door. And why was she mad? She'd been the one to push him away, so she couldn't expect this to be easy. Somehow, she had to get them back on track and fix this.

"Bush Jr, please," she said, and her begging demeanor dropping away. "I need to apologize."

Yes, she did. But did he want her apology? Somehow the apology meant less than the trust he longed for.

She waited for him to say something, but they seemed to be going through each other's psychological struggle. "Did I come at a bad time?"

Attempting to gather his self-control, he said with a mock amusement, but part of him wanted to go to her, gather her close and just hold on. "You should know."

His voice was still bitter, not exactly welcoming, and there wasn't much she could do. Each person had an attitude. But that's not why she gave up. "Bush Jr, please," she begged again. "I think I owe you an explanation."

He hesitated, summoned all his abilities to make his face impassive, white underneath his emotions seethed. Some rational part of his brain analyzed the situation. She had lied to him, not once but repeatedly. The only thing left now was to find out just how deep her deception had gone, and for what reason. Did anything else matter as questions, demands, accusations had to be answered? *Let's see what she has to say, and that was the only way he's going to do, so they're going to fix this for good was to deal with her.* The idea seemed to inspire him enough to accept.

Finally, Bush Jr sighed and swung the door wider in invitation. "Fine, come in."

Surprising his temper changed, and the tension had passed when he stepped aside the door. "Thank you," she said, sauntered in, and trying not to breathe out in pure relief. Trying to appear natural and normal, but her eyes widened at the unimaginable mess in the elegant living area. Discarded clothes littered everywhere, some were on the sofa, some were on the carpet, along with cups, glasses, bottles, were a little bit each place. The dining table was heaped with books, magazines and empty fast-food containers. He always been clean, neat and tidy, not like this. "What's been going on in here?"

Noticing her surprise, and to his discomfort, he told her. "I kicked the maid out for couple days."

But suddenly embarrassed by the mess when he's getting a clear look, "I guess I'd better let her back in. I've got coffee, if you'd like a cup."

She grabbed his arm before he could turn toward the kitchen. "No, thanks, I'm good. You look completely worn out."

"It hasn't been letting me sleep." He looked straight in her eyes, "or much of anything else."

"I meant food, exercise, fresh air. Your health is more important than anything." The chef in her stepped forward. "I'm going to fix you some tea, and some chicken soup." He stopped her by holding up one finger. "No, thanks, you don't have to do that."

"For the love of God, Bush Jr, don't act like I am pitying you just because I want to help you! I'm a chef."

He seemed about to argue then changed his mind. "Appreciate that, we'll get to it." He was calmer than he'd been little while before and determined to stay that way. "Are you sure you wouldn't like some coffee or tea?" he asked as he headed for the coffeepot was full.

He needed his coffee, she told herself. And she needed a moment to regroup. "Yes, I'm sure. You go ahead."

She wandered the room, one hand placed protectively over the life beginning in her womb. For the first time in her life, she knew a passion for something other than herself and her own comfort. She would protect that life, she promised herself. At all cost.

Pouring himself a cup, Bush Jr walked back to the room, and studied her. It's not her clothing or her hair that held his attention. Her exhausted and pale appearance was unlike her normal energetic-self, and he had already noticed how much thinner her face was, how dark were the circles beneath the eyes, and how frail were her hands. Christ. She was painfully subdued,

HUNG BUI

too. Guilt lanced through him. Is she ill? He thought. She had yet to take off her jacket. Or is she worried? Yes, maybe it was just worry, not ill health. No, she couldn't be. "Have you been all right, Tiffany?"

Her body hadn't changed at all, at least on the outside, and she didn't know how to answer. The truth was beyond question. She wondered how he react if she told him, no, she wasn't all right, she was miserable and because she'd been restless and pregnant. But she found it wasn't annoyance or even amusement she felt. It was pleasure, the rare and wonderful pleasure of being his care and worrying for her as she felt happy looking at him. How many people in his condition would have given a thought to her welfare? Touched by his expression concerned, she smiled. "Me? Are you worried about me?"

He should have backed off right then. "I don't want to, but I just asked when I see." And with an impatient gesture, he motioned her to the couch. "You should sit down.

You look very tired."

With that suggestion, she followed him into living room, cleared a space on his couch and made herself comfortable, wishing she could comfort the man she loves. And when he sank into the leather one of the side chairs, she weighted her words carefully and launch right into the topic they were both avoiding. "I know how angry and upset you were when you found out the truth about me."

He sipped his steaming coffee, watching her over the rim of his cup, and felt an instant souring in his gut. Was that from the coffee? Or from her voice that irritated him. He arched a brow. "Did you?"

How could he have misjudged her so completely? Judging people quickly and accurately was one of his most finely honed skills. He'd seen an intelligent, interesting woman. A classy one with humor and taste, but underneath her beautiful exterior, she was a liar, just someone taking advantage of the opportunity. "Do I look angrily now?"

"No, you don't. I'm glad you're not anymore." She said slowly but went straight to the point. "I have brought so much sadness to everyone. So, I'm sorry about what happened that day, and I'm sorry I hurt you."

Bush Jr silently and carefully examined his feelings. He wasn't angry now. "I don't know if I should congratulate you or cry for you. But I don't want us to get any more troubles, and not make things worse. So, let's forget it. We're both reasonable people." He suggested, but there was no guarantee he would be like that in the future.

"Yes." Relief flooded her as she took his hand, and wondered what's he going to do next, or maybe he was not one to bear a grudge for long. She decided to ask him. "So, what are you going to do for Labor Day, by the way?"

The change in subject with an odd question that surprised him, and he looked at her, puzzled, not understanding what she had in mind. He wasn't in the spirit of the holiday. "I don't know. I haven't made plans yet, since I'll surprise my parents a trip to Saigon."

"Your mom and dad are leaving town?"

"It'd been almost a year since they'd not traveled anywhere, and this seemed a good time for them to get away for a while, so I'm sending them on a cruise." He said in answer to her question.

"That's a lovely thing to do, but if you have nothing to do, my family organized a party." Tiffany said softly, sounding sincere. "You know you'd be welcome to come to our house in Miami. My mother would love to have you."

He sips another strong, black and hot of coffee. It made his mind more alert, but he found it too bitter, and couldn't stop the disappointment and anger that had burned through him. He slapped the half-drunk mug down so that coffee sloshed over the rim and onto the coffee table. His temper was less easily controlled than his grief. It was done before he could stop himself. He hated himself for it and her. The sense of betrayed was so huge, it overwhelmed everything. "You really don't have a clue, do you?" He murmured.

Tiffany felt as if she'd been slapped at his change of behavior as he glanced at her with obvious fury, and storm clouds gathered in his eyes, but behind the mad was vulnerable. He was not making any sense. What had she expected? "No, I don't," she countered, throwing his question back at him. "What did I say?"

"What you said was about how you figure everything's just clicked back into an acceptable position."

She wished she'd never asked. It made her ache with regret and shame, and she was sorry for it. She'd rather have felt annoyance than this panic that was sneaking in. She took a moment, trying to alleviate both, and held up her hand in defense. "I didn't mean to blurt it out like that, just trying to be nice. Besides, I thought you're not angry anymore."

He thought about controlling his temper as her searing blue eyes stared into his. He sighed regretfully. "Sorry," he said, pulling out few sheets from the Kleenex box on the table and wiped up the spilled coffee. "I am not angry with you if that's what you're wondering. Spilling the coffee was an accident, and I'm moody. I'm unhappy. You've been around me long enough to know that. But I am frustrated that you're dishonest with me in some way." She looked at him so sharply, and he knew he'd hit a nerve. "Or was that what your mother meant?"

Bush Jr was a man with such shifting traits that he sometimes appeared to have multiple personalities, she thought. When he was at his best, he was brilliant, and when he was not at his best, he was still far better than the average. He never lost his temper. She knew he was ruthless in business. He didn't raise his voice, didn't throw or break anything, and didn't threaten to do her bodily harm. And he didn't look exactly angry, perhaps a little indignant. It was combined with confusion and was no time for excuses. So, with an effort, she pulled her emotions back in and forced them to settle. "You don't need to explain that" she said quietly as his face was a mask of indifference, wouldn't accept them in any case. But she wanted him to know where she stood on the very awkward situation. "And you have every right to be angry, throw something. But I didn't come here to be insulted."

"Then what do you want from me?"

Desperation tore at her soul. "The chance to explain why I couldn't tell you from beginning, so you don't have to hate me."

"You're a day late and a dollar short! Nothing you say can change everything." He cut her off sharply. "And what if I said I'll never believe you again?"

Their conversation was growing decidedly uncomfortable. "But you do, I can see it in your eyes," she shot back, her inside quaking, but she wasn't going to back down. "And you make it sound as if I've committed some terrible crime."

Something flashed into his eyes. Pain? Or pity, that she knew he was concerned. But he had been unable to put them into words. So, she explained everything which she had to pay the ultimate price for her mother's secrets. "Please, Bush Jr, try to understand how it was. Try to see my side of things," she went on. "I know nothing of my past.

My mother created a whole new identity for me. Which isn't exactly my fault, and I can see why it also makes you angry to my mother."

It had been classic her mother behavior. She maybe was a user, but he still wasn't absolutely convinced. Though, Tiffany looked as if she was telling the God's truth. "Absolving your mother is not of my business and I'm not angry to her, but it was late to be out under any circumstances. And you must admit that I had reason."

"I do. The reason I didn't tell you what I was doing was because when I met you it changed everything. I loved being with you every minute that we were together. A force's so powerful that all reason becomes blind to it, blind to all things, even the truth. It nearly killed me if I leave you and scared that you'd reject me. It doesn't make a difference now, but you need to think about us, Bush Jr. We'll start over. With time, things will get better, like they were. I swear."

Oh, Lord, how he wanted to believe her, how he needed to trust her. A traitorous part longed to believe her, wished that she could take away the pain of the past few weeks, that they could pick up where they'd left off, but she was a liar, a woman with the secret past and hidden life, couldn't be trusted. He wouldn't let her fool him, not this time. "Save it for someone who'll believe it."

"It's the truth, damn it!" She closed her eyes for moment, trying to control her temper. "Just hear me out, Bush Jr."

"Why should I?" he demanded, and still those things couldn't be forced. "And don't push this, Tiffany. This is so much bigger that I'm not going to let you force that on me."

"Why would I do that?" infuriated, she shot back, but realized again how much pressure he must have been. "I'm just hoping we can both be mature enough to accept each other's opinion."

"Tiffany, did you come here to apologize, or demand that I do so?" He asked back, the fire in his eyes had frightened her.

She shook her head. "No, it's not something I want."

"Then don't …"

"Talk about this," she finished for him, reached for his hand, and lacing his fingers with her own. "I know. But we must. You are my…." She stopped.

She didn't say that part because she realized that again, she was putting her heart on her sleeve in front of Bush Jr again, and that part she probably shouldn't.

He felt himself reaching, straining for those words she didn't say. "Go ahead and say it," he snarled, his voice icy and his annoyance with her making his unexpectedly tense back, as he pulled out his hand, and brushed her words aside. "Lover, that's the word you were looking for or call me whatever suits you? But you're a Jefferson's, aren't you? And the fact remains that all you could give me is breaking my heart. It's barely had time to mend." He knew it was a cruel thing to say but thought only of defense. It was not a judgment he was making of her, or himself, it was a simple statement of fact as he saw it.

The accusation rang like a gunshot in the room, torn between what he'd said, what he'd meant and what she felt about it. She should have told him in the beginning. Hell, she'd meant it, planned to. She'd never intended to deceive him, not this way, but she'd had no choice. Now he detested her, and despite all her best efforts. Tears were more than she could fight, and saw the tear drop on the back of her hand when she looked down. Quickly, she reached up and brushed others from her cheeks. How could he talk to her this way, this lover she slept with, made love to, loved with all her heart? Struggling to keep her voice calm, she looked into his eyes. They were the same, intense, and impatient.

"You made your point, Bush Jr," she said, taking deep gulps of air between words. "I'm sorry. I can keep telling you that forever, but I never meant to hurt you. If you don't believe anything else, please believe that I never intended to cause you any kind of pain. I should've told you all this from beginning. But then? Then I was stupid enough to actually fall for you."

The tears that glinted in her eyes broke his heart, undermined him, and he hated this part of her. "Well, you're sorry that happened, but you're not sorry for what you did. And please Tiffany," he pleaded again. "I can't stand to see you cry."

She never allowed tears in front of anyone, especially him. And though she tried to dash them away, other fell quickly onto the table as lowered her head again. "I hate what I did. But to be honest, I was frightened the way you'd leave me, and it scared me. I love you. That's all there was to it, and how many ways do you want me to say it?"

Love her, just love her, his willful heart pleaded. *You'll never find a love like this again.* "The fact that we'll be facing isn't the problem to do with lack of love." He shut his eyes and turned away, furious with himself for having admitted it. "But in this case, love doesn't fix everything. You're a clever girl and you know that's humiliating."

He turned back, and the violence in his eyes was more compelling in contrast to the absolute calm of his voice. "Do you think I enjoy humiliating myself like this, or do you really think you could ever undo the humiliation I suffered?"

She stared at him with those huge, watery eyes, and there was a flicker of hurt in there too at the question. "No, I don't and I'm sure I can't, but I'd like to try." Tiffany insisted. "Love makes two people who forgive to each other, and who make the effort to keep them. Humiliating is giving up. What part of that don't you understand?"

"I'll tell you what I understand." He wanted to relent, to reach for her and hold her until those tears dried up, but he steeled himself against that reaction. Understanding didn't make him any better about the situation. "I understand that you expect me to tell you everything's just fine. Then we can pick up where we left off? But understanding and accepting aren't always the same."

Tiffany struggled to keep her composure, her tone as cool and impersonal as his. "I thought it worked because we love each other," she raised her hand to his mouth, her touch light against his lips. "And I thought you want to fight for."

How had he ever thought he loved her? She was a generation older than he, a woman who was his aunt. Couldn't she see what was right and the same or necessary for both? Desperate, he jerked his head away. "You never give up, do you? You just keep pushing and never stop."

"When something's important, I go for it."

"Don't push me. What seems simple to you isn't so simple for me."

But she made himself turn to face her and had his mouth on hers. Her practical words rang hollowly in her ears as her heart simply melted. "No, it's not something I try to do. Or meaning you don't trust me."

The touch was gentle, though there was steel beneath. Never trust her again, his mind insisted. *She'll only lie to you and hurt you again.* "Meaning that neither one of us really trusts the other." He admitted and dashed the angry away. "You can't have love without trust, Tiffany. I trusted you once, and I loved you. Good Lord, how I loved you. But you took that love and trust, turning it against me by lying to me from the first minute to the last. It was a calculated deception. We look like strangers now, and you still want to make myself trust you."

Tiffany hated his rationality and the excuses he made without trying. She hated him not wanting to fight for her, for them and for himself. Taking a tissue out of the box on the table, she blew her nose into it. "You were right, Bush Jr. I betrayed your trust. I should have talked it out with you."

"Yes. If you loved me, you should have. You don't hurt the people you love."

"Of course, you do." She defined. Love had too many sharp edges, able to cut through the soul like a razor. When the love is real and deep, you have the capacity to hurt someone more than you ever thought. People who love that deeply hurt each other, even though they don't mean to. "I know love and the pain it causes. Unfortunately, so will you. No one, not even you will get through life without it."

"I guess. But how could you not tell me what you were doing, day after day as I was sharing the most personal parts of my life with you. And when I saw that there was a part of yourself which you'd hidden from me. I felt terrible." He snapped.

The more she tried to explain, the worse he felt. But she had to push now, she told herself. She must have persuaded him to give her another chance, just one more chance. "Bush Jr, right now, you feel overwhelmed. I understand that. You're fearful about trusting again, and I understand that, too. But the answer still is love. It's a force so powerful that all reason becomes blind to it, to all things, even the truth. Lying had been wrong then and it was wrong now. It was too late to change the past. But it wasn't late to change the future."

Trust her, just once more, for God's sake, Bush Jr, you love her! He squeezed his eyes shut, struggling to be calm, to be objective, not to be hurt. "How?" He asked and kept his face impassive. "But for being fair and honest, Tiffany, I've lost faith in you." "Faith in us, you mean," she clarified. Bush Jr didn't even know the whole truth.

"Faith isn't something given, its connection, a source of the power of love. Losing faith how to get back, Tiffany?" he said, turning his eyes away. He couldn't risk believing her again. Not completely. Not when it came to matters of faith. He was too vulnerable. Just because she mentioned it wasn't any reason to run back to her or believe anything she said. "So, don't talk to me about faith!"

"Maybe I was hoping. Because I thought faith does not make things easy, it makes them possible. And I thought you believe in fate, why not in forgiveness?"

"There are so many things between us we couldn't start forgiving them all."

An awkward silence followed. She was handling it badly, but saw no other course open but straight ahead. The closer she came, the further away he drew, and no, she wouldn't beg anymore for something he didn't want to give her. "I screwed up, and I'm asking you to forgive, but if your pride stood in my way. Tell me what to do to make this right if there were a way to erase all my mistake, I'd do it and I'll fix it."

Slowly, the hope and life drained from his expression, and a bone-numbing grief took hold. "I don't know," he said, closed his eyes against it. "I honestly don't."

The hope shriveled and died. Everything she'd tried to explain had meant nothing, and she had run out of replies. She was weary of baring her soul to him. She was tired of hearing that he didn't believe in her as a person. Even if it was her own fault, he'd ever gotten those ideas in his head, she didn't care, she was tired of letting him see the real her and finding out It didn't matter. So, she was ready to end this conversation and just try to figure out how to push on through the rest of their problem from where they now stood. Maybe they both needed a little space and time to think. Next day, everything would be better, or at least it'll be clearer. "Would you like me to go away for a while?"

Thanks, God, for her offering. "That would be best for both of us, wouldn't it?" He swallowed back the emotion battling within him and wanted to let go of all his worries, all his fears as the thought of breaking up popped into his head. But damn, he needed the peace and solitude to find the way how an amicable settlement could be reached. "I need time to heal and think things through. I hope you understand."

Feeling bitter in heart, she had no choice, but to give him time to cool off and hope that he would think through what she had tried to do and what would be the best for them. "Yes, I understand," she said, standing up and looked straight in the eyes of the man she loved so much. It was just what she'd wanted, but she felt empty. "I do want what the best for you, Bush Jr, but how long?"

A life with Tiffany was all he'd ever desired. But could he trust her this time? Could he trust fate? He couldn't answer those and her question. He restrained himself from hugging her good-bye, even though every fiber of his being wanted to wrap his arms around her. "I'm sorry, Tiffany. I don't know if I'm up to it right now.

She nodded again, ordered her shaky legs to walk to the door, expecting to hear his feet following. But when she put her hand on the knob, she felt shame for being less than honest, for giving him less than he'd asked. She groped for control. She had wondered sometimes what she would do if she found herself in this situation. She had always known it could happen. But was there any chance of a future for them?

At the very least, he would need time to heal. And she would need a wellspring of patience, and she'd kept mum for good reason. Rushing him into the kind of intense relationship she wanted could worsen the damage. She'd already suffered and couldn't bear to witness the disappointment-even resentment in his eyes. She didn't believe he'd suggest abortion, but she couldn't begin to deal with the idea of terminating her pregnancy.

She turned around, and he was in the exact the same spot, his head down. She started crying copiously again. "You're right. We're different. Two different worlds now, but there's nothing I can do to change it. Nothing I would do. If you're finding that too difficult to accept, then I give you all the time and the space you need, but we'll have to come back to this. Let me know when you've made up your mind."

That seemed the best option; she opened the door but made herself turn so that their eyes met across the room. "Bush Jr, I've never asked you for anything until now. All I want is for you to consider what I've said. Giving us a chance to get back to lovers, you needn't give me an answer right away. These days it seems I have nothing to do but wait." She asked with a hopeful look.

God, he'd loved her, and the plea and the tears gleaming in her eyes would haunt him forever. But this woman was his aunt, and didn't expect that loving her would be painful. With that realization and it sounded like good-bye. He held her gaze for one long, intense moment, didn't know what move.

The silence was deafening as he stared at her, refusing to speak. "I guess you've given me your answer. Go and live your life. Be happy. I want that for you, even if you don't believe me." She said in bitter understanding, took a step backward, and another, until her back pressed against the door and there was a space between them as large and deep as Atlantic Ocean.

Bush Jr was torn. Part of him wanted to run to and put his arm around her. Part of him wanted to keep watching she left. He was halfway across the room before the heavy oak door closed and stopped himself. Why did he want so much that he'd cut himself off from and just tossed away something he'd searched for all his life? Tiffany had left. It was a feeling of loss and emptiness beyond belief, almost beyond bearing. He'd done it.

It took a few minutes for the shaking to start, and when it did, he collapsed onto the sofa. This wasn't what he wanted, either, but now Tiffany gone, and he was even more confused about their future than ever.

⁎⁎⁎⁎⁎

Fool that she was, she thought he loved her so deeply that he could toss everything away for her. She was wrong. But she shouldn't cry. What was the point? To make she felt better. Too bad she didn't have a styptic Band-Aid big enough to stop the bleed or ease the pain she was feeling. Yet, she stood by her motorbike on the street outside his house for several minutes, and watched the porch, hoping to see if he would come outside and stop her. But the porch was deserted. Was she expecting too much? How could she ever expect him to love her with that deep, soul- jarring love when the wound she inflicted on Bush Jr was so great. She absentmindedly wondered how difficult it would be to change his feelings toward her? How long would it take? All that was left now were pity and regret instead of letting him know her pregnancy and getting back his love, as she had hoped they would, instead they had broken up. Troubled, she felt overwhelmed with panic, and she had no idea when she would see him again. Bush Jr would never want her; he had made that clear enough. Love was one-sided, his way or no way. There wasn't room for compromise. And she had made any sort of trust between them impossible by approaching him with lies and an assumed name and making him the object of a sordid plan. How could a man with his pride forgive her such behavior? He couldn't. However, if he couldn't forgive her, then losing out on their second chance would be his fault, not hers.

Even though she was determined not to cry, tears flowed down her cheeks, drop by drop. Is it love? Is it hurt? This was all her fault. How could she blame him, though? She'd seen hints of judgment in his eyes, even when he'd managed to say all the right things, and she was lucky he hadn't just tossed her out without listening to single word she'd said. Now, times had changed. She decided not to think about the future, but she had to face the consequences. She'd prepared for the worst, but reality struck her cruelly than expected. She had never felt this kind of pain-persistent, heavy, and crushing out every fragile flicker of happiness inside her. How ironic when she herself knew the painful ending, but still deliberately stepped forward and took the initiative in this inherently painful love affair. What if he never saw her again? She asked herself if it changed her mind about the baby because of him, although his responsibility was not small, but she was also having it for herself, and thanks to God. She knew she was dramatic, but it was hard not to be. Her situation with him was completely unstable, and everything about the situation was designed to arouse her worst fears. Emotionally, she was like a terrified child, and total mess. A pregnant mess on top of it, with serious problems of her own, which he knew nothing about. She couldn't blame him for that, too. She couldn't have told him, if she wanted to, and she never should have let him go without mentioning the baby. But the news that she was pregnant would be supposed to remain a secret. Bush Jr would twist things around; think she'd tried to trap him into a marriage he didn't want. Out of compassion for him, she had no intention of telling him until everything settled down.

But it seemed everything was falling apart. Including her relationship with Bush Jr, despite her pregnancy. "It's over, faces it!" she told herself. Who else could be blamed for this ending, wasn't it yourself? However, she was suddenly and violently nauseous. In an instant, her stomach flipped hard, and threw up the acid and bile behind her bike.

As she spitted, straighten, she wondered. She couldn't be sick. Wouldn't be sick, one part of her argued.

No, she was certain. This had nothing to do with her pregnancy, another part screamed. She promised herself to be strong to protect her child. Somehow, she'd find a way to save them. She just had to work on it. Oh, sweet Jesus!

Weighted down by so many emotions, and despair stole into her heart. She couldn't allow herself to go down that path, nor give up hope. She should find a quiet place to stabilize her mind and physical. Determined and unable to bear any longer to stay here alone through the holidays, she wiped away her tears and brushed aside previous unexpected worries. She would turn down every cooking show and attend holiday parties by sending email from her cell phone to the people she had previously accepted invitation to and planning to meet. The excuse was that an emergency had occurred that had made her mentally unstable and apologized to them for having to cancel her filming sessions. Thinking back, she admitted that this was not her character. But then again, she'd never had a broken heart to nurse before. Now that the decision was made, and instead of heading home, she texts to her mom, I'm coming to see you, and then without carrying anything she drove away to Miami and began to sob, because the pain had only just begun.

Chapter 21
Love hurts more than hate

Even though her heart was broken, and the parts of her that were hope and love had died that day, but to run the business, she needed to handle it properly.

Smiling realized she had to temporarily put her personal matters aside, and because her position was not a job, but also a sense of responsibility. Both the models and the crew depended on her to do the best. Her name on the contract guaranteed she would produce all her creations. And she reminded herself as she rubbed an aching temple, being sad wasn't going to help. So she appeared back to work normally, and pretending like nothing happened. But when she was alone, she felt pain and cried silently, and on the contrary when she worked with everyone, especially those who made her suffer, she had to pretend to be strong. But it felt so uncomfortable and suffocating when facing them, and she felt silently sometimes and wasn't sure what to say with them. She had learned a lot about both in the past few days. Both had betrayed her and lied to her, he had cheated on her maybe during their entire relationship. They were a disgusting pair, both. And she knew she would never feel the same way about Shirley again. It had killed any feelings she had for them when they betrayed her, then could look her in the eyes every day, and pretended to be her best friend and lover. There's nothing worse than what they did. It was a double loss for her. Even though, Shirley could see how devastated she was, and she knew she had to do, to throw Shirley off the sense, but she had given her the impression that all the blame had been put on Mathew. And all she could hope was that the show would move quickly and complete their contract. She didn't want to live this charade with them for any more month. Because every time she looked at Shirley now, she would remember that she had lied to her, while sleeping with Mathew in his house. She felt sick whenever she thought about it. It was painful when discovered that your best friend had been sleeping with your future husband, she hadn't been married to Mathew, but she had lived with him and she loved him.

She wanted Shirley out of her life now, but she had to, also she needed her to finish the work. And working on the set kept her busy that she was grateful for her work now. It forced her to think of something else besides Mathew and his cheating on her, Shirley, and their betrayals.

Life without love is nothing.

Bush Jr had told her he needed a private space for himself so he could come to terms with the truth and get his mind straight. She'd been wounded, but couldn't do much more than agree. He should have felt relief and because getting drunk didn't make a damned bit of different and was never a solution to anything. So he must find the best method for him to proceed. First, he needed to deal with reality. Broken heart could heal. Maybe the cracks were always there, like thin scars, but they healed. People lived and worked, laughed and ate, walked and talked with those cracks. With that belief, he pushed all thoughts and images of her out of his mind and promised himself that he would pick up the life he'd led before knowing her. To achieve that, he needed to return to his job. With many sale meetings, client meetings, planning and strategy sessions. And then he did it.

All employees who met him all bowed their heads, and he still had a serious leadership look when he returned to his office at fourteen stories mirrored glass structure above the streets of Orlando. His briefcase was there with a mountain of work on his desk. Taking a seat, he returned to his schedule, made note of a couple of important client meeting, planned some necessary staff updates, then opened a file, and looked over the contract that would sign in the paper the following week.

But it was easier thought than done. Fifteen minutes later, he found it hard to concentrate. He looked thoughtfully out the windows as his thought drifted away from business. He shook himself, picked up his golden pen and ordered himself to concentrate. But he couldn't. His brain seemed unable to work the way it did. He succeeded in reading the first page of the current balance sheet, and images of Tiffany Stanley intruded. He would never get strong again if he began to lie to himself. Being weak and sentimental, he leaned back in his chair, pushing away from the paperwork, tossed the pen aside, and pulling his fingers through his hair. He'd never be able to concentrate on it now when the hurt wasn't any better. He admitted, rose, walking to the wide window behind his desk, and frowned out at his view of the city. The city he loved, the town he'd trust. It was a habit. It was going to be another beautiful day, he mused.

Another beautiful late-summer day with clear skies covered the renovated buildings, all the shops, restaurants and inns that drew the tourists in to sample the wares. The thick traffic weaved and changed on the street, the hustle of cars and people below walked around town, enjoying the weather, going about their business. But just now he didn't see any of it.

He was like a lord who reigned above, where power and money many people dreamed of. But it's not good to be on a high throne. The image reflected through the glass whose eyes showed sadness, like the mood in his heart. There was a knock on the door, interrupting his thoughts.

What now? Frustrating, he turned away from the window. "Come in."

His assistant opened the door and walked in, smiling as he came back to his chair, sat down, and looked across at her. "Mr. Bush Jr."

"Yes." He barked, trying to remember her name. "Any news?"

She's unfazed. "Mr. Brian wants you to call him back. Nothing urgent, he said, and I've brought you the papers as you requested."

"Thank you, Lilah." Bush Jr held out a hand for the papers, nearly smiling as she quickly passed them across the desk, and he glanced over at the Florida newspaper which had published an update piece today. And in an old habit, he checked his watch. It occurred to him, painfully, that he had rarely thought of time when he'd been with Tiffany. "I'm sorry, Lilah. It's a lunch time. You should take a break."

He dismissed her, but she didn't leave. She paused for a moment, and he realized she's expecting something from him. "What, Lilah?"

She'd worked for Bush Jr for three years, and for the first time she's worried about him when he had begun calling her by the first name or inquiring about her lunch time. Before, he often complimented her on the way she dressed. It's not like him. The change in him had the entire staff baffled, and she had noticed easily how unhappy he was after the incident happened. As his secretary, she felt obligated to dig out the source of it.

"Sir, there is something I want to ask, but I don't know if I'm a nosy person?"

Bush Jr stare at his secretary, silently observing and only seeing concern for him. Lilah, his grandpa's secretary whom he had inherited when Jefferson Bush had died. She was a pleasant woman with a sharp mind. She had always liked him and had helped him ease into his newfound role as head of the company. "All right, would you like to sit down?"

"No, Sir. I hope you won't consider this out of place, Mr. Bush Jr, but I wanted to know if you're feeling well."

A ghost of a smile played around his mouth. "Don't I look well?"

"Oh, yes, of course, a little tired perhaps." Lilah said smartly without missing a beat.

"I do? Are you just trying to rile me up?"

"Why would I do that? It's just that since you got accident, you seem distracted and different somehow."

"To answer your original question is no." He began rearranging the papers on his desk. "You could say I am distracted. I am different." Shaking off the mood, he looked up again. Distracted? What a mess he was. He was bogged down in work he couldn't concentrate on, tied up in knots he couldn't loosen. With a shake of his head, he glanced at Lilah again. "I don't think I am entirely well."

"Mr. Bush Jr, if there's anything I can do." She asked in her breezy voice. As usual she was showing her concern for her boss, as solicitous of her as she had been from her first day of working for Jefferson's.

Studying his employee, he considered her concern. He had kept her in the company because she was very efficient, quick, and had been enthusiastic. As he recalled, he had nearly refused to accept her as his secretary because she had two children, a boy and a girl. The girl had just turned thirteen and at that age, her mother's hair would definitely turn gray very quickly. It had worried him that she wouldn't be able to balance her responsibilities, but she was bright, ambitious and good at her job. And aside from an occasional over-adoring smile, she was a very good employee. That's why he'd taken what he'd considered a chance. It had worked very well indeed. "I have something to ask you."

"Yes. Please ask."

"Lilah, how long have you been married?"

"Married?" She asked back because of his change of subject. She blinked. "Fifteen years."

"How's married life treating you so far?" He couldn't resist asking.

She loved Trent. Being his wife made her so happy. Their life together wasn't perfect, but it was good and held the promise of bright future. "Trent and I are happy."

Trent, he mused. He hadn't even known her husband's name, hadn't bothered to find out. "Why?"

259

"Why, sir?"

"Why are you happy?"

"I... I suppose because we love each other."

He nodded, gesturing to prod her along. "As simple as that?"

"That's enough, sir. It certainly helps you get through the rough spots." She smiled a little, thinking of her Trent. "We've had some of them, but one of us always manages to pull the other thought."

"You consider yourself a team then. So, you have a great deal in common."

"I don't know about that, but whenever I feel like shipping him out, I think about what my life would be without him. And I don't like what I see." Taking a chance, she stepped closer. "Mr. Bush Jr, allow me to ask directly, if this has anything to do with Tiffany Stanley..."

"Tiffany Stanley?"

"Yes sir." She had seen the photograph of Tiffany, and details about her had emerged in Florida Today. "It was in all the papers."

He must have missed it. There had never been any mention in press about his accident. As far as the public was concerned, Tiffany Stanley who was daughter of Jefferson Bush, and the news was all over Florida included other things in the papers that had captured his attention. "Yes, I had been."

"You're not-upset?"

"About Tiffany? No." He lied. That fortuitous event had changed all their lives irreversibly, that was about as big as it got, and he had been thinking of her in weeks.

Love, Lilah realized, and if it'd had this kind of effect on the boss, he had all her support. "Sir, if something else is on your mind, you may be over-analyzing the situation."

The comment surprised him enough to make him smile again. "Do I over-analyze, Lilah?"

"You're very meticulous, Mr. Bush Jr, and analyze details finitely, which works very well in business. Personal matters can't always be dealt with logically."

"I've been coming to that same conclusion myself." He stood again. "I appreciate your time."

She realized she'd been dismissed again. "It's my pleasure, Mr. Bush Jr." And it certainly had been. "Is there anything else I can do for you?"

"No thank you." He turned back to the window. "Have a good lunch, Lilah."

"The same to you, sir," she was grinning when she closed the door at her back.

Bush Jr stood where he was for some time. Follow your instincts. Listen to your heart.

He told himself, but the messages coming from his heart were mixed with doubts and fears. One minute he was convinced he couldn't live without Tiffany, and the next he was sure the relationship had been a complete blunder on both their parts. It was so painful being apart.

He went back and sat behind his desk, then picked up Lilah's report. After one paragraph, he slammed it down. Grumbling and swearing, he rubbed at a dull pain around his heart. He wasn't accustomed to aches there.

Headaches certainly, never heartaches, but the memory of the way she'd slipped into his arms haunted him. And her taste-why was it that it still hovered just a breath from his own lips?

It would help if he felt like he could discuss this dilemma with his parents, get their advice. But he hadn't reached out to either his mother or his father. He was too embarrassed to admit that he might have one of the strangest loves in their entire family history.

So many images invaded him, bounced around in his head, and conflicting thoughts jostled for prominence in his mind. He hated it when he couldn't solve problem, come up with the right answer and get on with things. He sighed, closed his eyes for a moment, endeavoring to sort them out, and of course he needed some air, something to clear his head. Ignoring all things that he'd been working on, he reached for the suit jacket he'd slung over the back of his chair and slipped into it as he walked out his office, and then drove along the beach which he did something he hadn't given himself time to do in months.

"Damn women," Bush Jr muttered when he walked on the beach with his hands in his pockets, and his head down. He took a deep breath of the salt air, as the wind whipped through his hair. He loved being here, and it felt good to be out in the world for a few moments, to at least see others living even if he could not do much living himself as he focused on the pelican's flapping wings and the fish he held trapped in his beak. He just stood there, trying to take in the sights and the sound of the tide flowing in and out lull him into relaxation with the hot Florida sun make him forget all his worries.

But there were problems. People were talking and laughing or jogging past each other, and his gaze caught on a younger couple wrapped up in each other. As he watched, their hands stroking over each other as if unable to tear themselves away from breaking contact, laughs low and intimate, creating a bubble no onlooker or stranger could break. And he imagined them laughing at something no one else would understand.

Include the vivid blue sky reminded him of Tiffany's eyes that he wished she was with him. If she were here, now, beside him before time passed or the wind changed. She would smile, he thought. If she had been there, the beauty of it wouldn't make him feel so lonely, the mood would be better.

And there she was again. Invading his thoughts. Causing him to draw comparisons. He lifted his hand to push the blowing hair out of his eyes and bringing him sharply back to reality. It would be wiser for him to concentrate on the business rather than any of its occupants, or he could travel. If he could settle down a few moments, he could put some of those thought on paper. He'd get back to that. Bush Jr promised himself. Once everything would fall back into perspective, he would have his life back again.

That thought sent him flying to LA for few days. Just a few days away, doing what he was best at, and thought he felt better there, as he had assumed that with his business people at the Polo Lounge and played golf with them would ease his inner torment. But his mind hadn't been on business, and realized he's not that strong.

He couldn't get her out of his mind. He'd tried, but she kept swimming to the surface of his consciousness, toying with his thoughts. How could he escape what was in his blood, in his bone? No matter how he tried and pretend he had a choice, Tiffany was there. Finally, he gave up, and his heart yearned for home and for her.

He hadn't heard from her since, and she gave as much time as he need. But time was something he had plenty of these days. At this point, he thought, his whole life was a gamble. The money he'd earned could be lost. He shrugged at that. He'd earn more again. The power he now wielded could fade. He'd build it back up again. But there was one thing he was coming to understand, that if lost, couldn't be replaced. Tiffany. Even he should be seeing other women. He could and started to. But each time he tried to so much as think of another woman. Tiffany was there. She was so firmly planted in his mind that there wasn't room for anyone else. He wasn't going to get over her.

He had no doubt he was going out of his mind. God, he missed her, and missing her was eating him alive. Day after day he prowled the house and the grounds, wondering what she was doing. Night after night he tossed restlessly in bed as thoughts of her invaded his brain. When he slept, she was in his dream.

Why she haunted him like a ghost he couldn't live without and hadn't he stopped thinking about her, wishing for her? Why could he still see the way she had looked at him that last time, with hurt in her eyes and tears on her cheeks? Four weeks, he thought. He should have adjusted by now. Yet every day that he was here, and she was somewhere else, it got worse. He hadn't heard a word from her, and he never called her again from the moment she left the house. She'd left him for good. But he knew it was a lie. Now he'd lost her.

Not that it mattered now, and finally Bush Jr couldn't stand it anymore. He drew a deep breath then exhaled slowly. She couldn't change what she was, and he couldn't help loving her. He prayed they could find a solution to this, because now that he had found Tiffany, he couldn't let her go. She had every reason to lie, and he knew it, but would she really be that devious? He intended to find out and needed to see her, if only just once more, and the important thing was that he had to figure out to retrieve them.

How? That was one question he had no answer.

Chapter 22

Love is an act of endless forgiveness

Jean Vanier

The doorbell rang making him refresh. She'd come back, was all he could think. And all the pleasure died from his face when he saw his parents. "Mom, dad!"

He was immediately enveloped in soft material and strong perfume. It was his mother, a woman of unwavering beauty and unwavering opinions. She didn't like kissing on the cheeks, holding hard and long was the only way to show love. "Well, that's quite a greeting."

"Sorry." Dutifully he pecked her cheek. "I was…, nothing. I thought you're just enjoying your trip."

"There's no fun when our mind is full of worries." Brian said it bluntly, and before Bush Jr could ask more, he gave the reason. "Since you're becoming a recluse, and that's why we're paying you a visit."

"I've had other things to do," he said, stepped aside.

"Right, the other things you had to do." His dad said, taking his mom's arm walked in.

"Well." He watched his parents sit on the couch but couldn't relax enough to follow suit. "Can I get you something to drink?"

"No, thanks," his father gestured to him. "Come and sit here with me, let's talk this out, son."

It was his father's voice that put him on guard. "What's the problem?"

"You are, I believe. You're so damn tall, you're giving me a crick in my neck. Sit and tell me what you're been up to."

"Me?" Damn, he hated it when his dad turned the table on him. Bush Jr let out a deep sigh and complied, thinking how much his father had changed lately. Or perhaps he hadn't. Perhaps he simply saw him through different eyes these days, perhaps clearer eyes, and how he did annoy him at times. "I've been busy. I meant, I'm trying to do something to eliminate the need for brooding and self-pity."

"You've been hiding." His dad corrected and laid a hand on his. "I love you, son. That's the reason why we couldn't sit back and do nothing."

"I know. So, you've got something to say. Say it."

And his dad brought up the subject that lay at the heart of everything. "Two things became clear to me when I realized is that you're unhappy. First and foremost, is there any word from Tiffany?"

Not a question he wanted to answer and ignored his father. "I was thinking of taking meeting for you tomorrow."

That off-topic sentence annoyed him. "Stop trying to get me off the subject. We're talking about Tiffany." He returned stubbornly.

"I was talking about business," Bush Jr said with equal stubbornness.

It never paid to forget how quietly stubborn Bush Jr could be, too. "You know, son. You're beginning to annoy me," Brian told him.

"Does that mean you're leaving?" Bush Jr inquired.

"No!" Brian bellowed. "Nobody leaves until we come up with a solution."

"Then, what are you trying to tell me, dad?"

"I'll be blunt. You seem don't want to give her have another chance."

For his own peace of mind, Bush Jr didn't know if he could. "Of course not, Dad," he said, trying to sound calm, but his spirits were soaring. He gave his dad a guarded look. "And don't try to talk me out of this."

"That's the problem." He said, offering him a gentle smile. "You don't care about anything. This is your life we're talking about."

They studied each other in the following silence. "I won't deny it, but it's my problem, not yours."

"Well, I'm making it mine because you don't have the right mindset," he said, ready to fix this just the way he had to fix everything else in the family. "I want to resolve this issue once and for all, and I'm hoping that the pair of you will stop analyzing the steps and stages and accept what it is. You can't do it if you keep avoiding each other." Feeling regret, his dad was right. "I'll think about it." He promised.

"I know you're a grown man and don't need your father telling you how to live your life. But let me say this once, just in case it needs to be said. I believe that you love Tiffany, son. So are we all." Brian's voice cracked briefly. "The two of you can make a wonderful life together."

Bush Jr smiled bitterly but said nothing. So, his dad asked. "Do you still love her?"

He resented her for lying to him, but he still loved her. So, Bush Jr was honest with him. "Even though, I'm mad as hell at her right now, and a part of me would like to wring her pretty little neck, but yes, Dad. I still love her."

Brian shook his head as if the conversations were becoming too painful, but he restrained himself from offering the comfort, the sympathy, that stirred inside him. "You said you love her. But your actions do not match your words. Why?"

There was no way to avoid the truth, no reason for Bush Jr to lie. "Dishonesty, Dad. It's not for people like us, isn't it?"

"I see," his father said and a wounded look crossed his eyes. "People like us?"

"Honesty is high standard that Grandpa had taught us to become a good person." He said automatically.

"Nothing's worth being dishonest. We both know that. But the Jefferson don't solve family problems that way. I don't think all of Tiffany's motives are evil. I don't believe there was any malice in her action." His dad replied in a supportive tone. "Poor Tiffany, she's made it clear how much she regrets what she did or caused when she talked to me on the phone."

"She called you. Why?"

"She begged our forgiveness and ask that we allow her to make this up to you in some way. She'd do anything for that opportunity."

With that, Bush Jr cracked an ironic laugh. "How can you say that when it's obviously that you still haven't recovered from what happened and I'm the one who had to deal with her?"

"Yes, I know and I'm sorry about that," he felt an obligation to defend Tiffany, but he also knew that some of what Bush Jr had said was true. "But that didn't fit in with my plans. I convinced myself that it was the best if I set all that aside and started afresh. Successful people are tolerant and understand others. Tolerance is not about covering up other people's mistakes, not allowing them to make mistakes, but about creating a good opportunity for them to correct their mistakes. Can't you find it in your heart to forgive her and give it another shot?"

Forgive, yes, forget, no. When you hurt, you don't forget, he told himself. "I'll have to think about that. For a bit, I don't know if that's feasible. I can't speak to that now, and I would like not to."

"Fools," he muttered. "So, for that you'll never forgive her?"

He drew in a big gulp of air then let it out slowly. "Not exactly," Bush Jr loved Tiffany, he really did, but he hated the situation he was in. And he looked his dad squarely in the eyes, "I just can't trust her, and I just want to get on with my life, which she's making that impossible that why I thought it would be better for her if I cut the cord all at once, and find some peace."

His quite stubbornness infuriated him. "Jesus, is that your rationalization, Son? Hurting yourself by not giving her another chance?" He asked with a touch of anxiety in his voice.

Bush Jr usually admitted the way his dad asked questions, each one leading to the next, as if challenging. "Yeah. And let me handle it my way."

"Really?" Brian's chest tightened. "I think you were wrong. The situation is only going to get worse. Will you or she be happy? Just what in hell is it?"

Again, his question was hurting his head, and Bush Jr couldn't deny a growing irritation as his anger suddenly coming to the surface. "Damn, it is what it is, Dad and I don't care. It doesn't make any differences."

"I'm sick of your just rolling through life, letting it carry you along without any direction." Brian replied, with a sinking heart as he's staring at Bush Jr's grim profile. As far as he was concerned and worried about him was it couldn't be healthy for him, emotionally or physically. "You can't do your work properly. You're losing weight, which means you're not eating, and you look as though you're at the end of weeklong hangover. This is far more than wounded pride. From all appearances, your life is falling apart around you, and that's the way you want it?"

Bush Jr couldn't answer. Lying by saying 'yes' to his dad was one thing but trying to fool him was another. He was slowly shriveling up without Tiffany. His days felt like empty, wasted months. The hours dragged, especially when he was home alone. The walls seemed to close in around him, suffocating him. Normally he enjoyed his own company, but since he'd been without her, even every day routines seemed useless.

The happy, expectancy was missing from his life, as was the excitement. Without her, his future looked astonishing bleak. Didn't realizing what he was doing, Bush Jr's hand moved in a silencing gesture. "I'm fine. I'm capable of handling what needs to be handle."

The atmosphere seemed to swirl with hostility, and Brian gave a short laugh. "Your lips are saying one thing, but the rest of you are saying another. Who'd know that better than I do?"

His gaze held his dad's. The answer was so obvious that the question didn't require a response. He was lost without Tiffany, but he thought he would get over her in time. The only question that remained was how long it would take. A lifetime, his heart told him, but he refused to listen. "Dad, please stop talking about this matter."

"Stop lying yourself, dammit." He scolded, unable to let it go, and he reached out to take Bush Jr's hands in his own. "Where is my energetic Bush Jr? Show me your spirit, son. Don't be so depressed."

Feeling a little sorry, he said. "I'm sorry, Dad." And contrite for any harsh words. "I didn't mean upset you and understand. What you've got to do now is the same as everybody's telling me I have to do. Get healthy, get strong, and get back on your feet. I don't like hearing it either, but that doesn't mean it's not the simple truth."

At that a moment his temper died as quickly as it had flared, and when Brian calm enough to think rationally, a part of him couldn't blame Bush Jr. The boy had been raised with a sense of decency and honor. "I'm sorry too, son, I was angry with you for putting yourself in unhappiness way. You need to get your life back on track, that why now all we have to do is straighten out the mess between you and Tiffany."

Bush Jr didn't argue. Personally, he agreed with him. He valued so many things about his dad, and his honesty, all above. "I will be. But I don't want to ever be bound to anyone, anyone who could humiliate me that way. I don't like being lied to and used."

"It's a fact and it's a true lie." His mom broke in impetuously. "But your emotion's blocking all things, especially when it's so important that you just didn't want to face it. It's time to look at the truth."

She would have said more, but her husband's hand settled on hers, and squeezing it into silence while he kept his gaze on Bush Jr. "The two of you were so in love, and then puff! Suddenly everything went in smoke. Now I'm worried." He said and seeming touched by whatever he saw in his son's face.

"You don't need to be."

"As simple as that?"

"Why does it have to be complicated?"

"Because relationships usually are."

"Only if you let them be."

Maybe he should just trust them to take care of their own relationship, their own feelings. Brian only knew he wanted him to be happy, and to be open to it, brave enough to understand what it was worth. Age and experience had taught him a lot about the value of love. "That's not the way I see it. I've never witnessed anything like that. And I do sincerely hope the two of you to come to terms with the situation, try to set aside your differences, and be lovers again. Have you ever made a real commitment to each other?"

Bush Jr pulled his hands slowly out of his, and a deep sigh escaped him. "That's one of the things I neglected. And in any case, it's done now. We both understood commitment was out of the question."

"Is there any reason why?" He looked intrigued.

Feeling sick at heart and unable to sit, Bush Jr pushed himself up and began to wander around the room. "Because I wasn't prepared for it." He had been embarrassed by this, but that feeling had passed. "And I got mad what she had it all worked out in her head, one of her step-by-step."

Brian watched his son pace back and forth, which made him lift a brow. The Bush Jr he'd come to know rarely made unnecessary moves. "Hold on, hold on, and stop pacing, son," he commanded, and when his son did, he went on. "You mean, she hid the fact that she was your aunt?"

What a stupid fool he had been. She had lied to him. Bush Jr sighed. "Sure, and it was more than that. She had plenty of opportunities to tell me, but she never says a word to me and ever since, everything suddenly happened to hit me like a wall. I didn't know it could be like this. I've been in turmoil."

"I don't get it," he admitted. "How could she do this, and how could you not know?" *Because she's a lying witch!*

But he didn't believe it, and even as the ugly thought entered his mind, he tossed it aside.

"People do stupid things when they're in love you know," he said sensibly. "I know it sounds unbelievable now, but we had serious problems. And it was an assumption on my part. A mistake, I guess."

As if Jennies understood exactly what was going through his mind. "Then you won't make another one, will you?" she cut in and looked at him gently. "You are heartbroken and in pain. I see that. But if you found that was insulting. This proves you're fool."

She reached up and gently stroked his hair, liked she used to when he was small. The only place she would touch him. "How can you say that mother?" Bush Jr nearly screamed. What really was the fact that he was disappointed in Tiffany; not in the circumstances, but in Tiffany herself. "It's hard not to feel sad and angry and even hopeless when bad things happen. Do you realize what I've been forced to endure? And do you think I should act normally with a woman who does this to me or behave as though nothing had happened?"

"It's not fair, is it?"

"No. Do you think love is?"

"Love is the most powerful emotion on earth. It did crazy things to people, made them weak, but also made them strong, son." She took him by the shoulders, gave him a quick kiss on the cheek, endeavoring to reassure him as best she could. "She loves you. That's reason enough for her. Do you want to lose her? Or would you rather she'd have left you?"

"I'd rather she'd have been what she could be. What she might've been."

"The choice was hers, son. Just as your life is yours."

For a moment Bush Jr was silent. He understood fidelity, the need for it, and the lack of it. "It seems that we've come to different conclusions here. If you remember, she has now become my aunt."

"And that bothered you?"

"For Christ's sake, do you know what we're talking about here?" He said stubbornly. "Incest!"

The word hung between them. "It's not," Jennies didn't agree, but she felt duty bound to make Bush Jr understand the seriousness of all this and she moved on in a stronger voice than usual. "She is your aunt in nominally and she is part of the family, our sister. We all know that by now, but we don't care because it would be so easy for us to know that the two of you haven't had the same blood."

She saw Bush Jr flinch and knew she'd hit a mark. Good, she went on. "That could be fixed anything and besides, there's no motive for her to hurt us."

The facts are the facts. Bush Jr thought, but he didn't want to argue, even though it burned him to deal with it. "I'm surprised you don't hate her. But morally we are still related to each other. That's what I'm concerned about."

She could see he wasn't satisfied, so she tried to explain her theory. "We don't hate Tiffany Stanley, and we're not taking her side, believe us. We hate what she did to you, but look what that got her. And she's sorry for the results." "So, what's your point, Mom?" he asked impatiently.

"My point is, let not start this process in hate and excusing what she did, which you're still emotionally involved with her. You said you loved her, but why does your heart carry a rising wave, overflowing, resentment drifts away? It's time to heal the wounds by accepting that then you forgive her and move on. That was the last step you should take. She'll change your life."

A humorless laugh escaped. A laugh that contained torment. A laugh took away his tears. "Believe me, she already had."

"In a way, that will make your life better." She pointed out. "Don't keep watch in your heart, don't close yourself off to those possibilities, and don't make it more complicated. It isn't. Take it from your mom. Life is too short to bear grudges, to care animosity inside, so that it gnaws away like a canker. Don't let that happen to you. You both deserve better than that."

"But why?" Bush Jr asked, sounding unsure.

"Why?" She repeated, astonished. "Because we all want love and because you're my son. That's why. The two of you are perfect together."

Bush Jr flinched slightly, thinking of that. The four of them, Tiffany was the least to blame. It was the others who had created the problems, not her, and what Mom said made sense. He nodded in agreement. "Thank you for those words, Mom."

She gave him a pointed looked and concluded. "Well, it's time to stop deluding ourselves, all of us, and stop talking about it. You love her. That's the whole point of the mater, and your happiness is what matters to me more than anything in the world, son."

Bush Jr felt himself weakening. He hadn't realized just how far gone he was when it came to her. Or how lost in her he'd allowed himself to become. But he went through it. Completely lost in her and lost without her. He hadn't seen that coming, and he'd failed miserably. That wasn't the surprise. No, that honor went to the fact, that despite what she'd done, he was still in love with her. And he suspected, always would be. "Look, I know you meant well, but…"

"I meant the very best for you," Jennies said, reaching for her purse, opened it and took out a small white satin box. "I'd like you take this. If you decide Tiffany is the woman you want to build your home and family with. I hope you'll give this to her." She opened the box and informed him. "It was Great-Aunt Rosy. And it was when your dad asked me to spend my life with him and putted it onto my ring finger."

Sentiment and memories swamped her as she offered Bush Jr the ring. "I loved her, though. I still miss her."

He'd expect questions, but he hadn't guessed that they'd already planned it. "Mom, so do I." He told her. "But that's not part of the deal."

"I know, son. I'm not pushing you. I always meant you to have it when it was time. I wanted to pass it on to the next generation. Tiffany deserves it, son."

He hesitated for a moment, looked at the wonderful woman, who truly loved him. Marriage, he hadn't thought of before, but maybe it was time. Taking the box, he carefully slipped it into his pocket, also had a plan in his head. "If she will let me."

"Have faith, son. I'm sure you can find a way to convince her." His dad rose and put a hand on his shoulder. "Now listen. You listen carefully. This may be the most important advice I ever give you. Why is there a word of choice you know? Some things are forced to exist alone. Yes or no. You both resented and wanted her, it was just too vain ambition. So you choose, you are going to marry a wonderful woman in this world. You have our blessing, son, and a huge family here to cheer, tell her that when the time comes. I'm proud of you. I know you'll handle what comes next."

There was what he should do and what he wanted to do. "I wish it was that easy, and going well." Bush Jr whispered.

"But it is, it really is," his dad's hand pat softly on his shoulder. "You'll know. Do the best to what your head and your heart are trying to tell you. Can you do that?" Odd, he felt different already. As if a piece of his had flared to life, reminding him there was a woman who loved him for who he was and never asked for changes. Isn't that love? Had he ever loved her like Tiffany ever really loved him? If it did, he'd listen to reason. "Yes, sir," Bush Jr replied. "I'm certainly going to try."

Chapter 23
Family where life begins, and love never ends

H ome was the most peaceful place, and also she returned to. Parents were always the ones who opened their arms to protect them. However, the past six weeks had been difficult for her to keep her mind off Bush Jr. She tried not to wonder where he was or what he was doing, wonder if he ever thought of her. She tried not to wonder if he missed her, and since everyone thought she was away, there were no calls, texts, or emails even from Bush Jr. And why would there be? He'd been pretty clear. He hadn't wanted to see her again since the day after she left his house, and she made none. She spent most time sleeping, crying, walking on the beach and thinking about their unborn child that was the evidence of their love. She had finally seen her obstetrician, because she couldn't ignore her pregnancy. The gel was cold against her bare skin, and the doctor moved the wand slowly, glancing at the ultrasound screen, began to smile. The whooshing sound of the baby's heartbeat and the baby was growing well in a good size and seemed healthy. She had seen it on the sonogram, and she had cried when the doctor pointed the screen to show it to her, but she had refused to know its sex. She had carried the still photograph of it with her everywhere since. According to their computerized calculations and whatever information she could give them, she was four months pregnant, and the baby was due at beginning of March. She could see the future if she closed her eyes now and thought calm thoughts. There would be a room for the baby in her house where's something in sunny yellows and glossy whites, with fairy-tale prints on the walls. She'd have a rocking chair she could sit in with the baby during the long, quiet nights, when the rest of the world was asleep. But the whole thing still had an aura of unreality for her, particularly since to no one knew and suspected because it didn't show. It was the sweetest secret of her life, even she knew it would soon be time to go back and pick up her life again, but she was grateful for the weeks she'd had to heal, and for her family. For the first time in days, she felt some semblance of calm. This was where she belonged.

Opening her eyes and stretched her legs on the seat by the window in the living-room of her mother's house, she was much at home, and at peace, as she could be anywhere in the world. Through the opened windows, she could feel the sun on her face and her arm where her tattoo had been removed by laser treatment as she ran her index finger over where the tattoo had been. Nothing was noticeable.

That luminous sun seemed to belong only to Miami's Bay and a lovely cool breeze freshened the air. She could see the way down to the rugged beach and could hear the ocean waves rolling onto shore. By changing the angle, she could see the terraced lawn, the green with verdant grass scatter with a profusion of flowers that stirred in the wind, and dotted with the variegated pinks of the cherry blossoms from a lovely cherry tree in the middle of the courtyard that dominated the screen, and where she used to sit beneath it when she was a little girl. Leaves lifted by autumn breeze, skittered to the picket wrought-iron fence enclosing the lawn and the garden at the end of the courtyard.

This house had belonged to her stepfather, Martin Stanley, after his mother died. He and her mom had begun to raise a family here, and they had other two children, Danny and Tyler Stanley. The house now had belonged to her mother Angela Stanley when her stepfather, Martin suddenly and unexpectedly died of a massive heart attack six years ago after the company's shares plummeted. He was sixty-two years old.

So many memories and recollections of the past were constantly assailing her, but she could not dwell on the past at this moment when she could sit there for hours, dreaming, thinking about Bush Jr, and about moment they had shared.

When Angela hung up the phone, she went downstairs and saw her oldest child sat there on the long windows that lined the room. She was glad she came by. It's seldom Tiffany was able to spend long time with her. But she didn't seem to notice her approach, that something hadn't gone well. She looked completely withdrawn and as though she were in her own private world, and her attention focused on the garden outside. "Hi there," she said.

Tiffany nearly jumped out of her skin. "Oh, Jesus!"

She had been so lost in thoughts. It took her a moment to recoup, turned and saw her mother stood at the doorway, wearing a long flowery morning dress. "You scared me."

"Sorry. Didn't you hear me come in?"

She shook her head. "I... was thinking."

"Oh, let me guess, you were thinking about Bush Jr." She said, smiling and when she sat on the low sofa, she patted the cushion beside her. "Come, sit."

And when Tiffany sat next to her, she took her hand. She had never seen her daughter look like that before. "Darling, what is it that makes you look so tense, sad, even exhausted? Are you sure you're not ill?"

It was a cozy moment with a strange sense of peace. Just wishing that she could go back to her childhood now to be taken care of by her mother like this, without having to worry so much about life. Her mother had changed so little in the years between. Her hair was blond and thick as her daughter's, though she wore short and sleek around her face. Her skin was smooth, with the beautiful luster of her Spanish heritage. The cobalt eyes were often dreamier than Tiffany's, but in those eyes, she could feel love.

"I'm fine, Mother." She lied, looking at her, and had forced a smile. "You're so beautiful, Mother."

It felt so good to hear that from a grow daughter, but Angela knew that was a hiding compliment. "Tiffany don't digress. Something's happened. What is it?"

"Mom." She did her best to hide unhappiness from her mother in the past days, but she should have known she couldn't fool her. She raised a knee, and linked her hands around it, feeling cold. "I'm wondering how to explain to you that I and Bush Jr won't be spending much time together." "Oh, you mean because of his business?"

Taking a deep breath, Tiffany said. "No, he's leaving me."

She learned back against the cushions on the sofa, gaping at her daughter. For a split second she was rendered speechless, and then she asked. "You two had an argument, didn't you?"

When Tiffany nodded, she understood. "I guess about us then. Am I responsible for that?"

Tiffany shook her head. "No. No, it's just the way things are. And I apologized when he knew about me, about us, but..." Her throat knotted up. Dammit, what was wrong with her? She took a deep breath. "He made it clear that he can't accept my apology. I really don't blame him."

Her mother let out a rare sigh. "Oh, honey, why are you telling me this now?"

"Because I didn't want to upset you for, I was a dumb-ass. I should have told him from the get-go like you said a million times," Tiffany paused, felt weak tears fill her eyes again. She seemed to cry constantly these days, because she missed him terribly. But she tried to blink them away. "I'm sorry, my moods." And with a shake of her head, she rose. "I don't seem to be able to control them."

"Darling, I'm not upset. Everything you did was for the right reasons." Angela held out both hands, waiting until Tiffany had crossed the room to link hers with them. She was good at consoling and advising another woman. "But I can tell you're missing him even though he hurt you."

"Mother," Tiffany exhaled slowly, knelt to rest her head in Angela's lap as she always had when she needed comfort or conversation. She gave a tearful smile as her mother stroked her hair. "How did you know?"

"How could I not know?" Her mother rejoined with a touch of wry sadness. "Nothing else could put that look in your eyes."

Tiffany felt a rush of gratitude. It seemed that her mother's face was the only one she needed to confide in, and wouldn't turn her away, or condemned her for what she wished to talk to her about. She glanced up at her mother. "I've come to realize recently how very lucky I am to have you, to love me, to want me and care about what happens to me."

Puzzled, Angela cradled her daughter. "There's nothing more important than family. A place to be loved and cared for..."

It helped enormously to hear it, all the same. "But all families don't." Tiffany lifted her head, her eyes dry now and intense. If Bush Jr had come from a different family and a different life, he wouldn't be the man she loved. The man she was almost ready to believe was beginning to love her. "Do they?"

"The loss is theirs." Angela paused and shrugged offhandedly. "But what exactly happened to you?"

Tiffany had kept silent after that, gripped her mother warm hands again, and knowing what tormented her was not the disgrace she had brought on her family, but the pain she had caused Bush Jr. The memory of his face the day they had parted-so blank, so controlled had sent her into fresh agony every time she thought of it. "I've been thought about how it must feel to suffer for love..." Her voice trailed off and she let out a long sigh. "Can anything be colder than that?"

"No. You don't have to talk about that." Her tone gentled. "I know it hurts you."

She sighed. "He's been hurt, too, you see. He just thinks-Oh, I wish I didn't care what he thought. But I love him so much." Tiffany added and sobbed, unable to stem her tears. "I'll never love anyone else."

The ache in Angela's own heart swelled as she smoothed back Tiffany's tumbled hair. "Did you think I wouldn't see it? The fact our relationship had broken your love."

Comforted, Tiffany rests her head on Angela's lap again. "I thought it was the happiest day of my life, knowing the Jefferson's family, but relationships aren't always easy." She sniffled. The fact was only made she love him more. And the more she loved, the more she hurt. "Now look at me, crying like a baby."

The tears would help. No one knew better. "You have emotion, don't you?" She said as she reached for the box of Kleenex on the table, pulled out a few, and handed them to Tiffany. "You have right to express them."

She had to smile as she took the tissues, and her mother's words so closely echoed the ones she herself had thrown at Bush Jr. She wiped her eyes and cheeks. "I certainly expressed them before. I told him he was a wonderful man."

"You know, Tiffany, I don't need to know much about him. But from everything you're telling me, he sounds like a good man."

Tiffany got up to pace. "Damn right he is. He's also kind and generous and loving. It's just hard to see it sometimes, though that shell he's still got covering him."

"His life hasn't been simple, Tiffany."

"And mine has." She said, and without explanation, she started talking about her father. It had been a long time since she'd seen a photograph of her father, which was the only one her mother had ever had and kept secretly for a long time when she showed it to her. He was standing on the table at a Christmas party with a drink in one hand and her mother in the other. "Dad hadn't given me the kind of home every child should have. And then it came and completed the circle, he and the whole family. I know

Bush Jr was already a man when we come into his life, and it's the whole person I'm in love with, Mama."

She stared at her daughter, taken by surprise at this mention of the past, and Jefferson Bush's. For years she'd kept the name of her daughter's father a secret. Only she and her husband knew the truth. "Your father was a good man."

"Then why he abandoned us?" Tiffany had never asked her mother that before, although she had often wondered, and her mother startled.

"Goodness, Tiffany, how can you say such a thing? You know very well it hasn't been mentioned in years."

Her mother's face was suddenly crossed with an expression of extreme sadness and pain. "Then trust me enough to tell me, Mom."

"It's not a matter of trust." Angela tried to turn the situation around. "I wish we should put that chapter behind us and go forward."

"We can't go to the next step until we understand the last one. You told me that. Now tell me what happened. Why did you and Dad really split up?" She pushed.

Angela felt her resolve weaken. She learned back in her seat, crossed her legs, and stared into the distance, as if looking at times past. "I'd always considered it fate that we'd found and separated each other. Our destiny. Your father would have known me, and I never crossed that forbidden line. If not for circumstance." In a sense, that was what she was doing. "And as honest as I can possibly be, Tiffany. I owe you that. It's time for you to know the truth."

"The truth?" She repeated. How many secrets did she live with, unaware?

"Things were not all that great between us by then, but that wasn't the real reason we did."

"So why did you?" Tiffany probed, anxious to understand at last about her parents' relationship. Lately it had baffled her.

"I left your father," she defended him. "And he never knew he had a daughter."

Tiffany's eyes widened, momentarily startled. "You never told me any of that." Then she recovered herself swiftly to ask. "What happened between the two of you?"

"I know that sound like I did it on my own. I was young, but I was old enough to know what I was doing, old enough to be responsible. I can't even comprehend what my life might have been like if I hadn't given up the controls and loved him."

"But you didn't say anything about love."

"No, I didn't. I guess you should know how I felt about him."

"I think I already do."

"Oh, no. Do you think I just loved him from afar?"

"Then how did you get into this?"

Her mother was quiet for a long moment before she answered. She had always been honest with her daughter, which was one of reasons why their relationship was strong. And they had survived tragedy together, which made them even closer. They shared a special bond.

"It was a mistake, and I knew I was risking everything I owned to become a rich man's mistress." She continued with the only memory she hadn't forgotten. "Your father took me to the party on a night like none I've ever been before or since. It was one of those gorgeous spring nights when all the women are beautiful and men handsome."

Her mom's voice had grown soft and her shoulders sagged little as she reminisced. "He treated me as though I were something rare and valuable. He bought me a diamond necklace, a turquoise ring, a new dress of silk. There was a time when I thought that was love. We went dancing like we were the only two people in the world, and he kissed me." "Oh, Mom. He did?"

"Yes. I could explain my fascination with him at that time. I let my emotions run free and wild. When he first kissed me, kissed me liked I've never been kissed in my little apartment. I didn't resist. I kissed him back. We spend that night together after that he shoved me gently onto my bed and had sex without protection. From that point on, he was like a starved man given his first meal. His lovemaking was fierce, but no less tender, panting wildly, touching me everywhere."

"Just one?"

"No, but that was the first time I gave my virginity to your father." She smiled, remembering the passion, the soul-jarring explosion of desire; the afterglow that was just long enough for rest before he kissed her again, his arms wrapped possessively around her. Blushing foolishly as she realized that her daughter could read her thoughts, and didn't want to say further. "End the story."

"Except that you never told him. Why'd you do it?"

"For him, of course," she said simply. "We secretly had sex after that in the hidden places where he took me to. At that time, I had this silly illusion that he and I would… oh, well, you know…" Her voice trailed off in embarrassment.

"What?" Too stunned for reason. "Get married?"

"Something like that," she admitted, her voice rough. "I knew it was out of the question. I contented in our affair, but by then I also understood we couldn't really be happy, even we became involved very heavily."

"Let me guess, because he was Jefferson Bush."

"Not really."

"His family found out we were lovers, as well as I found out that I was pregnant with him."

Attracted and drawn to her mother's love story, she couldn't help but question it. "Then why didn't you tell him about the good news? What was his reaction?"

"At that time, I thought the same thing. But it was uncomfortable to be around with his relatives, and then a big incident befell him when his beloved daughter died in a car accident. Seeing him suffer in his loss, I promised myself I would leave him. It's not only that, but also because he was too perfect to ruin his reputation by bringing in to disrepute for your father was with me, a girl young enough to be his daughter, and the scandal of my pregnancy would be headlines on the news and was too much for his family to bear."

She wished she knew the words, the gesture, that would erase that cool dispassion from her eyes. "It must have been horrible for you."

Angela nodded, and her face became taut with tension as she continued to talk. "Terrified. I was scared to find myself pregnant by a man I'd decided was unsuitable, too scared even to consider your father will tell me terminate the pregnancy. But I wanted the baby, and once it shattered my illusion. I moved down Miami, and I'd managed to keep the pregnancy a secret."

Tiffany kissed her cheek, to soothe, to comfort. She saw the change in her eyes, and yes, the hurt in them. It explained a great deal, she thought, to hear her tell the story, to see her face as she did. She'd been disillusioned, devastated. Instead of giving in to it or leaning on her family for help with the burden, she'd taken her baby and started a like with her. "Tell me the rest Mom. Why did you marry my stepfather?"

"Since we ran into each other by accident at an art exposition, we had clicked, discovered how much we enjoyed each other that evening. We started to meeting for coffee, and that led to a quick date, and while we were having dinner together, he handed me a business card and told me to come his firm the next day for a job interview."

"I imagine you did." Tiffany said dryly.

"Yes, when I found out who he was, I decided to take a chance and go to see him. Everything happened at once. We became involved when I worked for him. But your step father, he was careful with me, so careful not to touch my hand too long or hold my gaze too long. Until one night we were sitting on the porch when I was three months pregnant. I've done everything to keep my pregnancy quietly. I don't have any family, and none of my friends know, No one in Miami here really knows who I am, either. But my body was changing, I broke down."

With a laugh, she ran a hand over her face. "It sounds so silly, but I hadn't been able to snap my jeans and it was terrifying. It made me realize there was no going back, and because of your future. All I had to do was make sure your step father would keep my secret. I confessed everything to him, but one thing I have to lie about is not mentioning your father's name. Lied that it was a tourist who I'd met and slept through the night. He bought it, didn't mind about that, because he let me see his heart. He gave it to me, even when he believed I couldn't or wouldn't take it. Therefore, besides that, he happily helped me going through by offering to marry me."

Angela touched the wedding ring on her finger. "Of course, I said no, but he began to reason it all out. The baby would have a name, a home, a family. It sounded so right the way he said it and I wanted the baby to be safe. So, we decided to get married quickly and quietly. I never went back to Orlando; I never look back. It was the best I could do."

"My step father must love you great deal. But why didn't you ever tell me all this before?"

"I never needed to."

"Then, how'd dad found you, found us?"

"I believe it's destiny, knowing that the course of fate, once set in motion, was nearly impossible to alter." She concluded. This was a right answer as their eyes locked together. "I thought that secret would be sinking into oblivion, but God does his way since your stepfather sold his shares to Jefferson Bush Jr, who took over our little company ten years ago."

"Did you ever regret not let him know." Tiffany asked.

"I don't allow myself to have regrets."

They were both quiet then, staring each other. Eventually Tiffany murmured. "I'm beginning to understand that suffering for love is a noble thing."

Angela smiled at her indulgently. "You must have hated me?"

The information had to be clear, the details of her mother's actions, of her dad's, even her own. It was what she had hoped to hear. "No, why would I when you did all the right things, and it had all worked out." Tiffany pointed out, reaching out to pat her hand gently. "And I'm honored that you could share your past with me, Mom."

Smiling and her mother's loving eyes looked right through her. "Good, I'm glad to hear you say that. How do you feel now?"

"Shaky," she admitted. "And you know. I had a carefully outline plan like yours. But it's not a simple thing, convincing a man to fall in love with you."

"Do you really want it to be simple?"

"I thought I did, but I don't know what I'm going to do." Tiffany started to cry again as she said it.

"For now, you can make one part simple." Rising, Angela took the tissue out from the box, patted her daughter streaming eyes, and reassured her as best she could. "Be yourself. Be true to that, to your heart, and be patience."

Tiffany rolled her eyes, but didn't say anything, so she continued to soothe her. "I know that's difficult for you, but patience, Tiffany. See what happens if you step back instead of bounding forward. Give it time, believe me Tiffany, people will change in time."

Tiffany shifted on the sofa. "Patience and time, I guess I could try, but..." She shook her head, knowing that time was something people couldn't choose. "There isn't time. I'm pregnant. I'm carrying his child." It was like a great mystery she had solved, or secret that only she had as her mother watched her in amazement.

All the soothing words Angela had prepared slipped away down her throat. "Oh, Tiffany! What did you just say?" She exclaimed in surprise. "You're sure about that?"

"Positive, and I'm serious, Mom." To prove her point, Tiffany lifted her T-shirt so she could see the bulge that was there, like a small round on her belly, and she insisted. "I'm twenty weeks pregnant, and I went to doctor last week."

"Wow!" All she could say, and think was that her baby was carrying a baby, and she was hurting by relating with her family, and Bush Jr stepping in her life. She was not handling it well. Worry clouded her face, and she peered at her intently. "Are you well?"

Tiffany smiled, pleased that this should be the first question. "Yes."

"When is your baby due?" She asked, apparently noticing the small bulge in Tiffany's tummy.

"The baby's due in March."

"That'll be lovely. After all, I'm going to have grandchildren growing up here." Angela rose to her feet to rock Tiffany against her. "And my little girl, do you know whether you're having a boy a girl?"

Despite the ultrasound she'd recently had, she didn't want to know if her baby was a boy or girl. "No, all I want is a healthy baby, but I hope it's a girl." "Oh, that's what I want, too," Angela agreed.

"Girls' clothes are much more fun."

For the first time in many days, she saw her daughter smiled as they broke apart. "I'm happy for you both, and sad."

"I know. I want the child. Believe me no child has ever been wanted so much. Not only because it's all might ever have of the father, but for itself."

"And how are you feeling now?"

"Odd," Tiffany said. "Strong one moment, and I'm terrifyingly fragile the next. Not ill, but sometimes light-headed."

Understanding, Angela nodded, and asked. "Why didn't you tell me sooner?" "Because I wanted to tell Bush Jr first," she admitted.

"I can't imagine how he reacts when you tell him you're pregnant. He'll be especially please."

"Mom," she took in a deep breath. "No, Mom, I can't."

She noted the way Tiffany glanced away and knew the reason. "Tiffany, he didn't know about the baby, did he?"

Suddenly, to her absolute astonishment and dismay, her eyes welled up with tears again. That was natural, she told herself. Pregnant woman wept easily. Their emotions ran on the surface, to be bruised and battered without any effort, and often without cause. Hers met her mother's eyes. "Of course not," she whispered, and then poured out hidden things. "I haven't had the guts to tell him and the way things are going, and he never will."

"Because of our relationship was sort of flush this out of your love and our systems."

"That was and because I didn't listen to you that I should tell him, before everything goes too far."

Her mother gave a sign with regret and tried put that away. "How is he?"

She could see the concern in her mother's voice. "We've been talked. But I can tell he'd changed. I feel like I hardly to know him. He's not likely to understand what I try to explain."

"Don't be so sure, sweetheart." Her mother's voice was reassuring. "He's been hurt, too, and it makes sense that he's changed."

"Mom, I don't think he'll see me."

"I don't argue with you about what's happening between two of you," her mother said in a supportive tone. "But sooner or later you're going to have to face this."

"I'm facing it, Mom." Tiffany said calmly. "I'm willing to accept the consequences of what I've done. The only reason I want a baby of my own was I want a family."

"I know the feeling. I can't believe you're in the same situation as I was before. But have you no regrets at all?" Her mother asked in concern.

"No, Mom, but one more thing was I don't know how I'd faced his family and parents. And it feels as if I'm living in the midst of a huge disaster."

"They'll get over it," her mother said knowingly. "As I remember, Mr. Brian and Miss Jennies were both nice people. It's nice to know we're related to them, and they both love you. It makes a difference. But I can't imagine they'd be shocked that the two of you find each other attractive and have a baby."

"Finding someone attractive isn't a license to tear up the sheet with him." Tiffany blew out a breath. If she had it to do all over again, she would behave so differently. She would have trusted Bush Jr enough to be honest with him, and perhaps he might have listened. She longed to comfort him, a ridiculous notion since she was the one who had caused him grief. If only she could see him one more time, to assure herself that he was all right, but common sense told her that such ideas were useless. She must let him go, and salvage what she could of her own life.

Unfortunately, that was becoming increasingly difficult. "Mother, I really want to tear up the sheet with Bush Jr."

"Okay, family relationships are complicated. We both know our own minds and have no problem pushing our opinions on others. But give it time. Let all the rest of this sort itself out and trust fate. When it's right, love can triumph over just about anything." "But unfortunately, timing is something we don't have the right to choose."

"Right," she agreed. "And that baby is my grandchild, I will do everything in my power to lead a comfortable life for him or her."

Tiffany was deeply moved by her mother's every word, and wishing, she had as much confidence as her mother, but she didn't. "I'm not as brave as you."

"Well, like I said," she told her, "Just have faith, it'll work out. But it'll take time to adjust, because in his heart. His pride's been hurt, but he'll come around."

So much for that argument, Tiffany mused, recalling her conversation with him that day in the past, and let she fill in. "What if he doesn't?"

"He will. Trust me, Tiffany." She said, trying to exhibit an optimism she felt. "Because I know how amazing love can be, and the reason he's hurting so much is because he loves you. So, crying not going to get you anywhere. In the meantime, go wash your face. You're going to make yourself beautiful-and made him suffer."

For the first time since she'd come home, Tiffany felt the faint stirring of hope. She set herself to stop trembling, blinking hard against her tears. "Good idea, Mama," she said as Ben trotted over.

At the sight of her, the dog wagged his tail, sniffed at her, and then rested his head on her knee for greeting. She smiled, put the dirty tissues on the table then knelt and put her arms around his neck, gave him a hug, for his presence to reach deep inside and soothe her. "Hello, big guy," she stroked his head, rubbed his ears, but talking to her mom. "I need some fresh air to think how."

"You should, and I'm going to take Ben out for a walk." She patted Tiffany's knee, slowly rose to her feet, and Ben's tail wagged enthusiastically.

Chapter 24
All are the best arrangements

Bush Jr wasn't sure he could do that by himself or didn't want to. And that was even worse. It couldn't mater that she was his aunt. It shouldn't matter that she was beautiful and kind and sexy. Because every time he thought of her it always made him desire many things. For home, for family, for laughter in the kitchen and passion in bed, he thought, and let out the long breath. Because it did matter, it mattered very much when he wanted to see her again. He was going to resolve this matter with Tiffany Stanley somehow. In fact, he had an idea that was going to turn the proposal into something she wasn't likely to forget.

He tried to call her, but he thought he wasn't going to get to the bottom of the problem over the phone. Therefore, he needed to tell her directly and decided to drive with an indescribable sense of peace to her quiet house. Parking on the driveway and got out of the car, he looked around. Everything was neat and orderly, but the house looked like abandoned.

Please, God, let her be home, he silently prayed, then peered through one of the garage's little window, cupping his hands around his face to block the glaze of day light. Her SUV Infinity sat inside, but there was no sign of her bike. He continued to the front door of the house, knowing goddamn well it would be locked, and though they had keys to each other's places. He tried a few knocks on the door, then a few rings of the bell. "Damn it," he growled, and instead the keys, he pulled his cell phone from pants' pocket and dialing her house number. He could hear the telephone ringing inside then it stopped when probably the machine picked up which had told him that. No one was home. "Damn it all to hell!" He cursed, clicked the cutoff button, dropping the phone back into his pocket, and then backed into his car.

Feeling helpless, he rested his elbows on the steering wheel and covered his head with both his hands. "Where the hell are you, Tiffany?" He whispered, trying to think what he was doing. He wasn't waiting to have a rational conversation, as he'd tried to convince himself he was over the past weeks.

He was waiting to beg, to promise, to fight, to do whatever it took to put things right again. To put Tiffany back in his life again.

Shutting his eyes, he focused all his concentration on her. "Damn it, you're not shut me out this way. You're not. Just because I was so idiot is no reason to…"

He paused as suddenly he saw a vision. Actually, he knew exactly where to go, and should thought of it before. He opened his eyes and pressed start on his car. "Meeting you is fate. No matter where you are, I can find you."

He jammed the gearshift into reverse, backing out of the driveway quickly, and was rewarded with a thud echoed through in the car, 'bam,' and following with a yell. "Hey, watch it!"

Bush Jr jumped as the automatic brake brought the car to a sudden stop.

Somebody had pounded on the trunk of his car. In his rear-view mirror, he caught a glimpse of a blur.

He gasped, looked again, just in time to see a bicyclist, one hand raised, middle finger extended. "Watch where you're going, you lunatic!" he raved.

And once he had passed, Bush Jr paused a few minutes to catch his breath. His heart was knocking so fast he couldn't think. Sweat bloomed over his body, and he felt his inside tremble. He couldn't afford to hit a bicyclist or pedestrian or dog or anything now.

Cautiously, his heart still jack-hammering, but he eased out of the drive and onto the street. Yet, despite inside he was quivering, his father's encouraging echoed through his brain. You'll handle what comes next. Setting his jaw and regulated his breaths, his tense muscles relaxing a bit as he clicked on the radio, cracking the window as he approached the bridge. And Céline Dion song of I love you drifted plaintively out of the speakers.

His hands tightened on the wheel, turned the radio up as high as his spirits, and listening to the smooth words of the song as he kept his eyes on the road. *I wish I could go back to the very first time…*

He'd handle it, all right. One way or the other, he thought himself. He knew where she lived now and had his own GPS system that would lead him to Miami. *I love you. Please say you love me too. These three words, they could change our lives forever. And I promise you that we will always be together till the end of time…*

Of course, once in the Miami city, he eyed his GPS. He wanted to make sure he was on the right track and he slowed his car to the neighborhood speed limit of twenty-five as he headed down a side street toward the beach, and finally, the car stopped at its destination, and he studied the iron electronic gates closed.

"Great! It's freaking great!" He must know the codes that electrically released the locks and swung open the gate. On top of that, they're massive, at least twelve feet tall and double that in width, and set in an ancient stone wall, with lichen and moss growing between the stones, and many tall trees were visible above it.

Annoying to know about that, he turned off the engine and got out of the car, trying to find another the way in. He moved slowly, inching around the perimeter, wondering if he could climb over the fencing, drop ten feet to the ground below, and then climb out again? He was about to give up. But to his utter amazement, he found an aluminum stepladder six feet high outside a warehouse. He thought that fate was on his side, so he smiled, looked around. There was no one around, and wasted no time, he placed the stepladder against the fence, but he stopped for a moment when he saw a PRIVATE PROPERTY NO TRESPASSING sign had been mounted on the fence and it said *Hell, what did you think you're doing?*

Ignoring the warning, even though his heart was pounding hard, but he made carefully, and without any difficult to reach to the top and over of the fence, but it's not easy to reach the ground. And he was secretly grateful for the cherry-tree branch bending slightly over nearby. So he had to hold the branch of tree to swing down, but his weight snapped the branch like a matchstick, and he fell, his buttocks hitting the ground hard when it broke from the tree, hit him on the head enough to see the stars, as well as he was sure he'd heard his own bones rattle.

"Idiot! Son of a bitch! Damn it!" He cursed as his hand touching his head. But he ignored the discomfort and was on his feet again quickly intent on his mission. But if he was honest, he was scared. He not only was he trespassing, but perhaps making a mistake of insurmountable emotion proportions. Suddenly his father's teachings echoed in his mind. Failure couldn't stop your determination. Giving up was the reason. With that in mind, he began to limp along the fence line to the house until he stopped dead in his tracks as he saw the dog began letting out a low, threatening growl, then barked madly and warning with the gold eyes looking upward to his, as if to say. *What do you think you're doing?*

Though on leash was holding by a woman in her long flowery dress, stood her ground, and watching him with bemused eyes, but the dog causing the hairs on the back of his neck to lift. He'd known about the dog, but God damn, that was one big German shepherd, and there had been no doubt if he'd made one more move, that beautiful son of bitch would have sunk his teeth into him. His hands automatically lifted up in the air.

"I'm not a cop, so put your arms down. Who the hell are you, and what the hell were you doing on my property? It's clearly posted."

The woman asked in a voice that was cold as the ice, but the visual was not her. Bush Jr eyes were on the menacing shepherd, who was showing him his teeth. He saw the fur on the back of the dog's neck moving in the light afternoon breeze. He put his arms down but froze in position as he wondered what it would be like to get bitten by the monster dog standing in front of him. He remained statute still, one eye on the woman, his other eye on the ferocious-looking dog. "Is he dangerous? Is he going to rip my throat out if I move?"

With a glance at the dog cocked his head, waiting for command, she said. "Yes, and loved every minute of it, if I give him the command."

"I'd appreciate if you'd not."

She leaned down to scratch the dog behind the ears and ordered softly. "That's okay, Ben." The dog hesitated for just a moment, but he understood he was the subject of conversation, and sensing the change in atmosphere. He cooperated by stopped growling instantly and stared sniffing the hem of his pants.

"He's harmless." She reassured him.

"That's what they all say. But he listens well." Bush Jr commented.

"He's a good dog. Anyway, talk to me and make it good, mister. You look familiar. Have we met before?"

"I'm not sure, but my name is Jefferson Bush Jr..."

"Wait a minute, wait." Her face alternately astonished and delighted, cutting him off. Then she closed the distance between them. "What did you say your name was?" "Jefferson Bush, Jr." He said his name again but began in protest. "Do I know you?"

"Yes, I believe so," the woman said. "And you're sneaking in my house, Mr. Bush Jr.

You should respect private property."

His mind concentrated on Tiffany too much to recognize, but now Bush Jr remembered when he looked over the documents he'd had, the deed and title for the real estate agency formerly owned by Martin Stanley, once a wealthy man who had fallen on bad times about ten years earlier. He had been quick to buy and had convinced Martin that the deal was sweet. Martin, a rotund man of sixty-two had looked upon the Jefferson offer to buy his real estate agency as a godsend. Not only would he be able to pay the IRS and his creditors, but he'd be able to pay the back-property taxes to keep his house at least for a little while. Bush Jr had watched Martin sign the papers with his wife, and stuff a check into the inner pocket of his jacket, pump his hand and thank him profusely, satisfied as if all parties to deal truly were happy.

And now, under the sunlight, he was in his house, and saw that her eyes were light blue and piercing, her pale blond hair mixed with gray, stands blowing around her face where it escaped her hair-clip. Her skin was so white it appeared almost bloodless. And because he was so excited and scared of the dog that he didn't recognize her at first encounter. "Mrs. Angela Stanley! Yes, I've broken the law. But I hadn't planned it this way myself, and I'm not a bad person like what you're thinking."

Never in a million years would she have expected Jefferson Bush, Jr to be standing on her property. "No, I'm not, and what the hell's going on Mr. Bush Jr?" Bush Jr offered a wide smile and his hand. "Forgive the intrusion, ma'am."

"Ma'am," Mrs. Angela repeated softly and chuckled. "We've known each other to long to be so formal. Call me Angela just like everybody."

"Yes, Mrs. Angela," he began nervously. "I didn't mean to do this, so you're welcome call a cop, kick my ass or anything else. But you'll have to wait until I finish talking with your daughter and apologize for everything."

She eyed him seriously, as he wrapped chilled fingers around her palm, and realized everything he said was true. "I can wait, and what did you think she would be here?"

"I didn't really know if she'd be here, but I decided to take a chance."

A smile flirted around her lips. "That's why you're here?"

"Yes, Mrs. Angela."

"And did she make you unhappy?"

There was compassion there, but not so much that it made Bush Jr uncomfortable. "Yes-No," he let out a heavy sigh. "She wouldn't do that, Mrs. Angela. I did that all by myself, not even sure exactly how. But what I know is I broke her heart."

"You're honest. I admire honesty in other people." She smiled at him, and he was reminded of Tiffany. "But do you still love my daughter?"

"Yes," he admitted. "Yes, I do, but …"

"But you hate me?"

"Oh no, Mrs. Angela, The only person I've hated was me."

"No hesitation there. I might just like you at that, Mr. Bush Jr."

Uneasy, Bush Jr cast out a look toward the house. "Please, is Tiffany here?"

She could see how much he cared about her, which made she like him better. "You're bleeding, Mr. Bush Jr. What did you do?"

Awkwardness was replaced by disgust when he noted the wet smear of blood on his palm. "Oh," he dug out a handkerchief, dabbed gingerly at the knot that was forming against his head, and saw some blood. "It's just a scratch. Don't worry about it."

"Really, I'll be the judge of that." She said, obviously determined to deal with his bleeding head, by yanking his head forward, ignoring his yelp of protest, and gently she pushed his hair from his face and pawed through to get to the scrape. "If not treated immediately, the wound will become infected." "Jeez, Mrs. Angela!" he said as her finger touched to it.

"Don't be a baby." Angela scolded, and annoyed at seeing the rough wound on his head, she gently took his arm. "Come inside, I'll fix your cuts and bruises then send you to her."

"I'm not, but I guess that puts me in your hands, Mrs. Angela." He said gruffly. "And I can't believe we're related."

Mrs. Angela seemed to read his thoughts. Another smile curved her lips. "When you know me a little better, dear, you'll have no doubt of it. Will you come with me?"

And before he could follow, the dog, having finally accepted him was giving his tail a couple of thumps in the air, streaked back, and galloped ahead to the house which was somewhat encouraging. The beast was warming to him. God, how he started loving this dog!

Chapter 25
God has made everything beautiful in its time

Ecclesiastes 3:11.

She was miserable and worried about everything. But now was the time to heal, was the time to rejoice over the birth of her son or daughter, was the time picked up the pieces of her life and move into the future.

Blowing her nose with a tissue, Tiffany got up and went to the bathroom. She leaned over the sink and stared into the mirror. Jesus, she didn't recognize herself. The woman who was gazed back was hardly recognizable. Looking older than her actual age, her face was pale, her blond hair was gray more than blond and mess; her usual vivid blue eyes were red from crying. She'd never worried about how she looked, but now everything was upside down. However, her mom was right. Crying wasn't helping anything and wouldn't make her any better. Maybe she and Bush Jr would never be together, but at least, God willing, she would have his baby. "I'm not going to cry anymore. I'm going to solve the problem, just as you solved your problems, Mom." Feeling better with the thoughts, she splashed her face with cold water from the faucet, patting it dry with a towel, and then she took out a compact, patted her cheeks with powder, and put light red color on her lips.

Putting the jacket on, Tiffany went out the door, and it was no surprise to her she'd ended up on beach. The ocean was a valley of blue stretching forever east. Sunlight sparkled on the surface, waves rolling and crashing to the shore. A few vessels were visible on the horizon.

It was where she'd always come when she had things to sort through. Letting the cool breeze blew across her face and sneak through her sweater and wound through the long blond hair she'd tied back in a tail. She liked the feel of it, clean and fresh, and it was so healing to see fall making its way back after the long summer. There would be other signs of it soon. In a few more days, she would be ready to go back and face reality again. Her life was changing, changing fast, and none of it seemed to be for the better.

With a small, helpless sound, she sat on the rock. Here, alone, she could admit it, had to admit it. She would never be healed. She would never be whole. She would go on and make a good life for herself and the child, because she was strong, because she was proud. But something would always be missing.

She was through with tears, through with self-pity. Miami had done that for her. She'd needed to come here, to walk this beach and remember that nothing, no matter how painful, lasts forever, except love.

Rising, she started back, watching the water spray on rocks. No more negative thoughts, she admonished herself. I've got to be positive, get on my work, and I must take care of myself for the baby's sake. Mom did it all alone, and so can I, if that becomes necessary.

After all, I'm also a member of Jefferson family. The women in this family are very resilient. We're also competent and enterprising, we can handle anything. And being her family, they will stand behind her and support her.

She stood for a moment, staring out to the sea as she thought how sorry she was that Bush Jr would never experience that kind of union. Desperate, she began to pray.

Prayer was another thing she'd let slip as she'd raced through these recent days, frantic to accomplish all that needed doing. She'd kept secrets and hid her doubts, even, at times, from herself. She'd struggled with the stress and doubts and confusion without remembering that she could give it all to God and trust Him with the outcome. She looked up at the blue sky above her.

"Please God helps me," she prayed silently, one of the most heart-wrenching prayers. "Please show me the way. I really lost my direction. Please don't let me go so far that You can't get me where I need to go. I've made a mess of things and I need You to make it right again for what I can't."

She whispered the word "Amen" aloud then stood in silence as the ocean wind blew wildly. She ran her hands through her hair, as if she was brushing away the mess in her mind, and that's when she heard his voice. "You never go for walks alone on the beach, unless something big is bugging you."

That all-too-familiar sound shocked her and she couldn't believe it. She thought she was imagining it or her mind was playing tricks on her, teasing her because she was pretending to be fearless. Very slowly, she turned, and looked in the direction where the sound came from, then Tiffany stood dumbfounded as if she had just witnessed a miracle. Her pulse hammering in a hundred places, her wide eyes caught sight of man that she always missed day and night, standing no more than ten feet away. She was almost certain that it was Bush Jr. His face was shadowed with a two-day beard, and there was a neat white bandage at his temple.

"No," she whispered. "How can it be you?" She knew that it wasn't possible, there was no way that Bush Jr could really be here, and yet she couldn't hold back the avalanche of emotions that crashed over her. Wonder and joy were coupled with absolute shock, making it impossible for her to speak. That it was an illusion. She couldn't convince herself that was a man she had dreamed of for. But he was still there. She could see him standing there to smile at her.

"You gonna stand there like that all day or you want to welcome me?" He asked and started toward her.

She wasn't often overwhelmed. But his voice cut a slice right out of her heart, so, she found herself struggling through waves of astonishment that nearly made her collapse. What in God's name how-how had he known to come here? Many emotions went through her at once: happiness, anger, longing, love. She did her best to hold it together, and in defense, she took a step back. The action stopped him cold, and neither of them moved, just stared at each other. It's like a thousand lifetimes they couldn't see each other.

His breath caught, and he stood there, unable to take his eyes from her as she stood trembling, staring at him in bewilderment, as if he was a figure in a dream. Her face was thinner, her eyes larger, and she looked tired, but the way she looked at him. Oh, her eyes were dry. There were no tears to tear up his gut, but there was a glint in them as if she was afraid him. How much easier it would have been if she'd leap at him, clawing, scratching and cursing. But she said nothing, and just stood there.

He hadn't moved any closer as seeing the recognition on her face. Eventually, he broke the spell. "Stop looking at me like I just came back to life," he paused, waiting for a response. But she didn't. He added quickly. "Tiffany, I have shocked you."

It'd been nearly two months since she'd seen him, and hearing his rough voice, her panic faded, trying to regain her composure, and she might have smiled to greet him. Instead, she steeled herself. She didn't want to appear overjoyed to see him, although she wanted to run to him, to feel those strong arms around her, and wanted to tell him how much she missed him. "Surprised is a better word, Bush Jr. I can't believe you're here."

The words were his expecting, and he had been starving for her body since he last saw her. So, he closed the gap between them, catching her waist with two big hands to draw her unrelentingly against his body and hugged tightly. Both of them choked in this touching atmosphere with a heartbeat stronger than ever.

"God, I've missed you terribly, missed everything about you," he admitted and leaned down to touch her lips. They were still sweet and soft, and then he let go and looked into her eyes. "I never knew a man could miss a woman that much, Tiffany. I couldn't bear my life without you."

She'd never thought to see him face-to-face again, certainly never to touch him. "About time you realized it. I missed you, too," she said in a rush, glad just to be in his arms again, feeling the warmth of his body surround her, and the magnetic desire that was ever present between them urged their hungry mouths to meet again in the kiss, as if it were the first time, or the last.

His kiss carried so many nostalgias for each day, like he was drinking after spending days in the desert, let her know how desperate he'd been without her. And it was so happy they were together again.

She didn't stop him because he was willing to give something she'd never asked. And that kiss with his touch was like a fire consumed all the passion, sorrow, sadness, loneliness and pain in her heart since he left. Her arms tightened around his back and kissed back, to feel the salty, bitter and sweet taste of the kiss.

She felt everything in her soul dissolve into his, and then they stood there for what felt like an eternity as he held her, and could barely pull away from each other, until she finally pulled back to look at him. Really look and noted the bandage on his head which was covered by his hair before. She felt her heart skip a beat as her eyes shot to his. "What have you done to yourself? Let me see that."

She was a great deal gentler than her mom had been. "I'm fine. It's..." Bush Jr touched his head where the bandage was. "Nothing. Really, I fell. Your mother put antiseptic on it. On my head, I mean."

"My mother!" she couldn't hide her surprise and her gaze flickered over his shoulder, toward the house. Her mother allowed and took care of the man who had broken her daughter's heart. "You've seen my mother?"

He managed a quick smile. "Yes. After I was wrongful entry, and her dog scared the hell out of me." He knew he was babbling, but he couldn't stop. "Then she was taking me in the kitchen, pouring some tea into me, and she apologized to me for everything."

"She did?"

"Apparently you told her a few truths that suddenly she felt very guilty that she'd caused us so much worry."

She braced a hand on the rock for balance. She was deathly afraid she was about to have a new experience and faint at his feet. But he wrapped his arms around and held her close. "Hell Tiffany, I didn't know where you were after coming to your house. Then I suddenly remembered that you asked me to come your mother's house for the holidays. I should have known. I should have known a lot of things."

She felt her eyes inexplicably well with tears. She swiped at them, embarrassed.

He lifted her chin. Long and short tears imprinted on hot cheeks with so much tenderness, love, respect and pain. "Are you all right?"

"I'm fine. I'm sorry for crying." She sniffed, but the smile widened. "But I just never really believed that you would be here."

"You're smiling," he said, looking at the long strand of hair which she unconsciously took into her mouth. He gently brushed her hair and smoothed it back. "I missed you so much, Tiffany in every possible way."

She nodded and felt frighteningly fragile in his arms as he pressed her still closer and found her lips again. This time her fingers, was roving, her mouth hungrier, her loins beginning to tingle, and suddenly she knew that she wanted him again. It was as though she couldn't get enough now, as though he might leave her again there would never be more.

She kissed him as if she was a starving woman who'd stumbled upon a Thanksgiving feast, as if she couldn't taste enough of him fast enough. With a moan and his hands framing her face, he kissed her with the same hunger, with the same intensity, until they were both panting, nearly oxygen deprived.

"I don't know how to say all the words you deserve to hear."

What could he possibly have to say to her after weeks of silence, or for something else? Something she could only dream about. But remembering what he had told her before, she struggled against him. "Let's not redo this scene. I'm not putting myself through it again, Bush Jr. I won't."

Her voice was choked with emotion. "No excuse, Tiffany. Please believe me." He took a hand in his own, and then with other hand brought her face back until she looked at him again. "And no walls this time."

When his eyes forced on her, everything else melted away. "I want to sit down."

"Okay." He let her go, and when she sat on the rock, folded her hands in her lap and lifted her chin, waiting for him to speak.

Where did he should start? How about where they left off. He touched a hand to her cheek. "I blamed you for everything from messing up my life. I was wrong about you.

Tiffany, I'm sorry for not understanding you," he heard himself say, and the petulance faded from her eyes.

His soft words threw her, and she had to look away to weep because she couldn't begin to explain all the guilt she'd suffered. But she knew what he was going to say, and she wanted to hear it. "I can't accept your apology until I know what it's for."

"Right. Let's start with this. When you asked me for another chance, I was too afraid because I didn't believe you to convince myself I was doing what was the best for us. But I was wrong, Tiffany."

"Why?"

She stared at him impassive or confused as she curled her fingers to keep them still? He didn't know, but he caught them in his. "Because since you've been away, I've had a chance to think it through. Fate had brought you into my life and without you, I have no motivation to strive. That's your fault. You've done something to my brain."

She drew a breath. It needed to be asked. "Do you want me back, Bush Jr?" "Do you want me to crawl?" He simply asked her back.

She nearly laughed, but decided to play it out. "You deserve to crawl a bit, but I don't have the heart for it, and I have no intention of letting you ruin your life."

He grabbed her hand as if it were a lifetime. "It's ashamed what we have to do. But it wasn't you, it wasn't me, it was life. We should be grateful. Grateful can be forgiveness."

"That's an excellent decision."

He took her chin in his hand so that she faced him and he noticed that her eyes could be as shrewd as her father's. "Tiffany, every time I reminded myself that I didn't believe in love or marriage or lifetimes, I remembered the way I felt with you." "How did you feel with me?" She insisted.

"Very fun and happy. But since without you, I can't see or touch anything," he said carefully. "I need you in my life, I want you to share it all with me. We can learn from each other, make mistakes together, and I love you more than I can say."

"I think you said it very nice," she couldn't prevent the overwhelming sense of glee, but she did manage to conceal it.

"Then please forgive me for not being brave like you, and not taking the leap you deserve, Tiffany. I just don't want to lose you. Let me make it right this time."

She'd been more than happy to extend forgiveness, seeing as how she needed some forgiveness of her own. "The truth is, you've done nothing to hurt me. In fact, I owe you for just about everything. I'm the one should ask you forgive. But it's not important anymore since the moment you're holding and kissing me. Everything from the past was gone. We have a future in front of us. This is time for future, and the only thing is coming right now is today, and today has to be faced."

He nodded, sucking in his breath, and pressed his lips to her brow then to her cheeks. "I've been afraid to face the truth about us. But I understand that better now, after I realized how important you'd become to me, and in my life. I know you've been through, and I don't even know I have to do the right thing." He paused and thought. This seemed like the right time, the right place. "Honestly, there is the right thing to do and make things right is what I have left is to ask you to marry me."

Startled, she looked at him with wide eyes, and her brain desperately struggled to understand what he'd just said. Had he... Was that... "Did you just..."

"Ask you to marry me?" Well, he certainly was asking her to marry him the way he'd intended to. "Yes."

Once again, she was fighting tears. It was like a dream coming true. "You would do that for me, or because you feel sorry for me?" she tried to be sensible.

His heart was beating fast. He hated to put himself at risk; the very word "marriage" sent a chill of apprehension down his spine any time he thought about it. But he was no coward. It had taken him long enough to find a woman he could love. He wouldn't shrink from any commitment she'd required. He smiled, kissed her. "First, it would ease my conscience if we married, and no, I'm doing this because I've finally loved you exactly as you are. I still remember the first time we met, I didn't know that would be the last time I ever loved someone in the world, I can't dream and love anyone. Now I have you here and will go with you all the way to life. No matter who you are." He paused, took her hands in his and carried on. "Marry me, Tiffany Stanley, and I'll promise to make you happy for the rest of your life."

Her throat tightened with emotion. She'd waited all her life for someone to ask that question, especially from Bush Jr. Finally, he'd given her the ultimate gift of love, one so precious and fragile she was afraid to move and break the spell. Hadn't she prayed for the answer? Surely this wasn't a coincidence. *God created all things having certain purposes. There's nothing this world exist without the reason.* And it was all she could do was pressing her head over his heart and hugging him hard. But for some reason she hesitated in her answer as she understood. His desperation. His guilt. He felt responsible for her. It was sweet and noble, but not a gesture of love. "That's a really nice thing to say, Bush Jr. But you're saying that because you know it's what I want to hear."

"No, Tiffany, I'm serious. And it was come from some very smart people who love me." He replied, smiling tenderly. "I want you to be my wife."

"And everything else?" she whispered, thinking of the deception in the past and the fact of their relationship.

"Doesn't matter anymore," he whispered back, didn't want to think of the pain before, nor the hindrance to the relationship between the families, nor of the fact she's his aunt. There was no room. His heart, mind and body were filled with only Tiffany Stanley. "Marry me, Tiffany."

Her heart took flight. He wanted her! He loved her! "And if I do?"

"You'll make me the happiest man in the world."

She smiled. "Loving you isn't easy."

"Will you marry me?" he asked again.

Couldn't describe how happy she was right now. With a smile mixed with tears, she nodded sightly. "Yes! Yes! I would love to marry you, Bush

Jefferson Jr, whenever you want." Finally, they'd crossed all the barriers between them, and she was where she belonged. And then, she couldn't help but embrace him, gently placing a passionate kiss on his lips as she realized he was finally hers.

It's great relief, he responded enthusiastically. He and she exchanged the honey of love in the middle of the blue see and sky, and when he realized how much he didn't want to stop, he pulled back. "I was afraid I might say something wrong or do something stupid and ruin any chance of getting you back."

In a moment, in the silence later, and for the first time together, they both began to grin. She brought his mouth down back to her. She couldn't stop touching him. "You could say just about anything as long as you said you loved me."

"I'm crazy in love with you, baby," he admitted, looked over the sea. "I love this spot and I guess you'll want a ring."

She glanced around over the sea, then pushed her hands through her hair. How could he think of that now? But her system kicked a quick boot. "Yes, I want a ring and you get down on one knee then ask, and I'll say yes or no. That's the right way to propose."

"Do you believe in miracle?" He asked as realized the ring he'd carried back home in his pants pocket.

"You know, miracle happens once in the lifetime, so I not always do."

"You're right, but if I say there's a diamond ring in my pocket that I'd planned to ask you to be my wife. How does it strike you?"

"What?" She exploded, stared at him. For one long moment, she assumed he was teasing, but their life in his eyes assured her that he was completely serious. "Don't make me cry again. I hate that."

"You know we both do."

"Well." She angled her head. "Then prove it to me."

He nodded with the corner of his mouth tilted as he pulled a white jeweler's box out of his pocket. "Let's make it official."

Her mouth dropped open, but then she cried out loudly. "You got me a ring!"

"Of course, I brought this for you. I want you to wear it always."

Emotion totally swamped her as he thrust the box at her. She found herself gripping it with both hands. "Bush Jr!"

"Please, open it."

"All right," she said, holding her breath with fingers not quite steady as she opened the box. It was impossible not to guess what was in it, even he told her that's a ring. But when she saw it, she gasped in amazement. It was a traditional single two-carat, emerald-cut diamond gleamed seductively against a circle of platinum engagement ring with baguettes on either side, nestled in velvet. Instinctively she ran a fingertip over it as if it was cool to touch. Then her gaze lifted to his for a beat before swiveling back to the ring. "Bush ... Oh, my God, Bush Jr!" she breathed and put a hand to her chest.

He beamed at her. "Do you like it?"

"Of course, it's the most beautiful ring I've seen, but are you proposing to me, Bush Jr?" She was pleased that her voice could sound so steady, so mild, when her heart was still somewhere in the stratosphere.

"It's a ring, isn't it?"

"Yes, it certainly is a lovely one." She lifted her gaze from it, stared into his eyes.

"What? It's not big enough for you?"

"Idiot, I didn't say that. I'm waiting."

"I don't know what you're talking."

She sighed. "All right let try this. I didn't plan this. I didn't want this. It wasn't the deal. But I'm in love with you."

He opened his mouth, his arguments ready. "Now you're making a joke of it."

"I'm not. That's wasn't the most romantic proposal. Hear me out."

Enjoying herself now, she sat back on the rock, laid one arm out. "You're an extraordinarily attractive man. You have your own business, and though apparently you occasionally under value yourself, you have a healthy ego, a good brain." She pressed her lips and nodded in a considering way. "And you come from strong stock. I believe-if we're going to use your idiotic turn of phrase, you're good enough for me." Romantic, that's it.

"You're in love with me." He could manage.

She wondered if she would ever again, in the long life she planned for them, have him at such a disadvantage. "Completely, Bush Jr. And I've been very brave and stoic, I'll have you know, accepting that you weren't in love with me. But since you are, it's different. And if you had the sense to ask me to marry you instead of showing a box in my hand, I'd say yes."

He was still staring at her, but his brain was clearing. And his heart, it was lost. "I had really good argument planned to talk you into it."

"This is supposed to be serious," she chastised him, but no matter how hard she tried, she couldn't keep the laugh out of her voice.

She was right of course, but he tried to stand firm. "No. I'm not getting down on my knees."

"I should hope not." She got up, hand him the box. "Try again."

Plucking up his courage, he sank onto one knee and Tiffany caught her breath and her hands flew to her mouth as he held the opened box up for her.

"Tiffany Stanley. I love you." It wasn't hard to say it when your heart was full of words, he realized. "I want love, cherish, and have a life with you, a family with you. I will protect you for the rest of my life. Be mine. Marry me." Oh God, he can't believe he's saying that.

"You've no idea how relieved I am to hear you say it." For the first time, her happy tears come. "So, let put the ring on me, kiss me. Then it'll be perfect."

"Well, I still haven't heard 'yes', Tiffany."

She laughed with emotion flooded her heart, poured into it, out of it, warm and smooth and real. "I did say yes before," she reminded him. "But I can say it again. Absolutely yes!"

That made him laugh too, and she leaped, throwing her arms around him, found his mouth with hers to cling sweetly to seal it, offering him everything, her lips, her tongue, her compassion, and her love which was more than perfect. "Here," he took the ring out, tossed the box aside, and took her hand.

Her heart filled her throat, and happy tears pooled in her eyes when he slid the diamond ring onto her finger. It was the right fit too, and unable to believe that this happened. "Oh, I love you so much, Bush Jr. Nothing would make me happier than to spend the rest of my life with you."

Sunlight shone through the stone, sparking as beautiful as her smile. "It was a family heirloom. It was my mother's. She would want it to be worn by someone I'd love. They married for love and they stay married for life that I think we've got years to make up for."

She held out her hand, couldn't take her eyes off it. Once they committed themselves. It would truly be forever. Nothing else mattered.

"Yes, we will," she said, let her forehead rest against his. "Thank you so much."

"Don't thank me," he growled against her ear, "show me how much you love me."

"I will-oh, I will," she whispered, and resting her hand on the bulge created by her baby. "Ouch! You're like your father, aren't you?"

The odd expression on her face made his heart lurch in sudden panic, and he followed the movement of her arm. "What is it?" Bush Jr asked.

"I feel the baby kicking." She said in wonder.

"What baby?" Bush Jr stared at her in amazement despite circumstances. His face went utterly blank, and he stood as still as stone.

She discovered she liked catching him off guard that way. Her smile widened, wanted him to feel the minute vibrations of his child moving within her. Taking his hand, she pressed it against hers. "Feel that? Someone's in there. Incredible, isn't it?"

Oh, Holy Jesus, she wasn't kidding. "Now you're freaking me out."

"I know it's a shock, but it's true." As if she had anticipated his reaction, she brushed tears away, and pulled back her jacket to show him her gently protruding stomach.

"Our baby," she said softly. "I know this is hard to take in, but Bush Jr Jefferson, you're going to be a daddy." For a moment, he stood there and stared at her, but didn't say another, word. Just kept quiet. She was aware she was holding her breath and her heart clutched. She wanted to beg him to say something, but she waited patiently, allowing him time to absorb the information.

He put a hand back on her stomach where he could feel the stirring beneath his hand, gentle at first, then the baby kicked again, seeming to prove Bush Jr to know the issue. "Whoa. I'm not sure I know what to say. You're insane … oh my God … You're been pregnant for all this time and you never told me." "No, that's not true. I tried to tell you from beginning."

Bitterness seeped into him; Bush Jr hated to taste it again. "Then why you kept it from me? I have to know why you did what you did."

Time of holding back bubbled inside her and burst out. "Please understand, if I kept it from you, it was only because I was more worried about your reaction. I'd been prepared to talk to you, to confess, and then when Steady had a problem, and next thing was we got trouble right after you found out the truth about me. You'd already burdened me with enough difficult information. To upset and worry you further didn't seem right for me to pull on you, too."

He remembered those brief flashes of strain he'd seen in her from time to time. And guilt flared. "My reaction?" He hadn't expected it. "Damn it, Tiffany. There's nothing you don't know about my life. I wouldn't have left and let all those happened if you'd told me, or because you think I don't want the baby?"

Tiffany moistened her lips. "No, I'm not going to force you to be with me, because I'm having your child. I understand you'd have doubts. This wasn't planned by either of us." She said evenly. "Shit happens as they say, and I want to apologize about that." Nothing made sense. But the only one was he wanted this child.

"I hope you won't." He suddenly grabbed her shoulders and kissed her again, hard this time. "This child is loved, is wanted. This child is not mistake, but a gift. I'm glad you did."

Sighing, she let her worries slide away, "Really? Do you mean that?"

"Don't you know me by now?" His dark eyes flashed in that sexy way that always made her throat catch and couldn't help but grin. "Yes. I always mean what I say. And I'm going to need a long time to show my gratitude. I want the baby, and you, and everything we made together."

Her relief was enormous with a mist of tears. *Yes, she thought, this time I finally got it right.* "I've been waiting for this all my life."

Pampering, he fixed her hair. "We made a baby, and I'm going to be a father." He said it slowly, jestingly, then let out a whoop and scooped her off her feet. Panicked, she threw her arms around him, clinging to his neck. "Yes."

Bush Jr smiled, thinking of his genes, her genes. The two of them ran in the Jefferson family and seemingly she was carrying on the tradition. "We're a family."

Tiffany had nodded. "Absolutely, Bush Jr. That's what we are."

He kissed her long and hard before he began to walk. "If we do a good job with the first, we can have more, right?"

She smiled, knowing he spoke of the children. "I guess you're right, but where are we going?"

He would take the risk of loving her. It wasn't as if he had a choice, anyway. "I'm carrying you back in and putting you onto the bed where I'll make slow, beautiful, soulful love to you."

"My mom's house, and I can still walk. Let me down."

Bush Jr listened, but still didn't care, just carried her away. "Things have changed, I think she's allowing me. And, no, because you're having a baby, my baby."

She knew what he intent to do which she was intent on letting him, and how good it could feel to be carried with the baby kicked hard again that Bush Jr obviously felt it, too.

He paused, his face whipping around to hers. "Oh, boy, it just hit me again. What are the chances? I mean how likely is it that the baby will, you know, inherit your talent?"

Smiling, she curved a lock on his hair around her finger. "You mean, what are chances of the baby being touchy? Very high, the Jefferson genes are very strong."

"Would you mind telling me the baby is boy or girl?"

She understood his sudden curiosity. "I really want to tell you the sex of the baby, but since I firmly do not want to know, waiting until the day of birth. But now I hope we'll have a beautiful girl."

"Oh, I do, too." He said proudly. "Isn't she strong?"

Chucking, she nuzzled his neck. "Of course, she is. But I bet she has your brain."

"Yeah," he took another step and found himself grinning. "I bet she does, and we need to get married soon."

She kissed him again. She had never been so happy. It was amazing how much life could change between yesterday and tomorrow. Is it true that when you love, all things come to life?

Chapter 26
Trust is more valuable than anything

As soon as she solved all of contracts, Smiling flew back to Florida, and her dad picked her up at Miami International Airport. He was shocked when he saw her that afternoon.

First, without Mathew and she looked awful and like she'd been through the wars. She'd lost weight, her face was deathly pale, and her beautiful eyes shadowed and troubled. Brian knew that something had happened, and his heart started pounding and worrying. But he waited until they came to her house and sat next to her on the sofa of the living room. His eyes went straight to his daughter. "Are you okay?"

"I'm fine, just tired after traveling and plane changes." She lied to reassure him as she met her father's worried gaze and forcing a smile. But no matter how much she wanted to pretend everything was normal, it wasn't. Tears welled up when the repression was broken and she turned away from him, hoping he wouldn't see the wetness in her eyes. What the hell was wrong with her? She couldn't seem to stop crying. And of course, her father noticed.

He knew her better than that. She had never looked, or sounded, quite like that. Her eyelids were puffy, and he could tell she'd been crying. He'd never seen her cry, not for herself anyway. The few times he'd seen her shed tears. they'd been for other people. It made him sick. And angry. "No, you don't look fine to me." He said, reach into his pocket for his handkerchief and handed it to her. "Here, honey. Dry your eyes and what are you hiding from your father?"

She dabbed at her eyes, looked at him thoughtfully for a moment. At this point, she couldn't hide anything anymore. "It's over, Dad. I and Mathew broke up."

Surprised, he asked. "So what's the big deal between the two of you that you had to come to this way?"

She pulled herself together enough to tell him everything that had happened, sparing nothing. He looked totally shocked. "Oh, God. That's awful."

Mathew had cheated on her and what was wrong with Shirley? How could she do a thing like that to her employer and friend? He was disgusted with them both, and sorry for Smiling. It was a terrible blow. He pulled her into a fatherly hug. "What a stupid, rotten thing for him to do. He wasn't the man I had thought him. And how could Shirley?" He said practically. "You don't have to shed tears for such traitors." He was livid and Smiling laughed through her tears.

"Yeah, that's pretty much what I think too." She said, blew her nose and wiped away tears.

"Why didn't you tell me? It must have been terrible for you to go through all this alone." He looked sympathy.

"It was too much to tell you on the phone. I wanted to wait till I saw you. So there it is. Not a pretty story."

"What about Shirley? What are you going to do with her?"

Shirley's betrayal weighed heavily on her too. She saw clearly her true nature. Looking back at what happened, Smiling couldn't understand how she had trusted her so completely, and over the years developed so much faith in her, that she blindly did whatever Shirley told her. She thought that Shirley had been making her life easier and protecting her. Instead, she was the silent enemy in their midst, stealing her trust, even sleeping with her fiancé.

"I don't need her to work for me anymore. She's the person I've trusted most in the world for many years. I can't imagine she slept with Mathew, and for how long? With that grounds I guess I can fire her. It's not a happy thing to do, but I have had the heart to deal with it."

"Good, what about Mathew? Did you talk to him?" He asked her quietly. He was very sad about him and he could see that his daughter was too.

Nothing was easy right now, and hadn't been in well over a month, nearly two, since she moved out. Even though she knew that Mathew was apologetic, but she still couldn't accept it, because it happened so quickly. She met his eyes with an effort. "Not really. I must see him since it happened, but I don't want to. And I'm afraid," she admitted in a whisper.

Afraid that I'm not over him, that he'll beg her for forgiving his ignorance, and I'll do that. Her thoughts run on. "I'm still reeling over Mathew."

He knew immediately what she was thinking. "What are you going to do about the Milan Swim-lingerie Summer show with him?"

Her father was genuinely concerned, because he knew her fashion show schedule. And that question reminded her of their last conversation on the phone.

✿⋆✿

"Smiling, you can't be serious. That's crazy. This is about our career not our love life."

"That's right," she said coldly. "And both are over. I am no longer in the mood to work with people who betray and deceive me." She sounded bitter, but she was tired after a long day, and still hurting over what he'd done. "Do you realize what you're going to cost us both?"

"That's too bad, Mathew. Maybe you should have thought of that before you slept with my assistant for how long which proved that you didn't really expect me to work with you anymore."

"You thought wrong about me. Can't we separate the two parts of our lives? We do such great work together. You can't erase everything just because you can't forgive my mistake."

"No, it was you who caused it. Let's be clear about this. I won't work with you again. I have fulfilled my contract."

"Look, Smiling. I know you're still mad at me. I'm sorry. I was wrong. You don't deserve that consequence. But our careers have proven the point that we are inseparable."

"That point of view is now outdated, Mathew. Either of us can develop our own career. Besides, you've got Shirley. I completed the last contract and that's it." He suddenly panicked about it, once she made up her mind, she would do it. Besides, he also knew how principled and fair a person she was. Combined with her stubborn temperament, he knew he couldn't convince her. There was no moving her off her position now, although he hoped she might reconsider it later, but he doubted she would. And then he thought of something else.

"I still love you, Smiling, even if I screwed up. I will prove it to you again."

"I don't expect that from you. Time will help us overcome this situation. That's all I have to say about it. Thanks for your call. Take care." And with that, the phone went dead in his hand.

✲✲＊✲✲

"I will never cooperate with him again. I told him that last time when I finished that last show with him. And that was it. End of partnership and romance."

"I'm sorry about that. Everything is not as expected," her father said, touching her cheek with his hand. "You two were so crazy about each other, in a lot of ways. I always thought he was such a good guy, and can't figure out why he could do such things. You were everything to him. But anyway, people like him now, just throw away, don't mourn. If he cheated on you, maybe this is a blessing in disguise," he said, trying to cheer her up, but she wasn't ready for that yet.

"I'm little tired of this kind of blessing, the ones in disguise. I like the ones that sound like good news, not the ones that break my heart."

"I know, I know. But if the relationship ended, it might free you up so you can meet someone who truly loves you, and takes care of you for the rest of your life." He said convincingly, although Mathew hadn't been that for her, but he had been very important to her. They had been comfortable and happy, and she had loved him a lot. "Only then, I'll rest in peace."

"That's the lasting I want," she said somberly. "I'm sure I'll be happy, don't worry, dad. But I think I'm done, and I thank my lucky stars that I wasn't foolish enough to marry him. Now, I just want to spend time to treat my heart wound.

"Good. That's right. At least you weren't married to him. So there won't be much legal trouble and complications. And you never bought any property together. That's always a disaster when things go sour, and you have to take it all apart." He had always told her not to, and she had listened to him. Her father gave good advice. "I think you ought to fire Shirley immediately," he added. He was furious with her. Smiling was less angry than deeply hurt.

She was profoundly wounded by what Shirley had done, her affair with Mathew and her lied for years. "Life never happens as we wanted it to be," she said sadly. "I'll deal with her on Monday officially." She couldn't imagine life without Shirley either. They had worked together forever. Thirteen years, it was almost like a marriage. They were best friends, as well

309

as employer and employee. And Shirley made her life run so smoothly. It was chaos now. She didn't have heart to look for a new assistant either. Her whole life seemed to be upside down and broken to bits, like her heart. "My lawyers are doing it. She will get the letter by e-mail. And they'll send a hard copy to her home address."

That would be a relief too. She wanted to get Shirley away from her now, any vestige of their friendship and trust had been destroyed, and in spite of that she'd to fake it for two months. Now all she wanted to do was get it all behind her and never see Shirley again. She didn't allow herself to think of the friend she had lost, or what she had done to her.

Seeing her silent, her father asked her about the Winter Fashion Show was coming up soon in Miami, and he wondered if she was going. "How do you plan to do about it?"

"Like I said, Dad. I don't want to do and run into anything with them, especially with Mathew," she explained as his betrayal weighed on her like a concrete suit. "My lawyers will communicate about business issue. And during this time, I'll come up with new designs and sketch many new fashion models from home, and then working with mom to compete their brands with our own production. And because they're new styles of the spring collection designs. I want to send them to few exclusive boutiques I sell to and see how they go before I take a risk putting them into the show. I can give them a trial run before I commit myself to other buyers."

He grinned to agree, particularly if the other woman was with Mathew. "Anyway, it's a good thing that you come back here to develop our family's business."

She nodded. "Isn't that what you and mom always want me to do?"

He smiled at that, feeling some of the worry evaporate. "But the best thing is you should get them out of your system once and for all. Memories are dangerous, you know. And although, I don't know what your future looks like, but I will stand by you."

"Thank you," she brushed a kiss on his cheek. "I'll try, dad." She hoped it didn't take too many years.

"Next time something bad happens to you, don't wait to tell me," He admonished. "Now, go take a shower and rest, if you need anything, let me know." He kissed her on the cheek, and left her house a little while after that.

※ ☀ ✳ ⁂ ※

His mind was restless and heart full of worries on the way home, and as soon as he got home, he immediately told Tommy. "Jennifer's pretty shaken up. She needs companionship and protection."

He was talking about Smiling and couldn't help but care, Tommy asked. "What's happened to her, sir?"

Brian heaved a gentle sigh. "Her fiancé is cheating on her, and apparently, he slept with her assistant, whom she considers her best friend and who worked for her for thirteen years. Nice people and people in her position are such targets for every kind of bad behavior, exploitation. What happened is the biggest shock in her life. She needs time to get over it. That's why I want you're moving into her house tomorrow as a watchman guard and look after her for me."

Tommy stared at his boss solemn face on the rear mirror. What he was asking of him sounded difficult and uncomfortable, and while he tried to decide whether or not he'd misunderstood him.

"You heard me," he said, reading the question in Tommy's eyes. "If you're obviously living with her, Smiling will accept, and besides, her ex-fiancé won't dare make a pass at her."

Being in the house with Smiling was asking for trouble, big time for himself. "I understand, sir," Tommy replied. "But do you think I have to actually stay with her? I can call trusted agents come to protect her."

There was only man he trusts with his life was Tommy. "I appreciate your honesty. But I think it's best if you're where you can keep an eye on her, at least for the time being, also prevent others from hurting her again." Brian said. "Please help me. I'm begging you."

Tommy thought a long moment, but gave no reply to his boss, he seemed to acknowledge that none was necessary, and he generally stayed out of other people's business. Besides, he understood what Mr. Brian meant and why he should want to be involved. He knew very well that one of the quickest ways to become vulnerable to someone else was to become concerned with their problem. With the military had instilled in him a sense of loyally, and he, upon joining Jefferson family, had transferred that loyally to Mr. Brian. "But Miss Jennies, Bush Jr your entire family, what are they going to think?" Tommy countered to his silence. "Everyone will know!"

"It would hardly be effective if it's a secret," Brian reminded him. "If you're worried about that or afraid of what people will say, you needn't be.

You must have noticed by now that you're not my employee. You're our family. They will understand and know better."

Tommy hoped. He was overcome by a strange mix of worry and anticipation as considered just how he'd do that. "But what about her?" he asked. "Will I tell her the truth?"

"You might as well when the right time. However, keep that between you and me now. I'll call to let her know you're coming. Do what you can do, and keep in touch."

Knowing that he couldn't refuse, he nodded to accept the assignment of task. "Yes, sir. I'll be there, and I'll do what I can."

It was like entrusting Tommy with his daughter, but he knew what's good man he was, and something in his voice and what he had said to him told him that he cared about her. That made him relief. "Good, I'm glad you handle this for me, son. This is personal, and like I said, she's physically, mentally and emotionally exhausted, also she needs to focus on the other important stuff, too. So no matter what happens, I'll accept it, as long as Smiling can stabilize her mind."

Tommy understood what happened, then quickly reassured him. "You don't have to worry about that, sir. She will be safe with me. I promise."

On the way of our life, everyone has moments of ups and downs, sometimes happy or miserable. But the most important things are we are surrounded by relatives and friends, reaching out to help others when they need it and receive help from others when we are having problem ourselves. "I know, son. And I really appreciate that." He said without giving it further thoughts. He knew Tommy would be in good hands with him. And if they developed feelings for each other, that's fine. Then he had a delight smile as he rushed off the car to enter the house himself.

Sitting alone in the car, Tommy closed his eyes, willing the image of Smiling's beautiful face from his mind and concentrating instead on everything his boss said about her. It sounded to him like she was facing a crumbling relationship with her fiancé and a personal betrayal from her assistant and was being mental breakdown on top of it. She hadn't had great luck with men, or made good choice perhaps. And yet she seemed like an extremely kind, decent woman and down-to-earth person. But she lived in a complicated world full of untrustworthy people, dishonesty and superficial values. He felt bad about how vulnerable she was to people like that. It was hard for some people to resist taking advantage, like her assistant. And he knew it couldn't easy for Smiling. His heart ached as he felt badly for her, and deep down, he knew the reason he was considering taking this task was Smiling. It was that simple and that complicated.

Chapter 27

Everything happens for a lot of reasons

Smiling was slowly adjusting to life without him and tried to put the past behind when she moved back to Florida. Being busy with work kept her mind off Mathew, but for thousandth time, she wondered about him and Shirley's relationship. How had it started? and cried every night when she returned home. Lying on her bed now and stared at the ceiling, she was thinking about it that day, and feeling the ache where her love for him had once been, and now it was all so painful. It had been that way for three months. She had only called Mathew once when she wanted to be making sure he got all his stuffs, and didn't want to contract him anymore since, but was having his lawyers call her and beg her to work on next show with him. Her cell phone took that moment rang. She nearly jumped and tried to ignore it. They could leave a voice-mail message, but she plucked it anyway from the mess of her bed, and recognized the number of the traitor, Mathew Neilson. Her heart beat a little faster, and she told herself to let the call go to voice mail. He betrayed you. Remember? There was nothing left to say. Her heart was in conflict between hate and love. But it's not good to rebuff. So finally, she made her choice by pressing the answer button. "Mathew, is there anything else to say?" She asked without preamble, hoping there was no trace of emotion in her voice.

She finally answered the phone. "I just wanted to hear your voice. It just seemed so important to me right now. At this point, I think you've calmed down, so I mustered up the courage to call and talk to you." "If you have something to say, just say it."

She heard his sigh before he spoke. "I miss you. How are you?"

"How would you expect me to be? You cause me a great deal of pain." She said honestly. She had no intention of letting him off the hook or easing his conscience. After almost four years living with him, she deserved better than she'd got from him in the end. "I'm falling apart and we have nothing to say to each other." At this moment, her tears could not be contained anymore, everything was falling apart.

He sighed as the tragic sincerity of her words hit him especially hard. He had regretted it terribly. "I know Smiling. I'm so sorry. I understand why you feel that way, but we shouldn't have ended up like this."

⁎⁎⁎⁎⁎

Tommy walked around the house, double-checking everything to see if there's anything wrong, as well as checking the security system which he'd been able to control some of the fear for her with a security company that patrolled her house from dark to dawn, a state-of-the-art alarm from the first day when he came to stay with her. The perimeter of the fence was wired to detect a breach, had placed motion detectors at every entrance and exit, all windows and with remote access in her hallway. That way, he controlled when the device was turned on and off and knew every time someone would break in. As well as he changed the codes every two or three weeks, just to keep the house more secure. For him it was necessary to be careful, even the smallest detail. He also brought a secure laptop, a portable security system, an extra weapon and some clothes. He didn't know how long he'd be here so he added some toiletries and stuff. When he was satisfied that everything was still secure, he went to the bar, making Smiling's favorite drink that made things easy for her. He put limes and ices to the shaker, adding tequila and the juice. As he shook the drink, he smiled to himself, thinking of her. Funny, he was here to do a job that he didn't want, but for the first time, he realized that staying with Smiling seemed natural and right, and how much he cared for her. She was no longer herself, being aggressive about everything, but looking for alcohol on its own. He could see her mood, but didn't ask anything. Just silently taking care her more. No wonder he was attracted to Smiling since she kissed him. It had been the flaw in his character to be attracted to vulnerable women. Or rather, she was changing his life. He hadn't been the same person. It was as though everything that had ever been important to him had abruptly been taken away. After three years, he hadn't been interested in another woman since his wife passing. And it was time to get over it. Maybe his interest in Smiling was a good thing, a signal that he was back to his old self. And yet he had to watch his step. He poured it into the glass then headed to her bedroom. When he went there, before, knocking on the door, he heard she was talking on the phone, and that made him stopped doing. Though his mind told him, respected her privacy by knocking or walking away, but his legs disobeyed, because of her angry voice. Every muscle in his body tightened, but if he reacted, the conversation would end. As much as it was a private family matter, he'd been pulled into this, and it was always to his advantage to know as much as possible about those who interacted around him. Besides, he knew that eavesdropping on the private conversations was rude. But the rules had changed. She was not as active and happy as before. He often put her on her bed when she wept and drunk at night, to lay awake if she slept. He knew the stories, the scandal. So, he just stood quietly by the closed door and listened.

⁂

"You should be. It was such a rotten thing to do to me, for the whole time we were together." Tears seemed to have dried up, now they were full again.

Hearing she sobbed, Mathew felt like a total bastard. If it was before, he never let her shed a single tear.

"I slept with Shirley," he confessed to her. "Which was extremely stupid of me. She tricked me into it. I swear she did it on purpose, while you were away. She wanted what you had, Smiling, even if that meant sleeping with me. And when I told her it couldn't be anything more than a one-night stand. She didn't take it well, because she's the one who's setting me up, and got me in her web and threatened me to tell you if I didn't keep seeing her. It was a miserable situation."

She suddenly chuckled, scornfully, just because he portrayed her as someone evil and himself as her victim and was absolving himself from all responsibility and blaming Shirley. Smiling thought he should have had more balls than that, and never gotten involved with her in the first place. She hadn't held a gun to his head after all.

Bewildered, he further explained. "I was upset with myself that I let it happen in the first place. But I didn't want her to do that. I thought I'd lose you, and I did anyway." His explanations were all about defending himself, not love. "Stop giving those bogus reasons. That makes me hate you even more."

"Yes, you're right. I was such a fool. This isn't her fault, or yours, I guess. It's mine. I did the wrong thing all the way." He said, sounding remorsefully.

"Yes, you did," Smiling agreed.

316

"Does everyone know what happened?"

There was a long pause, and then Smiling said. "What do you think I did? Just pretended we were okay?" "How did they take all this news?"

"They were shocked, and pretty pissed."

He was embarrassed to have her entire family know how badly he'd behaved. "I'm making a mess of this, but I want you to know that I'm really sorry."

Mathew regretted but refused to admit his mistake. His ego was so big, how could she accept it. "An apology doesn't solve any problem, when I lost trust, lost love. What is left to reconnect the old love?"

"Don't be that way, Smiling. You're just looking for an excuse." He sounded annoyed by what she'd said, and shocked. She'd never acted this way before. She was always independent, but he could hear that he'd hurt her with his adulterous affair with Shirley. He'd never meant to be unfaithful. But it had happened violently, passionately and treacherously. Because of that lust, he lost her trust, and he regretted it now. "I just wish I could turn the clock back, so you didn't have to deserve to suffer for my mistake. I hope you will forgive me. Is there any chance we can lay that to rest and start over?"

"Do you think it's really that simple?" She mocked. They had been so happy; they had been so close. They had considered themselves special, and among the lucky ones, touched by the hand of fate. And even, she'd tried to make him miss her, to make him regret ever cheating on her to the depths of his soul. But once a cheater, always a cheater. And didn't the ending taught her a lesson for life? "Do you think I should trust you after what you did to me, Mathew? I haven't heard from you in two months, and funny enough, that doesn't work for me anymore, the way it used to."

"I just gave you time to calm down." He explained, but knew that there was no way to undo it. He knew it now, much to his chagrin, that Smiling would never let him forget it. And perhaps he deserved that. He accepted his fate at her hands and always wished that there was some way to let her know how much he still loved her. "But hear this. I'll do whatever is necessary to make it up to you, if we start over and spend sometimes like the old times sake. We've always had such a good time together."

Damn Mathew for throwing away everything they'd worked for, and for sex with Shirley? Was it a ridiculous midlife crisis, or had he truly, completely stopped loving her to the point that all he felt was disdain? "Yes, we did, but I just can't do that, Mathew. Shirley would jump at the chance. Cause our love is over."

"No. You're a star in the fashion industry. That's what she hated about you. She wanted to be you. It didn't matter what she tried to do, she still couldn't be you. She didn't have your talent or your looks or all the things that makes you, you."

"Unfortunately, you realized these things and you still treat me badly."

"I know I can't do anything but ask you for your forgiveness. I love you, Smiling. I have determined in my heart that there's only you. It killed me when you left me. I need you in my life. I need what we'd planned to have together. We've got a second chance. All we have to do is take it."

She felt weak. Hurts could be healed, she knew that well. But even though the mirror was broken, trying to put it back together, still left scratches and cracks clearly visible. As well as all faith in him was gone. So, she didn't want to continue because of those sentences. "No, there aren't any second chances, Mathew. Do you understand what is most important in Love? Trust is more valuable than anything and it's not something you take on and off, like a hat, so just leave me alone."

Because he was still in love with her, he had to hold on. "You think that's a wise move? We belong together," he murmured. "Oh God, Smiling, we've always belonged together."

For his sake, for her own, she had to make him see and leave her. Pain flashed into her eyes before she controlled her expression. "You're wrong," she said flatly. "That was yesterday. Today our love of old days is dead. Now no matter what you say, it doesn't matter to me anymore." And there was nothing left to say except. "Take care, Mathew."

Mathew sighed and felt like a monster by the time she hung up. He didn't know how he had expected to end, he had considered calling back, but figured out he's got nowhere. Because he realized now that she clearly had no interest in giving him another chance, and probably, he'd never see her again. He wondered if there was someone else. But he knew now, if you were involved with two people and lie to one of them, this was what happened. *Sometimes the things that rob the happiness of us in our life are not catastrophic tragedies. But it is out of the trap of lust and desire. Desire doesn't always make us feel enough.*

✳✴✽✵✻

Disconnected the call and put down the phone, Smiling slumped back down on the bed, curling on her side, then buried her face in the pillow and wept. If Mathew really loved her then he should confess and repent, maybe she would forgive him and give him another chance. But on the contrary, he excused himself and blamed others. It's hard to get those thoughts out of her brain, but all she needed now was a glass of wine. And when she opened the door, she immediately distracted and startled. "For God's sake," she murmured, putting a hand over her racing heart and staring into Tommy's light blue eyes at the hallway. "Cut that out! What are you trying to do, give me a heart attack?"

Tommy tried to hurry down the hall before Smiling could catch him listening, but too late, and he froze, searching for the right words to explain as he watched her hand cover the spot where he presumed, her heart was pumping wildly. But her swollen red nose and see the mist of tears still clinging to her lashes, surprised him. And when she dropped her arm to her side, he immediately asked.

"Sorry, I didn't mean to. But what's wrong?"

Oh lord! How much of their argument had he overheard? "Nothing."

"But it seemed like you're crying."

A wave of heat washed up her neck. "Oh, yeah? What are you doing so sneaky like that?"

Her face drawn in irritation as if she was about to argue with him. He thought he about lying, making up some excuse. But her unstable mood and sad appearance forced him to ask. "Are you all right?"

"You just keep asking that." She said, resenting him.

"It's my responsibility."

Must and couldn't be denied that his concern warmed her and to break the tension, she pointed at what was in his hand. "What's that?"

Knowing it was important to talk, and this was going to take a while to explain. "I think you could use a drink I brought to you." He handed her the glass. "And I just wanted to check on you." He lied as if he had every right, and maybe he did after she came back here with downhearted.

It sounded like the truth, but she didn't quite believe him. "Is that so?" She laughed, trying for sarcasm. "Well, it doesn't need explanation, does it?"

Doubt was evident in her eyes. "I think it does." He said, motioned to the sofa. "Why don't you sit down?"

She wouldn't have obeyed, but the sharp snap of his voice warned her it would be less complicated if she did. "All right." Holding the glass, she stepped back, allowing him room to enter, and waited for her to sit down on the sofa, then took a sip of her drink to calm her anger.

"Better now?"

"Yes, I think so." She exhaled. "I hope so."

Tommy knew lying would be pointless. He joined her, sitting on one of the chairs perpendicular opposite her. How should he begin? Taking a deep breath, he explained. "You have a right to privacy. And I'm sorry. I didn't mean to invade your privacy, you know. As my job is eyes and ears, and I wasn't really eavesdropping, but I couldn't help but overhear."

No one bothered her, especially when she was alone. Until his presence in her life. At work, she did her job with Tommy at her heels. Like a trained guard dog, he was constantly by her side. He practically snarled when anyone came too close. At home, he invaded her privacy from time to time, bringing in the various drinks or Chinese specialties he knew she loved, and other tempting things to stimulate her failing appetite. One morning with a full breakfast which his own excellent chef had prepared and woke her from a sound sleep on the bed, after a night she had drunk to much whiskey on an empty stomach. Because at that time, she just wanted to drink. The wine was hard to drink, but when she got used to its taste, she found the pungent taste more pleasant than the tormented thoughts in her brain, and could dispel the pain in her heart. And he fed her every spoonful himself. It was such a thoughtful act. She had never felt more vulnerable in her life. And yet, silly as it was, Tommy's presence was comforting. Why did she feel like family with him? It was pleasant, comfortable and strangely warm. This feeling had never appeared in her before. And because it sounded so reasonable, she nodded. Still. "Okay, that explains why you take such a personal interest, but I think you carry it a bit too far. Because there are somethings you don't need to know."

He rarely argued with privacy, but he had to. So mixed up with everything Smiling made him feel. He remembered first time when he looked at the bottle of wine in her hand, the whole body stood unsteadily, and smelled strongly of alcohol, making him go to take it out of her hand and tried to catch her. But she pushed his hand away. "I can go. Don't pity me."

"Drinking too much alcohol is not good for your health. Let me help you to your room to rest."

She still won't let him help her. Just staggered away. After taking a few steps, one foot crossed the other, could not keep balance, so the whole her body fell down. He caught her, but accidentally, his hand embraced the side of her breast, the soft breast that fit in the palm of his hand like he got an electric shock. "Come on, Smiling. Why do you have to torment yourself like that?"

She looked at him with heavy eyelids. "I really can take care of myself. You don't have to worry about me."

"You're very drunk. Don't be stubborn to keep trying to argue." He said, and had no choice but picked her up, swinging her off her feet as deftly as if she weighed nothing, then carried her up to her room and put her on top of her bed and turned to leave, but he paused and looked back at Smiling curled up on the bed, still with her clothes and shoes on. This was a situation he'd never dealt with before. "Come on," he said softly as he stood at the end of the bed, picked up her feet, and removed her shoes.

She smiled, half asleep. "Look, Tommy, I guess I should thank you for helping me, but I really don't want your pity, Tommy."

"I don't pity you," he said, wondering how he could undress her more yet keep his sanity. "If I get your nightclothes, will you get into them?"
"Sure," she said and began to undress her dress.

"Wait, I'll go get it for you." With that, Tommy went over and rummaged through her chest of drawers and withdrew a long white nightgown of soft cotton trimmed with rows of lace, then he was lying it on bed when she was wearing only her lacy panties and was sound asleep.

Tommy's first thought was that he should leave the room, but he didn't. Instead, he lifted her to a sitting position, slipped the gown over her head, put her back down, then pulled the gown to cover her body. He folded the big coverlet over her and stepped back to look at her. At that night, alone in his bed, he thought he would never have believed himself capable of such a thing. Caring for her wasn't in the game plan. This was just another assignment. She was just another assignment. It had to be that way. But if he wasn't careful, this would turn into something much more than a job.

"I'm sorry, Smiling. I didn't mean to get any of it. It was an accidental eavesdrop."

It was a simple enough explanation, but not good enough. She took a bracing swallow of sweet and sour combined, and then put it down on the table, clearly still pissed off, but trying to make it easier. "In that case, forget about it. That's not your fault."

Maybe not directly but he felt guilty all the same. But tell her the truth that was his surveillance duty and under obligation to her now when she was already lit up with temper wouldn't help her. It would hurt her. It was the last thing he'd ever do. Hurting her would hurt him, too. At her silence, and rather than brood, he focused in on her, and would have offered her a smile, but she didn't look ready to sign any peace treaties. "How are you feeling, are you …?" "Total fine," she said. "Thanks for the drink."

He recognized the anger that was still darkening her eyes. He let out a sigh. "Look, I have no intention of snooping into your past, Smiling. I just want you to know that. But Smiling, are you and your fiancé... Did you...?" The sentence wandered away, unnerved by her calm brown eyes.

"Ex-fiancé," she corrected and responded. "And yes."

He knew that, of course. Still, whatever was going on between Smiling and her fiancé was certainly none of his business. He had no intention of becoming involved in her personal life. But since knowing her until now, everything related to her, he wanted to find out. After all, why? He didn't know. He just knew that there was some nameless feeling that urged him, wanted him to learn more about her private life. "You're not very kind to him. Do you mind telling me what happened?"

It was his voice, she thought, so calm, so persuasive, that nearly had her opening both mind and heart. She could almost believe as she looked at him that he really wanted to know, to understand. But could she trust her secret with Tommy? "You're funny, Tommy. My private matter has nothing to do with you, so why should I tell you?"

"I don't know. Maybe it's the look that comes into your eyes. It makes a man want to stroke it away. And could probably help."

Her chin came up a fraction. "There's no need to feel sorry for me."

"I don't think sympathy's the right word." Abruptly weary, and tired of trying to find answers, Tommy advised her. "Just let them out, Smiling. That might be the best solution."

"Yes," she stared at him. "But I can't. And you don't want to know."

Clearly it was a sensitive subject. Her hard look warned him not to press for more, but he was her bodyguard. Concerning to discover secrets was part of his mission, too. "For some reason I think I do. You know, you've prodded my curiosity. Also, that's something else we're going to work on."

He's challenging, and there's no easy way to talk it with him. But suddenly, she remembered the memories from the day they'd spent together in Miami before. And because Tommy not only her father's trusted associate, gained her trust, but also gained her trust as every instinct inside her told her this was a man, she could share it with him. This man, every gesture was very kind and gentle toward her. From her point of view, Tommy was a pretty complete man. He didn't make her uncomfortable. From almost the first minute, she'd felt as though she could talk to him, depend on him. He was a kind, considerate man. A smart, logical one, she supposed, or else he wouldn't be a bodyguard. He had a wonderful smile, eyes that paid attention, and handsome appearance, although he had been broken in marriage, but it was certain that this man was the focus of other talented young women. He seemed to understand her very well, her feelings he could see through, and he was right. It was better to tell him and have it done with. Gathering up her courage, she told him her entire embarrassing story.

He listened as she struggled to remember the details, put them in order when she explained about the argument with Mathew and found out about her assistance Shirley. There was so much emotion, huge waves of emotions. Anger, shock, a sense of betrayal and fear.

"Can you imagine how I felt when I saw them?" Emotion tremble in her voice as her eyes filled with tears quickly again, couldn't blind them away. They always did when she talked about Mathew.

Hurt, of course. He knew every moment of it would be painful that he could tell and hear it in her voice. Because he had a lot of experience with females who used flowing tears and gulping sobs as they were broken heart, just liked he knew what it was like to live with pain. And because of his concern, he hadn't noticed what she wore, or didn't wear. He did now. Her feet were bare, slender, with smooth, shapely calves and her thighs where she kept her knees and ankles pressed together.

It was dangerous to his libido, but he took in the rest of her in a loose, short-sleeves nightshirt that landed mid-thigh. The shirt wasn't snug, but he could still see her breasts, soft and full, beneath the thin material. Her hair hung over one shoulder, she hadn't been as careful with her makeup as usual, but she still looked good. Beyond good, he knew she was gorgeous.

But the pain in her eyes hurt him. Wanting to soothe or comfort her, but the best way was to let her face this pain. And in the courtly manner he could draw out without warning, Tommy rose from his seat, armed himself with a box of tissues and sat next sat to her.

"I can't imagine it." With gentle expertise, he mopped at her face, and because he felt a possessive need, he closed the distance between them, put his arms around her, and pulled her into a comforting embrace. He wasn't sure if his motives were suitable? Maybe somewhere deep inside him, he had believed that she needs a shoulder to lean on, and apparently so. She didn't resist as she wrapped her arms around his waist and laid her head on his chest. Hell, he wasn't sure of anything except at this moment, there was nothing more important to him than the woman he held in his arms. "If you needed to cry, go ahead and cry. I'll hold you. You're safe. I won't let anything bad happen to you. Not ever again."

Tommy understood the moment of her weakness, and he held her so close that she felt his breath mingled with her own. Over her back his hands rubbed gently, soothing and pressed his cheek against the top of her head. Along with his comforting words were her undoing. She wept in his arms, her body trembling as she released the pen-up emotions that so desperately needed release. "But sorry for him is one thing, blaming yourself for what he did, or for what happened to him is another."

His comment and the embrace were shockingly intimate that it took her a second to figure out what he was saying or doing. Strange how much pleasure the caress endearment gave. She couldn't explain why she suddenly felt so safe, why it seemed that as long as Tommy held her, nothing and no one could ever hurt her again. But she needed to stand on her own. She was the kind of woman who stood on her own feet and faced her own problems. She lifted her head and gazed up into his eyes. "You sound just like my mother. And that's the trouble."

"So, you're going to torment yourself for it?" He didn't know why the hell he asked her such a stupid question. wasn't the answer obviously? He should draw her away, but thought that it's better this way in his arms when she was soft and vulnerable. Even though, there was no passion, no fire, just comfort.

She'd been doing just that, Smiling realized as she was just inches away from his gorgeous eyes and his mouth. Love wasn't all it was cracked up to be. How long was she going to be miserable? Since she'd never really loved anyone the way she loved Mathew, and she hoped that phase one of getting over him was feeling sorry for herself, because she was now wallowing in self-pity.

"I'm dumbfounded now," she'd blamed herself for not preventing something she knew in her heart had been inevitable. She jerked back, unable to face him, and hastily looked down the floor. "I believe that if I tried hard, I would overcome it. I also believe the time is what heals all the sore wounds. I was wrong, and strangely enough, I can't set it aside."

He brushed a strand of hair away from her face. That's the first time he dared. He wondered if that was good or bad before he cupped her chin between his forefinger and thumb and lifted her face so that she couldn't avoid looking right at him. "I can look at you and see it. But what did make you can't?"

Yes, she was fighting over whether to let go and forgive Mathew? And imprint of his warm touches and gestures, as well as his sincere eyes, couldn't resist the entanglement. She sighed. "I can't tell you how many times I've asked myself the same question that I don't have the answer; except that I still love him too much to care."

Tommy frowned at her voice broke on the last word. "Yes, it shows." But the more answers he found, the more questions that arose. "Do you think his love will still be completely for you?" That was important for him to know.

"I don't know," she answered his question as honestly as she could. "But I think he'll do if I give him another chance."

It was easy to see that the relationship was broken, but equally so to see that Smiling wasn't ready to let it go. And it irritated him. "I think you're already made your choice. But don't be so stupid. In love, once a crack appears, if you still persist in being together, you will only end up hurting each other."

She hastily pushed him away from her, stood up and distanced herself from him. Talkative men were annoying. Sometimes. But God, why didn't Tommy annoy her? And she wanted him to know how she felt. "I understand your sincere advice," she said plaintively, tired of explaining it to everyone, and trying to justify it, even to herself. "But he was sorry."

Since she wanted to stay away from him, Tommy followed her, and suddenly she stopped in the middle of the room. He knew she still had feelings for Mathew. But he didn't trust Mathew, not at all, and he didn't want her continue clinging to someone who was obviously betraying her, and those thoughts would have to get out of her head quickly. He came forward from behind her, mere inches separating their bodies, but he didn't touch her. "Sorry doesn't change what he did."

"I know," she replied. Part of her hadn't grown past that day. And that part, the hurting part, wanted to bring him back. It's not true to say that she still loved him, but it's also wrong to say she no longer had feeling for him. It was something inside her that she didn't fully understand, but it was too strong to ignore. And what if she believes in him again, would he hurt her a second time? She would never survive. "But I'll do whatever is necessary to give up trying."

When someone hadn't loved you anymore, even you kept holding firmly and not let it go. You would still have nothing eventually and the one who got hurt the most. "Smiling," he took her arm. "Why won't you let go?" The sympathy he'd been feeling changed to a wave of anger rose up, against himself for getting caught up in someone else business, against Smiling for dragging him into it. "You should be wise. The man like that only makes you unhappy." And he regretted right away. Hell. He hadn't meant to say that last part aloud. It was too personal as her anger dissipated.

In defense, she slapped him hard enough to make his head snap back. He was hurting her now, but not his hand. The words cut her deeper. But his expressions didn't hurt at all. "That's my business," she snapped, more irritated with herself for reacting to his words than she was with him. "Don't give yourself the right to decide on my private affairs, as well as, don't tell me what to do or what I feel."

She turned away from him. But he caught her arm, then whirling her around, gripping her hand hard in the way that was both abrupt and proprietary. He no longer knew why his anger was so fierce, only that he was past the point of controlling it. And the emotions were running too high for two of them, but he was not going to let Smiling sway him.

"I don't blame you for being angry." Tommy said, released her hand, trying to control his temper. "Why don't you let go of the things you can't keep to keep the things you can't lose?"

This question made her think deeply. This was a difficult question that she couldn't answer for him. "You ask a lot question and don't get smart with me." She shouted at him. "I make my own decision. I run my own life, such as it is." Then dropped her eyes to stare at the floor again. She didn't want pity.

"So it is," he agreed. "But you don't make sense, Smiling. And even if you won't, you can't go back. I won't let you."

Her own mood quickly shifted from pity to annoyed, she jerked her head up, fought not to cry, but tears leaked from beneath her lashes anyway and slipped down her cheeks. "Don't. You don't have to say what I was thinking or doing. My father sent you here to protect me, to help me, not paying you to judge me and to insult me."

Every word out of her mouth seemed to upset him. Yes, he was paid by her father to protect her, and he's trying to keep his boss happy. There was nothing personal here. And he didn't mean to say that. But seeing her eyes swam in tears again that was made him angry. He could fight her anger, but he couldn't fight her tears. So, he pushed away the anger. Anger had nothing to do with what he was feeling now, instead, something comforting. Calm down, he drew her against him and let her sob out the pain. "I'm sorry if I overstepped with my concern," he said apologetically. "I have no right to tell you what to do or influence what decisions you should make about. But for God's sake, I don't fake feelings when I care a great deal and I'm simply giving you advice, not to humiliate or hurt your feeling but out of the feelings of someone who doesn't want you to get hurt again."

Feeling the sincerity of his apology, and the words he spoke immediately knocked down the wall surrounding her, causing her temper to disappear as quickly as it had arisen, and wondered fleetingly if his concern was genuine or if he was just fulfilling his duty. Taking a deep breath, she stepped back and look at him. "I understand, and I'll keep that in mind." She said, understood the implications that he hit some nerves in her. But she wouldn't admit it to him.

"When you realize it, don't forget that you're an intelligent and strong woman, Smiling. You've had a shock, a bad one, but promise me that you must not fall."

She couldn't summon the pride to draw her away or to seek a private place as she'd always done in times of crisis. He didn't speak to tell her everything would be fine; he didn't murmur quiet words of comfort. He was simply held her and encouraged her. But there was more, something in his eyes, in his voice that she wondered, and wishing she could know. She reached up and her sad eyes stopped where the slap had the red mark. She felt regret, touching that place. "I understand your concern," she said seriously. "Shedding tears could make me weak. But no, I won't fall apart."

Despite his good intentions, his gaze shifted, and he found himself observing her firm nipples pressing against the material of her T shirt. He couldn't help himself to calm her, until she had to look at him. "This is a mess, and you have to face it. But it doesn't have to be like this" He reminded her and pondered. He'd protect her, protect her in every way he could. "And to be honest, I won't let anything else happen to you. It's not going to work for me around to see you like this." He caught her waist under her shirt, then holding her hand in place against his chest.

This chest area of his was really strong. "No! I can take care of myself." She jerked her hand away and tried to take a step backward to fight her rising panic, but his hand was strong, holding hers so tight that she couldn't move, and his features set. "You needn't feel obligated to look after me. There's absolutely no reason for you to worry about me."

That wasn't smart, and his concern, apparently, was something she didn't want. "I'm sure you're very capable of taking care of yourself. But already you're showing me signs that you'll step into a situation that could possibly be more miserable than you're aware."

His gaze held hers, and for the first time she saw some deep emotion he hid, a flicker of desire in his dusky blue eyes. "Therefore, you worried me that I can't."

Without moved her head, Smiling shifted. "Can't what?"

Tommy knew that Smiling had loved Mathew and that he had hurt her badly because Smiling had cried her heart out on his shoulder one night after too many whiskey sours on an empty stomach, one those rare occasions when she drank hard liquor. But he'd never learned exactly what Mathew had done to her to cause her so much pain. All he knew was that whatever the cost, he'd never let Mathew hurt her again or he'd fight whoever stood in his way to keep her. Even if it was Smiling herself who stood there. "I can't ease your feelings about it, but let it go with wind. You should not let your pain of yesterday at beginning of every day or every dawn.

She lowered her gaze to the strong hand holding hers, then up to his eyes. He didn't look as if he were kidding. His face showed nothing of what he felt, and his eyes were haunted. But beyond that, his rapid shift of moods left her baffled and upset. She wondered; did men behave in this inexplicable manner all the time? And if they did, how did a smart woman handle it? She had a feeling it would take a long time to learn. "You're a nuisance. Has anyone ever mentioned that?"

That made him smile. "Once or twice," Tommy said. "Smiling, I just trying to get you to see the possibilities. So, I won't back out."

She felt the sting and accepted it. She'd never expected knowing Tommy to be painless and she asked seriously. "By holding my hand?"

He stared down at their linked hands, intended to keep it. But he released her hand, only put them on her shoulders. "That's just a side benefit of my job. You worry me." He repeated, then feeling greatly daring, he slowly slid them down her arms to her waist, sliding his gaze from the change in her eyes to her lips curved, just enough he felt bereft.

She felt a shift in the atmosphere, she suddenly knew he was going to kiss her. Before she could think twice, both of their face was shortened by him, until their lips touched each other.

He meant for it to be quick kiss on her forehead and cheeks and must have tasted the salt of her tears to comfort. But instead of ending the kiss as he'd planned, he sank in, tasting the softness, feeling the heat rush over him like a fiery wave.

Her body went rigid from shock. She could have resisted. She meant to. But this kiss was filled with indescribable emotions. She didn't respond, just popping her fist against his ribs, not holding but not protesting, or intended to push him away. Because, it meant nothing. Could mean nothing. No heat, no desire, but fear and anger become more confused with passion, and knowing if she didn't free herself quickly, she'd be lost again. Somehow, he seemed to know that her struggle was against herself, not him. And because she waited too long, in the next second, she felt his mouth demanded both submission and response. Begin slowly, gently, testing them both.

The way he kissed her at the night in the past went beyond trying to make a point. They had unfinished business, and he couldn't wait to finish it this time. He held her closer. His mouth demanded more, until, despite fears, despite doubts, despite everything, she gave. Stop! She'll hate you afterward, she'll hate you forever. You're one of the good guys, so you absolutely would not take advantage of her. She's also Jennifer Jefferson, you idiot!

He hated the nagging voice that persisted in his brain, working its way through the fog of lust, then let go of her lips, but he still wouldn't let go of his arms. "I'm simply trying to protect you. You are my only concern." He murmured the words against her mouth, then again when his lips pressed to her throat. "That includes taking care of you when you need it. I do nothing out of a sense of obligation. Especially not with you."

She lifted her head, met his eyes, finding nothing more than a patient kind of amusement. It was as though some memory was stirring inside her. This wasn't the first time, she thought. This man, his breath, his face, his body were familiar to her. She knew him. She knew how he worried about living up to the heavy responsibilities that had been placed on his shoulders. He worried about her and her family. If anything happened to her, she knew his soul would go with hers. How did she deal with him now? She could handle the arrogance, the flamboyance, even the demands. But how did she deal with the kindness? "I don't understand you."

"Why? Because I force things out of you that you don't want to admit, not even to yourself."

"You sounded as if you did. As if you only came to me because you felt you have to." She tried to pull away from him, but he held her fast.

He knew the way he felt for her. He had known it for some time. But she belonged to someone else, and that would never change. He managed to block those thoughts. He couldn't leave until this situation was completely over and he knew for sure Smiling was safe. "I did what I thought was best," he admitted. "And because you're not fighting me. You're fighting yourself."

True. "I never thought about it." She admitted. She'd never experienced anything like the sensation that had rammed into her because of Tommy. It was more than physical. She could admit that now. Still, it made no sense. But at least her battle with him had helped her over the grief. It was hard to be sad when your temper was being constantly pushed to the boiling point. "Tommy, I'm sorry being a bitch and we can talk about this later, okay? My mood is unstable right now. I need some time alone." Her voice to be strong, but it trembled. She wanted to escape from the sensation that she was completely helpless. "And I want you go away now." She commanded him, hoping that Tommy understood her responsibility as the boss.

He would, because she needed privacy, but he had never abandoned a woman in distress. He was happy to give Smiling all the privacy she wanted, so long as he could make sure she was all right in the end. Beside he knew she was lying, and he hadn't taken offense and thought she was serious. "Believe me. That's not a problem. But how can I when your mood is unstable?" he burst out. "And yes, you want me to leave just as much as you want me not to."

Damn him, how he always seemed able to read her mind. She wanted him to get lost and leave her alone, but she couldn't. He'd been nearby when she'd needed him, she didn't know his motives, but she doubted they were pure. She'd thankful to have his strength, his presence during her suffering for love, though she was certain she could have handled the situation herself. "I appreciate the thought. And yes, I love having you here."

Her admission told him that he'd nailed it. "If you said so, then please understand why I'm saying that because I have ulterior motives," he assured her. "I don't want to see you're trapped forever. But I can't protect you from life, no matter how much I might want to. There's something called trust in any worthwhile relationship. You've been making your own decision for a long time, Smiling. It's time I'm making one for you. And if you let me, I could help your scars heal."

Tommy's expression was so earnest, he was so deeply concerned, but how could he? "I'm not your responsibility."

"Aren't you?" He said simply with some measure of control. "But can you see I want you to be happy, Smiling? Happy and safe. That's all that matters."

"Why?" she asked quietly and searched his eyes deeply while she waited for him to answer her.

"Because every time I see you cry over someone who's hurting you, and how much you'd been holding it in. It cut me off at the knees. I knew I'd do anything for you."

She looked away from him for a moment. "You're confusing me."

"How can you're confusing for what I go through every day with you? To be so near you yet not to be allowed to touch you and said comforting words. It tears me apart. I lie awake at night, in the room so close to yours, and dream of going to you, and pulling you into my arms." These sentences, whether accidental or intentional had a hidden meaning. Only who spoke would understand, but the listener was completely blind. And then he could restrain himself no longer, he wrapped his arms around her and pulled her close.

In response, she wanted to push him away, but the familiarity of this man prevented her movement. She put her face up to his. "Tommy," she whispered, but maybe because she didn't resist, he didn't let her speak as his mouth closed fast over her warm, soft and pliant lips.

The panic came first, a choke hold that snagged the air from her throat. Simply she wasn't prepared to meet it, and she knew in her heart that she should stop him. But avoidance of Tommy hadn't helped her so far. The intensity in his never altered, and she knew he was absorbing her mood and testing it.

He knew it was madness to want her this way, to forget his priorities, but it was already too late. And each time, it was a little sweeter, a little sharper, a little more difficult to forget. He was about to cross a threshold from which there was no return. And life would never be the same.

She struggled against him again, and more frightened than she'd been. She wanted to pull back, to shove him away and prove that he meant nothing to her, but her furious protest was lost, and so on, letting his kiss toke her breath away, letting his arms tighten, and as every coherent thought in her mind tumbled out and scattered. Why was she clinging to him when she knew deep in her heart it was wrong and crazy? Why did his touch thrill her as no one else had? But it didn't matter, because she was drowning, and she knew she couldn't save herself. Drowning in sensation, in longings, and desires. Equally strange how quickly she forgot Mathew, letting herself go astray. In a trance, she felt his hand slipped under her sleeping shirt, hesitated then claimed her breast with the swift experience. This was more than temptation, more than surrender. Her sadness, her guilt, her regret, her fears; all disappeared. What she felt now wasn't a need to give but a need to take as she moaned against his lips.

And her cooperation was a great deal more difficult to resist than her protests. He lost himself in her and experienced the shock of being helpless to do otherwise.

Her lips were like a flower petal, light as silk in the breeze, bringing with it a lovely fragrance, it was like the faint sunlight filled the bottom of his heart, and he was infatuated with the sweet feeling that she gave to him. He grabbed, gently penetrated, took away the sweetness in her mouth.

So was she. The intense sweetness pushed her heart to make it vibrate. The fist she'd struck him with relaxed, and her open fingers slid around, up his back, hooked possessively over his shoulder, let the kiss deepen. Until she began to lack oxygen, pushed him away, then he just let go and shifted back. They stared at each other in the dim light, two strong-minded people who'd just had their worlds tilt under them.

"Your manners continue to be crude," she managed and fell back on dignity. "Do you know what you're doing?"

"It was mostly to shut you up," he answered, could still see the dregs of passion in her eyes, still feel it vibrating from her, or himself. "I'd apologize if I'd read you wrong, but it changed."

But she saw it, that tiny flicker of passion that he tried vainly to hide. "Yes, and it was my fault as much as yours. I should stop you, but I didn't. Oh!"

To her surprise he pulled her back, strong arms surrounded her and his mouth, hard and unyielding, pressed firmly over hers. She opened her mouth to protest, but his tongue slid past her lips and beyond the barrier of her teeth.

Her resistance fled. Common sense failed her as his tongue touched hers, explored the roof of her mouth and a thrill, hot and wanton, swept through her blood.

From gentle persuasion, there was no urge to devour or possess. But the kiss quickly escalated into a dark, moist mysterious invitation that he could feel the desire growing and his blood roaring through his veins. Blindly. Recklessly, his hands moved over her thin cotton nightshirt, and dipped beneath the hem to explore naked skin and subtle curves, then reaching one hand up, touching her breast, tested the size, and felt her nipple harden beneath his palm.

She shuddered, knowing that he wanted her as much as she wanted him.

He wished he'd never touched her, never kissed her, causing now he wanted her so much. "Smiling, my mind is not clear right now, and you have no idea how much I want to have sex with you and damn the consequences?" He admitted to her ear, and the words were torn from him that he urged her to step back, until she bumped and sat down on the edge of her bed close by.

While following him, a thousand warning bells rang through her mind as she realized what was about to happen. She stared up at him. "Tommy, please..." she whispered, but her words caught in her throat. Yes, she was fighting herself. She had to fight herself before she could fight him.

He saw the confusion on her face, but he also watched the shock and arousal flare in her eyes. "Stop holding yourself away from me," he whispered and guided her very gently to lie back on her big, comfortable bed. "And there's a lot I haven't shown you. But I need to hear you say you want me."

She had always felt disgust when she'd heard that because no man had come close to making her forget herself for even a second. But Tommy did. Dear God! She was weak where he concerned. So damn weak. All she could do right now was feel when her body so willing and her mind losing hold fast. "Yes. So, do your will."

In hearing it, sweet pain spread through him. They understood that there could be no more waiting. Finally, the moral barrier was removed, instead with madness and heaven became one. He slid down her body then his mouth found her again.

The feel of him on her body, of his delicious heat, of his tongue darting into it, taking possession and avid. And driven by her own demons, she immediately opened for him, greedily taking what was offered, selflessly giving what was demanded, and making her own small, desperate sound of need. She couldn't fight, it was too devastating with her too.

They forgot everything in each other's arms, and regardless of the consequences as he felt his already stiff cock was ready to satisfy lust which he'd thought was long dead.

She arched once in defense, in desperation, but it wasn't a moment of protest as the pressure was building in her the same explosive was it built in him as his tongue thrust slowly, deeply into her mouth with a demanding pressure that made her body curl into his. This was a lover's kiss that had kindled fires her body that she hadn't dreamed of. It had faintly shocked her to find out how passionately she could respond to him. She'd never felt that way with Mathew. In all honesty, she'd never felt that way with Tommy either. It was just that things between them had heated up so quickly and unexpectedly in their short time together and had become so unexpectedly complicated. Want me, she seemed to say. Want me for what I am. Her tongue mated anxiously with his, touching, exploring, and her fingers were light against his back while his hands were roaming, finding all the secret places. She'd known his strength before, but this was different.

His hands didn't press. His fingers didn't grip. They skimmed, they traced, they weakened. But she didn't flinch when he tried to discover them, and instead she moaned softly as her body arched in reaction, there was only pleasure. Waves of it.

She was wild beneath him, but no longer in resistance. Every moment was a demand that he takes more, give more and bolder, no longer hesitate. His fingers inched up her ribs, cup the underside of her breast, found her nipple and gently rolled it between his thumb and finger.

Don't do this! While you still can. She doesn't know what she's doing! She's reaching, damn it. She'll hate you in the morning and you'll regret what you're about to do for the rest of your life!

Don't trust how you feel. Trust what you know. But he didn't heed. His body was aflame with long banked desire that had been quiet for so many years. Now it came upon him again like a torrid wind through thin glass, destroying all his defenses. With a desperate groan, he stripped her of her nightshirt, ripping the buttons from their holes as the seams of the soft fabric gave way. Then his gaze glued to the mounds of her full breasts. They were soft and firm, with erect pink nipples that pointed eagerly upward, rising and fall with her rapid breathing. A beast inside him that had been caged too long, he bent his head and began kissing and taking her rosy peaks, one by one, into his mouth. That made she drew in a swift breath. Leisurely, as if he were drinking his fill, he teased and suckled at her nipples, tasting of their sweetness, ignoring the fire in his loins as he leaves all of her. She was anxious and hot, more than willing, and wearing only a tiny pair of blue bikini panties. No man alive could have resisted it; any man alive might have wished for it.

Desire thundered through his brain, racing in electric currents through his blood when he felt the shirt rip away from his back. And just as slowly, just as ruthlessly, just as devastatingly, he slid lower, letting his tongue trace a path from her breasts to her navel, rimming the small indentation and feeling her hard, flat abdomen against his face, then lap at the subtle curve just above the lace.

Wherever his lips went, bringing his hot breath there. She leaned in for him to touch her closer. She wanted this. There was no denying it now, not when this feeling drove her crazy, unable to escape, wanting to experience an intimacy she'd refused to allow herself. "Tommy."

When she called out his name, he vowed to bring her the thrill and the glory of madness. He kept working his way, slipped beneath the waistband of her panties then exploring the soft curls and the hot moist cleft between her legs through the lace.

She gave a sharp cry again as he touched the most feminine part of her, and twisting the body to feel the ecstasy of lust. No one had ever made her feel this way. It terrified her. It delighted her. It was easy, almost too easy, to forget the rules she had set up for their relationship. There was only now and the way her body experienced explosions wherever he touched, wherever she wanted him go on touching. With a murmur of confuse pleasure, she offered more. "Oh... please... Make love to me."

With something between an oath and a prayer, he pulled on her panties with his teeth, deftly removing them before inching back up her legs with his mouth.

She was completely naked, but she didn't feel vulnerable. She felt invulnerable and understood why as her fingers found and unbuttoned the buttons of his shirt, quickly pushed the soft cotton fabric off strong shoulders and down long arms, then tossed the shirt to the floor. But she hesitated at the waistband of his jeans, and he held her hand.

No hunger had ever been so acute, so edgy and keen, as this for her. He only knew if he didn't have her, all of her, he'd die from waiting. He unbuckled his bell, and once the zipper was sliding down, he kicked off his jeans, then removed his boxes with the speed of light. Naked at last, he rubbed gently against hers.

The heat of flesh on flesh ragged through her like a firestorm. Her hands and mouth were no less impatient than his. Her needs no less brutal. At once, her curious fingers touched the magnificence of his erection and heard him moan with deep hungry pleasure as she whispered into his ear. "Is it safe?"

He propped on his elbows, staring down at her with lust-glazed eyes. "S-safe?"

"You know... precaution."

He didn't expect that at this moment, she would still keep her mind so clear. Yes, she was right. They couldn't risk making love without precaution. "With you? Yes." He said, but wanting her to continue to touch him, and moved to slide next to her, giving him access to her body. With his hand dipped between her legs, and his fingers gently separate her two petals, then teasing.

Every time his fingers delved into her moistness, making her groaned, and her hips thrusting upward, anticipating. Until she couldn't take it anymore, she had to beg him to take her. "Get the condom, Tommy."

He flashed her a devilish grin and his blue eyes danced irreverently. "Yes, ma'am."

As soon as he got up and fumbled hastily for the foil packet he kept or hidden in his wallet buried deep in there, she wrapped the pillow in her arms, hugged it to her chest, and watched he tore the condom open with his teeth and rolled it on.

The bed sagged when he returned to her. He tugged the pillow away, and she didn't resist. She rolled onto her back; her gaze locked on his. And soon he moved between her thighs and stretched on top of her.

His knees parted her legs impatiently, poised for entry, and he hesitated for moment, staring down at her innocent, beautiful eyes staring up at him with infinite trust and hunger, her lips parted in desire. At that precarious moment he hated himself. For what he'd done to her, for what he'd done to himself, for that frightening and overpowering need to claim her in a way as primitive as the very earth itself. Yet he couldn't stop himself. In that heartbeat when he should have told her that they would never have a future together, that it would end up hurting them.

"Christ, I should be hung for this," he growled, before his lips claimed hers again, strong arms held her hard and possessively. His entire body tensed and he groaned savagely, thrusting his erection into the slick, hot softness and comfort that she so willingly offered. She was tight, hot and wet and as her body grew accustomed to his size and length. He stayed completely still inside her and groaned from the sheer bliss as he watched her face twisted in pleasure and she gasped while her fingernails digging into his shoulders. He took her from there, with more care than he'd ever shown a woman.

He showed her what it was to burn and was very delicate, noticed her every move. She frowned a bit, he would immediately slow down, making her even more excited.

He tried to go slowly, meant to, but she wrapped her legs around him, moved her hips to his rhythm, driving him deeper. "Don't stop!"

He was helpless to refuse as she felt so good and hanging on to his control by a thread, he started to move. Out and then in, letting his animal urges take over in the rhythm increasing.

She moved with him, danced the intimate dance of lovers.

It had been so long. He tried to wait and wherever he could draw in the taste of her while they moved together in merciless, driving rhythm. But he couldn't, and within a few more short strokes, her mouth couldn't help but groan loudly, then bit his shoulder as she came swiftly, and the hot spasms pouring through her body drove him over the edge. He gripped her hips, braced them, then drove them both hard and fast.

He cried her name, throwing back his head and spilled himself into her while she clung to him with her body shaking, and he fell against her, breathing hard.

Long seconds passed and neither of them moved. Staying clutched, joined and shuddering. When he felt her grip slacken, her hands slide weakly down his back, he kept his weight on his elbow, bent and kissed her softly one last time, then lifted away and settle himself beside her. For several moments, neither of the spoke, thinking about what happened.

She closed her eyes, waiting for the shame to come, and the self-disgust. But there was only the soft, lingering glow of pleasure. She could have told him she'd never intimate with a man so quickly. Or that she'd never felt so in time, so close to anyone, as with him. But there didn't seem to be a point. What was happening to them was simply happening. This was sex.

He rested his forehead against her shoulder a moment as a thousand questions went on in his head, a thousand contradictions struggle within him. For the love of God, he'd had sex with Smiling. A woman could make him weak, even he found that making love to her was bittersweet. As perfectly attuned as they had been in bed, as sweetly erotic and wickedly demanding as the night after. But this wasn't supposed to happen. He'd crossed the forbidden threshold, and sooner or later he'd have to face up to what he'd done. Oh, Jesus, what was he going to do? Disgust scraped at his soul. Guilt tore a hole in his heart, sighing he moved away her warm, naked body long enough to deal with the condom and thought what could he say to her?

And when he returned the bed where he'd left her and stared at the ceiling, appalled by what he'd found inside himself. "I'm sorry, Smiling," he said, wracked with shame.

"Why are you sorry?" she asked, looking truly puzzled. "For what?"

"You. I took advantage of your trust and hurt you," he said, racked with a kind of remorse. "That wasn't what I'm supposed to be doing."

How quickly warmth could turn to chill. She closed her eyes, felt cheap, and hurt by his defection. *It's true that when the fire of lust arises, defilement will come to you in turn.* "You didn't hurt me," she lied, managing to keep her voice steady and forced her emotion to drain. "You regret what we just did? If so, the best thing to do is forget it and move on."

The fire in her eyes intrigued him. Which was odd, after what they'd just done. No, since the day he'd stepped into this house and onto her life, nothing had been normal. "Can you?"

Should she feel regret? Yes, morally she should. She'd given more of herself than she'd intended, shared more than she'd imagined, risked more than she should have dare. But she'd be condemned to hell before she accepted sole responsibility for desire that sizzled between them. She refused to feel an ounce of remorse. She hadn't tried to seduce him and what had been simmering between them for over time was just starting to ignite. "What do you expect me to do? It's too late to change anything." She said, not sure if she was relieved or disappointed. Her pulse was still beating erratically and the sexual scent that the two of them created still clinging on her skin. She thought she would shower, hoping the hot water would ease the memories. Pushing back her hair, she landed lithely on her feet. "I'd like to take a shower."

Torn between puzzlement and fury, and with on a long breath, "Smiling." He sat up quickly, caught her arm, yanked her back before she got away. But she shook him off, and stood naked in front of him, standing naked, too, as his groin tightened.

His gaze ran the length of her body, and a familiar hot gleam came into his eyes. "I meant, this has gone too far, Smiling. What happened between us was a mistake."

"Stop right there." She angled her chin up defiantly as his eyes moved from her face to her breasts and lower, then backed to her eyes. She thought he might kiss her. "I did it for the same reasons you did, Tommy. We just had sex because we're two restless people who needed a release."

Damned common sense, sex had muddled his mind, that explained everything, but it didn't change the facts. She was on one side of the fence and he was on the other. He couldn't fix it now, except to try to make an excuse. "Look, we can't do this anymore." Saying that, but seeing her full naked body was harder than he'd thought it would be. A lust hit him so hard as he started getting hard again, and she realized that. It was crazy. He just made love to her, yet he wanted her again. A faint streak of color rose in her cheeks and he knew she had read his thoughts.

His tall and thick erection pointed up her belly, and for that moment, if he asked, she'd open her arms and invite him back to her. But instead. "That's beside the point. But you're an idiot if you think it won't happen again and don't make this any worse than it already is." She said, turning her back on him, walked to the bathroom.

He watched her walked away, his gaze going from the brown hair around her shoulder to the nip of her waist, down to the swing of her smooth sexy rump, the curve of her calves when coordinating her steps. "I'm not trying to complicate anything," he tried to explain further, and shamelessly, he admitted. "The back of you is as beautiful as the front."

That made she stop. "Is that so? And you are hard again. Don't play the green-bearded devil anymore." Then she put a little more sass into her walk and heard him laughed.

When she was into the bathroom, she closed the door behind her, but she's not bothering to lock it, because it didn't matter when they already got over the limit. She stepped into a large glass shower, and turned-on hot water, tested it before stepping under the spray shot out of the shower-head. It was nice and hot, and letting water stream over her face, flattering her hair, and let her tired muscles relax. She nearly moaned as she touched herself between her legs and felt a small triumph. True, she'd always thought her love should save for Mathew, but she didn't regret making love to Tommy. In fact, standing here in the hot spray, she was viewing the situation with a jumble of emotions. What had transpired between them was pure animal lust. They were trapped, forced into intimacy, and they found each other darkly alluring. All that sexual tension had explored into unbridled passion, and there was nothing more to it, no complicated emotion, no need to make promises for a future that didn't exist.

❦❦＊❧❧

Standing naked with lust raging, Tommy heard the shower running loudly in the bathroom. He wondered if he was losing his mind and how he'd been unable to fight temptation he'd come to giving in to his lust and how much restraint it had taken to keep from making love to her over and over again. For the first time in his life, he felt genuine remorse about his relationship with her. But that wasn't the hard part. Facing Smiling would be the real test ever since setting eyes on her again in her house that first night, he'd been compelled to be as near her as possible. However, having her around even more would be such a blast of temptation. Night after night, he had told himself that he could control his emotion. But he was no saint, only a flesh and blood man and he hadn't been with a woman in too long to count since his wife died. He tended to keep his personal life out of his sex life. And his personal life hadn't been a priority, in any sense of the word. His son had been his entire world. But *straw near fire will catch sooner or later.* That's why everything was mixed up now after letting his emotion off their usually taut rein, and taken her regardless of the fact that she was the lovely daughter of his boss.

Worrying wouldn't improve his situation. A smart man would run as fast as he could in the opposite direction, but he guessed he wasn't smart *because lust was like a bottomless cave. Neither could be filled nor satisfied.* Physically, they clicked in the way he never had with another woman, and he could tell by her body's response that she had felt it, too. He'd hope that once he'd her, his hunger would lessen. But he hadn't able to put on the brakes. "God, please help me," he muttered as thinking of the folk saying that once a man wanted to fuck a woman and wanted to protect her at the same time, then he's in love. He didn't know if that's true or not, but it sure was how he felt. Let the future bring what was to come. Right now, all that mattered was Smiling. Answering to himself, he walked toward the bathroom, pushing open the door where the smells of shampoo and water were heavy in the air. And in the mirror, he caught a glimpse of her body through the steamy glass doors.

* * *

"Silly girl," she chided herself as her mind was filled with blistering memories of passion she'd never known existed, passion hidden deep within her. Blushing at the vivid thoughts, she poured shampoo into her palm. Tommy was a complication she hadn't anticipated, a wrinkle in her life she wasn't prepared to deal with. Their lovemaking had been so explosive, so fierce and savage, that she felt drained afterward, as if she'd been in an emotion battle in which both sides were victorious. Even Mathew hadn't been able to stir her body the way Tommy could. Guilt swept through her. Comparing the two men was wrong and completely unfair. She had loved

Mathew, she only lust after Tommy. Or was it more than that? In fact, a silly little part of her thought it might be just the beginning. Lathering her hair, she wasn't sure what to do next, just let this love affair run its natural course.

He had given her the comfort and pleasures of their sweet lovemaking, each moment together a reaffirmation of life itself. But she could hardly call them lovers, and the consequences of falling in love with Tommy would be dire for both of them. She used to believe in love. But deep-down true love must not exist. Mathew seemed proof enough.

Rinsing the shampoo from her hair, and let the hot water drizzle down her back. She didn't want to think about that. Not now. She should have waited, been surer of him, been surer of herself. And after days of suffering, crying for the broken love, she deserved to enjoy a satisfying physical relationship. At least, it eased her heart broken.

Through the hot mist he saw a flash of long legs, her hair spilling down her back, her skin pink from the hot water, her white breasts swelled gently at the waterline, her rose nipples erect little buttons pointing proudly above the lapping water. And when she was bent over, rinsing her hair, he noticed a flash of her rump, two firm cheeks. God! She was beautiful. So perfect, caused his manhood to swell, and hard as stone. And all his qualities turned sick when he was attracted to her again, his hand reached for the handle of the glass door.

❧❀ ✽ ❀❧

But with Tommy now, the complications would be tenfold, and still she couldn't help remembering everything that had led to their being together in the bed. Leaning against the wall of the shower stall, her knees were suddenly weak when she thought about how easily she'd given herself to him, how much she'd wanted him, how easy love had made every touch magic, every kiss joyous that there had been no holding back for either of them. She'd felt so safe, protected, and loved. Don't be silly, she told herself. She didn't love him. She couldn't. And he wasn't the loving kind. Whatever he'd once shared with his deceased wife, he wasn't about to share it again with any woman or even with her. It was just sex, nothing more.

While she was trying to work out her emotion, the glass door slid aside, pushing her thoughts out, letting in a draft of cold air, and shooting out a jet of water. She pressed a hand to her chest. "Tommy! What are you doing...?" Her voice trailed off as she saw and took in his nudity with his lustful eyes.

He bit back a grin as the warm water trailing over the tips of her breasts, cascading into her navel, sliding through the dark curls at the apex of her legs. He cleared his throat. "Can I shower with you?"

It seemed natural, as if he'd been her lover for years. And oh, Lord have mercy, she couldn't answer as her eyes were helplessly riveted to his magnificent body. "But if you want me to leave, I'll leave."

Her stupid heart did a little flip at the sight of him. It certainly wasn't the first time Smiling had seen a man without clothes. But her memory of Mathew's lean, pale body even her male's model that had occurred to her that a man could be call beautiful. But they were no match for what she saw in front of her stunned eyes. Tommy was the sexiest man she'd met in a long, long while. His big, muscular body was solid and hard from workout, perfectly sculpted, without a single curve or angle in excess, adding his erection was magnificent. She could be happy to look at him for an hour, and damn it, this wasn't supposed to happen, this lust, but she couldn't seem to control her emotion.

Because she's saying nothing, he decided as he stepped into beside her, and drew the sliding glass door closed, eagerly running his hands down her body under the hot water, touching her gleaming skin was wet already with soapy, then lowered his mouth to her ear. "Want me to wash your back?"

She felt shock waves all the way to her toes, ripples of sweet sensation. Tommy determined to drive her out of her mind when the shower spray hit her side, his hot mouth was against her nape, and his smoky voice sent shivers down her neck that she felt like moaning. Damn! She wasn't supposed to be this vulnerable.

She hadn't been able resist him either. Tommy was her weakness, and let he kneaded soapy hands down her back, then his thumbs digging small circles on either side of her spine. She bowed her head and this time she did moan aloud as he moved back up her spine and then over her shoulders, loosening her muscles. And after he rinsed her back, she started to turn around, but he halted her with a touch.

"Don't move."

She waited, not even caring what he meant to do next, she was so relaxed, so tired emotionally and physically. Then she felt the touch of his fingers in her hair, working shampoo in. He massaged gently over her temples and at the base of her head where she hadn't even known the muscles were tight, and then he tipped her head back so that she rested against his shoulder, carefully, cupping his hands against her forehead to prevent the soap from streaming in her eyes, he rinsed her hair. That was a new torture all its own. The man was so thorough.

She could feel the lust, now and again, of his erection as he moved behind her. It was a peripheral reminder, not urgent or rude, that he want her. Tears gathered in her eyes, surprising her with her defenses down. This was nice. This was wonderful.

Her eyes closed and lifted her face to the spray, letting the salt mix with the hot running water. So many sensations buffered her at that moment, she couldn't keep up. So, she wasn't going to spoil this.

He reached around her with his soaping hands caught her hands, and lacing their soapy fingers together, then surrounding her abdomen, drew her tight enough that her spine pressed tight to his chest and abdomen, and she could feel his erect penis against her smooth rump cleavage, but still there was no pressure. Simply, let water pouring over their naked and slick bodies.

He unlaced their fingers and trailed his fingertips up her arms. "Lift," he whispered in her ear, and she obeyed.

He soaped under her arms and let the running water rinse the bubbles away. She watched as he soaped again and then lifted his hands to her breasts. She groaned and let her head fall to his shoulder when he touched there, and then he circled her breasts with his fingertips. The light tantalizing touch in contrast to the heavy beat of the shower. When he at last circled into her nipples, they were tight and aching. He pinched them between thumb and forefinger, both at once, and made gasp. At the same time, she felt the brush of his lips against the back of her neck, and his hard penis wedged into her bottom cleavage now, thrusting just slightly, hardly noticeable, really. But it made her knees weak.

His hands left her, and she watched, hypnotized, her eyes half lidded, her breath coming faster, as he soaped them for third time. Now he laid them on her belly, making gentle, maddening circles around her navel as his hips thrust behind her.

"You're enjoying this, aren't you?" he asked deeply, his voice as sensuous as a caress.

"Enjoying this?" she asked innocent, but she couldn't stop a smile. "I'd enjoy it more if you'd help me."

"It would be my pleasure." She heard he whispered in her ear as his hand moved down to her little fine black hair and below, then threaded his fingers into her wet curls, gently exploring, and she moaned softly and widened her legs to encourage him.

"Like this? Or... like this..." He teased her as his other hand traced tickling patterns on her insides of her thighs, then his middle finger found her clitoris. She arched into his hand, gasping as he tapped it. But he seemed to be enjoying it himself that he twitched his right hand free suddenly and reached behind her, and at the same time he bent his knees. She felt his cock pushing through her legs, rubbed against the wet of her folds, teasing just right or letting her feel how much he wanted her?

"Close your thighs," he said, hot and urgent in her ear, and she did, trapping his hard erection between them, rocked slightly, and feeling the slide, so close to her center. Water and soap acted as a lubricant, allowed it moved silkily against her skin.

She felt his breath hot on her nape and the brush of his lips against her neck as he kissed her damn skin. She moaned low in her throat, and his right hand moved slowly down, seeking out her clit white his left flicked at her nipples. It was so much, all the disparate sensations all at once, and she had to hold on to something for support. So, she gripped his arm with both hands as he played with her. She felt swollen, engorged with heat and want, and her hips jerked helplessly. The head of his cock was showing up against her clit from below while he pressed gently down with his finger from above. She mewled, arching back against him.

"That's right. That's the way." He whispered, then suddenly turned her, rinsing her, and then sank to his knees. As she stared down at the top of his wet head, seeing the way he looked at her with such absorbed concentration. He kissed her belly, then his masterful tongue was delving over her clit.

Her smell was different from any other woman he'd been intimate with, pure in its humanity. She was sweet musk, unadulterated by the chemical stink of perfume or fancy shampoo.

She tossed her head back, parted her thighs, moaned in sheer ecstasy, her hands combed through his hair, and one her smooth, slim leg coiling around the firm muscles of his shoulders for balance.

He gave more, two his fingers joining in the play, going deep, just as he sucked on her clit between his lips again. And with each firm stroke of his fingers, each soft pull of his mouth, he pushed her higher and higher made her shaking and moaning.

Then pleasure, the sharp edge of it tipped toward pain. At that point, between glory and devastation, her body simply shattered.

While she was still panting, her orgasm still sparking within her, he switched off the water, pushing the glass door so hard it had banged against the surrounding tiles, reached for a towel from the bar, wrapped it around her, then pulled her into his arms, darkly pleased that she was limp, and with a lustful need to claim her, he's carrying her into the bedroom and set her down beside the bed without bothering to dry off, and leaving a puddling trail of water behind him.

She gave him a wicked smile as he took the towel away from her, letting it fall to her sides before he fell on the bed with her, let the fire inside him rage, but he pulled back just enough to take a good, long look at her, and letting out a rough groan. "I can't get enough of you, Smiling. All I can think of is having you again."

She watched him impatiently fish a condom out from his wallet and curse steadily to himself as he rolled it on. Her mouth curved uncontrollably, a giggle bubbling at her lips at his swift movements. But all desire to laugh left her when he climbed on the bed and felt his broad, hard thighs parting hers, easing between them. Her arms reached up to draw the full weight of his warm, bare chest down over hers. He kissed her again, deep and thoroughly, and with a single deep thrust, he was inside her.

Both of them stilled, but she gasped, clinging, a wild little cry escaping her throat. She loved the way he filled her. Each time they made love, it was more thrilling, more beautiful, with the pleasure that was so exquisitely sharp, it was nearly painful. Her fingertips digging into his shoulders. He was her mate, her companion, her opposite. Need for him would never fade, and he was a man who should be by her side for the rest of their lives that she could at last admit it. *I love you,* she thought, but didn't dare utter the words. Instead, she wrapped her legs around him. She wrapped her soul around him, too, if it were possible.

Her face was buried against his throat as her breath heaved in and out, but he inched away, watched her face, withdrew and shoved back into her, hard, and almost cruel. He was telling her something with this love making.

She was his match. God damn it, and if nothing else, he would remember her until the day he died. Because she'd leave her mark on him, burn it into his very soul.

Frantic for each other, lost in each other, and trapped in pleasure with the shock of that ragged peak, her hips meeting his almost brutally, and he rubbed against her with each close thrust, driving her higher, faster, then moved with her. Her eyes closed as the pleasure built inside her, and she came with a shuddering moan that trembled through her body, but Tommy didn't stop, just pounded into her until she came again.

With a groan, loud and awful as he pumped heavily into her. She bit her lips to keep from stating her love-words he didn't want to hear. They lay breathless, having been swept away by a tidal wave of love and emotion. And when the rage of pleasure waned, he slowly sank down to her, his head beside hers on the pillow, his strong heartbeat thundering against her breasts.

Neither of them moved for the longest time. She held him close and thought that only this one man could protect and satisfy all her needs. He took care of her and comforted her sincerely while she was suffering from love. And his way making love was not to demand sex, but to pamper her and show her what her true sexuality was.

Tommy gave himself a minute to remove the condom, turned out the lights. And when he slid into the bed next to her, he eased her back against his chest, holding her spoon-fashion against him. He kissed the side of her neck, and heard her soft purr. His erection started to stir. He wanted her as he always did, but she needed to sleep as much he did. "Sleep, Smiling." He murmured into her hair.

Closing her eyes, she consoled herself that for now he was hers. Tonight, she would enjoy their time together, and in the meantime, she would sleep well and enjoyed the novelty of having Tommy all to herself for the entire night. Tomorrow she would face whatever the morning might bring. "Good night, Tommy," she whispered through a smile.

Tommy grabbed the edges of the blanket and sheet, pulled them up over their damp bodies and kissed Smiling once more time. After that, they fell asleep wrapped in each other's arm.

✿❀✻❀✿

Her iPhone vibrated on the nightstand table early on the morning, pulling her out of the deep sleep. She sat up, and as the covers fell to her waist, she realized that she wasn't wearing a gown or anything else. Recalling the night's lovemaking, she smiled. She'd never meant to let that happen, but she discovery that how two people could give and get so much, could please each other in ways that bothered on euphoria. She looked down at Tommy in half of light in her own warm bed. He looked peaceful in sleep, content, and unworried. She resisted the urge to touch his hair or kiss his sleepy mouth.

He was a terrific man. She had never experienced anything like last night. He cared for her very much, always brought her joy. His sincerity brought a feeling as if she was falling in love with him. No. She was enjoying this man, enjoying making love with him, but she wasn't in love. She wasn't about to mistake lust for love. Yes, she cared for Tommy. She liked him. But that wasn't necessarily love.

Satisfied, she didn't want to bother this matter anymore. She checked the calling ID that had awaken her. It was a text from Lisa Bronson who's fresh out of fashion design school in Atlanta and was hired by her mother to work for her and became her new assistant. Lisa was a dear sweet person. Reading the text that was asking her to come little early to check the setting out for the show, she texted back that sure and thanks for the text, and then she felt Tommy drew her closer.

Amazing how quickly life could change when it was an entirely different matter to wake up with someone beside him. Especially, he felt her naked body against his just the way he liked it. He hadn't wanted to sleep with a woman since Lydia. There had been times when he'd wanted sex, but never had he wanted that emotion commitment of spending the night with another person, waking up to see a new day begin together. With Smiling, he felt differently. The more they'd been together, the more sexual their banter had become. It left him frustrated and at times, annoyed. But there would be more to the fusing of their bodies than the physical; there would be a bounding at a deep level, a level he wasn't certain he could accept, and a level that he wanted to avoid. But it gave him the opportunity to see what sex and a good night's sleep had done for her. She looked like less sad and no more painful than the evening before. "Morning."

"Good morning." She felt foolishly. "We slept later than I intended."

In one smooth move, Tommy wrapped his fingers around her wrist and brought her hand to his lips. "You should relax today. I'll show you around Miami."

It would be nice to wake up to this every morning. She could enjoy the combined scents of breakfast, and him that filled her head. So, racing off to work would be the wrong move. But she already answered yes. And she didn't want to lose the client's trust. She laughed and nuzzled against his throat. "I wish we could, Tommy. I truly do, but I have …"

"A business to run," he finished.

"Exactly. For the first time in weeks, I feel I can run it without having this urge to look over my shoulder. I'd really like to shower and change."

Understanding and there wasn't a choice, he sat up and kissed her. "Why don't you go to have a shower yourself, and get dress, I'll prepare breakfast, then I'll take you there after we eat."

"That sounds perfect." She managed a smile, then got out of bed, walked naked to the bathroom.

※ * ※

When he was alone, Tommy mentally kicked himself repeatedly. He had sex with Jennifer Jefferson. Not once, but twice within twelve hours. How could he have been so stupid? He'd always been cool when it came to women. Only Lydia had turned him inside out.

And now was Jennifer. So what are you going to do about it? he asked himself, ran a hand through his hair and felt remorse tear at his soul. He was supposed to protect her. That's your duty, not climb into the shower like a lusty beast. He threw the covers over and reminded him of how he'd put himself and his needs above hers.

His stomach hurt. He overstepped. Smiling had come into his life wounded and desperate for affection. His plan was to bring her a lighthearted, or maybe she could intimate to him or confide in him as a good friend. But he'd taken advantage of that which he honestly hadn't meant to do that in bed.

Oh, God, this whole thing was bad, very bad. From the moment he accepted this mission, he knew that sooner or later this would happen. This was the cause of suffering and unhappiness that he couldn't avoid. Sighing for his sins, he told himself that he could not let that happen again.

This was crazy. Yet he couldn't blame only himself. She was responsible, too. And she had been more than willing. But that didn't explain anything. She was breaking all his rules, the one he'd formed for personal survival. Even now, when he knew better, and yet he'd still imagined kissing her again, touching her and making love to her until they were both exhausted.

In a flash, he remembered the texture of her slick skin, how it looked in the shower and rosy from the hot water. How easy it had been to press her back against the slick tiles and enter her sweet moistness. Now the images disturbed him. He closed his eyes. If Mr. Brian ever got wind of what had happened, he'd come at him fists flying. He didn't blame him; he'd do the same. Even in these days of equal rights, women's open sexuality and guilt-free sex, he believed that a man should live by a strict moral code, as should a woman. He didn't believe in casual sex, and thought he wasn't old fashioned enough to think that a person had to be married to have sex. It was probably best to love a person before knowing them physically, just like he had with Lydia.

Although and he felt guilty for acknowledging the fact, his lovemaking with Smiling had been every bit as satisfying as sleeping with Lydia, maybe more so. Before last night, he wouldn't have believed that he could be so emotionally attached to a woman, but Smiling had changed all that.

Damn her, still being in love with Lydia had been safe, and it had helping assuage the guilt he felt wherever he thought of her and little Jason. "Forgive me," he said, reached into his back pocket, withdrew his wallet and flipped it open to a picture of Lydia and Jason taken years ago. Their images had faded with time. Behind the photograph, in a secret pocket, was his wedding ring, a wide gold band. What a sentimental fool he was, and hypocrite. The same wallet that held his gold band also held a small supply of condom just in case. He wondered what Smiling would think if she knew the direction of his thoughts. Did she want more from their relationship?

Carrying a truckload of guilt around him, he whispered curses himself. "Son of a bitch." And closing the wallet, slapped it into his back pocket, and then he put on his pants, but no shirt, left the room to prepare breakfast for her.

***

She took a quick bath, trying not to remember what happened in the shower last night, but letting her thought wandered. It was just that she'd come to count on Tommy's company so much, too much. He made her smile; he made her ache. He made her want things, things she'd been afraid to want. But he was still kind of a romantic fantasy for her, and her life was complicated now.

Maybe this wasn't so bad. Yes, she'd made a mistake. So what, other people, normal people, slept with people all the time and she didn't see anyone else angst over it. For all she knew Tommy hadn't given it a second thought, and in fact would laugh off her worries.

But you've slept with him now, as in slept, snuggled in his arms all night long. And that was more intimate than anything else and it changed things for her.

Had she ever felt like this? Like she just wanted to climb into the man next to her and stay there?

Being with Mathew had been good, but she wasn't for him. When they'd slit, he'd moved on with shocking ease. And the truth, so had she.

But it'd left her feeling broken and more than unsure about love in general. But then Tommy had come into her life. She knew that she had no business feeling anything for him at all. But apparently, some things like matter of the heart; not only happened in a blink but were also out of her control. And what if he thought she was cheap, that she was easy, or even worst. What she ever had with Tommy, maybe just sex, she wanted it. But if their relationship turned out to be a short affair, so be it.

She switched off the shower-head, toweled off and wrapping it around her body, tucked it in between her breasts as she stepped back into the bedroom, and when she tossed the towel aside, grabbed a fresh pair of underwear from the dresser and tried them on. The scent of coffee and frying bacon made her realize how hungry she was. So, she quickly put a kimono on, cinching the belt tight around her waist, followed a tantalizing aroma, and found Tommy in the kitchen, was frying eggs. "Smells good."

Tommy turned. "I know we don't have much time for breakfast..." And trailed off, staggered as he watched Smiling bustled in. Her hair still damp, piled haphazardly on her head, her face flushed, and she's wearing a short, flowery kimono that was loosely, almost carelessly knotted, so that it gaped intriguingly down the center of her body nearly to the waist, and barely covered her ass. Oh man, she was even more beautiful than when she was all done up, and he liked it when she looked natural, clean and sexy, and the scent of shampoo drifted from her, filling his nose, reminding him of the shower they'd shared. His mouth simply watered, and his cock harden, straining against the fly of his jeans. It made him want to snatch her up and carried her back to the bedroom. But he really had to stop thinking things like that.

She smiled as he was bare chested, his jeans hanging low over his hips. All her worries went up in smoke as a nice flush of heat began to work up from her toes. "I don't know why you're looking at me like that, Tommy. You've seen me naked."

"Yeah. Maybe I've got a weakness for long women in short kimono," he said, pulled out a chair for her, and when she sat down at the kitchen table. "I made eggs and bacon."

Tommy went back to the stove, brought a plate he'd left there then placed it in front of her, containing two sunny side up eggs, toast and several strips of bacon. "This is the only way I can fix you fast," he said, laid a hand on her shoulder. "Eat."

He was taking care of her. And how the hell did he know she liked her eggs sunny side up? That made she smiled in happiness, and touched by his concern, she would make time for this morning. "I have time. And I love what the server wear." She said, admiring his bare chested and muscles that she had trouble dragging her gaze from him.

Her smile was so wide that touched his heart and lit up the room more than the sunshine. Delight filled him to overflowing. Last night, she'd been sad and desperate. Now looked at her. Radiant, happy and delicious. He brought a fork for her. "I think apple juice's better than coffee."

"Yes. Thank you." She picked up her fork, scooped up some eggs on the toast, then took a bite, closing her eyes to savor the mouthwatering taste.

After placing her glass on the table, he leaned against the counter-top with his mug of coffee. "Smiling," he said.

"Yes," she finally said, once she'd swallowed it, and looked up at him. He looked sad and vulnerable now.

"I think we should talk about what happened last night," he said forcing the issue that hung him like a cloud.

She put up the fork to stop him. "I thought we already had this discussion."

He sipped his coffee, watching she continued to eat. He would love to have sex with Smiling again, but he was honest about himself. He was no good for Smiling. His life was complicated already, and his sole responsibility. "We have," he said tightly. But it would be better not to repeat what happened last night or avoided getting involved any deeper with her. "It happened, Smiling. Whether you want to think about it or not, I didn't mean to …"

She placed gently the fork on the plate, knowing it was important to talk. "No need to explain. We've all over-act."

"The problem is that there, Smiling. You see things the way you want to see them. But I see them for what they are."

She lifted her glass. "And what was this?"

"This was a mistake. I should have handled things different, or I shouldn't have touched you or kissed you or let things get so out of hand."

"Or, or, or. But what about in the shower?" she accused and lowered her glass back down.

To her amazement, a blush crawled up his face and he set his mug on the counter. "Believe it or not, but damn it all, anyway. Look, I'm trying my best to apologize here."

She looked up from her eggs into his serious face. And it struck her right then that Tommy could be so much more than a bed buddy, although God alone knew sex with him was nothing short of incredible. He had heart, he had soul, he was smart and accomplished. And sometimes he had the ability to see right through her. However, her feelings about him were still confused. Sometimes she was sure she loved him. In other, more rational hours, she thought she hate him, or should hate him. "My God, why do you keep dancing around the issue? There's no reason to be sorry."

Staring, he dragged a hand through his hair. How could he have convinced himself he understood her when she was now and always had been an enigma? "Yes, there are a thousand reasons. I didn't want you to think I'm some kind of man that I go around bed hopping and jumping in the shower and …"

"It's nice that you have standards, but you did." She interrupted. "So, I don't want to hear your apology, your excuses or your pitiful reasons. Because I believe we both understand perfectly well the status of our relationship. I could have stopped you if I'm in charge of my feeling, Tommy. But I wasn't some whimpering female who couldn't say no."

"There's no need to be noble, Smiling. The fact is I took advantage of you." He admitted, wishing she could hate him.

"No, you didn't. It seems to be fair to tell you that this isn't your problem. I'm not in the habit of what I did. I don't throw myself at men just like that. The truth is, I couldn't pretend I don't feel it. And it was time I got my body parts was involved." She pointed out. "It's as much my fault as yours."

The corner of his mouth ticked up. "It's no one's fault, Smiling. It just happened."

353

They were fantastic together in bed. But eventually the sexual attraction would fade. She understood that. She'd be prepared for that, be able to handle it when the time came for things like this. "Then why do you always think you have to apologize?"

"Because whether you admit or not, I'm trying to say that …" "What?" she cut him off and pushed him to answer.

Her eyes besought him and he wanted to tell her that she was special, that whenever he was around her, he got a little crazy, wanted to hold her all night long, to touch her hair, to kiss her lips, to whisper his most intimate secrets. Instead, he cleared his throat. "You need to know that we shouldn't let that happen again."

"I see." Her courage weakened, so she turned her head to stared out the window, determined not to let him see the frustration in her eyes. Her feelings were evident in them. Guilt and remorse washed through her, along with a family sense of shame was one side, and the other, sex with Tommy was not what she wanted or one-night stand. But it had been a memorable one. Besides, she believed in fate. She'd been destined to leave Mathew, as she was destined to spend last night with him, and learn what it was that made she give her heart and felt free to do whatever she wanted now, and that was important to her. She didn't know if the changes were for the better or the worse. "If I don't have any regret, why should you be?"

Shock came first then pleasure. She had a way of turning his thoughts around, but he sucked in a swift breath, and his hand reached and gentle turning her face back to his. "No regrets?" He whispered.

She wasn't even sure what she was doing. Nothing made sense anymore. She was trying to do the right thing, and instead, everything she did seemed so stupid. "No, and I don't want you to regret that, either, or worry about it. I want you to just let things happen as they're meant to happen."

The impression was so strong, that her suggestion was a kind of forgiving, and would give more than asked. "I've never met a more confusing, complicated woman."

"That's the nicest thing you're ever said to me. No one's ever accused me of being complicated."

One way to another, he had to convince Smiling to see his way. "I didn't mean it as a compliment. It's not going to solve anything until you start listening and stop anticipating."

That made her grin and relaxed again. "This means we're finished feeling awkward around each other."

Sure. Maybe, but the excitement that knowledge brought was tingled with a trace of fear he struggled to ignore. He couldn't think about tomorrow and tomorrow's consequences when he wanted her. "Look, that this has gotten way out of control, we both know it. Therefore, we should find whatever it is that does to get back in control."

"That's fine, but how?"

They both would have a problem, because nothing's going to be quite the same again if whatever path they chose. It could change their life in a negative way forever. Smiling should be returning to the life she'd had before. A life that suited her as this one never would. And if they ended up, they knew it would be painful. It was all so confusing. But from now on, the more distance between his body and hers, the better, he ordered himself. Honor and loyally to a person's family were more than lust. And yet, where she was concerned, he was able to toss away his deepest convictions. "I can't think of it right now, but it doesn't matter. Soon or later, we'll both have plenty to regret."

"Maybe you're right," she admitted. "But look. Just because we made love doesn't mean you have some kind of responsibility or a duty to me."

He knew that Smiling didn't understand why he needed an acknowledgment, but that didn't matter to him now. From this moment on, they were going to go back to the way things used to be. It would be the best if he stayed away from her. But right now, he couldn't. "I have to," he said, looked at the clock on the microwave. He had to get out of here. Already aroused, if he touched her again, he might forget that. "Finish your breakfast then get dressed. I'll take you to work."

The sudden change from lover to employee hit her like jet lag. But she realized that after what he'd done to her, she had a different view of him. In all those years, not a single pass, not a touch out of the way, but overnight her whole relationship with Tommy was different, exciting. But still his glum mood bothered her. Somehow, she had to get on with her life. Without Tommy messing it up. He was doing this to her, she realized, but he resented his action. She did feel something for him. She wasn't sure what or why, but she felt it so much that she wanted to push him out of her mind, but on the other hand, she wanted to pull him closer, making her thinking that maybe, just maybe, what she was feeling was... No. That was beyond ridiculous to imagine. He needed to go back to his life, back to his world. That's why she was going to have to rethink her entire relationship with him after today. And after time had passed, if he thought of her, he'd think with gratitude that she had begun to open doors for him that had always been closed before, just like hers. And more than that. She felt like a woman again, her own woman, able to make decisions regarding her life on her own. It was a very nice feeling indeed. But that was crazy. Just because they'd made love, she was already fantasizing about their future. Looking down at her plate, she said. "I'm doing."

Chapter 28

Home is the story of who we are and a collection of all the things we love

Maintenance of good relationship, sometimes you need to keep a safe distance. That's the only way to stop it. Time and distance were what both needed to ease back far enough and analyze their relationship. Tommy reminded himself that he couldn't afford to let himself get in any deeper. It was better to stick to the present and the future. For that reason, he had begun to keep a safe, professional distance between them pass few weeks for the job. But the hard truth was he and Smiling had done that night, it had been more than sex. And he wondered how long they could keep up this circumstance, pretending that the attraction they felt for each other didn't exist.

His conscience twinged as he considered that he had deeper, ulterior motives, motives that had more to do with sleeping with her than keeping her safe. Don't lie to yourself, Tommy. A voice deep in his brain nagged. *You're falling for her. Face it, man.* No, he couldn't fall in love with her. He assured himself. It might have been a little like caring. That was almost acceptable. A man could come to care for a woman without sinking in overhead. But not a woman like Smiling.

He felt emotionally disintegrate beneath the weight of that realization. But because they'd be working together, he couldn't avoid her so much as he watched her and recognized that she seemed so wary, so secretive. Not once had she opened up to anyone. Not once had she talked and laughed with anyone. She'd kept to herself, jumped at the slightest noise. Tensed when someone touched her. Except him. And at some point, he knew they were going to have to deal with each other. Besides he also wanted to put that off, if possible, most because he had no idea what she was going to say.

He was more than confused, he was lost. How many times had he thought of her in the past few weeks? Too many. And the hardest of it was the desire. It shifted and rippled continually under the surface of his thoughts. He often caught his mind drifting back to the scent of her skin when he took off her clothes to expose her body so sexy that he buried himself into the moist heat of her and then to have all that sweet paradise wrenched away so violently, had been excruciating as her hands gripping his shoulders and she'd cried out in pleasure and pain. It had been heaven, also hell. He shouldn't have wanted her. It had been a sin. But he'd never wanted any one thing the way he'd wanted Smiling. Maybe he'd never so completely satisfied in his life as he had with her, and he'd never felt so guilty for seducing someone. Jennifer Jefferson was different from any of the other women he'd had in his lifetime. Very different. And that was a problem. A big problem.

Clearly, she didn't trust anyone since. And just as clearly, he'd done nothing to earn her trust. Quite the opposite. That hadn't bothered him much before, but it bothered him now. Trust was a precious thing, and he wanted hers. As much as he wanted her body. He wanted more from her. He wanted her beautiful eyes to regard him with interest all her time. He wanted to know what she was thinking, to share his own. He wanted to protect her, to make sure nothing bad ever happened to her again. She deserved happy. She deserved love. He wanted many things for Smiling, but was he capable of that? For the first time in he was thinking about a future, with an adventurous, frustrating, warm, sexy woman he couldn't seem to get enough of. How much she meant to him. He was in deeper with her than he'd been with any women since Lydia. The converse to be true, relationships always seemed complicated to him. What he felt from Smiling had to be something else. Obsession and its very high risk, also he realized that he was starting to fall in love with her. "Don't," he warned himself. "You're not allowed to have feeling for her."

He didn't want to love anyone. Because the prospect was not going well. Retrospective, love was a disaster. Love hurt. He couldn't afford to make the same mistake he made with his wife, Lydia and didn't want to hurt someone or to be hurt. He never wanted to go through that kind of pain again. It was better to be alone. He'd decided that a long time ago; and decision had served him well. He'd been happy until Smiling who brought a sensation, he'd sworn he'd never feel again. He knew who she was, and yet she was drawing things out of him he'd promised himself he wouldn't feel again. He was perceptive enough to know she was a woman who could draw out more. Making love with her again was inevitable, so inevitable he knew he'd have to weigh the consequences. Prices always had to be paid, and who would know that better than he?

Stop examining your feeling and for God's sake, forget any silly romantic fantasies you have about this woman! He told himself he could handle this. He just needed to keep her at a distance, had always found an excuse to break off their relationship before it deepened into something emotionally dangerous. He and Smiling could enjoy each other for as long as it lasted. Hell, at best what he felt for Smiling was lust. Wanting her was all right. Making love to her was okay. Because two people making love didn't necessarily love each other. But sex could also create love. Trying to find a solution for himself when he glanced around, and he admitted that the consequences of his actions had come as the housekeeper Margaret waved him over and said, "Mr. Brian is looking for you, he wants you in his office right away."

Uh-oh, his boss had found out? "Thank you." He said, feeling his stomach drop to his toes. This was going to be bad.

⚜ ✳ ⚜

There was nothing that took the edge off a day like the sound of margarita ingredients mixing with juicing limes, tequila and ices in a good quality blender. Smiling moved her hips in time with the beat of the music, coming from the speakers into the kitchen wall, then flipped the switch on the blender.

Since she went home, she felt peace and happy to help her brother's wedding plan, and when the drink was ready, she turned off the blender, pouring the slushy mixture into four salt-rimmed glasses. Her mother took first the first one, smiling and thanked her. She smiled back.

Yes, there were things to say, maybe things that might never be said. Was it better to get everything in the open and deal with it? Probably, but so what? Every family had problems. To be honest, she could go her whole life without having to deal with who did what and when. Better to just accept there had been a problem and move on. "I pass," Tiffany announced as they took seats around the island and poured her a glass of iced tea from a pitcher on it instead. "I'm pregnant."

She knew Bush Jr loved and pampered Tiffany like thin eggs, eating and drinking now all had to be according to the menu. "That's right." Smiling took a long drink of her margarita. "I forget about that alcohol can be a bad influence on baby. But did you know that alcohol also enhances the aging process." They all looked at her.

"That was cheerful." Tiffany told her, sipped her iced tea. "My doctor said I could drink in moderation, but I only sipped the sparkling wine. Are you okay? You don't seem like your usual self."

"I'm fine, better than fine, because you know what?" Smiling studied her glass and frowned. "If I start to look ugly, I can get plastic surgery."

Steady moved close and touched her sister's arm. "You seem so pessimistic. What happened?"

Smiling tossed her head. "Nothing, I'm fine, just being weird. Ignore me." Uncomfortable with this conversation, she turned to their mother. "Let's talk about the wedding, Mom. What's new with that?"

Because of Tiffany's pregnancy, their wedding was rushed by two family and set the wedding date at beginning of next month.

Jennies grinned. "Well, there are a few things I want to show you." "I want to see them all," Smiling told her.

Jennies got up and hurried from the room; Steady got a large bowl and dumped chips in it while Tiffany collected the takeout containers of salsa and guacamole. By the time Jennies return with her lap-top, they were passing the bowls along the island.

Because she was always attentive and thoughtful, so after sketching out the designs, she also wanted to hear Smiling's opinion. "Here are three wedding dresses I'd picked out for Tiffany. But with your design aesthetic, can you add ideas for these wedding dresses?" Jennies said, and they all put their heads together, looking at the screen. Tiffany beamed the moment she saw them. "Do you think these designs are pleasing to you?"

The wedding dresses she personally had designed for her looked incredible. A narrow column which fell from the shoulders with a slightly lowered neckline in back, and a discreet drape below it. The lining was white and pale pink and strapless, but the sheer ivory lace came up to the collarbones. The same overlay created long sleeves and fell to the tea-length hem. The bodice was fitted with the skirt flaring out. It swayed and moved with every step. Adding with the bouquet was white with hints of green, so it would show up against the dresses. They were beautiful dresses she had ever seen, beyond her wildness dreams. Proving that her mother-in-law really loved for her. "You're doing a wonderful job with the wedding dresses. I love all of them, mom." Tiffany said, feeling a special interest in as Bush Jr's family was already in deep planning mode. "Thank you. It's going to be an amazing."

"I think it is." Steady thought about mentioning the Vietnam tradition Ao Dai dress, but when she'd told her mother about the change. She told her that she had insisted on keeping Tiffany's choice as her first one for an officiating. So Steady had let Smiling contribute ideas.

Smiling looked thoughtfully at each wedding dress and thought for a while, then came to a conclusion. "They are simple design, not too modern or outrageous or so classic to the point of being different from other people's designs, while still maintaining a look of dignified elegance and lovely." Smiling told her. "But to make an impression, in addition to the main wedding dress for the church ceremony, I think we should combine with a traditional wedding dress and a headpiece go with it, just like your wedding dress you wore on your wedding day, mom. My idea is that we should coordinate Western and Asian tradition, so the lucky red color will replace pink color and loosen trousers will conceal her bulging belly with six months' pregnant by then, also make she feels comfortably for moving. The dress is both modern and traditional that we'll use all the techniques to create an unforgettable impression of high fashion." "Makes sense to me." Jennies agreed.

"That what I was suggested." Steady interjected cheerfully. "The dress should be both modern and traditional. But Tiffany needs to choose her own choice, because this is her wedding dress. Is the color okay? Is it what she imagined?"

"I have no idea what you and mom are talking about. But it would be amazing, because you are all experts." Without thinking, Tiffany leaned over and hugged her future mother-in law to show her gratitude. "Thank you for loving me."

"This is my special gifts to a special woman. It's not every day your precious only son gets married. I can't wait to welcome you officially to the Jefferson's family. My Bush Jr is a lucky man."

Smiling raised her margarita. "Now that we have that out of the lists. I think I'd like to know everyone's opinion on who should be my best man?"

"How's Tommy?"

Good question. Smiling sipped her drink. "Why would you ask me that?"

Steady shrugged. "Because I'm just pointing out a simple fact. Everyone knows how perfect you two look together, and I wondered if you've decided to pick him."

She thought of Tommy, her deepening feeling for him, the way his smile somehow warmed her inside. The way he steadied her, helped her deal with the problems she was facing. "Yes," Smiling admitted, took a healthy swig. So close and yet so far away. "At least we're getting along and I'm comfortable with him."

All three women turned to look at Smiling. They all knew that was undoubtedly a lie. The words were all correct, but there was something in her tone.

"Honey, I think you did more than that." Her mom said.

"Any spark?" Tiffany asked next, cutting right to the chase.

"What?" Smiling looked away, realized the meaning. *Lovable and romantic?* The sparks between them could set off a dynamite charge. But love? She couldn't determine. He was different now, or maybe she was as well. "Of course not, I have my career to think of, Tiffany. I don't need any man now."

"Needing and having are two different things," Steady said by the way Smiling answer. "And I don't mean that you have to take him seriously."

"I'm glad to hear that."

"But what's with you and him anyway?"

Should she tell them she slept with Tommy? That she was in the middle of an affair, a one-night stand? Besides, in the past few weeks since that night, she noticed he was keeping his distance. She felt him slipping farther away from her and avoiding her, making excuses that he needed time to take care of Jason. And anything that could lead to physical contact between the two of them. He always reacted swiftly, pulling away and breaking contact. He wouldn't talk about what they'd shared that night, and if she ever brought up the subject, would say tersely. *It was a mistake. Don't make a big deal of it.* Once in a while, he seemed to let down his guard when she approached and hoped he would kiss her, but he always moved away. When he did that, she saw another side to him, one that felt regret.

"At best, we could friends, but that's all." Smiling explained. "I don't get the feeling he's dying to date either. I think he still missed his wife."

That all sounded very strange. Jennies had never heard that phrase from her before. "Smiling, if you want to lie to yourself, go right ahead. The vibes between you two were so intense. If you were, you wouldn't have acted and said the way you just did." She pointed out. "And that's pathetic. You're both ridiculous. Don't waste your lives." "Mom's right, sister." Steady said fairly and sipped her drink.

Smiling held up her hand in the shape of a T. "Come on. Stop trying to embarrass me. I just want to be myself for a while, and just because he stays over that means we have..." There was more than that, she paused, letting them think whatever they want, and didn't want them to spy on her.

"He's been with you day and night." Steady corrected and came up another question. "So, help me, if you tell us that the two of you are just friends, I'll disown you. The real question is, any sex?"

Her sister swung around, and her eyes were huge in her face. "What nonsense are you talking about?"

"I hate to ask that, but exactly you two are so close, how could something like that not happen? Especially, you and Tommy are attractive and charming people."

She didn't like the way this was heading. Yes, their relationship had shifted. they'd gone from wary adversaries to wary lovers. She couldn't pretend that nothing had changed when her entire life was turned inside out. And letting her family know the truth would spoil everything, especially now. No matter how much she like him, and was attracted to him, she didn't want to attach any emotions to it. Not yet.

"Really?" She retorted and changed the direction. "Sex does not bring to me true love.

That's something I didn't think would happen to me."

Smiling looked worried as she said it, and not a surprise, Steady could see that Smiling didn't want to admit it. Since breaking up with Mathew, Smiling had always hidden her feeling. With more questions than answer. Steady asked. "If you don't give yourself another chance, why not? Also, do you have feelings for Tommy?"

Smiling rolled her eyes, had no idea which of her sister had tattled. She didn't have an answer for that. "Are you serious? We're not talking about me. We're talking about
Tommy."

"Look, I can tell you what I really think is going on." Overreacting seemed to be in the air. "That man loves you. Any fool could see it. Stranger things could have happened. He's single, and you're not bound anyone now. You deserve a good man in your life, and Tommy is surely all that. Why not go for it."

She didn't bother protesting any further and silently cursed herself for wearing her heart on her sleeve. It had always been her failing, she supposed.

She'd had trouble hiding her true emotions. Pride prevented her from stepping back. Dignity prevented her from continuing what was, despite logic, becoming interesting. Besides, Steady was right. She and Tommy were both single. She'd slept with him, and that was giving her a hard time forgetting about their one-night stand and the pleasure he had given her, and she missed him more than she would have thought possible. After Mathew and Shirley's betrayed her, she had vowed she'd never fall in love again. But she's been wrong. Dead wrong. What she felt whenever Tommy was around was his sincere feelings and a feeling of extreme exhilaration, although she often she'd tried to talk herself out of this ridiculous feeling of euphoria. But he'd become a part of her life, the first person she thought of when she woke up and the last one before she went to sleep. She spent her days avoiding him and hoping to run into him at the same time, although they always a carefully maintained distance between them. But she's also decided it was time to trust again, to love again and she believed that he was definitely worth the gamble. However, this was too personal to share with her family.

She gulped down the last of her drink. "For one thing, he hasn't confessed his feelings to me, for another, he is my bodyguard, and yet another thing, I want to say that the evidence is pretty convincing my judgment that I don't want to have a relationship with a man who only has sex. This must be more, like trust and love. That's hard to come by."

"Stop analyzing love like that, and just follow your heart, sister." Steady said, trying for mock surprise. "There's no joy in life without risks. You are willing to take a few risks, if you feel strongly about something. Moreover, how he would hurt you while he protects you like a mother hen, no matter what. That's what love was."

That's right, Tommy was taking care of her, but he did because of his job. "I think so. He is one of the nicest men I've met, but protecting me that is his job responsibility. If because of temporary feelings you think it is love. That love only hurts each other."

"I was afraid that was the lesson you'd learned, but that's not the point." Her mother took her hand. "Love is messy sometimes. We get hurt, we got broken, we make mistake, but we must take the risk. Life without taking those risks is meaningless.

You've been to terrify to move forward since the day Mathew broke your heart and decided it would never happen again. But Smiling, if Tommy is the right man for you, you'll know it. But after knowing, you have to accept."

Smiling didn't want to protest, because she was considering it. She liked him a lot. She wanted to be with him. The list of his good qualities was endless. But that wasn't love. "Call me old fashioned, but that's the way I feel." Her fingers curled tightly around her mother's. "I want him. He wants me. But he's not ready to cross the line of friendship."

Smiling said that, but her voice sounded damn insincere, so Tiffany cut in. "How can you be sure? Have the two of you expressed your feeling for each other?"

Smiling frowned and thought about her question. "We're still shy about it."

"Doesn't that make you wonder, Smiling?"

"Yes, but maybe I'm not sure of anything. And when we're together, it's all about the business. Frankly, I think I ought to keep it to myself. See how he feel about me, and what we're not getting."

"Someone has to take the first step," her mother patted her hand. "You're the only one who can answer that. It's never too late to take a chance on someone you love. Look at your brother with Tiffany."

Smiling laughed. One of the reasons she loved her mom was that she saw things clearly and knew about getting over the complicated things. She would take her advice and get through it. Be honest, that was nice to think about being with Tommy again. He'd fundamentally changed her, and she had a bad feeling there was no going back. And while she thought they were headed in that direction, she wasn't sure. Because neither of them had said the words or made any offer. She knew why she hadn't, but what about him? That was her biggest fear. She was the only one considering trying to make it work, and hopefully not for a while. She wanted Tommy and her freedom. When she figured that out, she'd be willing to make a move. Her breath caught, and from the corner of her eyes she saw him stepped into the room with his long legs, warm eyes, and broad shoulders as he's walking up to her father office. "It's a good suggestion, mom. I should take the initiative first."

"No matter what others people think, I advise you should follow your heart when you want to be with him."

Her heart was broken open. She wondered why everyone couldn't see what was in it. Loving Tommy was easy, as she could well attest, but if that love was thwarted by class ties, she or Tommy might lose a part of themselves, unable to grow into the person they wanted to be. "It sounds so easy, but I think I don't have a gut to do it." "Never know until you try, and I think you do, because I have a strong daughter."

"And I have a wise and beautiful mother." Rather than continue the no-win argument, Smiling turned their conversation to other things as she picked up her glass. "But for now, I think we should focus to the wedding. Shall we?"

Tommy thought thoughtfully, not knowing what his boss called him for. Walking slowly to the front door of the big room, trying to calm down his emotions before knocking on the door three times. Then pushed the door and stepped inside. "Margaret said you were looking for me."

Mr. Brian looked up from his computer and nodded. "I was. Please close the door and sit down."

Tommy did as he was told then took the seat across from his boss and told himself that, whatever happened, he would accept any final decision. "Is there something you called me up here?"

Mr. Brian slipped off his reading glasses and folded his hands together on the desk. He had been observing Tommy and Smiling lately that something was off. "It is completely ridiculous that you continue to act like this," he began. "I don't know what you have in your head that you have to keep doing. But it must stop right now. I'm not putting up with this anymore."

That was it? They were going to talk about Smiling. The slightly higher pitch of his voice told Tommy his suspicions were valid.

"I don't know what to say," he admitted.

"I want you to know how much I appreciate everything you've done for my daughter and for me." Mr. Brian continued. "I'm sure you'll continue to do. That means a great deal to me. I also realized that there was something wrong between the two of you. I've been waiting for you to come to your senses after you brought Smiling back here. But you won't and you're still hiding. Why is that? Better tell me what's going on, or I find out for myself."

Tommy looked down at the desk; obviously wondering what to say, how to avoid his suspicious. "A lot of reason, some I'm still figuring out. When I have them, all of them, I'll tell you, sir."

They slept together, he was sure of it. Ever since he sent Tommy to take care of Smiling, he knew for sure that this situation was going to happen anyway. But he was not angry with him, instead glad that he'd accepted him from the very beginning. However, it seemed love was playing an important part in between them. He could see and understand. But maybe because the role of the class was a barrier between them. But love would get them through.

Time would prove it. *True kindness is helping others without forgetting to leave others with dignity and self-respect.* With that experience of his own, he saved Tommy's matter by making up a new position for him instead. Because he felt strongly about loyally, and that was a man whose opinion he trusted, and loved him like a son. "That's just fine Tommy. I just want to give you in different position. You'll understand my way of thinking. I want you selected and formed a security team to observe and keep order for the wedding party, so giving you time to be a groomsman."

Heard this, Tommy breathed a sigh of relief when the stone in his heart seemed to have been removed. "Yes, sir. I'll do it right away."

People need encouragement rather than reprimanding. If you want to help a person improve, always look at their strengths and advantages.

Chapter 29
"What God has yoked together, let no man put apart." Matthew. 19:6

The big day they've been waiting for finally arrived. Today, Bush Jr and Tiffany's wedding took place at Faith Fellowship Church that the whole family was working on it and had attended. This wedding was important matter. There were five bridesmaids, five groomsmen, three ushers, two altar boys, and the church was packed to capacity. The Jefferson's were such a large family, along with all her family and relatives were present as well. Tiffany loved the thought that her new family had so many members, in law, and friends who had come all the way from different States, to celebrate the marriage of them.

This was a big day of her life, every detail had to be exactly what she wanted. Her wedding would be perfect. Miami would be nice for the wedding. But it would be easier for her family and his big one to have it here. And to arrange a wedding in that short a period would take a miracle. She had been so busy herself and scarcely had time to go see her personal fittings, but they had a miracle. First, the fall weather on Melbourne was divine, as though it had been made up in a fairy tale. Warm but not hot; cool but not cold; sunshine but not blistering; constant breezes that refreshed. Second, her mother-in-law had been a godsend for her who had put in a lot of effort to organize and prepare the wedding, and every detail of the happy event had been meticulously planned. From the big thing liked the wedding party, to the small details liked the invitation card design, the caterers, cakes, musicians, flower girl, bridesmaids' dresses, the hairdressers for all of them, and makeup artists for those who wanted, even their honeymoon had been arranged. Also, Smiling was a great helper and organizer. She was given the responsibility of dressing up the church for the occasion. She'd put raspberry pink roses and creamy white magnolias everywhere, both inside, outside and lined the stone walkway of the church. Their lovely scent greeting guests as they arrived. Pink and white roses delicately intertwined with baby's breath in large wreaths with wide, lace-trimmed satin ribbons hung down on each side of the old weathered double doors. She knew that, as a result, everything would go smoothly. And so far, it had. But she was too nervous as she grasped the fragrant bouquet of lilies and roses, tied with white pear-studded ribbon with both hands when Smiling handed it to her.

It's beautiful, plus her favorite flowers, so careful she held them slightly below her waist the way Smiling had suggested. With the lines of her dress, the column of the skirt, and the beautiful bead-work on the bodice, the more contemporary bouquet could be stunning. "You look stunning. The dress is everything I promised, and I want you to see the full effect when you look."

"Yes, and more. It's also thanks to you and mom had designed this wedding dress for me, so it makes me so sparkling. Thank you."

"It's been a pleasure." And a relief to be done with it. "Bush Jr is going to faint when he sees you."

Their eyes met in the full-length mirror in the church's waiting room, then Tiffany studied herself, and smiled a stunning reflection of the woman who was about to become Mrs. Bush Jr Jefferson. Victorian in style lovely dress, extremely formal and fit her exquisitely. And all the more precious because Smiling and her mother had designed and made it for her. But she'd never thought a wedding dress could be comfortable, that she would feel like herself as she walked down the aisle to meet her groom. "I hope not. I wouldn't mind him being blown away, but not that excited about him fainting."

"Good point. He'll have trouble catching his breath. How about that?"

Tiffany raised her hand for a high five. "Perfect. You are the best, Smiling."

"That's what I'm here for. I'm so happy you're going to be my sister-in-law."

A wave of joy percolated through Tiffany, and they hugged for a second time. "Thank you for everything." "But you look so worry."

Tiffany looked again in the mirror. Her hair had been styled in an up-do and her veil was waiting to slip on a heart-shaped face, wide blue eyes, long lashes, and naturally rose-colored lips, she knew she had been blessed with good features. But Smiling was right she did look worry. Not worry, exactly, but nervous. She forced herself to smile. "I'm not worry. I was just nervous."

"It's normal to be nervous as any bride would be." Brian said when he knocked softly on the bride's room door, showed up behind them.

She turned around to find her future father-in-law had never looked more handsome in his black tuxedo, crisp white shirt, and red rose boutonniere Smiling had pinned to his lapel an hour ago. His dark hair, graying at the temples, was fresh cut, calmed her jittery excitement. His eyes filled at the sight of her and the smile that creased his face was filled with genuine admiration. He swallowed and blinked. "I really hadn't realized how much you look gorgeous today, Tiffany."

Tiffany felt an inner glow. He was complimenting her. "Thank you. And it's hard to believe you're representative to give me away." She whispered tremulously as a look of tenderness on his face she swore she had never seen before. "It's almost as good as having Daddy with me."

There was absolutely no doubt in either of their minds that she was his daughter in law. And he knew, as he looked at her, that neither of them would ever forget this. Because her father had passed away, so he offered to take that role and take her into the aisles on behalf of her father, and the bride's family approved. It was his duty today. A simple task, one he told himself he could do well for her and his family, and he took pride to play this part, be who he hadn't been before, and assume his role today as father of the bride. His eyes went bright with tear, but Brian blinked them away, smiled, and bent his gray head to kiss her cheek. "Honey, I'm greatly honored to stand in for you, and I can't wait. It'll be a wonderful part of the family to tell. I love you, daughter in law."

She brushed away a happy tear, and gazed up at his face, an older version of her dad's, a visage she'd thought never to see again. "I love you, too." She admitted.

Smiling left the room, let the two of them talking, stood in the vestibule in her bridesmaid dress, clutched her bouquet in her hand, and waited for the bride to appear with her father, until it was her turn while Steady and Gloomy, two her sister-in-law, Linda and Spencer moved next to her. The five of them would be walking down the aside one by one, in order of age. Bill Nguyen walked by with Cathy. He grabbed a quick kiss from Gloomy then winked at her before walking inside with other groomsmen and taking their position at the altar.

"Are you ready?" Brian asked. "I'm sure Bush Jr is anxious to see you."

Everything she had been waiting for rushed toward her and she told herself that if she nodded yes to this, then it meant she wanted to be with Bush Jr, she was ready to be. To him and to that life, she nodded yes, took his arm, looking up at him and squeezed it. "I can't believe this is happening, daddy."

Brian smiled down at her. "Everything's going to be just fine and let me give you to my son."

Tiffany nodded yes again, and he tucked her hand in his arm as they walked out of the room to lobby, and toward the main doors. She could feel him tremble beside her as they were waiting in the center of doorway.

Gloomy, smiling as the maids of honor went into first and reached the end of the aisle to the flowered altar. Smiling was the next in line. They had purposely placed her last so she wouldn't steal the show because she had the kind of looks that took people's breath away, and there were lots of whispers as she glided down the aisle next to Gloomy, came Steady, and then Linda and Spencer. They took their places on the dais with a bouquet in both hands then turned and waited for Tiffany and their father soon come into view.

The vibrant strains of the organ filled the church for the processional began, and the entrance doors opened. The moment they both knew they would remember for lifetime. "God bless you," he whispered as the signal came from one of the ushers. "Now walk proud. You've earned it."

"Here comes the bride," the hostess said in the peaceful ancient church filled to overflowing with freshly flowers and morning sunlight, with other people present as witnesses, Tiffany Stanley was married to Jefferson Bush. Jr. "The bride in white, more beautiful and elegant than flower."

She took a deep breath and they began stepping forward, entered under the arched doors. The aisle seemed a mile long as he kept them at a slow and steady pace.

Everyone rose to their feet, and at the altar, Bush Jr turned, and gasped at the sight of his stunningly beautiful bride who came toward them on his father's arm, with measured steps and eyes cast down beneath her veil.

The scene was playing out as she'd imagined it for month, exactly as planned. All the attendants were in place, each pew decorated with white baby's breath, greenery, and white bow. Her gaze drifted to her mom on the left side of the church, which was filled with people who'd chosen to sit on the bride's side to keep the numbers in the pews fairly equal, and glanced at people she loved on the others. And through her veil, she could watch Cathy who was Gloomy and Bill Nguyen's six years old daughter, walk before them down the aisle, scattering rose petals over the burgundy carpet to blaze a trail for bride. She was darling in a lacy white dress, with her sable curls bouncing over her shoulders. Ahead of her, James' son John was the ring bearer. He looked so cute, a miniature of his father, and took his role very seriously. But she could keep her eyes from drifting back to her soon to be husband, the most handsome and wonderful man on the planet who waited her seemed unable to wipe the happy smile from his face.

❦ ⁂ ❦

She looked at her beautiful daughter in the beautiful formal wedding dress and was so happy that she had tears in her eyes. Years later, she no longer had to worry about this daughter, also felt Bush Jr's love for her daughter that she could rest assured and be happy. She used to think that family ties would always get in the way of two families. But love was God cooperated and raised by two lovers.

Jennies was moved, unable to hold back tears of joy, pride and blessing that filled the air as Brian was holding Tiffany's hand, taking her step by step toward their Bush Jr in her fairy princess gown was touching the floor with the white cloud of heirloom veil which was a picture her life to look like once before. But she couldn't miss the fact, so proudly displayed, that Tiffany was exceedingly pregnant. There was love there for a lifetime, and more. Her husband was the one who gave Tiffany to her son. She was proud to have her as part of the family, and when she looked across at Tiffany's mother was standing with her sons in her lovely gowns with pearl drop earrings. Her honeyed steaks were pulled back into a sophisticated twist, and saw the tears shimmering in her eyes then pressed the handkerchief to dry them, she could tell she was feeling the exact same way how lovely her daughter was, after so much pain, finally enjoying the sweet fruit. She pressed her palm together as if in prayer and lifted them to her lips. Caught her eyes, they shared a happy smile even though the happiness tears on her face were telling that everything worked out for Tiffany and Bush Jr in the end on that perfect fall day where they stood and watched the ceremony. And their hearts were filled to overflowing as they all witnessed their son and daughter marring the one, they'd always loved.

Today was proof positive that a loving family-no matter how bound by relationship and pull apart was the greatest gift in life. Beneath her breath, she continued to repeat. *God is Love. Love really does conquer all.*

Tiffany was a dreamlike creature on this perfect day, her wedding day as Bush Jr stared at his beloved. The gorgeous creature coming toward him.

She was willing to spend the rest of her life with him, just the two of them, forever and ever. And there, Bush Jr stood to the right of the altar, in his black, western-cut tuxedo with his best men who were his brothers and waiting with Pastor Steven stood beside him, holding his Bible with both hands. It had been one of pure love, pure joy.

She took his breath away as Bush Jr's heart was in his eyes. There was no other way for him to describe it, and he never took them off his love while she completed the journey with his father. They all turned to face Pastor Steven who started the ceremony by asking. "Who gives this woman to this man?"

"Her mother and I," Brian answered, and everyone burst into joyous laughter.

Tiffany found herself beaming. This casual and comfortable atmosphere suited her and Bush Jr perfectly. She had spent so much time dreaming about her perfect formal wedding. But now that she was here, she knew this was exactly the wedding she was meant to have.

"I love you," her future father-in-law whispered through tears, and after she stood on tiptoe to kiss him through the folds of her veil. He took the groom's hand and placed her hand on his, gave her to the man she loved, and went to join his wife in the front row. Tiffany took Bush Jr's hand with a joyous sense of rightness. And he smiled at her, telling her without words that he felt the same emotion.

The pastor opened the bible. "This happy even is Heaven's own design for lovers meeting," he began. "Love is everything. Love is mainspring of human action that can be opening yourself and accepting each other. Acknowledging there will be both good times and bad times but believing both is better when you're together."

Smiling felt the tears spill from her eyes. She knew that everyone would think she was crying because her brother was getting married. But she was crying for what she'd lost. She had no one to blame but herself. She probably would have gotten through it all if Mathew hadn't. She thought no one had noticed her red eyes, but at that exact second, she saw Tommy looked at her, and she remembered where she was and what was happening. Of course, he'd noticed. He never missed anything.

"I've seen Bush Jr and Tiffany together," the pastor continued. "I know they were led by God so they could find each other. More than that, they were brave, and willing to risk the unknown, to make the attempt to reach out, to find their way to their well-deserved happy ending. This is just the beginning. From the moment after they're wearing rings each other, they will step out into most wonderful and blessed journey."

The church had a beautiful altar, and the three stained-glass windows set high above it were quite something to behold with the light streaming through them in the rainbow, where their Bush Jr and Tiffany intertwined his hand with hers.

It was her moment. The moment every woman dreamed about as she stood at Bush Jr's side, prepared to pledge her life to his while bridesmaids and groomsmen all each side of them. She'd never felt more uncertain-or, at the same time, more confident of anything she'd ever done.

"Now that Bush Jr and Tiffany have exchanged traditional vows, they would like to share a few thoughts they prepared on their own," the pastor said. "Bush Jr, if you're ready."

His eyes held hers, slid his arm around her waist, drew her close and said his own vow. "From this day forward, I vow that I will never leave you. No circumstance is great enough to keep me from you. We will raise our family and grow old together."

"I love you with all my heart and I will never stop. You are the greatest gift in my life, and I will cherish you for as long as we both live."

This was the perfect moment for her to know; she chose this. She chose him. This was her life. She did not think it would be possible for her. But it was. It would be. So, she vowed back. "My dear Bush Jr, God created all things having certain purposes. There's nothing this world exist without the reason. I'm thankful to Him for His intended path, guiding us back to each other." She paused and swallowed back the lump forming in her throat. "You are my soul mate, and the love of my life. I promise I will love, cherish, and honor you until death do us part."

Brian and Jennies watched and listened to the solemn exchange of vows. Life is a circle and love is what gilds it. And two of them began their own circle within those circles forged by all the generations before. Their heart was filled with overflowing.

Listening to the words that would bind Bush Jr and Tiffany together then beautiful wedding rings to be worn on their ring fingers, like a sweet bond that Smiling couldn't hold back her tears. She felt a sense of loss for herself. She never heard those words, never knew the overwhelming joy of pledging her life to a man who would love her back with equal passion.

The rings in place, the vows spoken solemnly, Pastor Steven closed his Bible, smiled as he looked at them. "By the power vested in me, I now pronounce you man and wife. You may kiss the bride."

"Thank goodness!" her mom said with a burst of applause followed his words. *Happy to finally be part of a family.* And Tiffany leaned forward as Bush Jr lifted her veil and kissed her as if she were the only woman on earth.

Tiffany melted against him. Finally, they were together, and nothing, nothing could tear them apart. They turned and smiled to a big gathering of friends and family who were clapping hands.

Organ music began to throb through the church again, and a surge of true joy ran through Smiling in rush. Involuntarily, her eyes turned toward Tommy where he was smiling with happiness for them too. Longing she didn't dare soften to swelled in her chest as she snapped her gaze back to Tiffany. She and her Prince Charming practically floated together down the aisle hand in hand along the flower-strewn runner and guests threw rose petals at them. It was a happy time, a happy day, it was the culmination of a lifetime.

Behind them, the bridesmaids and groomsmen followed in orderly, and Smiling's gaze flicked to Tommy again, took his arm and walk back down the aisle with him.

"They made it," he said, smiling as he held his arm out to her not nearly enough seconds later. She slipped her hand through his arm, and they started off behind Gloomy the maid of honor, and her husband Bill Nguyen, the best man.

"Like a fairy tale." Smiling said, keeping her gaze locked firmly ahead of them.

Walking with her husband, she sneaked a glance at him and remembered the time when she met him, then it was time to fall in love with him, and the whole time that seemed to be apart. Now, holding hands with him walking down the aisle, she didn't believe this was real. Many things happened, so now they could happily go to the goal together, really not easy. This happiness, this love, him and the presence of those who she loved the most. It's her precious gift.

As soon as they made it to the last row, and formed a reception line outside. Tiffany accepted kisses, hugs and handshakes from friends and relatives.

Smiling slipped her hand out of the crook of Tommy's arm. "Tiffany," she said as the line dwindled and hugging her sister-in-law. "It was such a sweet wedding. Congratulations."

Tiffany sniffed. "It was, wasn't it? I'm so happy."

Smiling laughed. "So why are you crying on a good day?"

"I know it's crazy, isn't it?" Tiffany smiled. "Happy tears are wonderful, though."

"Happy tears are always good." Tommy stepped in, hugged her, then pulled a handkerchief out of his pocket. "Here, has a good cry. You're entitled." "Thank you, Tommy." And the tears fell.

Bush Jr grinned, pulled Tiffany into his arms, and brushed the tears from the corners of her eyes. "As long as they're happy tears," he said, kissed her then winked at them. "I'm happy one."

And Smiling felt Tommy watching her, but she refused to look at him. She didn't trust her heart, couldn't trust her heart.

And then they all thanked everyone who came forward to offer congratulations again. Bush Jr received handshakes, accepted claps on the back, and listened to well-meaning advice.

"I'm happy for two of you." His dad finally said after hugging him, and then kissed Tiffany's forehead.

"You are the most wonderful family I could ever hope to have, and I have you to thanks for it all." Tiffany replied, smiling at her father-in-law, a man she had grown to love, respect, and admire. He was so kind to her, the most considerate person she had ever known.

They'd gone full circle, but one thing remained the same. That was the love of family is one of life's greatest bless. "No, you should thank Jefferson Bush, your father in a crazy kind of way. If he hadn't demanded a DNA tests, you never would have met Bush Jr. And by the way you look lovely, and how to address you."

"Life is full of wonderful surprise." Tiffany said and kissed his cheek to answer. "Despite there are different ways in which to address a member of family, but I want you to know that I hold in high respect as parents in law.

Having said that, neither I nor my mother will ever apologize for our actions prior to your family…"

"We love you, Tiffany." Her mother-in-law cut in, and she kissed on her cheek. "You're our family now and being part of this family means you are loved and always will be for the rest of your life. No matter what! This is now. I hope you will always be as happy as you are today. And I'm proud to have you as my new daughter and think of what beautiful children you'll have."

Tiffany could feel her eyes star to burn again, and she hugged her tightly, her voice emotional. "Thanks mom, thank you dad, thank you family for forgiving me."

And in turn, her family congratulated with all the right words, all warm, affectionate sentiments, and hugged each of them. Her mom was crying, of course. "I love you, mom." Tiffany said. "Coming to Melbourne is the smartest thing I've done."

"True." Bush Jr pressed a kiss to her forehead reassuring. "Tiffany and I will go back and forth to visit you, mom."

"I'd love that," her mother said, beaming and glance from one to another. "And right now, I'd like to wash my face. I must look a mess." "You look just like your children to me," Bush Jr replied, "but help yourself."

"I'll do that." Mrs. Angela Stanley touched Tiffany hair, and his cheek, and then went off.

In this moment, happiness and joy have spread everywhere. No more pain and regret, joy was evident on each person's face for the love of today's young couple. And after additional photos were taken, his dad said to everyone again on the micro. "Thank you everyone, we couldn't have done it without you, and we'll be happy to see you all at the reception."

Chapter 30

Love and laughter are best remembered when surrounded by family and friends

Following the main ceremony at the church and as they discussed before. At 4:00 pm, the first limousine pulled up to the Jefferson House's portico where Steady stood to greet the guests. Bush Jr emerged, wearing a traditional black tuxedo, and then turned and helped his bride out of the car. Tiffany wisely wore an outer gold lace rode over the Vietnamese's traditional bright red silk wedding costume style elegant, flowing with gold silk trim of Chinese's character along the collar and cuff, and embroidered with the gold Chinese double joy words as an outward expression of happiness when returning to her husband's home. On her feet she wore a pair of red boat shoes and on her head, her blond hair was tied into a high bun and held tightly by an elaborate marching red and gold circular headdress that looked like a flying saucer. The dress was killer, but the most beautiful thing about Tiffany was the happy smile she gave to her husband.

"Hi," Bush Jr said. "Everything has been arranged?"

"Good according to the plan." She smiled up at them, and Bush Jr winked at her.

"Good job, sister. We'll see you later." He said, then they walked into the romantic scene.

Even though she wasn't a professional planner, she had done most of work to put this wedding together. A lot of the ideas and suggestions had come from her family, but it had been Steady who put endless hours and lost sleep to pull it off. The house was large function space, but wasn't enough to hold four hundred wedding guests, so a tent had been erected to cover space for more additional ten-person table rounds. Within minutes later, the rest of the wedding party arrived, and they were ushered through the lobby to the wide expanse of back lawn, where was for the cocktails, open bars for anyone who wanted something different, also where the professional photographers proceeded to take a million photographs of happy couple, families and friends.

And Tiffany's relatives were the second to arrive, then wedding guests did next soon after, with a long line of chauffeur driven cars outside, drawing up to the portico one by one. They could join all of their family and friends in an open big tent for diner where the champagne fountain flowed with rosé champagne next to wedding cake with topper that spelled out Tiffany & Bush Jr. Tables were set with white chairs had been draped with pink covers, ready to receive them. DJ had embraced the spirit of the event. And because this one was Vietnam traditional and formal public marriage; Tiffany had been invited a real cordon blue cook from Japan who would be listed the side dishes offered and the appetizers on the menu for them.

Oh, a happy day it was for the Bush Jefferson's that God couldn't have blessed them with a prettier day. There wasn't a cloud in the sky, the high temperature for the day was seventy, and constantly had a gentle breeze. They could have drinks and appetizers out with sunset and under stars. Everything was perfect, just like it should be. Perfect like they always wanted it. It was beautiful, and the fields on the lawn were the color of emeralds under the sun when they spent the entire late afternoon greeting their guests who looked wonderful. The women in all their elegance, the men in their tailor suits, and accepting the many gifts offered them.

And at six-thirty when the last of guests were seated. The master of the ceremony began with stories was told about both families; both of their families were present. There were many speeches were given and many toasts made that they wished them a lifetime of love, joy and happiness and many, many children, and then the scene erupted into a chorus of laughter and cheers, and the glasses clinked busily as frothy champagne was poured, and the supper began to serve as well.

Steady sipped her champagne and scanned the large crowd inside the tent. Right now, nearly four hundred people had come to the wedding seemed to be happy, eating, drinking, and laughing. Despite being dateless, even she wasn't sure that any man had ever really loved her. But thinking about her brother was blissfully married to a wonderful woman, she felt pretty good. And they were called to the dance floor by bandleader said over the microphone before the music started with the song they chose 'I Will Always Love You' for the first official dance as a man and wife. Everyone stood in rapt admiration. They were the best-looking couple they'd ever seen. And then "switch," the bandleader instructed, and Tiffany dutifully danced with Brian, who seemed quite overcome emotion and guided her easily around the dance floor, making her laugh at all the absurdities, and the fun of her wedding just as always. As if they've done it a hundred times before. And after her father-in-law, she danced with her brothers, and her new brothers in law, then Tommy, and their friends, and Bush Jr again, and at last they finally had dinner.

Chapter 31

You never know what you have, until it's gone

Invitations had been sent to the rich and the beautiful, from Florida to New York and LA. Local celebrities, the press and few Hollywood types were to attend.

Leo had received an invitation, and had respectfully declined, but in the end, he must attend, not in his dad's place. But because he believed it was a good cause. He'd deliberately come a little late as he locked his car, and glanced the limos were parked at the curb, and a few reporters lingered on the steps. Guess the Jefferson was big shot in the news, because no one else pulled in such a crowd.

Music floated through the night as he touched his tie to make sure it was centered and smoothed down his hair before he approached two cheerful attendants stood side by side at the doors, handing his invitation to one of them and stepped inside the opulent foyer. Men looked sharp in their dark suit and surrounded by the bright colors of women's dress include noise and movement filled Jefferson House with the good mood to meet and greet any latecomers. The wedding was being held in the largest ballroom, which was located on the first floor at the end of a long wide corridor. Outside with a magnificent fountain, complete with marble base, spouted water eight feet high and overlooking the serenity gardens.

The party was in full swing. He could hear the electronically enhanced music and the voices trying to yell above it. Four bars were set up one in each corner, and people thronged around them as bartenders generous with their pours and rushed to fill their drink orders. Servers passed among the crowd, offering dainty canapés or glasses of wine from their silver trays. Through the double doors to the adjacent ballroom were open, bejeweled guests talking, dancing, laughing and drinking, and there was station with every kind of delicacy to eat, the best of everything. Guests were encouraged to help themselves to whatever they wanted. He grabbed a glass of champagne from server's tray as he walked past, sipped it, and lifted his glass to examine the color of the liquid. Rosé champagne, expensive wine, he guessed as he scanned the room where a man walked in carrying a heaping plate piled with oysters, crackers, and a mound of caviar, and many members of the wedding party were chatting. There were dozens of people he knew, dozens more he recognized. The rich, the powerful, and the famous, but he didn't think to stop and talked to them. Because his biggest pleasure came from spotting his cousin Bush Jr in the distance, who probably had escaped from the loud music inside and now clasped his wife's hand outside the pavilion. She laughed at something he said. The way he looked at her and the way she looked at him. They loved each other. He hurried toward them, holding his glass of champagne.

❊❊✲❊❊

While Bush Jr and Tiffany, stepped outside for fresh air, Jennies and Brian were dancing nearby, and they were going their own thoughts.

Bush Jr and Tiffany will be happy, and they'd best be seeing about giving their mother a baby to bounce on her knee. Jennies is already fretting for a great-grandchild.

Brian felt much more relaxed, going to enjoy himself, as if a heavy load had been lifted off his shoulder. It seemed like the whole world had paired up into couples, but he ached deep in his soul as his daughters who still needed him. They were serving as maid of honor at her brother's wedding, and they looked lovely, in a slender, vanilla satin gown with a red rosebud in their hairs.

Lovely. Yes, they really were. But what bothered him now was the fact that at age thirty-five and thirty-six, Smiling and Steady hadn't found their way in life and was still unmarried.

Single. Oh, how he'd come to unhappy that word. When a man reaches sixty-eight years of living, he didn't have time for that kind of nonsense. He looked forward, had always done so. He was a Vietnamese who had lived most of his long life away from the land of his birth. America was his home. He had made his family and raised his children here. He'd watched them and grand children grow. How could he be content with his lot before he had seen them through something?

And of course, there was Jennies, the love of his life, the mother of his children. Between them-well, they'd had a hell of time.

Now he could turn his attention to his sweet Smiling and Steady. Pretty, with a strong spine, a serious nature and a romantic heart, and a brain? God love them, they were bright as the sun. Still, they were unhappy and didn't need a man beside them after they broken heart. So, it's up to him to see that they hadn't had the right men. The men had solid stock, good mind and fine heart. He could buy houses but couldn't build the home for them. Thinking suddenly of this, he sighed under his breath, then immediately clamped down on these negative feelings, focusing instead on his daughters. So, he'd considered this carefully with a plan for them found the man of her heart. Pleased, a smiled played around his mouth.

⁂ ❋ ⁂

Outside, it's a mild night at pavilion, they stood hand in hand for a moment to admire the view. The air was sweeter there, the moon light dimmer. The music became more romantic with distance, and watching their families and friends have a good time. As always, there was a silent, peaceful bond between them. They had an understanding that had surpassed everything for the past time, opposition, stress, fear, loneliness and hatred. It was band of love that brought them together and kept them there. But what she had not even dared to believe possible for her was coming true; marrying a man she had chosen for herself and the wedding was coming together wonderfully. Tiffany wished her dads had been alive to see it. How proud they would be, how happy to attend the wedding of their first grandchild and daughter? But tonight, even their absence could not dull all she had graceful for, and beneath her breath, she prayed in silence, *all thanks are to God. You are great.*

"This is the right time. This is when it was meant to be. I love you." Bush Jr said gently as he looked down at her, puzzled. "Who are you, by the way? Are you Mrs. Jefferson or Miss Stanley?"

"I hadn't thought about that. I'm not sure that at my age. I could change it. Thirty-four years as Stanley is a little hard to wipe out in a single day." Tiffany saw something sad but resigned in his eyes then. "But on the other hand, I tell you what, why not go for the big time?"

"Jefferson?" He looked amazed and touched. It had been an extraordinary day in their household.

"Mrs. Jefferson," she said softly. "Tiffany Jefferson."

Tiffany smiled at him. "Did you do it for me or for them?" Bush Jr asked gently.

"It's funny," she said quietly. "I did it for myself in the end, right? I'm Jefferson."

383

He kissed her lightly on the forehead. "See, it wasn't so bad, Mrs. Jefferson. You've made me incredibly happy."

She angled her head up at him. "Are you going to show me how happy?"

His lips and tongue found hers and he poured all the anxiety that he's feeling into the passionate kiss. She's breathless and panting when he released her. "Oh, yes. Later, all night long if you want."

❋❋ ✳ ❋❋

"Congratulation," came from a cheerful voice, interrupting their thoughts, and they looked around to find a man approached with a wide smile at them over a glass of champagne, which he held in graceful hand. "Nothing tastes so sweet as happiness, especially when you mix it with champagne."

"Leo! Good to see you." Bush Jr said held out his arms. "Thank you. It's been a long time."

The two men hug. "You right about this and good to see you, too. But I wouldn't miss this for the world."

The greeting between the two men was a bit humorous. They hugged like gentlemen. Leo clapped fondly Bush Jr on the back, and Bush Jr retaliated in kind and accusatory. "But you're late."

"I know, and I'm sorry about that." Leo replied, drained his glass of wine to apologize, and well-timed putting the empty glass on the tray when the server walked by, and then his glance slid to Tiffany.

Tiffany recognized him from the cover of *Florida Art and Design* Magazine. It was obvious that Leo liked Bush Jr. He was a charmer, too. There were a few similarities to Bush Jr in bone structure, high cheekbones and square jaw, and he had the same smile. And from their conversation and their ease with each other, she concluded they had been friends for some time.

"You're here, that what counts." She said and threw her arms around Leo for a hug.

"You look especially lovely tonight." He kissed her cheek for pleasant exchange. "Charming beauty in this wedding dress."

"Thank you. So, do you."

"I hope you'll both find a great deal of happiness in your marriage."

She responded with a warm smile. "Considering how it began, I don't see how that will be possible."

384

Leo clucked in sympathy. "Yours isn't the first marriage to begin under less-than perfect circumstances; nor will it be the last. I believe that having a wife and a child will benefit Bush Jr in ways he doesn't begin to suspect."

"He'll never forgive me for what I did," Tiffany said. "And I don't blame him."

"Nonsense," Leo smiled, following her gaze to Bush Jr. "I'm certain you must realize that Bush Jr was married you because he accepted you for what you are. To me, he was fortunate to acquire a wife like you, Tiffany."

Bush Jr laughed, putting his arm around Tiffany's waist, and pulled her closer. "So, I've been told. A hundred times, at least."

Tiffany looked at Bush Jr with adoration and kissed his cheek. "And we couldn't be happier now. I can tell you."

"I can see that and my best wishes to both of you for a long and happy marriage."

⁂

Brian could see Leo's face in distance where he shook Bush Jr's hand then hugged and kissed Tiffany on both of her cheeks for congratulation. His appearance was the most anticipated. This instantly cheered him up.

"Leo!" he cried, delighted.

The sound of his name calling came from behind, causing them turned in unison, and a smile struck his face when he saw who was walking toward them. "Uncle and aunt, lovely to meet you," Leo said, smiling to greet them.

Brian embraced his nephew and stepped back to study him. "Leo, how nice to see you, I was hoping you would be here!"

As he spoke, his glance returned to his wife, and following his gaze, Leo grinned. "I'm so please you're here, Leo."

Leo thought his aunt always looked so put together. She remained the most beautiful woman ever created. She had never had any face work done, but with her genes and her bone structure had aged beautifully. Her crystal-clear eyes never missed anything, and her smile could melt the coldest of hearts. Leo was so proud of his aunt. Cheerfully, he kissed her on both cheeks. "I never did tell you how beautiful you look tonight, Aunt Jennies."

On closer inspection, Jennies was forced to admit that Leo was the spitting of his father Jayden Tu, an old family friend. With a grin, Jennies leaned forward to kiss his cheek. "Leo thanks! You look pretty smashing yourself. Did you come alone? Where is your father? Doesn't he get a vote?"

"Yes, and actually, he got sick with stomach flu." Leo corrected. "He's feeling better, but he said he still wasn't completely over it and didn't want to spread the virus to everyone. So, he's sorry he couldn't be here tonight to celebrate with you, but he sends you his best wishes."

"Tell him I'm wishing him better very quickly, and you can also tell him I'll come to see him on Monday."

"That'll please him, and I will tell him that." Leo replied, smiling up at him, but his uncle patted his arm, changing subject. "How does it feel to be back?"

So much had changed in ten years. Leo had known what turning him back on Steady and Jefferson Bush's meant. They here had long memories, and they loved Steady. Taking their cues from her grandpa, they'd been distant with him from the moment on. They'd behaved exactly as he'd anticipated. He was prepared for it and not for the first time since he had decided to come back his hometown which would never be the same. Did he feel foolish? He'd been born here, raised here, and he'd fallen in love. Was it possible after all this time to win back their affection? But there was something else to do first, something he'd already known he would have to do. There were no secrets this time, and with their typical generosity of spirit, the entire family had welcomed and made him feel at home amongst them that why he was attending this wedding. "I don't know yet. It's odd, mostly. Everything was the same. Nothing was the same."

"But we're glad you're back and could be here to share in our celebration. Why don't you take your seat and drink champagne?"

Immediately he shifted his attention to the people gathering in the ball room as his thoughts swung to his cousin Steady Jefferson, hopping to spot her. When he didn't see her, he shot them another smile. "I'll grab something later. But you wouldn't know where I might find …"

"My daughter, Steady?" he finished for him.

"Yes, so I can say hi to her?"

"You're not going to start hitting on my daughter again?" Brian asked him with a strange little smile.

It's embarrassing. Leo knew it wasn't the mouth that showed his uncle mood. It was the eyes. When they smiled, he meant it. He and Steady had been friends once, lovers briefly. She'd other lovers since, and he had a wife. But he could feel as if they might be accepting him back. Maybe not in the same intimate role he'd once played, but at least as their relationship.

He looked at him, feeling that question in his gaze. "Is that what I'm doing, Uncle?"

"Look that way." Bush Jr cut in. "And speaking of which, buddy, we're about to start taking bets on how long it will be before you and Steady get back together."

"I'm afraid it's not that simple, bro. But did she find anyone... serious?"

He winked at him and answered kindly. "Not as far as I know."

Leo smiled with relief. "I have something else to ask you. Do you have a problem with me flirting your sister?"

Bush Jr laughed and nudged him. "No, but buddy, you better watch out."

Relieved they had no objections, Leo grinned back. "Thanks for your warning."

"Shut up, Leo." Brian commanded. "Last time I saw her was playing piano. You know how she is."

Trying to disguise his embarrassment, Leo said. "Thank you, I'll go find her there." Brian nodded and Jennies smiled in response and Tiffany and Bush Jr waved up as Leo began making his way through the throng of guests toward the ball room, into the music, the voices, the lights, and felt an immediate lift of mood.

This party was success as far as he could tell after one quick scan. The room practically glowed with the maze of ribbon tied chairs and ruffled tables topped with vases overflowing with an array of beautiful flowers, and all around him people were laughing, talking, and dancing. The noise level was a wonder on a wide, platform, under those flashing lights, the DJ worked with a piano stood against one wall and was played, everything from tropical remix by various fingers at various times. He turned in to the music was flowing out of the speakers. He liked it, the hard, repetitive beat; the pouring of drums; the rough metallic scream of guitar, and the way different dancers chose to move to it. Arms in the air, arms cocked like a boxers with fist hands, elbows jabbing, feet plated, feet lifting. Adding the scents of cooking wafted through the air. Wine was poured with generous hands, and nobody seemed to stay still for more than five minutes. He smiled at people he met, managed a few words to those he knew, but his eyes were forever moving, hunting, seeking for a familiar face.

Immediately, he caught a distant sight of the face he recognized at once. She was so lovely. He thought she looked like something that had stepped out of a dream. A woman he'd tried to forget, but every time her image filtered into his mind, he felt regretful for what he had done and that cut him straight to the bone.

The first time he met her, she'd been about eight, a little China doll. Cute, sweet, harmless, and he loved her. Of course, he did, in a purely family way. The fact that she'd grown into a woman didn't change that. He was still two years older, her more experienced cousin. But the woman over there didn't look like anyone's cousin.

Had she been beautiful long time ago and had he just not noticed, or had she done whatever it was women did to make them allure? It had been years since they'd last seen each other, but the view of Steady, his cousin was sitting at the lovely old spinet, hypnotized him, and she looked as though she was having a good time. For the life of him, Leo couldn't force himself not to stare at her and letting her music run through him. *The power of your love is all I need tonight. I know there have been times that I have caused you pain.* She was still had thick hair, gleaming like black silk that was piled in loose curls atop her head, and it showed entirely too much of slender neck and smooth shoulders. Her eyes had always been wide, brown, and glittery with emerald earrings, shaped like teardrops, matched the bracelet encircling one slim wrist, and one big tear-sharped diamond nestled comfortable between the curves of her breasts. But her skin seemed more luminous and, in a body, skimming red silk dress that emphasized her curves was pure magic. He could barely control his need to touch her again. He meant to run to her, but his feet seemed rooted to the spot, and wondered if she noticed his distraction.

What was it about her that pulled him so? She looked classy as hell. Perhaps that had been true years ago, when a young boy first saw those restless brown eyes on the face had been just as attractive. A classic oval with peaches and cream skin, a mobile and shapely mouth tinted with a soft pink. Sexy eyebrows they were dark and well arched to match the hair was longer than he remembered. She'd tucked it behind her ears, and it bounced against her bare shoulder. But now those innocent features had changed over time, so that she became an attractive woman that attracted the eyes of any man.

How's about her manner? That made him smile. How kind and lovely Steady was. She rarely hurt other people's feelings. If so, she simply forgot about them, but she must have sensed his scrutiny at almost the same moment.

Leo sighed. None of those questions could be answered today, or even in a week. All he knew for sure was why he hadn't asked these questions before? Shaking his head to dispel the nonsense, he asked himself. So what do you expect from her? Definitely wanted to earn her trust and respect again. After that … Well, time would tell. Luckily, he had time on his hands as the lyrics spoke for him. *I'd turn them all around if I could start again. There's something I must say I know it's overdue. The sweetest thing I've known forever called my own. Begins and ends with you. How I love you.*

Chapter 32
Flee love and it will follow you

Finally free, Tommy eased away from the group, and headed to the bar. The bartender was dropping a slice of lime into a glass and flicked a glance his way then placed the drink in front of a woman and smiled when it was his turn.

"Tommy. What can I get for you?"

"Vodka, please, easy on vodka," Tommy answer.

"You got it."

So far, he'd managed to avoid Smiling, which meant he tried and failed at shoving thoughts of Smiling from his mind. He still hadn't figured out what he was going to say when they are next together. And he drank more than he should have. "Well," the bartender placed a glass on the napkin in front of him and said to him. "It's early to try to get drunk."

Tommy chuckled, tossed a couple bills on the bar. "This is medicinal. It's going to be a long night."

He picked up the money, and said thanks to him, then hurry to serve the others.

Tommy drained his vodka, and unable to keep his attention off Smiling as she drifted from table to table and group to group. He turned his back to the bar and leaned against the counter, looking around for a distraction, and he saw she stood there, addressing everyone in the crowd where all eyes were on her. Except for him, who was watching her? She looked freaking amazing, he noticed. Hell, he noticed everything about her. Not just the sexy, sloe-eyes, curvy, golden-skinned, masses of curling hair, soft, full lipped amazing that was killer enough. But to add in the heat and light she just seemed to emanate. She made one hell of package.

He shook his head, as if to clear away cobwebs, and reminded himself. Get a grip, she was Jefferson Jennifer. In any case, she was a famous model, always surrounded by people. They were people accomplishing things. They talked about interesting things and they were in fact interesting people. Just like now, with a man.

When a woman looked like Jefferson Jennifer, there was always single males could flirt with her, but Smiling never flirted back, at least not in a way that any guy could take seriously. Her flirting extended to everyone, male, female, young and old, but except with him. He wasn't sure what to do about it. Still, it never hurt to look. He was a man who appreciated lines and curves in the woman. In his estimation, she was pretty much architecturally perfect. So, he motioned to the bartender for another drink, then pretended to listen to the conversation, and watched her slide and sway through the room.

Looked casual as the bartender placed the second one for him. He brought his glass to his lips, sipping his drink and continuing to watch her over the rim at the way she'd stop, exchange greetings, pause, laugh or smile. But he'd made a kind of study of her over the years. She moved with purpose.

Then some guy, he didn't know who, but seeing the quick, flirtations grin, the easy did a lot of his hand movements from back stroking to shoulder draping. And yeah, her body language wasn't signaling reception. Tommy stiffened. A predatory instinct jumped to life inside him. "Son of a bitch." Putting his drink on the bar, he tried toward her. But saw she did attentive smile at him, laughing up at him from under that thicket of lashes she owned that meant she was avidly interested. Then without moments, she gave a quick, almost imperceptible signal, the man found himself chatting with another woman.

Then he heard her call out Elizabeth! And follow up with that sizzle-in the blood laugh of hers before she grabbed a very fine-looking blonde in a hug.

They chattered, beaming at each other the way women did, holding each other at arm's length to take the survey before. No doubt they told each other hoe great they looked. Liked you look fabulous. Have you lost weight? I love your hair. And from his observations, that female ritual had some variations, but the theme remained the same.

Then Smiling angled herself in a way that put some guy to the blonde face to face. He got it then, by the way she sided back an inch or two then waved a hand in the air before giving some guy and thought the blonde would distract him.

Why did all that bother him? He wasn't the jealous sort. And certainly, had no reason to be jealous. But why did he get an uneasy feeling when he with her or around her? He didn't have an answer. How could he explain what he didn't understand? One thing he knew now: he didn't like the idea of any man getting close to her.

❧ ❧ ✳ ❧ ❧

Smiling did not so much as glance at Tommy, but she knew that he was nearby and watching her. Always watching. And while she glided between guests and stopped to hug women and men she had not yet greeted, she tried to meet his eyes between conversations, tracked his movement across the crowded hall, checking his face for any displeasure. She knew he watched people without being obvious, not because cared, and in watching them, he was able to learn their secrets. That why she turned away to meet his eyes. Not because she didn't trust her heart, couldn't trust her heart, but because she understood that an agreement had been made between them; they knew who they were here for.

Chapter 33

The ones who love you will never leave you. Even if there are hundred reasons to give up, they will find one reason to hold on.

Some sixth sense drew her to aware of someone watching her. Turning her head left, her heart lurched as her eyes flew instantly to a pair of gold-brown eyes met hers, whose was brazenly focusing on her. Where had she seen those eyes before? How could a stranger's face seem so familiar? He was tall and distinguished looking, wearing a well-cut tuxedo, a white shirt, a navy Hermes tie, and he had an aristocratic air of command that instantly caught her eyes. At once he smiled and nodded his head in recognition. It was a smile of such surpassing sweetness, of such compassion that she had to restrain herself from rushing across the room to his side. But she forced herself to look away and followed the music.

Leo continued to stare approvingly in her direction until she turned her head and their eyes met, knowing she had spotted him and he remained where he was, watching until the crowd cheered when she stopped playing, stood and walked to him.

She and he had been more than friends for what seemed a lifetime, yet somehow many years they hadn't seen each other. Her heart began to thud as she wondered how she should greet him. A hug, a handshake, the stiff, distant, arms crossed greeting he deserved? But he was leaving her no time to think as he took her into his arms and gave her a casual, bear hug. The nearness of him, his smell and touch, caused her skin to tingle, her heart to race, as if she were thirteen years old again and first realizing that she was falling in love with the boy who'd been her cousin and her best friend. She had waited for this moment since that last awful conversation between them.

God, it felt wonderful, and the heat was immediate. It was like a sinking sense of having been played by fate as the body that pressed firmly against his reminded him, uncomfortably, that his relationship with his ex-wife had been based on their being a sensible match. Since the divorce, he'd avoided entanglements of any kind, so it had been years since he'd experienced the dark, sensual, visceral burn of desperately wanting any one woman.

Her confidence lifted a full notch at his reaction, and the feeling so familiar and comforting that for a moment it was just like old times. She rose on her toes to kiss him, just a bit too hard and too long for a casual greeting.

He backed off, smiling, and shoved his hands into the pockets of his pants. It was the only way he could keep them from touching her. If he had been any younger, he might have blushed. For him, it was like turning the clock back. And he'd been right about one thing: there was still that attraction between them. When they opened their mouths, they both spoke at the same time.

"Hello, Steady."

"Hello, Leo."

"You first," Leo said, gesturing with his hand.

The way he looked at her and the way he had used her shorter nickname brought back memories of a time in her life she had tried to put behind her. "What a nice surprise!" She said, striving to sound as nonchalant as possible. Why wasn't it that her emotions were always so raw whenever he was near? "And how have things been with you?"

Her voice was sweet, her smile acidic. "Fine, just fine," he answered stiffly. "And you?"

Something kindled in his brown eyes, something new and pleasant. "I'm okay, wonderful actually."

Steady was the only woman who'd ever been able to light up him inside like a glowing Christmas tree by doing nothing more than looking at him. No matter what else had changed in his life and in their relationship, that one fact remained the same. "You look lovely."

Complimented by the man who she'd forgotten and his bubbly personality. He loved practical jokes, bawdy humor, and having fun. A pang pierced her deep. She'd really lost him these past years, and so much had happened in those years, so much to talk about, but only now she was beginning to realize he had just been a ghost of his former self. Although, it made her happy, but also a bit shy, So she took a closer look at him. "Thank you. You look very handsome yourself," she said, admiring him with genuine affection, and stepped back staying away the deliciously expensive scent of his cologne settled around her like a sensuous mist. "You really do look good, you know."

"You're not supposed to look so surprise. It's not polite." He said, chuckling, as their eyes met. They shared the same memories, the same dashed hopes, and once upon a time they had shared the joys and laughter. It was hard to remember those days now. Only the regret remained. He had come here to add the new memory to their album.

"I just forget how good-looking you are sometimes. Are you staying for good?" She asked suddenly, changing the subject. "And have any plans?"

"Oh, I've got a few of them." He smiled and wondered what she would think if he mentioned that the biggest plan of his life was to woo her. "But right now, I work for my dad, and I've got big contract coming up."

"I'm glad to hear that. And tell me ..." It was a struggled, but she kept the eagerness out of her voice and spoke matter of-fact. "Have you ever discovered how much you miss me?"

"Huh?" it made him nervous with her question. But even after all these years, just one glance at her plum-sweet mouth, her big eyes with curly dark lashes, and the sweet scent of her had him couldn't resist taking and hold of her arm, leaned toward her, and kissed her cheek. "It's been a long time since we last talked. So, the answer is yes."

That was exactly what she'd wanted to hear. So much had changed, for all of them, in this past year. She'd been perfectly content in Melbourne, with her home, her work, her routine, but Leo had not changed much, she decided. He looked well, approachable and relaxed. He'd done this many of time before, but this felt different, more intimate. Therefore, in reaction, or defense, she pulled away almost at once, afraid he would hear the pounding of her heart. Why was it always this way with him?

"Yes, it has been a long time," she agreed. "And you really mean that, don't you?" It was a statement, not a question.

"Of course, I do. I've missed you." Swamped by memories and needs, he scrutinized her once again. Damn, she was lovelier than his memory of her. He'd hoped it would be different. He'd hoped his fantasies of her would be exaggerated as so many fantasies are. But he pushed those thoughts aside. They were useless to think about after all. She was here, flesh and blood in marvelous form, and beautifully groomed and dress were taking his breath away. Then again, he reminded himself, if he wanted Steady to take him seriously as a man, he had to take himself seriously first.

With that in mind, he smiled. "But anyway, you amaze me."

"Only because you're finally starting to pay attention," she told him, trying to tell him that she'd been right in front of his eyes for years. It had simply taken him a long time to notice how incredible she was, and his hands were lean, and there were no rings on them. "I haven't changed, Leo. You have."

"Of course, you've changed," he argued. His gaze roved over her face. Her glossy chestnut hair was longer than it'd been the last time he'd seen her. But the color was instantly recognizable. "Your hair."

She felt an uneasy fluttering in her stomach, the way she always did when he stared at her intently. Leo had seen her hair before. Of course, he would notice the change even she clipped it up. "Yes, I wear it long back. What do you think?"

"I can see that. It suits you."

She smiled. "And because I never figured you for coming back, not for any length of time."

He laughed, full and rich and delighted. "Neither did I. But things change, Steady. They're meant to, I guess. I've been itchy the last few years, and I finally figured out I was itchy for home. How are things with you?"

My feeling for you hadn't changed. "They're okay. I assume you'll be finding out later."

There was so much to ask, so much that couldn't be answered. If he had had one wish at that moment it would have been to reach out and kiss her. Just to kiss her once and remember the way it had been. "I will. Otherwise, I wouldn't have come."

"Great, welcome back," she tucked her arm through his in an intimate way, and together they walked to a grouping of chairs near the stage. "How about we grab some wine and trade some stories."

It was obviously she was plotting out their future as women always did. He thought as they sat down and asked her, "about what?"

"My plans," she said. "I'm going to find myself a house."

"Sounds like you're moving out of your parents' home."

She managed a small smile. "Every bird needs to leave the nest."

"Then seem like you need a favor."

Leo's a designing engineer, and a wonderful architect. He'd done a few plans for their business last year. And his dad had promised to a look at a new house which she insisted on the best. But so naturally, she thought of him. Steady nodded and leaned forward. "Maybe, Leo, I would be grateful if you show me a new house at your father's development on the outskirts of the town."

"I see. And if you ask me to, I'll do my best to find your dream house."

"Sounds great," she said. The first requirement of her new house was that it should have some sort of view, second one was it would have to have a balcony. She wanted to have a pleasant, sparsely home that was the most up-to date electronic equipment and artistic. That was a third point on her list. Her fourth requirement was that the new house should have plenty of space, closets, a proper office, and a big bedroom where she could spread herself out. The last one was she wanted the bathroom to smell fresh, and to be able to open a window. "I think I'd like a house with a balcony and view of the water, at least four room, large closets, big bathroom with window, and utility room."

"To you, I'd be more than happy to help you out." He offered and was rushing things. "Tomorrow, if you're free, I could give you all the tour, okay?"

The lights in the overhead chandeliers suddenly dimmed as the band began playing a new song. The music slowed to a moody ballad and the singer launched into some classic pop song asked for bride and groom walked onto the dance floor for dancing together again. When the strains of "I want to know what love is" filled the air, Steady watched Bush Jr took Tiffany in his arms, led her into the middle of the floor and began to dance.

Then other couples joined in the music, eager to display their own facility, until the floor became crowded with many friends and dozens of distant relative and cousins who truly knew how to move.

"I'm glad you're excited about it," she kissed him on the cheek for his willing. "But let's not rush things. Just enjoy the party, shall we?" "Your wish is my command," he mocked.

Steady laughed then, and as she watched their bodies entwining and moving slowly together. "Hey, I love this song. It's time for us to lead off the dancing. Join me?"

He liked the sound of her laughter, but since she didn't wait for him answer or come up with some kind of excuse, she grabbed hold of his hand and pulled him into the warm room where couples were gliding around the dance floor. For the first time since he'd come back to Melbourne, he felt their relationship was back on the level where it belonged.

Chapter 34
Love will find a way

"Look like you didn't take your eyes off her." A voice said just behind him, disturbing his thoughts, Tommy jerked himself back, turned, and watched the bartender placed the Manhattan in front of a noble lady then he moved down the bar to start filling drink orders for wedding guests. "Oh, Miss. Charity," he broke into a smile. "What? I didn't get you."

"I don't see how you could have." She said as her glass halfway to her mouth, "since you didn't take your eyes off Smiling."

Smelling of Chanel perfume, and he smiled into her blurred eyes. If even she could see that he was brooding, he'd better watch his step. "I always look at her. My job is to protect her in every way."

Ugh. That wasn't true, she took a sip of her drink, and studied his face. "I don't see that you have any problem. But don't play stupid with me, mister handsome. I read people very well. I saw the way how you look at her, and I saw how she look at you, since the day we met. People are falling, Tommy." She argued him as she glanced over where Smiling and new partner were dancing with couples danced, moving slowly, holding other tightly, and surrendering to the dreamy mood of a melodic ballad on the dance floor. "Denying it is stupid, and one thing you aren't and never have been is stupid."

Despite his best efforts, Tommy picked his glass and his lips curved against the rim as he glared at her. "Okay, now you're just being ridiculous. Especially, you really think she could fall for me?" He said, finishing off his drink, then set the glass aside. "I don't think so. I try to keep my professional life and personal life separate. And I don't mix business and personal feeling." He made it very clear for her to understand. But he couldn't forget Smiling's unexpected kiss, the feel of her slender body pressed against him. That's amazing, heart stopping, and gut tightening.

Smothering a knowing smile, Miss Charity pulled the cherry from her drink and popped it in her mouth. A moment later she said. "I know it's

none of my business, and I wasn't criticizing you. Just telling you've got to
…"

"Stop, yeah… yeah I know."

"No, that isn't what I meant," she said quickly, taking another long sip of her drink then her eyes serious on him. "I meant; you're better expressing your unspoken love."

His chest convulsed, couldn't dare to believe that she actually said that. "Oh no, I can't not fall in love."

Understood his confusion, she held up a hand. "You're being deliberately evasive, Tommy. You'll feel better if you're honest with me and with yourself."

A strange expression passed over his face. "What's that supposed to mean?"

"Meaning's if you could ever quit putting your job long enough to think of that, you might surprise yourself."

The old woman's observations had been right on the money, and he had the horrible feeling that Miss Charity was as good at reading body language as he was that it was so damn obvious. He had been in love before, but things with Smiling were different.

Somehow… richer, bigger and more confusing. And though he wanted to believe that Miss Charity was right, that he had feelings for Smiling, but he knew those hopes were only foolish fantasies. "Honestly, I tried to tell you that it's easier for me to work for her if we keep personal relationship out of it." "Logical. I find you consistently logical, Tommy."

He wasn't entirely sure it was a compliment. "Like I said, I'm not going to let my personal feeling interfere with my job. But the problem is, almost everything I think or feel connects with her."

"And the way you're caring more for her could make the problem seem bigger, right?"

"No. I wouldn't be able to tell you, because of all the women in the world, I could fall in love, could love, except Jennifer Jefferson." He was amazed that the words had come out. "Look at her. She could date all kinds of famous or power men. She wouldn't be interested in me."

"I know she could," she admitted with a grin. "But wealth, honor or status are external things. The virtue is real basic and root of a human being." Nonplussed, she gulped down the last of her drink, then went on. "Generally, I'm not big on advice, but I'm going to give you some anyway.

The love of your life might slip away if you don't do something, and I don't want to see either of you hurt."

Tommy stared at her. "You think I'd hurt Smiling?"

"Not intentionally. But I think, perhaps, you listen to too many voices that aren't your own."

She was speaking the truth. "I'll remember that."

"And here's another piece of advice, if you're worrying about something like you aren't worthy of her. You are wrong because love is not an option or brought from destiny. It must be combined from God. Evidence is her love before. Of course, she would. She'd be lucky to have you. I believe so."

"Thanks, looks like we're in the same boat," he said quietly, hoping against hope that it could be explained away. "She's been great to me. And such a good woman like that, I can't reach. I can only cherish. However, I'll be crushed when it ends, and it will. So, I should put that aside and move on. Don't you agree?"

"You're sure of what you do?" she asked, her face quite serious. "Why would you have to force yourself within a limit flame for the rules that made you gradually become emotionless and forget your own feeling?"

He wished he could answer that. "No, I can't. Even though, love between man and woman does not rules. But in this situation, love was a different matter, and my head hasn't clear, that why I need time."

She knew what he was saying but she wasn't worried. "Time's what you need, Tommy, but take love when it's offered. Let it live with you." She said in consideration, but distracted by the lyric of new song from Kenny Rogers. *Lady, I'm your knight in shining armor and I love you.* "Oh, this is one of my favorites."

The knowledge was so clear, so right that he could almost hugged this woman for showing him. Almost, instead, he smiled and held out his hand. "Would you care to dance with me, Miss Charity?"

The faintest of blushes tinted her cheeks. "I'd love to, Mr. Tommy." She took his hand and he led her onto the dance floor.

⁂

Something had changed, Smiling felt it. Ever since from that day, Tommy had seemed different, desperate and was very careful to keep his distance with her. They didn't touch, didn't even brush arms. It was as if the past few weeks had never happened. Something was on his mind, but she had no idea what, nor did she know how to ask. She wanted him, physically, but he was like miles from her reach, emotionally, but he'd distanced himself from her feelings. Worry returned and with it fear that she was going to lose Tommy before she'd truly had a chance to be with him. She watched Tommy lead Miss Charity onto the floor. Her heart softened. She tried to harden it again but found it was a lost cause. It was a sweet thing to do, she thought, particularly since he was anything but a sweet man. She doubted that noble and dreamy old ladies were Tommy's style, but Miss Charity would remember this day for a long time.

What woman wouldn't, Smiling mused. To dance with a strong, mysterious man on the wedding was a memory to be pressed in a book like red rose. It was undoubted fortunate he hadn't asked her. She figured he was trying to keep his work from their relationship. So, the only question she was left with was the one that needed asking before she went any further, but the one question she couldn't scrounger up the guts to ask. The question dogged her through endless hours of temp work, she was so torn between dying to know the answer and refusing to acknowledge the inevitable ending to the sweetest thing she'd ever known. Of course, she wanted there to be more to their relationship, to see it go on and on.

She couldn't possibly see how it would ever work. But she wasn't going to let him walk away until he told her everything. With a sigh she herded a group of children into the television room, giving them cupcakes and pushed some games on.

⁂ ✦ ⁂

Tommy saw Smiling leave and saw her come back.

"That was lovely," Miss Charity told him when the music had stopped.

"My pleasure, Miss Charity." Then with all charm, he took her hand and kissed it, made her pleasure completely. And by the time she had walked over to sigh with her sister she had forgotten her, Tommy was back thinking of Smiling.

He noticed she was laughing as an older man who led her onto the floor. The music had changed. It was up-tempo now, something brisk and Latin. A mambo or samba, he thought. He wouldn't know the difference. Apparently, smiling knew well enough. She moved through the complicated, flashy number as if she'd been dancing all her life.

As they moved quickly around the dance floor, the others began to stand back to watch them. Her dress flared, wrapped around her legs, then flared again as he spun her out to arm's length, then back. She laughed, her face

401

leveled and close to her partner's as they matched steps. Once again, the prick of jealousy infuriated him and made him feel like a fool. The man with Smiling was matching steps with was easily old enough to be her father. But there was something infinitesimally intimate about the way they dance. It was nothing he could put a finger on, but it was just a feeling he got as he watched them. And then, before he could pursue the thought at all, the music ended, he had managed to suppress the uncomfortable emotion, but another had sprung up to take its place. Desire, he wanted her, wanted to take her by the hand and pull her out of that crowded room into someplace dim and quiet where all they would kiss each other. He wanted to feel the incredible sensation of her mouth softening and heating under his.

Feeling uncomfortable and wanting time to think, he lifted his glass to his lips, and let the taste of vodka race over his tongue. If thinking of her ate at him, touching her would have driven him mad. He didn't want her love, he told himself savagely. He couldn't, wouldn't be responsible for the range of emotions Smiling was capable of. He couldn't love her in return. He didn't possess those kinds of feelings. Whatever emotions he had were directed exclusively toward his work. He'd promised himself that. But he ached for her, body, mind and soul. Tommy took the rest of his drink, then slipped quiet out into the lovely view of the garden. But his heart was still heavy with the thoughts in his head. Was he and Smiling not suitable for each other? Was it better for them to separate? Was his feelings for her wrong? But asked and asked again and again, he still couldn't find a suitable answer.

"There you are." A soft female voice intoned, distracting him and quickly lost his train of thought. Tommy didn't have to look over his shoulder to know Smiling had found him.

"Uh... what..." He stammered as saw her walking towards him. "What are you doing here?"

"Looking for you. And because we need to talk." She simply answered then asked him the question that had been nagging at her about his attitude. "But first. Did I do something wrong?"

Damn he hated stuff like this. "No. Why did you ask?"

"Because I felt you're been avoiding me."

"We're together all the time, Smiling. But yes, I've been avoiding you." He admitted, starting with the one thing he did know what to do about.

"Why's that?" She asked bravely. A small part of her wanted to know, while the rest of her was certain the truth would hurt.

She asked too much recently, but it wasn't a coy question. It was a direct one. Tommy looked at her and kept his eyes on hers. "I told you before. I don't mix business and personal feelings. The other reason no longer exists. Leave it."

"That was not a good reason to explain. And you expect me to believe that?"

Why should she see so clearly what he'd managed to hide? He let out his breath very slowly, very carefully as his hands sought his pockets. No one knew better than he how destructive his temper could be. "You're right," he agreed. "And you can believe what you want to, but I've done it for only one reason,"

He came no closer, but his eyes still locked hard on hers "I did because of you."

Her eyes flew open. "Me?" Then wrapped her arm around herself. "That why you afraid of me?"

She saw him flinch. "What makes you say that?"

"For one, you won't stand near me, and for two, you never asked me to dance."

"No, I didn't." He admitted, "with good reason."

At that moment, the music changed into Elton John song. She held out a hand in a gesture that was as much a peace offering as an invitation. "Miss Charity claims you're very smooth."

Unable to resist, he took it in his. Their eyes stayed locked as she stepped into his arms and found that his embrace felt surprisingly right. Her hand slid gently over his shoulder, his around her waist. With their face close, they began to dance. Don't go breaking my heart. I couldn't if I tried.

Even though the song was a quicker tempo, but he ignored it and moving in the slow rhythm. The wounded romantic who lived deep in her heart started seeing rainbows. Something warm and sweet and utterly intoxicating flowed through her blood. Intrigued, she continued to sway with him.

Every time being this close to her and their bodies brushed, caused his blood to fire, his heart to pound. Desire made him hard. Hot and wanting, he pulled her against his body and she complied. He could feel her heart beating against his, quick now, and not too steady. And to wish she could belong to him.

It wasn't easy to ignore the heat that raced up in her as she felt his hand slid up from her back, fingers spreading until they tangled lightly with the tips of her hair.

He wasn't sure when that thought had sunk its root in him. Perhaps it had begun the first moment he had seen her. She was, should have been, unattainable for him. But when she was in his arm, warm, just bordering on pliant, dozens of possibilities flashed through his head.

She wanted to smile, to make some light, easy comment. But she couldn't push the words out. Her throat was locked. The way he was looking at her now, as if she was the only woman he had ever seen or ever wanted to see, make her forget that the dance was supposed to be a gesture of friendship. She might never be his friend; she knew no matter how hard she tried. But his eyes on hers, she understood how easily she could be his lover. Ooh, ooh, nobody knows it.

Maybe not what she thought, but it didn't seem matter when they danced together. Right from the start, I gave you my heart. She felt her will ebb away even as the music swelled inside her head. No, it didn't seem to matter. Nothing seemed to matter as long as she went on swaying in his arms. Oh, oh, I gave you my heart.

A dozen memories flooded her brain. In that swift moment, she remembered the feeling from the night they made love. That, she would never forget. But had it been just lust for him? And deep in her heart, she wished that Tommy might desire her all levels, and not for sex. Right now, all she wanted was to melt into him and be one with him. She pressed her lips to his. And now it's up to us babe.

This teasing, seductive kiss with the passion he remembered all too well of what they'd shared the night before, and it made him forget every promise he'd made.

Instantly her emotions went from one state to another, then merged in a torrent of need when his tongue joined hers, the pleasure was so intense that the greed flashed through her.

This was how drove people to do mad, desperate acts with their tongues tangled. This wild, painful pleasure when once tasted, it would never be forgotten, would always be craved. She wrapped her arms around his neck as she gave herself to it. Oh, I think we can make it.

He drove them both to the edge. It was more than desire, he knew. Still, those thoughts were jumbled, and all of them were forbidden. Desperate, he run his lips over her face, while wild fantasies of touching, of tasting every inch of her whirled in his head. It wouldn't be enough. It would never be enough. No matter how much he took from her, she would draw him back. And she could make him beg. The certainty of it terrified him.

She was trembling again, even as she strained against him. Her soft gasps and sighs pushed him toward the brink of reason. He found her mouth again and feasted on it. *Oh, you put the sparks to the flame.*

He felt helpless with Smiling so near. She was scary. And he wanted her. All hers, in every conceivable and pleasurable way.

She felt a punch of desire as the sounds of the music faded into the background and her world was filled with nothing but Tommy, his mouth, the sudden blast of heat.

Love, first experienced, was devastating. She heard her own quiet moan of surrender. And she tasted the glory of it as his lips played gentle with hers. Then she remembered everything about them being together, their kissing, their touching, and the feel of his hands on every inch of her body. She would always remember that one instant when the world changed, the music, the air, the scent of fresh flowers. Nothing would ever be quite the same again. Nor would she ever want it to be. Shaking off the feeling, she drew back to lift a hand to her spinning head. "Tommy …"

Smiling was delicious in so many ways. Her unbelievable scent, musky and sweet at the same time. And Lord help him, he wanted to do it again. He couldn't prevent his mouth from trying to devour every inch. He'd broken all the rules with her. A man who had vowed to abstain, and when they could and should be ignored. He'd had no right to ignore them with her. He pulled her against him. "My head keeps reminding me of where this is heading, but my body won't listen. Being so close to you every day and not touching you... It's driving me crazy."

There was a fury of desire in him. He was as aroused as she was. "It's been like that for me, too." With a moan, she pulled his head down, and pressed her full, anxious lips to his. *Ooh, ooh, nobody knows it. Ooh, ooh, nobody knows it. Right from the start, I gave you my heart.*

What they were feeling, all the longing, the desire, the need of each other was in that kiss. But the pain of the coming separation was also in the kiss. They were standing still, but everything around them was moving. Around and around, faster and faster. The lovely scents intensified, the music became louder and quicker, but all she cared about was the man who was kissing her. She never, never wanted to break apart!

"Smiling, Tiffany wants to…" Steady stopped dead, and after clearing her throat, she stared at the fountain the opposite way as if it fascinated her. "Excuse me. I didn't mean to…"

It was Tommy who pulled his lips away and Smiling had jerked back like a spring and was searching for composure. "It's all right. What is it Steady?"

"Sorry if I interrupted the romantic times," Steady said, not looking sorry at all. She smiled at Tommy. "It's well … Tiffany's going to throw her bouquet and ask you could come to join."

"Yes, all right. I'll be right there."

Steady rushed back in, grinning herself. Who would have thought that would be happen?

"I should …" Smiling paused to draw in a steadying breath but managed only a shaky one. "I should come." She stepped back. "Once they get started, they need …" She broke off when Tommy took her arm. He waited until she lifted her head and looked at him again.

"Things have changed."

Indeed. What happened that night had changed all of their lives. Her feeling for him was even more undefined and confusing than they had started out to be. But it sounded so simple when he said it. "Yes, they have."

"I don't mean the past," he said. "Right or wrong, Smiling, we'll finish this."

"No." She was far from calm, but she was very determined. "If it's right, we'll finish it. I'm not going to pretend I don't want you, but you're right when you say things have changed, Tommy. You see, I know what I'm feeling now, and I have to get used to it."

He tightened his grip when she turned to go. "What are you feeling?"

She couldn't have lied if she'd wanted to. She couldn't have said when she'd gone beyond her own borders and fallen in love with him. She couldn't have said why it had happened despite her determination to prevent it. "I used to think that you stayed with me because you felt pity for me, but I'm not the one you feel pity for. The feeling you have for me is protection. It's bigger than love. And I never thought I'd fall in love again." She said bravely. "But that's the problem. Because I love you, Tommy."

The words hit him with power of a freight train. He felt physically battered. His fingers uncurled from her arm and released her as if it were hot, as if he were retreating from some dangerous beast. "Oh, Smiling, you can't," he said firmly. "You know it's impossible, isn't it?"

"Is it?" She said. "You love me, too. You think trying to hide it makes it any less so?"

"For God's sake. You can't, I can't. He said his voice strained. "But I don't understand why, why me?"

"Tommy, don't ask such superfluous questions. The big problem with you is that you try to think more than feel. That's why you don't realize it."

"Feelings don't change facts."

"Tommy, feelings change everything." She contradicted his words. "Maybe we should have a clear talk."

"No," he sighed. The conversation was twisting in directions that he couldn't control. "Smiling, let's not get into this, okay? I don't think this is the time or place. All we need to do now is focus on doing well for the wedding party. You should go inside."

She read the shock on his face. That was understandable. And she read the distrust. That was painful. "When would be the time and place?"

"I don't know, Smiling. Later."

She was willing to wait, just not forever. "Alright. Whether you know it or not, I want your decision." She gave him a last unsmiling look before she turned away. *Don't go breaking my heart. I won't go breaking your heart.*

Chapter 35

Time doesn't heal all wounds, but Love does

A t almost midnight, shortly after wedding party was over, the guests gone and the newlyweds off on their honeymoon, Tommy went to the guest house where his boss prepared for him to stay. It hadn't mattered that he'd spent only a handful of days in it or stayed overnight over nearly three years. This house was just for him. Like the main residence, the guest house was done in an elegant, traditional motif, with a burgundy overstuffed sofa and chairs in front of white mantled fireplace, and bedroom with four-poster bed. What had happened to his life? He wondered with a sense of desperation. No matter how firmly he ordered his mind to stay calm and blank, it just kept opening to one single thought. She was lying. It didn't make sense, he couldn't allow it to make sense. He told himself as he removed his bow tie, shoes and socks, took off his vest and shirt, and then paced the floor into his solitary bedroom. What's hard for him to understand and impossible for him to believe was that she could consider herself in love after matter short time.

Things didn't work that easily. Thinking of that, he walked over to the window, looked out at the main house, then jerked the window open to breath in the damp, cool air. He needed something to clear his head. She made him like this. Annoyed, he turned away from the view and started pacing again. He knew how he'd felt toward Smiling all doing, but he'd hidden it from her or tried to. And every time he drew back, every time he denied what they had together, it hurt him more.

Thoughts swirled and danced, leaving him confused and with a headache and couldn't find an answer. He dropped on the bed, telling himself since he'd never be able to sleep; he'd just lie there until he came up with a solution. She'd given him time to hear his decision, which he admitted, he hadn't made yet. Invariably, whenever he set his mind to a problem, he solved it. It was matter of thinking through all the levels and establishing priorities. There seemed to be too many levels in his relationship with Smiling for him to deal with each or any one of them rationally.

She was mistaken. He had made her want, and she had justified her desire for him by telling herself she was in love, but if it was true. He himself felt pain. Did she really love him? She'd chosen him, she wanted him, but love would only complicate matter. It was undoubtedly the reason he'd avoided any long-term or serious ones up to this point. But why couldn't let himself love her? The woman he wanted and now she was his. She said she loved him. Why didn't he accept her love for him? "Because I have to. She's Jennifer Jefferson." A monologue to himself. No, because you're scared, Tommy. Scared of loving too much, scared of admitting that Smiling has always owned your heart, scared of future that you've never dared dream about, scared of not being able to keep your promises. Face it, Tommy, you're a coward. But he'd do exactly what he hoped to avoid hurt Smiling.

He dragged his hand through his hair. Okay, if that's being the case, they'd both to deal with it which he couldn't allow himself to think that. Leaning back against the headboard, he stared at the blank wall. If he couldn't successfully analyze Smiling, how could he hope to analyze his feeling for her? Desire, he'd little experience with that feeling since his wife gone, but he recognized it. How would he recognize love? And if he did, what would he do about it? But if he gave in, if he threw caution to the winds and confessed that he loved her. What would happen to his life or hers?

He couldn't allow himself the luxury of wondering what it would be like to be loved, and especially not what it would be like to be loved by a woman to whose love would mean a lifetime. He couldn't afford any daydreams about belonging, about having someone belong to him. Even if she hadn't been part of his assignment, he would have to sidestep Jennifer Jefferson.

You would never be any good for her, Tommy. His mind was in a fierce conflict. It's always on the wrong side of the tracks, and a questionable past, an uncertain future. There was nothing he could offer a woman like Smiling. He knew that. It made him a coward, but it was still true. Being with her would mean risking everything. He would have to believe in her, trust her. Worse, he would have to trust himself and he couldn't do either. He'd been taught to be wary his whole life. And because he feared hurting her as much as he feared being hurt.

But God, the only thing he became certain of during being with her was that he wanted her. It's plain and simple. She was a drug to a man who had always been obsessively clear-minded. He knew she was upstairs in her bedroom now, maybe dressed in scanty lingerie, curled up in the big four-poster, under white blankets perhaps waited for him, listening for his footsteps, eyeing the door until he stepped into the room. He was familiar with the house and could sneak into the house, walk up the stairs into her room without making a sound. If believing herself in love, she wouldn't send him away, then open her arm for him. He ached to be in them, and they'd ended up in bed, making love over and over again.

But he couldn't. Because that's what he played out that screen in his mind. It didn't matter anymore. But either way, he would hurt her by casually taking what love urged her to give. He could feel himself sinking in deeper. If he wanted to get out this unscathed, he was going to have to be a lot more careful. That meant living half a life, and Tommy didn't think he could do it. If he refused her and went on with his plans, would that mean half a life, as well? Those were the question he found and tormented him. But he rejected answer for. So, he made no decision, knowing once it was made, it would be final. He hoped to God he could stop thinking of her long enough to sleep.

⁂

While in her bedroom, with a sigh, Smiling tried not to think of Tommy and emotion he evoked in her as she peeled off her gown, threw her jewelry into the case and stuffed the velvet box back into her safe. Put on her white nightgown as she stared the night scene outside the bedroom window, The dark sky, where stars winked in the dark heavens. And unable to shake her feeling for Tommy, she continued in thought. In the last four months, she had come to trust him, but she'd been almost hilariously mistaken about him. He was quite a complicated man. Not easy to predict. His attitude was always cold, but knowing how to care and understand for others. As for herself, she'd been honest with him, and that hadn't worked. She'd been deliberately provocative, and that hadn't done so well. She'd been annoying, and she'd been cooperative. She wasn't sure what step to take next. But only one thing she could be certain that the fact he's beginning to accept that she loved him was a giant step. And eventually, Tommy would accept the fact that he loved her back.

He did love her. She couldn't be mistaken about that, correcting herself. But he was too honorable to take advantage of the situation, and too stubborn to admit that he and she belonged together. She was in love with him, there was no doubt of that. That speed with which she'd fallen only increased the intensity of the emotion. She'd never felt for any man, include Mathew what she felt for Tommy. This emotion that cut clean through the bone, and melded with the feeling of passion, which she could have dismissed, was a sense of absolute trust, an odd and deep affection, a prideful respect, and the certainty that she could pass the years of her life with him. If not in harmony, in contentment. And if that mean taking risks, she didn't have a choice.

Smiling smiled wryly to herself. Was that love? It didn't sound like any of the definitions she'd ever heard. It wasn't like what her brother had with Tiffany. Just looking at them she could see they belonged together. They were happy. But love didn't come to everyone equally. Maybe this was her version of love.

Lost in thought, she didn't notice that she was flipping her feet into the flip-flops, slipped quietly from her room down the stairs, and tiptoe through the front door. The breeze was warm through it was the coolest part of the day, and it whispered through her nightgown, pressing the silk to her body as she walked quietly along a flagstone path that weaved through the rose garden still fragrant and heading toward the guesthouse until she stopped at the front door. God what was she doing? She was trying to be a decent woman, but it was hard. Maybe sex hormones had fogged her brain, or she wanted to address her own needs. She could fight it. She could pretend that she didn't want what was happening between them, but the truth of it was that she did. She wanted Tommy to make love to her, wanted him to possess her as he once had. She hungered for it illogically, in a way that ignored past hurts and present problems, in a way that didn't give a damn for the emotional consequences.

She stared blankly at the door, shivered, and stepped away. No, it's best that she didn't. She should go back her room and get some sleep. She might do anything in there, would be very, very foolish. And yet the unusual mood swings that were evident on his face made her more reluctant to leave. In addition, there were still so many unanswered questions, and she hoped that they would be able to get to the bottom of it all. Well, it was why she'd come to talk to him, wasn't it?

Struggling with her thoughts, she saw a silver of yellow light peeking out from under of the door. Obviously, he wasn't asleep, although no sound came from the other side of the heavy door. She took a deep, sharp breath, gather all her courage and instead knocking, she twisted the doorknob and turned to open the door, and found it unlocked. She stepped inside before she had time for second thoughts and closed it behind her.

He got up out of bed as he heard the creak of the door, and it opened further. His heart jolted as he saw her entered the room. And he caught her arm. "Smiling!"

She was startled and stood speechless, and even though his grip wasn't hard, she could've pulled away had she tried, but she looked up at him in the dimly lit room. He looked sad and lonely. She suddenly remembered what her father taught her. *People who always appeared strong and cold outside, are actually trustworthy. They tried to create a thorny cover so that no one dared to come near, but actually they have a warm heart.*

"What are you doing here?" he demanded, spying her on the window ledge, one leg tucked up beneath her as she learned against the casing and her eyes involuntarily touching every powerful line of him.

"To see you," she'd seen him without a shirt many times before and she loved his masculinity, but she hadn't been able to stare then, not with him so aware of her and her family around them. Now her eyes could look directly at the hard muscles of his massive, bare chest, then over his shoulders, down his body to his flat stomach, skimmed her gaze over the bulge inside his pants to glace along the length of his long legs and down to his bare feet. Tommy was attractive on more than one level. "What do you think?"

He didn't want to see her in the middle of the night, didn't want to be tempted by her wide eyes, soft lips and in white silk robe. "You shouldn't be here. Someone will find us together."

She didn't argue, just stared up at him with those round eyes.

"So? For so long you and I have been together. Don't tell me you're afraid to be alone with me, Tommy," she said, wandered around the room and accidentally, she saw a framed photograph of a bunch of men in desert army fatigues on the bookshelf. She walked over and picked it up without thinking.

"Is this you?"

"What?" He glanced over and something in his face seemed to close.

He reached for the photo, but she snatched it up before he could. There were five men in the photo, loosely standing as if captured after a day of work, or whatever one call being at war. For it was obvious from the background that the photo hadn't been taken in the USA. It was some foreign place, somewhere with sand and rocks and very little vegetation for human to survive on.

She looked up. "Is this Iraq?" she asked, gesturing to the picture.

His mouth thinned. "Afghanistan."

"You were on the war?"

He didn't answer, and wished she'd turn his way so he could see her face. But she kept staring at the evidence of his life as if it was of the utmost importance to her.

She examined the photo. In it, Tommy was wearing a helmet, his arm draped over a slightly shorter, stockier man with sunburned cheeks and red stubble. The shorter man grinned, while Tommy had half his mouth cocked up. Two of other three men were sitting, arms draped wearily over knees while the fifth man was half turned away from the camera, a water bottle tilted to his lips.

"How long were you there?" she asked and somehow her voice had gentled against her will.

"Three years." He said, snatched the framed photo out of her hand and setting it back on the shelf. "I was career."

She frowned. She knew very little about the military; her own family tended to be on the opposite side of things, generally, but even she knew he was much too young to have retired. Had something happened in Afghanistan? She winced at her own naïveté. Of course, something had happened to Tommy. No one returned from war the same. "That's ..." she considered her words, choosing them carefully. "Isn't that a long time?"

He glanced down at the picture of his Special Forces team. "Yes."

There were questions she wanted to ask, but that would only lead to more of her business anyway. She'd given up right to Tommy's secrets when she'd made it plain that she didn't want anything further from him than that one night of sex.

She frowned, feeling vaguely melancholy, and then realized that the room had grown silent.

When she looked up, he was watching her, his blue eyes shuttered. "Okay? Is there something you want to know?"

"Just to know where I stand." When he didn't answer she added. "With you."

"I thought I made that clear." His heart was pounding and he kept his distance, certain that if he walked any closer to her, he wouldn't be able to resist the fragrance of her hair, the feel of her skin, the throaty sound of her voice as she whispered.

"But I haven't figured out." She countered, turning her gaze from his face to stare out the window, thinking their relationship. But as she turned back, noting that he was watching her, paying close attention at her hair tumbling to rest on her collarbone, and his eyes traveled from there down the peach silk dressing gown fastened around her slender waist, with just a hint of lace from her nightgown peeking out of the low neckline and the parting at the hem. "Talk to me," she murmured.

"About what?"

"You. I hardly know anything about you," she smiled. "Other than that, you were in army and worked for my dad. I think it's time we found out a little more about each other. Tell me about your wife, Lydia."

"Well, that's quite a change in topic. But I don't want to talk about her."

"Why not?"

A thousand reasons why not? And one of them was. "Because you never asked before. Why the sudden interest?"

"Because you never really wanted to tell me about her," she admitted. "And because all your life it seems that you've either been running from, or racing to something, I just wondered what it was."

"I don't mind telling you, but I just forgot." A lie. They both knew it. "Besides, I still loved her very much." He cleared his throat and stared at her, hoping that in so doing she would get the message and leave, not that he really wanted her to go. It would just better, safer, and for both of them.

Her big eyes searched his, and instead of making her unhappy, it made her laugh as she leaned closer, whispering. "Then you'd better tell me how she was died."

Her demanding seemed to bounce off the walls and ricochet through his heart. "You're the most infuriating woman I've ever met."

"Good!"

With a growl, Tommy said. "If I do, will you leave?"

Why she'd decided that she had to know about the wife he adored? She didn't really understand. She'd come to this room, not to discuss Lydia, but because she couldn't sleep, and knowing Tommy was so close had made it impossible not to want to be with him. So what, the new Jennifer Jefferson could take a relationship and her life one spontaneous step at a time! The old Smiling was long buried, the new Smiling was taken over! "Yes. After I know what I want to know, I'll leave."

He closed his eyes for a minute, as if gathering thoughts that ran in painful jumble through his brain. He loved Lydia; he couldn't deny that. If she hadn't died, he'd be with her still, a dedicated husband to the bitter end. But what he felt for Smiling was as different as night to day. And it wasn't easy for him, nor had he planned to speak of it. Now that he'd began, he discovered he'd needed to tell her all along. "I remember everything about Lydia. I remember the day she died." He choked on the words but went on anyway. "She was ... different from anyone I'd ever met before, she seemed more vital somehow. Anyway, we began seeing each other and one thing led to another and we got married. Simple ceremony," His voice lowered. "But her parents didn't approve and accused me of that I preached happiness at all costs to their daughter so that she tossed aside all her responsibilities, her education, her values and married to me. Though she should find someone ... different."

"Different?"

It annoyed him to admit that, he realized. To be honest with Smiling was face the truth without excuses. "Different from a man who'd joined the army a little while after high school, became career military."

"Oh," she said as if she understood. But she didn't. Any parents should have been pleased to have Tommy for a son in law, but then parents rarely were satisfied with their children's choices; she only had to look at her brothers and her father to prove that point. "But the main thing is that you loved each other."

"Loved each other." He repeated with a snort. "Do you know Lydia's folks were from San Francisco, old money, and had big plans for their only daughter? Thought she should marry a doctor or lawyer or at least someone with money and background. But Lydia was a stubborn thing, told her parents she was going to live her own life. Once she married me, they cut her off, never called or wrote, not even when our son was born." His voice had lowered to a grim whisper. "I only saw them at the funeral. They just mourned and cursed at me in front of everyone that Lydia was their only child. She would still be alive if they'd kept her away from me." His gaze became dull and he couldn't manage to hide the pain in his voice.

Saying these words, his eyes seemed to be dumbfounded. It was easy to see and recognize a combination of grief and fury, his unhappiness with the memory. It's like a dark part of Tommy that he never wanted to confide this story to her before, but saying it all, he could completely erase it. And though she understood, but she hated knowing she'd helped put it there. "I'm sorry. I didn't know such a situation happened and didn't mean to bring up bad memories." "Don't be. You don't know what happened."

"I know you lost a family you loved." She ached to hold him, to say she understood just like the way he did that to her. But she didn't dare.

Showing his hands into the back pockets of his pants, he scowled. His face turned suddenly savage and quiet fury burned in his eyes. "Lost her. That's nice way to put it." He crossed the room and stopped bare inches from her, close enough that she could feel the angry jets of his breath. "Don't you know what happened?"

His eyes blazed blue and it took her a moment to realize there were tears in them. "Only if you want to tell me," she said, suddenly feeling as if she was prying into a very private part of his soul, a part he wanted to keep hidden away from her and the rest of the world. Apart no one should dare question.

"Well, it turns out her folks were right; being married to me was a big mistake. Since I was severely wounded in a bomb blast, bad injured. I was sent home and stuck in the wheelchair. She was the only one taking care of me."

Love hurts, always and every kind. If you loved someone, you were going to get hurt. It was a given. Something she would have to remember. The thought stabbed her, leaving her nearly breathless, and her mind refused to know more as she wanted to get out of his spathe by withdrawing. "Tommy, I'm sorry. You shouldn't have to…"

"You asked, damn it."

That's how she felt guilty for bringing it up. "But I didn't mean to make you rehash everything."

"Lydia's car got hit by lorry in the raining day on the way refilled my painkillers," he went on, ignoring her.

Smiling covered her mouth. It was more than grief. "Oh, God."

"That what traffic police told me after I opened the door." He rubbed his eyes with his hands as if to wipe out the memory. "So, in a way, she's dead because of me."

His voice was so low, but she could hardly hear it, and saw the ravages of sorrow carving deep grooves in his face. She reached forward, touching the side of his face. "It happened. But it's not your fault. Not any of it, and it wasn't anyone's fault. So, you can't blame yourself."

"Who, then?" He grabbed her hand and squeezed. The first and only sign of emotion she had seen from him. "Who Smiling?"

She couldn't answer his question, even though she could recognize that he was still blaming himself for something that happened years before. Time hadn't healed his wounds; the scars were still fresh and bleeding. He dropped her hand, but she reached up and touched his face again, her palms pressed gently to his cheeks. He stiffened, but didn't move, and she let her hands slide down his strong, inflexible shoulder muscles as she leaned her head into the crook of his neck. "I don't know what to say, except I'm sorry that you were hurt and that you lost your loving wife." She murmured again.

He shook his head. "It's all right. There's no point talking about that now, and thank God, it's over." He ended the story, closed his eyes, and looked away from her, but didn't want to tell her the rest how he tried to kill himself and her father had rescued him.

She understood him now, perhaps too well for her own good. "Memory is the source of pain. It belongs to the past." She tilted her head up to his then took the initiative to kiss him on the lip. "Don't let the pain of yesterday make you regret your whole life."

His hands went on her shoulders. "Smiling, don't do this to me."

"We've done it before." She didn't stop, until she reached then stood on her tiptoes, ran her fingers up to his chest, and pressed her full lips to his. This time he didn't protest. His lips crashed against hers in repressed fury and he dragged her close, one hand on the lower curve of her back, the other twining in her hair which responded enthusiastically.

The intensity of what went between them surprised both of them. It was sparks, a merging, a flowing-an union. But it was Tommy who broke away. He pulled his mouth off hers and buried his face in her neck. "Smiling, please..."

"Please what?"

"Please, don't tease me," he begged, his voice hoarse and rough. "I'll screw that up, too."

He was looking into her eyes and she saw the pleading in them as if he'd known what she was trying to do. But damn, she felt good in his arms. "I'm not."

Swearing under his breath, he tried visibly to get control of himself when he was starting to get hard. Because touching her was torture, because touching her only made him want to touch more. He wanted her, but he would never risk the closeness he had shared with Lydia that was fogging his mind. The hands on her dropped so quickly. "Don't you have any idea what you're doing to me?"

"Probably about the same as you're doing to me."

"Don't tease me, Smiling," he repeated. "We can't, not here, not now."

"When?" she demanded, refusing to let go.

"Maybe never."

"I won't believe that."

"Smiling, it won't work."

"Why not? Why do you keep avoiding me?" She came right out and said it, but she had to. "What I told you and my feeling for you are still unclear?"

He closed his eyes as if waging a silent battle with himself. His muscles grew taunt, his jaw tight. Caring for her left him only one answer. He had to back away and give her a nudge in the opposite direction. In the direction that was right for her. He should do it quickly for her sake, and yet, for his own. "I understand what you said, but you and I are not compatible." He said, unhappy to be asked about it. "You are Jennifer Jefferson, rick, noble, and I'm from the wrong side of the tracks. Fate has destined me and you to not share the same path."

"I don't understand what you're saying," she stopped him, hurting inside. "And who needs it?" He didn't say a word, just looked at her with hot eyes. "I just wanted to talk to you whatever we could not grasp specifically, Tommy."

Silently he called her a liar, but took a step backward leaned against the wall, crossed his muscular arms over his chest and waited. "So, talk."

"I love you, Tommy, and you just need to know that."

Oh, God. There it was. Words he'd longed to hear but which scared the stuffing out of him. He knew she was a good person, but he really didn't deserve her, with her family background, compared to someone like him, it's the complete opposite. But the thing he didn't understand here was why she chose him like this. Was that the right choice for her? "You didn't know the meaning of the word. And I asked you why?" "Because … because …" Words failed her.

"We made love," he finished for her.

"Yes! You can't expect to just walk off after a statement like that."

"Finding out about our bodies was easy, but sex won't mean anything. And don't mix up lust and love."

"Don't lie to me, Tommy," she accused. "The way you had responded to my kiss tonight proved me a lot of things. You kissed me because you wanted to. Hide it any way you like, but felt what I did."

He stared at her, the woman accused him of lying. But she's right and why not? He had stepped over this threshold before. Or was that just an excuse? To hope that he would forget who she was long enough? "I've never given you a reason to distrust me," he reminded her.

"You have now," she said. "What you did was worse, like every time you held me, every time you kissed me or pretended to care!"

Every defense crumbled, feeling as if she'd slapped him. "Smiling, let's not argue. And please stop doing this."

"Do what?"

One curve of her lips, a tiny sparkle in her eyes, a mocking lift of her eyebrow and he found himself doing things he'd sworn to avoid. "Make something more complicate than it already is."

"Tommy, I've only complicated things by not doing so. But that's what I'm going to do now," she said, her temper exploding. "Tell me, right now you want me. The truth, please."

She was right. "Yes. I want you. That's the honest truth. But hell, that doesn't make it right."

His honesty shocked her. "We're two adults."

"I know. But I was supposed to protect and soothe you, Smiling, not slept with you. You were broken heart, and I took advantage of that situation. That's not the way it was."

How the hell had she forgotten that part? "Yes, you are my bodyguard," she said, giving impulse to say what was on her mind. "But the way you care about me is like a lover."

He closed his eyes to block out the anxious, loving look shinning in her eyes. "Don't try to make me into something I cannot, Smiling, because it won't work. Making love with you would be easy. Falling in love with you wouldn't."

"I think you're not being honest with yourself."

His smile was cold. "Really?"

"No. Is it her, Lydia? I know you took her death really hard. But she's been gone three years. It's time to move on, take the next step with me, Tommy."

"No, once is enough. I'll never go through that again."

She considered his fervent loyalty to a wife who had been gone over years. To what purpose? Would he never find a woman on whom he was willing to take a chance? "Locking the past is also bleeding your heart."

"Enough. Good night, Smiling." He shifted. "You should leave."

She looked him in the eyes and caught the need in his face clearly. He didn't want her to leave any more than she wanted to. "You really want me to go?"

He lowered her gaze. "Things are already so complicated."

"Sometimes the best things in life are complicated. But that isn't an answer."

He swallowed hard, sucked in a breath for courage. "Smiling, I've never been a particularly fair man. We won't be good together, and I can't take that risk."

He forced himself to stop talking. While his nature instinct was to keep going, he knew he had to give her a second to process what he'd told her. She was going to be angry. He had to be prepared for that. No one wanted to be rejected this way. Regardless, he knew he was making the right decision. Whatever he felt for Smiling, it wasn't love. It couldn't. Yes, he was afraid of what everyone would say, but so what? This was his life and he had to get it right.

She looked at him for a long time. Her expression was understanding, even kind. She didn't seem angry at all. But it was not an explanation that satisfied her. "You don't want to make our relationship today because of the obsession of your wife in the past. That doesn't sound like happy to me." She persisted with an interest that seemed casual, but that Tommy knew wasn't.

He had thought sex would make him part of her life, part of her family. Instead, it had led him feeling something had gone terribly wrong that he couldn't explain to her. He shook his head. "The other way is worse."

"But then for what? Let you continue to be the same person? Only disappointed and give up with a new love in life?"

"Not necessarily so. I intend to stay alone to raise my son. My life is far complicated already to have to deal with an affair with you or anyone else. If that sounds selfish, I'm sorry."

She met his eyes, along with the memories came back of the few good times, of the first time he'd kissed her, of the making love, she realized that Tommy had shared his body, but not his heart. "That would be all well and good except one thing is you just need to tell me, do you have feelings for me, Tommy? Other things I don't care about."

It was all there, in his heart, begging to be said. But remember, Tommy, you can't love this woman. You just can't. His brain argued with him. "What good would it do, Smiling?"

"Truth would certainly make for a change." Her voice was quiet, without its usual edge, and her gaze passed over his face in a slow search. "And because I keep getting mixed signals from you. One minute I feel like you want me, the next you're pushing me away."

Smiling asked this question to him, hoping to get a proper answer. And yet, there's nothing more heartbreaking than being in love with someone you couldn't have, especially when that person wanted to love you back. "Smiling, I won't tell you I do, because the thought of it terrifies me. I wish we could go back to what we had before. There was no pressure. When you make mistake once, you better be careful not to repeat it. So, it was simple to just let go and forget about it. That why I'll always push you away."

Simple? Was he crazy? He might think he could pick up his life where he'd left it off before her. She was going to prove him wrong. "Running away won't solve your problem, Tommy," she drew him against her and wrapped her arms around him. "You're constantly worried that you are and how things were going to work out. Because the risk is too great, but once you realize the mistakes you have made, you need to change to improve, not depend on them."

He didn't understand why this beautiful, incredible woman was willing to give him everything and so much more? He drew back. "That's something I cannot do."

"Cannot do?" She took his hands. "At least you're honest in your phrase. The more I'm around you, the more I realize you never lie to anyone, but yourself."

"You haven't been around me enough to know who or what I am. And you're much better off that way."

"I or you? Or is that your way of telling me to back off?" she countered, then shook her head when he didn't answer. "You're scared that you don't love me. You're concerned that you're making a mistake. You don't know what you're supposed to be feeling, but you're just as wildly in love with me, but you don't have the courage to face it." Practical and logical. How could she have figured all that out? He barely knew what was going on. How could she be more in tune with him than he was with himself? "Maybe I'm a coward and I could get over it."

"No, Tommy, you're not a coward and you couldn't. It's hit you between the eyes. But I guess because you have an inferiority complex with the social class, or my family is a multi-multimillionaire that weight on you." She pointed out and teasing. "Or just because that's really why you never want any woman in your life?"

He felt hesitant. In some ways he had never completely recovered from the death of his wife. Even now, four years later, the thought of a wife and children with anyone else seemed incomprehensible. Which didn't mean he couldn't have an enjoyable relationship with a woman. He'd had few over the years and still considered the women friends. "Yes, and because you never did understand me."

"That's not the issue."

"Damn right it's not," he told her, closed his eyes, prayed for patience. "I'm trying to lay out my cards here. You come from a different place than I do, and because you're Jennifer Jefferson. You're famous and you've had other important people in your life."

So, it's because of her fame and status, not because of any other factor that made him avoid her. Thinking like that, she had a little peace of mind. "Is that what you're in the middle of? Jennifer Jefferson?" she asked, teasing and stared down at their hands. They fit so well, didn't they? She noticed. Just slid together, as if they'd been waiting for the match. "And yes. The only people I love, and trust are my family, which now includes you. Also, I've been called a lot of names but never that."

"Smiling, joking about it doesn't change the truth. The truth's I've done thing my own way for a long time, I've avoided complications that I wasn't interested in. It's been easy to evade attachments. Until you," he continued. "But I've been afraid of that since my wife die."

"You want to be reasonable where reason doesn't fit. I know the feeling. We're stuck with other. There's no getting past it for either of us." Frustrated, she asked him for the first time. "Or you just never want to give us a chance?"

"What a hell of question!" He chuckled softly, sounding more like the friend he'd always been than like a lover.

"You don't understand what I mean, or deliberately don't understand?" She persisted, frowning. "I'm in love with you. In love with a man, I'm holding right now. You're exactly what I want, what I need," she kissed him lightly. "You have no idea how much. If you did, it might scare you."

He sighed as if trying to stay calm at her words. "I'm not scared of you, Smiling."

"Good, because I'm the kind of woman who goes after what she wants. I don't stop until I get it. So, this is it, Tommy. Either you love me, or you walk away. It can't be anything else."

This was the question that only he could answer and made him reflect on his time alone with all her seductions or the few precious minutes of making love to her. All that time he'd fought his feelings, telling himself that she wouldn't love him, that he wouldn't allow himself to love her. But deep in his heart, he could never really do that. It seemed like he was wrong about a lot of things.

He drew in a deep, slow breath, staring into her eyes as lies had only amused her. So, he would try the truth, he decided to be honest with her about his fears that she would understand his hesitations. "Smiling, I didn't want you to my life. I didn't want you love me. Perhaps that sounds strange to you. But it doesn't mean I did not love you. I just have a hard time to saying it. I did not know how to say to be true to my feeling. After my wife died, I thought there's no one out there could replace her, until that day. You're the beginning and end of my whole world. We started mutual affection, express concern, but it would have been cruel to try to hold on to you, for both of us, because you are a daughter of my benefactors. I tell myself I can't hurt them. Also, I'm afraid I'll never be able to give you everything you want. I'm more afraid that I'll try. So, it kinder to you to simply let go, to let you move on your life. This way, you had nothing to look back at. Only the future."

She dropped her hands, knowing that he was evading her. No matter how intimate they became, he still refused to take the next step and closed the final gap. "Think again," she said matter of fact. "Love cannot use reason to analyze, but use heart to feel. But I need to know why."

He'd imagined the conversation going any number of ways, but he'd never pictured anything like this. "Because I am frightened," he confessed. "About us falling in love each other, about my conscience's sake."

She understood his loneliness, his scarred-over pain, and his pride in his own skills. But he had kindness and cynicism, patience and impulse. He lived his own way, making his own rules and breaking them when he chose. And that was what worried her. Finding herself thinking of marriage, permanence and making a family with a man who not obviously ran from all three and had run from them most of his life. There was no way of truly understanding what had made him let go of her, but at least she knew now that it had been his own feeling, his conscience's sake, his own inadequacies that had convinced him it was the right decision. And at least now she had heard him say it. "Just because you doubt your own worth, are you afraid to open your heart up to me, or even to yourself?"

He hadn't thought about it that way, but it sounded kind of right. Of course, his wife's death would have affected him. Why after what happened between them, he still measured Smiling by her?

He was silently seething. Good. She knew she'd hit a mark, so, she took his hand and led him to the sofa. And when she sat next to him, she brought her hand up to touch his face, but then let it fall to her lap. "Tommy, don't let the past bind you but miss the good things that are waiting for you in the future. If you don't step outside, you won't see the sun ahead."

"Is your world always so cheerful and optimistic?"

"You are the one who taught me that. It's all in the past. Don't let it affect the present.

I hope you can distinguish between compassionate and love."

Her thoughts made him take a different look. Why did he always keep that fixed mindset and bury himself in the painful past, then regretted and got angry? Why not free himself from that so he could see the happy path of life. Smiling loved him. He should trust that. Trust her. Maybe in doing that, he would learn to trust himself. He believed in destiny, and if Smiling was his destiny, he would break mountains to have her, the one he loved. He loved her. There was no denying that now. He was putting her emotional happiness above his physical satisfaction. How could he not love her? Smiling was special. The most special woman he had ever known, and she was everything that he'd never known he was missing. He didn't think he could fall more deeply in love, but once he'd let go on the past, he was completely toast. Because Smiling had shown him the way past it.

He flung his arms around her neck and hung on. Just like she'd asked him to. "I can't tell you what you want to hear. I can't make you promises, Smiling. You're got me so messed up. But I do know this much. I have never, never wanted a woman the way I want you and never put my heart out there for anyone the way I have for you."

Now she wanted to weep, because it was everything she wanted to hear. He'd hidden his true feelings for her since they'd met, which made her very angry. And now that he'd revealed himself. It was sweet, but not a gesture of love. "What made you change your mind now?"

"You and willpower."

"So much for my powers of seduction," she teased.

"I'm serious," he said softly, his breath fanning her face. "You've got them, and I'm not immune. Until I saw you desperately in pain. But I can't bear the thought of you leaving and it will break my heart, if I let you walk away in pain again."

She looked away from him for a moment. It wouldn't do either of them any good if she wept. But his words had touched her in a new part of her heart and tears stood in her eyes. "No, I'm not walking away from you," she trailed off, glanced at his mouth. "Because you're a part of my life, Tommy. So you're never getting away from me. And you thought I was one of those women in your life pushing for a commitment. But that's not truth. I won't pressure you."

Joy touched his heart as he saw the tenderness, yearning and something that even his hardened heart recognized was overflowing love for him. So let's face the future together. With the first true smile of the day, he grabbed her around the waist and kissed the tears from her eyes. "Pressure me? It sounds like a good start, honey."

Heard him change his address, she felt strangely happy. "You called me honey."

He'd called her honey. The word had just slipped out his mouth. He didn't call honey to any woman, except for his deceased wife. "I did, didn't I?" He answered and frowned a little. "Is that a bad thing?"

"No, it's not." She liked the endearment, and it had come out of Tommy's mouth so naturally, without pretense or forethought. "But I need a man who can love me with his whole heart, love me the way you love Lydia. I deserve that, and I won't settle for less." She said as her gaze dropped to his mouth, and then she lifted her eyes to his where they held hers.

She was right. She deserved a man who love her with all his heart. "After all these lonely years. I'd finally found someone I loved the way I loved Lydia. That's you, Smiling. I love you."

Smiling rejoiced, a feeling of happiness crept in her. Tommy said he loved her, words were not romantic or literary, but from his mouth. It made her really emotional. It felt completely different from the previous Mathew or is this true love? And with Mathew, it only fleeting because of innocence and impulsiveness. She slid her arms around his neck and brushed her lips over his. "Oh, God, Tommy."

Through the fabric of his pants, his penis began to harden, he pulled her close, and kissed her passionately. Refusing to be denied.

His kiss deepened and the sensual beast deep in the most feminine part of her stirred and awakened, sending out pulses of heat, creating a moist, hot whirlpool between her legs. It had been like this between them. Hot. Needful and lusty.

Both of them were deeply immersed in the kiss. Tongue sliding, lips melding, bodies arching into each other in a slow rhythm, until she let out another of those delicious little whimpers and practically climbed his body. "God, you know make me lose control," he whispered into her mouth as the pressure his crotch was already hot and urgent against his zipper. "And I can't keep my hands off you."

She could feel the thick, hard ridge inside his pants, and a sharp stab of need cut through her. Her body burned for him the way it always did. "Works for me."

God, he loved this woman. He would do everything he could to make Smiling happy for the rest of their lives. He knew there were doubts to overcome, hers and his, but it was as good a time as any to start by laying the past to rest. And no matter how difficult the road ahead of them, he believed that because of love, they would overcome everything. His chest was aching. He had never really understood how painful it could be to love someone. He understood it now. The only thing he could give her now was sincere love. But desire made him hard, hot and wanting now. Kissing her softly, he scooped her into his hard arms.

"What are you doing?" She demanded, laughing.

The woman in his arms was the only one he would ever love, and tonight was his chance to cement their relationship. "Relax," he carried then set her on her feet near the unmade bed. Thank God, she didn't seem to notice. And pulled her against the V between his legs to let her feel the heavy erection throbbing beneath the fly of his pants. Jesus, he was on fire for her. "I'll show you what I mean."

She moaned, knowing precisely what he wanted. All the emotions of the last few weeks running rampant through her willing body. Her skin aflame, her breasts aching for his touch. "Don't let me stop you." She said, responded with equal passion, her hands reached up to his neck and drew him down to her, giving him a kiss, and bit by bit his warm hands began to move against her back, slipping her robe from her shoulders, easing down the straps of her gown so he could link more kisses, and then stopped on her breasts.

"Smiling, I've missed the taste of you."

She wiggled out of the gown from her waist, letting it land down to the floor, leaving her clad only in her lace panties-a tiny thong that barely covered any of her. "You can taste all you want."

The screen was clear in front of his eyes and they'd never touched again after that night, yet he recognized the texture of her skin, knew the smell of her. No exploration now, but exploitation. He kissed the side of her neck, trailed kisses over her shoulder, down to and tasted her pretty breasts, first one then the other, rolled his tongue over the pebbled tip, felt her trembling as she reached for his shoulders to encourage him to give her what she needed. What both of them needed. "Make love to me, Tommy. I need you."

Getting desperate himself, too, he lowered her to her back on the bed, pulled the last piece of lace out of her body with his teeth, and while he shucked off his pants, his dark blue eyes ate every inch of her, running up the long, smooth curve of her legs to the curve of her hips, the slender waist, the thrust of her pretty upturned breasts. She was so beautiful. But it was a deeper sort of beauty than he had noticed when he had first seen her. There was a kindness, a boldness of spirit and giving heart in Smiling that made her lovelier than he'd first realized.

He came down, parted her legs and knelt between them, kissed and nipped his way from her breasts to her belly, then lower, tasting her and making every nerve ending in her body jump. She was shaking, wet, hot, and needy at the feel of his mouth and tongue, teasing and tantalizing, driving her to the brink of climax.

She wanted to freeze time and enjoyed the feeling of pleasure forever, knowing that this night was theirs. But trembling all over, she laced her fingers in his hair and the wave of need washed through her, her breaths choppy, and her hips twisting against him, urging him to stop. "Tommy..."

He drew back and looked at her. Her hair was spread out on the pillow, tangled around her face. Her breasts heaved. He wanted to bring her everything. Man's love and sex were two different categories. Having lust didn't necessarily mean having love. But with love, the desire would soar to the sky. Once you had tasted the taste of love, you were unable to stop wanting more. Yes, love was something very strange. It changed people to the point where they no longer recognize themselves. It could also transform yourself from being cold and emotionless into a romantic version. "I want to please you."

She seemed to be floating in the clouds, "You are pleasing me," she whispered into his rough, hungry mouth. "But I'll enjoy that, later, I promise. And I want to please you, too. Right now, I just want us to be one."

Looking into her velvety eyes, he saw they were filled with love and promises. He nodded in response. They'd have plenty of opportunities. Hopefully a lifetime. So, he reached for condom, and after rolling it on, he opened her with his fingertips, then positioned himself against her, watching as his cock was filling her, sliding deep inside. For a moment he paused, letting her tight, wet heat envelope him, and felt her fingers dug into his shoulders as he started to move, then clutched at him, her head back, her hips were moving with him, meeting him thrust for thrust. They now lived true to their own feelings, enjoying each other's pleasures, the sound of skin rubbing against each other, ragged breathing, pleasurable moans. The two of them kept entwined with each other and didn't want let go, like they were craving a dish but kept eating it without getting bored.

Her body tightened around him, sucked him even deeper, and heard her moan of surrender and demand as he watched her cry of release, gloving him so sweetly, it drove him over the edge. Pleasure rolled through him, deep and saturating, washing away the pain and the darkness as he received it and happiness. "I love you." His mouth clamped on hers, drank from it. "God, I love you." Then poured himself into her.

They realized that the other person was very important to them now. More important than everything. "I know."

When both were tired, lying next to each other, hugging each other with sweat, the smell of sex, clinging to their bodies, and basking in the moment, the first real love either had ever known. Tommy gently stroked the stray hairs from her forehead, then leaned down and kissed it there lightly. Suddenly, she was feeling very sleepy, which made sense, as they'd been taking the wedding all day. Although, she wanted to open her eyes, but now she was too tired to fall asleep when the familiar sound of Tommy was whispering in her ears. "Smiling, do you know how much I love you?"

It was the love from his heart. And it's true that a man had to feel loved not only by God but by a woman as well. Yes, he felt it from Smiling. "I don't think I can..." He broke off because he saw her eyes closed as if sleepy. He just smiled and kissed her lips. "Sleep well, my love."

With their bodies entwined, tonight the two of them sank into a beautiful dream when happiness rushed in, overflowing like waves. Let's close everything in the past of their lives. The future was something that needed to be cherished and protected. So they would write new chapters themselves.

❦❋❦

PS. Love is great gift from God. Life without love is nothing.

Author's Note.

Dear readers.

We still mistakenly think that we ourselves are convenient and sufficient, have a lot money, good health, good appearance and have many other new materials that can make us feel confident and satisfied with our life or to be able to help others. However, life itself is never perfect, and so do humans. No matter how many accomplishments we try to achieve. It certainly doesn't make us always happy. And because, we have forgotten what it means to help out of our heart, and is a sincere desire to share the burden of suffering with others. Whether the helping is small or large. It's not as important as our mentality or our intention to do so.

A measure of a person's wealth is not material possessions or what he or she owns. If we want to know how rich we are. Perhaps, we need to count how many things we cannot buy with money.

Everyone's life is a long journey with so many experiences. Have a cheerful laugh, have sad tears, have faith to win or have lessons about failure. A carefree mind or keeping a tolerant and positive mind will bring richness in life. A simple and loving heart will make life a better place.

Human life does not need too much fussy, full of everything. Because in life if we do everything with a sincere heart to treat everyone with the honest nature inherent in who we are, willing to protect and sacrificed your personal interests for others. There is no better in this world than bringing happiness to others without minding our own problems. For that reason, when we share happiness, happiness is doubled. This is the content in my next story, And I've saved the best for the last one. *A loving heart always possesses miracle that cannot be understood by reason.* Using that heart to enjoy the joy in life.

Though the story, Love Conquers All is finished. But I'm sure you're wondering about some loose ends that were not tied up, some relationships that were left in limbos. I don't know if you wonder what happens next with Tommy and Smiling, what's going to happen between Steady and

Leo? So I'm now at work on a new mystery, thrillers and romance. The Love of Love, that will take up where Love Conquers All left off.

In The love of love, you'll meet again Mathew and Shirley, also the new character, Jessica who are definitely in for trouble trying to possess love which will only yield dire results in the end. Because anyone has a dark side. When that dark side is too big to fill the mind. They will do terrible things.

Hoping, you'll look for and read **The Love of Love.** As for the actual dates of publication for this next project, I'm not sure at this point, but I'll keep everyone posted on my Facebook and all the social platform, so check in often. In the meantime, very best wishes and happy reading on for a preview of **The Love of Love**, available now.

Warmest regards,
Hung Bui

Chapter 1

Use your heart to enjoy the joy of life

Steady yawned widely, looking at the high ceiling when she woke up, and contemplating the sunlight filling the room. She considered pulling the covers back over her head that she could sleep another hour or longer. But something strange was happening to her, had been happening to her since he came. She was looking at things, feeling things differently. She felt comfortable on the bed, thinking about her life and where it was going. For the first time in many years, she felt comfortable with herself. She felt comfortable with her wants, and right now the smell of coffee had stirred her mind. When there was a choice between sleep and coffee, Steady faced her biggest dilemma. She tossed the covers back as coffee won the battle, and scrambled out of the bed. Fresh coffee always made the morning wonders. She wore a simple white athletic T-shirt and silk boxer shorts in electric blue, headed for the bathroom. Then after she did her private things, she jogged downstairs, trailing her fingers over the satin finish of oak railing, into the quiet house now and told herself everything would finally get back to normal. The cleaning service would be by first thing Monday. She glanced briefly through the etched-glass window in the front door that she liked the brilliantly sunny fall morning, and then with a wicked smile, she thought Smiling and Tommy together, and they seemed to be well on their way to a new romance. She happy for them, and it made her think of Bush Jr and Tiffany again when she swung down the hall toward the kitchen.

They had spent the night at their home before heading out on their honeymoon. Though the house big enough for her brother or sister could come and stay for visits. Each of them had a fine mind, conscientiously applied to their individual areas of expertise, and none of them would stay overnight. Brother Justin's family had spent the night at Brother James' house. They would catch a flight from Melbourne up to Boston. Gloomy's family stayed in a hotel where the family had arranged for guests could stay overnight. And they were leaving tomorrow night, too.

Steady missed and thought of them, too. She had always been grateful that all of them had melded so well. Bush Jr was her closest friend, as well as her brother. Along with the rest of Jefferson brood, and the extended of Brian and Jennies were a solid unit. Husband and wife, parents, business partners, thirty years of marriage, the raising of seven of children and building of one of the most respected business in Orlando hadn't dimmed their devotion.

She couldn't conceive of the amount of effort it took to make it all work. Much easier, she decided, to concentrate on one thing at a time. For her, now was the house of her own that could build a family home for herself. Shaking her head to quiet her thoughts and came back to reality for coffee and omelet time. She grinned as she dug a bag of coffee beans out of the cabinet, and began to fill a coffee maker much like one she'd used daily at her office.

While machine hummed, she snagged the iPod lying on the counter and slipped on the wireless headphones. A little music with the morning hot meal, she decided. Great, just what I need to hear. She turned up the volume, started humming, and took eggs, cheese, ham, onion, tomato, mushroom and strawberries out of the refrigerator. And then put an omelet pan on the stove to heat. While it did, she put some strawberries in a little colander to wash, French bread in the toaster.

Leo woke and found himself alone in bed. As the morning light poured into the bedroom, it took him a moment to orientate himself. Turning his head slowly to glance at the luminous dial of his clock, and the headache behind his eyes told him that he'd had a lot, may be too much, to drink. It wasn't there that made him remember. His house and his own bed were miles away, and he'd spent a wild night party with Steady. Just thinking about the intimacies they'd shared the night before, made him want to see her again. He stretched out his arms, took a deep breath, and heard the familiar voice of singing, coming from somewhere caught him attention, someone else was up.

Concerned, he swung his legs over the side of the bed, appalled that he was still wearing the same clothes yesterday without tie bow and vest. Damn, he must have really been out of it. He hadn't fallen asleep in his clothes since his college days. He wondered if he was on his way to becoming an alcoholic? But his curiosity turned on as he buttoned up his shirt, started out of the room with bare feet, and when he was halfway down stairs, he smelled coffee. Strong, fresh coffee. The aroma was so welcome he nearly smiled. He continued to follow the sound, winding through the house toward the sunny kitchen, and paused in the act of it as another scent wafted toward him. Bacon? As well as found a pleasant surprise on the singer that made him smile before he recognized who.

He followed the sound, winding through the house toward the sunny kitchen, and paused in the act of it, found a pleasant surprise on the singer that made him smile before he recognized who.

Holy shit, Steady was standing at the stove, sautéing onions-mushrooms-tomatoes and peppers in preparation for the omelet, and the smooth, golden length of her leg more than made up, and speaking of music, he had absolutely no vocal talent.

She was concentrating so intently on the music piping through the earphones that she wasn't aware of his presence and he couldn't make a sound, just stood there, enjoyed the view and listened to the sound of her voice. My God, the woman had slender legs in a pair of her silk boxers wasn't covering up much, and left her indecent. He tried to breath and almost let out a moan as cocking his head, and watched Steady was bending over, head in the fridge, hips bumping, grinding, circling, presented such an entertaining show, no man alive or dead would have complained that she sang off-key.

Besides, he always knew Steady's body held amazing sexy curves, but he hadn't seen them on such stunning display like now. Her hips were slim, but had enough flesh to grab onto and hold tight, and her ass? It wasn't big, just nice and round. He liked round. So in this case, it's his preference. Her hair was black as midnight, straight as rain, and tumbled to waist that just begged to be spanned by a man's two hands. For Christ's sake, man, she wore no bra, no panties. He had trouble keeping his eyes off her breasts were unrestricted, and visible beneath the sheer shiny cloth. Nothing under the sexiest bed clothes to make lust shot through him. But his crotch was suddenly uncomfortable and his arousal stiff. Why it was hot in here and he couldn't gulp air fast enough as his collar felt too damn tight, so did his pants. And could also fantasize about how delightful it would be to touch her, to kiss her, caress her and thrust into the deepest, most feminine part of a woman was dressed like Victoria's model on the counter of kitchen.

Caught in her own world, she hadn't noticed him yet, which suited him just fine. Leo took a last look, shifted painfully, and managed to croak out a few words. "Good morning." He said to her, but she continued to take the jam out from the fridge and sing. Her hips did a quick, enthusiastic twitch that had him whistling through his teeth. Then she reached for a note that should have cracked crystal and turned to set the platter of toast and bacon on the table she'd already set.

"Good morning," he repeated, louder.

She changed position then her eyes met his. Her face immediately crumpled, stopped singing, didn't jolt, but she did scream as her hand flew to her chest and her eyes opened wide. "Leo, you scare a crap out of me!"

Leo held up a hand, palm out, and began to explain himself. "Take it easy. I didn't mean to scare you."

But with a music still blaring through her headset, all Steady could do was seeing her cousin with rumpled hair, sloppy dressed and face that held enough wickedness to fuel a dozen devils.

Very slowly, he tapped a finger to his ear, ran it over his head to the other and said. "Take off the headphones."

She's just become aware of the music over the blood that was roaring in her head and ripped them off. "Oh, sorry, and what on earth are you doing in my house?"

"Okay," he pulled his hair back and tried an easy smile. "Your mother and father insisted after they waved and watched the bride and groom got into their car to leave for Bush Jr's house where they'd be spending the night before getting on his private plane to Hawaii for their honeymoon next day. They didn't want me driving home as they saw I walked staggering slightly because I had had more to drink than I probably should have. Rather they didn't want me to have an accident or DUI ticket. They also knew I could stay in the suit at Morgan Hotel closed by. But you surprised me to grab my wrist, solving that problem by offering me a bed in the guess room, and explained that it's much more comfortable. Remember?"

That much was true. But he didn't remember anything after he shrugged out of his suit jacket and let it fell to the floor. His tie followed then his shoes and socks off. Then she pushed him on the bed. "Go get some sleep, and if you wake up before me, let yourself out."

He remembered he wasn't drunk at that time, but he was on the verge, and he'd leaned in and pressed his lips to her cheek, her nose and her forehead before she could stop him. "Thank you."

"Anytime," she wanted to say much more, much of it along the lines of take me, take me now. Luck was on her side, she did her best to smile then closed her eyes, waiting for him to start kissing her lips, undressing, laying naked and touching her. But he didn't do any of those things, only she could hear he just breathed heavily.

Too heavily, the deep breathing became a loud snore as she opened her eyes. Leo had passed out. Was that just exactly her life? And that's another story in the making.

"Right. Have a sit," she ordered, gesturing toward the table. "Coffee?"

He grinned, a knowing look in her eyes, and the scent drew him to the island and pulled up a stool at the corner to sit, but he eyed her the way a man might a favored pet that tended to bite. "I wouldn't mind it."

She walked to the coffeepot, poured the thick brew into one of the mugs, and set it in front of him. "Cream?"

"No. black. Thank you."

"I hope your room is suitable."

"It's great, and you were right about spending the night at your parents' house. How did you sleep?"

"Like a rock," she said with a smile. "Did you sleep well?"

"Fine. But I'm not sure if I fell asleep or passed out."

Finding out he hadn't remembered about last night had been both good and bad. On the one hand, at least she knew he hadn't been ignoring her. On the other hand, seriously, he'd forgotten that? "Drink, caffeine makes things better." She expressed her concern, and she poured the egg mixture into the omelet pan.

"Right." But at least he'd felt great today when he'd awakened. He lifted the mug when he noted, with some fascination that as she moved, her breasts shifted and bounced. He actually felt his fingertips grow warm with the urge to touch them. He sipped the coffee, letting the first hot taste of coffee seep into his system, and focused on her fully. "By the way, do you believe people can reveal their personalities by the clothes they wear?"

"Hmm?" distracted, she gave the fluffy eggs an expert flip, grated the wedge of cheese, turned off the griddle, then twisted around, crossing her arms firmly under her breasts, and met his gaze. But he wasn't looking at her now. He was staring at her chest. "Hey, what are you staring at?"

His gaze locked on her perfect breasts. His eyes seemed popping out his head at the delicious shadow and the hard buttons of her nipples were clearly displaying beneath the innocent silk. They made his mouth water, and his hand twitched with the need to touch them. Snap out of it. He swore under his breath and forced himself to sip his coffee again and focused on her face instead. "Your food, it smells great that I can resist."

"What are you talking about?" She asked as realizing that his eyes were fixed on her breasts. She wasn't easily embarrassed, but the longer he stared, the more uncomfortable feeling she became. "You're awful, Leo."

It was tricky as hell to act normal when he wanted to be all over her. He found himself sneaking glances whenever he could get away with it; because he couldn't help himself, and because if he couldn't touch, at least he could look. "Sorry wrong angle, and just an observation," he barked, set his coffee down. "But it's your own fault."

"Oh, is it?" she grunted, but was not going to fight him. "You like omelet?"

"Sure, anything."

With a smile, she turned back to the stove, transferred the omelet into two plates, adding bacon and toast to both then brought them to the island in front of him, next to a bow of washed strawberries already sitting there along with honey and butter, but she stood holding the spatula. "And I suppose you got a real eyeful, didn't you, Leo?"

"God save me," Leo put a hand to his heart, looking down at his plate, and then carefully, he forked in the first bite of the omelet, and nibbled a strip of bacon. God the cousin could cook. "I wasn't eyeing on you, just come across. And if you don't want a man to look, then don't bounce up and down in front of him."

"Oh, really," she cocked her hip and looked suspicious. "In that case, I'll get dress then."

"Ah, come on," he laid the fork across the edge of his plate, and in a move too unexpected for her to evade, his hand grabbed her arm, pulling spun her around so quickly snatched the spatula out of her hand. It crashed against the wall, and her eyes were going wide. "Steady, don't go away mad."

"I'm not mad," she said, and for lack of something better, her elbow jabbed into his stomach, and threw them both off balances.

His breath whooshed out on a laugh as he ended up with his hands at her hips and hers gripping his forearms. Then he stopped laughing when he realized he was pressed against her, and her eyes fired up at him. They were so wide and deep. "Look. Steady…"

She loved the feeling of his big body against hers, and she wanted to lean her head against his chest. If she did, she'd be able to feel the warmth of him, hear his heartbeat. For a moment she'd be able to imagine that this was real and the he belonged to her. But she mocked him with his own choice of words. "I've been looking, Leo Tu."

He jerked back. It was the safest move. "Sincerely apologized, Steady, I shouldn't have teased you like that. I meant you look fine just the way you are." Perfect. That sounded like a good reason.

She managed a smile. "All right, your sincerely apologized accepted."

He looked down at her mouth. Her lips were full, just parted, very tempting, and just looking at it had his own skin go hot and his muscles tense. "Now you look even more attractive than you did ten seconds ago." She rolled her eyes. "What do you mean?"

He tried to drop his gaze away, but it landed on the roundness of her rump beneath T-shirt, the shallow rise and fall of her breathing, and ignored the fact that his body went into a full aching attack as his eyes came back to hers. "I meant that I'm not going to mess up your morning breakfast, and don't want you to change those sexy pajamas I never seen before."

"Um, I …" And the words hung in the air as the memory flashed back, and only she heard once again in her mind the music she loved, the noise rising around them, the movements and the smells that she didn't hear Leo asked softly. You what?

She recalled, a good crowd at wedding party last night when she put it down to the wine they'd been drinking after the announcement blared over the mike, and then unmarried ladies lined up, waiting for Tiffany who stood on the stage with the band, turning her back on them and prepared to toss the bouquet.

"Reach for the flowers. Really reach," her mother called, holding her own arms up in the air to show her how to catch it. Steady wasn't interested in bouquets or giddy young women. Her life was on the line. Distracted, she glanced around for Leo. And she looked back in time when Tiffany threw the bouquet high above and behind her. It flew through the air and landed in Smiling's arms first, but she shook her head and tossed it away again, and this time it hit her in the face, but she caught it as her sister laughed over it. Embarrassed, Steady accepted the congratulation and well-meaning teasing as her mom pecked her cheek. And she replied back to Tiffany and the participants that she would soon catch up with them. Then when she indulged herself with burying her face in the bouquet, Leo asked right away.

"What do you think about this?"

"They smell nice," Steady replied, knowing it wasn't the answer Leo wanted. But there was something tender and warm in the way he looked at her, and he led her again onto the dance floor a moment later without saying a word where they were playing an old song that she had always liked. And she was surprised to find that Leo was not only a wonderful dancer, but he seemed to be in perfect harmony with her.

Being enfolded by Leo's muscular arms again, dancing beneath the softly glowing lights, had not been in her plans. She knew the room was beautiful decorated for wedding party. It was filled with gorgeous floral arrangements, cream roses and an array of pale flowers that mixed elegance and country so as to give the room an extremely romantic feeling. But all of it had faded to the background the moment his hand at her waist was so aloof, but so possessive. While one her hand was warm in his, the other resting on his powerful shoulder, her nose very nearly brushing his chin as they moved together to the beat of music, and they grinned at each other like the lovesick fools they were. Had she ever felt like this? Buoyant or happiness? She thought as she matched her steps to his naturally. She loved to dance, but preferred to do with someone she knew. Leo was comfortable, and she glanced around. Approving what was her, studying the guests to be certain they were impressed by their smiles, the nods, and the whispers that was making clear, they considered them a couple.

⁂⁂*

She fell silent as if immersed in nostalgia, and he kept staring at her, trying to probe her mind to find out what she was thinking as her faced flushed. "Steady, what are you thinking about?" He inquired. "You look like you're a million miles away."

She forced herself to look him in the eyes. "Not that far? I was thinking back about the wedding last night."

"I probably drank too much."

"No, not about that." Wasn't it strange and fascinating man who was related to her, should have such a strong effect on her? It wasn't that she was shy around men-far from it. She was selective. She had fallen in love with Leo when she'd been eight years old and he ten when they first met at the reunion party when looking into his deep brown eyes under his dark eyebrows. And through childhood and into adolescence she'd never looked at another boy. Leo had been her friend and cousin. But did that mean she couldn't love him or enough to become his lover? Of course, she'd pretended to from time to time hoping it might make him notice her. Yet, they were in love as only the young can be, carelessly, heedlessly, innocently, just held hands to drink coffee, watched movies and kissed her on the cheek. Until one night in the summer when the air was sweet with wild grass, they stop being children and their love stopped being innocent.

All her young dreams had been wrapped up in one strong, very virile man who she could so completely and wholeheartedly trust and who was always there for her when she needed him. And then, like summer lighting, their relationship had all gone sour in the day she'd never forgotten, and Leo had suddenly become her hatred.

She'd always been so good at staying in control, at distancing herself from attempts at seduction, from resisting the persuasions of physical attractions. But with him, each time she could feel herself slipping a little further and a little deeper. So, this time, she would do the logical and practical thing. She'd settle herself down, clear her mind. Then she'd begin to plan the best way to get him there.

Rather than keep his gaze, she stared at the front of his shirt, remembering the feel of those broad muscles beneath it. God help her, she wanted to feel them again. So, she told him the only truth she could right now, something else that burned in her soul and at the moment, seemed more relevant than her own secret anyway. "But can I ask you something?"

"That depends on what it is?"

Fair enough. "It's not about the business." "Okay. Shoot," he told her.

He hadn't hesitated. His tone so sincerer she felt sure she had been right to ask. "Well, I guess we don't know unless I ask. Do you ever think about kissing me again?"

He couldn't answer right away, because all his resistance had crumbled to that mouth of her, that seemed ripe and willing and close. Her eyes were dreamy and dark, he could see. He had only to lower his head, or better, yes better, to yank her to her toes. Then his mouth would be on those seductive, complacent lips of hers like the intense flame of sexual chemistry scorched both of them last night. Memories of its debacle on the dance floor came flooding back.

✻ ✻ ✻ ✻ ✻

He was immediately aware of her full breasts pressing against his chest, and feeling completely schizophrenic. It was funny, he broke her heart once before, she hated him, and now suddenly his mind wandered down the dangerous, sexual path as thigh brushed thigh. But he didn't care about, didn't give a good goddamn about anything, except the touch and feel of her. It was comfort. It was lust. It was heaven. God, it had been so long. Heat spread through his blood as thoughts of bare, fragrant skin and hot sex flashed through his mind. He remembered the first time he'd made love to her, how her back arched upward with the length of his body stretched across hers. How warm and tight she'd been as she'd so willingly offered him her virginity, how she'd trembled, just as she did now, draped in the luxurious dress in his arms. I want to know what love is…

He hadn't touched her in years, and so much for being able to concentrate on the dance every time he held her like this with the music of love. Besides, the sensation of her skin under his hands jolted through his system. It electrified his skin, turned his veins to paths of fire, melted his brain. An animal moan rose up from his chest, ready to escape his lips in an agony of need. I want you to show me. I want to feel what love is… He buried his face in her curls, grabbed her waist and pulled her tight, feeling his growing erection and rode against the V of her legs, and then pressed upward to meet the soft juncture of her thighs. Though layers of clothes, the kind that let him feel exactly how soft she was in that particular spot. He knew she felt how stiff he's gotten for her, too as she gasped, and he wondered if she'd move away, stop the dangerous game they flirted with, but once again she surprised him. Wrapping her arms tight around his back, she arched into him full power. I know you can show me…

Erotic images played through her mind as she remembered all too clearly how it felt when his knees impatiently pushing her legs apart and entered her body, how much she ached for him. She licked her lips, felt a familiar yearning deep wishing that they were in an empty room; hell, a dark corner would do. She wanted to strip off his clothes and feel the hard muscles inside hers so intimately again. He was staring at her and she sensed his own thoughts were following a similar path.

Shit. His damned cock thickened painfully, pressing hard against his pants and the soft heat of her groin. I want to know what love is … Their feet moved in a faint parody of dancing, allowing each body part to touch, tease, and slide against one another. If she hadn't had her dress on, he'd have been inside her without thinking twice. And the worst part of it was the song was ending and the smattering of applause. He lifted his head, froze and she opened her eyes. "What happened?"

He dragged in a long regretful breath, chest was tight, dick was so hard and swollen as his hands were still on either side of her. All he had to do was lean in and steal a kiss, but he fought for sanity, and it did stop him from thinking about that. He had to be patient and wait for her to trust him. "Song's over." He said, and reluctantly he released her to applaud. And yes, it was over at the last minute when the heat of wine made him pass out. It got a bit out of control.

⁂

Noticing he looked thoughtful, she asked again. "You're thinking about what I ask?"

Oh, dear Lord, it had been ecstasy sinful. He had to touch her. He would go mad if he didn't, as he realized their noses were nearly touching, warm breath mingling. "Yeah. About as much as I'd like to take the next breath."

The smell of him was overpowering, and so emotionally dangerous. Stop going, Steady before you do it. Otherwise, you wouldn't be able to stop. But she didn't move, couldn't.

She swallowed back all her emotions and his gaze flickered to her throat. "Oh, really Leo?" she asked her tone teasing, and instinctively, her body swayed closer to his and she tilted her face upward, bringing her lips close to his. "Prove it."

Her eyes told him the facts. She hungered for him to share. Shit, he wanted her as much as she wanted him. But he forced himself to wait. He needed to hear her say the words first. "Are you challenging me?"

"Just shut up and kiss me." She ordered, unable to stand the tension a second longer. Before he could react, she threw her arms around his neck and pulled his head to hers, kissing him hard. He kissed her back like a drowning man, his mouth open and hungry, his tongue seeking hers.

Warm, wet and demanding as strong arms surrounded her and he held her against him.

Hot, wet, demanding, the thrill of her touch, the fact that she wanted him again and was all so damned heady that he couldn't stop, and let the storm of emotions that had shadowed him since he left her.

Love for him was dead, she tried to tell herself. But this was Leo who was holding her, Leo who was kissing her, Leo who was acting as if he couldn't resist her.

The unique flavor of her seared through him, sizzling the nerves, smoking the senses. His arms surrounded her, grabbed her butt and pressed hard her long, lean body against him where her breasts were contacting with his chest. The scent of her, darker than he remembered and somehow forbidding, slithered into him, twinning through his system until desire ran hot through him, centered between his legs, causing him to think of nothing but the pure sensual pleasure of her.

She started to feel intoxicated, like she'd been last night. Her blood began to heat and her body began to respond. And somewhere in the back of her mind, the kiss was awakened her old emotion, and she knew that kissing him would only lead to more. Touching, caressing, pressing hot skin to hotter flesh that she couldn't stop herself as the hunger spilled out in response, and experienced the new. She pulled him close to the juncture of her parted legs, his pants-clad thighs inside hers, his erection hard against her lower abdomen.

He thought he'd killed his need for her years long before. But God he wanted her. Right here. Wanting nothing more than the feel of her naked body against his own.

Her need for him was almost embarrassing. She'd never been a sexually charged person. She preferred a good kiss to sex, probably because she'd never actually had good sex. But something told her that she wouldn't have to settle for one or other with Leo. He more than capable of delivering both. She was playing with the fire here. How stupid was that for a woman who'd already been burned? But she'd take what she could get while the getting was good. With her whole heart, she returned kiss for kiss by the way she'd only dreamed about. No kiss in her life had ever been more welcome as she stroked Leo's lips with her tongue, and he bit her lower lip.

He angled her head so that he could deepen the kiss. And just like that, she tried to gasp for air, and her fingers tremble with the urge to reach for his arms in protest, slid possessively around his neck, and revealed in the wild flash of heart and wanting more.

He couldn't explain, even to himself. Never in his life had he been involved with Steady, hadn't ever considered it again or wasn't sure that was what he wanted anyway. But Steady was wrapped in his arms now, and giving him everything he'd forgotten he could have. He's going to take what he wanted, to touch her, to feel that sizzling connection they'd experienced fifteen years before by filling his hands with her, to mold those pretty curves through the thin silk of her clothes.

How could she have known her life had such avoid in it? She'd tried to close the door on the part her life that included Leo, though she'd known it wasn't possible. He was still the only one who had been worth the wait and matching her passions. And this, just this, she promised herself. Whatever the risks, whatever the price, she'd had to know.

"Steady," he whispered into her open mouth as if the years were trying to separate them again.

She felt his lips slide down her throat, hungrily exploring the thin, vulnerable skin. Heat was pouring from her flesh and her nipples tightened to even harder points, while her legs wobbled beneath her, she leaned against him for support, and rub them his chest. Desire, she could taste it on him with the full, ripe and ready to explode desire of a man for a woman. He was aroused, his erection thick and long against her belly as she pushed her hips forward.

He lost his head, lost himself completely. Her hunger was unexpected. Her mouth was a banquet of flavors- the tart, the sweet, the spicy, and he was ravenous. There was so much there, the scent and taste and texture of her, so much more than the expected, so much richer than dream. All of it opened for him, invited him to feast.

Desire burst through his body, like a forest fire licking through dry tinder. He was so aroused that the twitch in his pants became a rock-hard erection. He wanted her now, here.

It was insane, she thought, absolutely insane to get this involved this quickly. But this wasn't the time for thinking, only a desperate leap of emotion that consumed her, even as she avidly consumed him. She slung a leg around the back of one of his, allowing the most sensitive part of her move fully meet his uncompromising muscle.

She wanted this, too. And the need for more slashed through him like a whip, he followed the urge to taste and touch her everywhere. He cupped her ass and lifted her high up onto the counter so that his hands were free to touch and take while his tongue never stopped diving in and out of her mouth.

Everything intensified. His touch. The heat. That primal tug deep within her as he crossed that invisible barrier between them. His free hand found its way under the hem of her shirt to touch her bare skin and sliding up the curve of her rids, cupping to feel the weight of her firm breast, and then tightening in a grip that was almost painful.

She met it with her own and he heard a soft moan from her, it made him groan along. Part pain, part of pleasure when he caressed her hard nipple with desire, then rolling and pulling it between his fingers.

A rush of pain, pleasure hurt her heart, a reaction to being touched after so long without his contact. She hooked her fingers through the bell loops of his pants and dragged him to her, so that his hard sex ground against the soft, wet part of her body.

It was good. Too good. And because it only made him want the rest of her. His hot and hard hand from her breast, her curves traveled down her body, making their way to her waist, her ass, and then his fingers slid under her short pants to palm her soft valley between her thighs, and his mouth moved, too, breaking free for a breath, and then running along her cheek to her ear. "Steady, oh, God. I want you," he whispered against her lobe. He didn't know how to tell her what she meant to him, what he wanted her to mean to him. What they could be together. So he only repeated what words he had. "I want you."

At that moment she realized what he was going to do, what she was about to do, but suddenly realized it was a ridiculous act of recklessness. Maybe for both of them, it should be stopped. But she was afraid it couldn't be stopped, as she was vibrating like plucked string, then she clamped her shaking hand over his. Stopping him. "Oh, Leo, wait," she reminded herself and the sound from her brought them out of the sensual haze. broke them apart.

He cursed, both thankful and angry that he'd scared her. Berating himself, he pulled backward and away from her, and then he plowed both hands through his hair and let out a long, ragged breath. "I'm sorry." He said in painted confusion, but he pointed out. "This is insane."

But it was happened, he knew it. And the moment had turned awkward. He should slowly regain his affection for Steady, and not be in such a hurry. But he couldn't help. He knew it was inexcusable, to drag her against him, to plunder that teasing, tormenting mouth with his. Shame washed over him, a cold gray mist over red-hot lust. Staggered by what he'd done, by what he'd wanted to do, he broke hastily away from her.

Steady said nothing, could say nothing, but she could think. Why had she let him kiss her? Why couldn't she resist him? Damn it, Steady, stop analyzing this thing to death. It's what it is. You and Leo kissed. You both got hot and bothered. That's the situation would happen.

"Steady, listen," he had to stop. But Lord, he wanted to do it again, he realized. He drew her back to him as she was looking lost and helpless. "If I've mistaken your feelings, Steady, I apologize. I'm not a man who finds it necessary or pleasurable to pressure a woman. And believe it or not, I usually have a lot of self-control, but every time I was close to you. I couldn't handle and resist the ways you still make me feel."

She touched her finger to his lips, silencing him. "Stop. I won't accept apogees for what just happened," she hated the fact that he was absolutely right, but what kind of a man thinks a woman wants an apology after she's been kissed boneless. He wasn't acting as if it were over. He had pulled her into his arms and kissed her with growing passion a minute ago. Was it really his fault? Or hers for not fighting for what she wanted? She was glad it was he who had made the first move and not her. His sudden and unexpected action surprised her so much that she felt right into his trap and arms. But she the initiator again with a stronger emotion. She wished she could explain herself completely to herself, to him. She had clung to him and kissed him back, and her heart had been clattering as erratically as his. "But to keep thing simple and to be honest it's not your fault for kissing me. We were kissing each other. That proves something that we still have heat and feel these strong physical attractions between us."

At this, a laugh burst from his throat, and was glad she'd managed to lighten the mood. "Just what every man wants to hear." He said, pulled her back to him. "You're very straightforward."

Their kiss was rather a new promise, a fresh start to their relationship, and their certainly about their future. She flashed him a smile. "And I've discovered recently that you're awfully good at what you do."

An invitation to her heart and soul as Leo stared at her in disbelief, but he didn't think she would say that at all. So, he was a bit nervous and flirtatious. "I've been saving up."

As if she knew exactly what he was talking, and viciously aroused. "Somethings never change," she said gruffly. "Kiss me again like you mean it."

Frustration, need, temper, lust, they'd all been bottle up inside him since the first moment he'd seen her. His cock remained hard enough to cut stone, and the passion poured out. He took what he hadn't allowed himself to want. He didn't wait a second longer, just lowered his head and captured her lips, ravaging her mouth to feed the hunger.

This time it was her own tongue that plunged past his lips and discovered its mate.

They plundered, each of them equally greedy, until they were both breathless when he tore his mouth from hers. For a long moment, they stayed as they were, staring at each other, with his fist hand in her hair, and her fingers digging into his shoulders.

His blood was still humming. He couldn't quite silence the tune, and he felt that basic need claw to a new level inside him. Their mouths were locked again, a reckless war of lips, tongues and teeth.

Burning up and craving the feel of his skin, his muscles, his bones, she placed her palms over his chest to the front his button-down shirt. Blind to anything but the roar of greedy need in her blood, she undid it by touch, her fingertips rasping against his bare, warm and hard muscle skin as she felt his hand rushed into her shirt again, desperate to touch, frantic to feel.

If he was going to hell, he'd make damn sure it was worth the trip. Instantly his hand tightened her bottom as the need to rip her clothes off, tasted her everywhere, and gave her pleasure. He brought her into firm contact with the hard ridge of his erection. "Let me have you."

The expression on his face serious, the need in his eyes naked. "Here?" she whispered, swallowed hard, knowing it was dangerous. Anybody could come along.

Looking at her hesitantly, he said. "If you're not ready, if the time isn't right, I'll understand, but I swear, Steady. I'm about haft out of my mind wanting you."

Her eyes wide, her expression filled with longing. "I don't care anymore if it's the right time or right place, if I'm ready, if I'll regret it later, if all you want is sex. I just plain don't give a damn."

Her face glowed with the brightness of her smile as the decision was made. No more thinking. No more questions. Just need and demand to satisfy it. His mouth found hers again.

He parted her lips, with his tongue and swept into her warmth as his hands stroked her body, fiercely, possessively, up and down her spine, exploring her, discovering her all over again. She gave herself up to the amazing sensations that only Leo could create and offered him more.

***

"Steady, is that fresh coffee?" Brian's question died on his lips and stopped dead in the doorway, slapped hard in the heart completely shock by walking right into an assignation where the sight of his baby girl wrapped like a vine around his nephew. Automatically, he spoke. "Oh. Excuse me."

Panicking in the climax, suddenly hearing her father's voice, the two of them were afraid to sprung apart like guilty children getting caught with its hand in the cookie jar. "Dad," she blushed faintly, to see his immediate jolt of embarrassment. "I was-we were just…"

He sent Leo a pained look then, man-to-man, as his face turned an ugly shade of red, and for an awkward, endless five seconds no one spoke nor moved.

Both annoyed, ashamed of watching, and without another word, Brian backed out, walked quickly away.

Leo let out a long breath, dragged his hands through his hair, and fist them there. "Oh God," there was one thing he hated more than feeling guilty. It was feeling ashamed. "Get me a gun. I'd like to shoot myself now and get it over with."

"We don't have one." She gripped the edge of the counter. The room was still spinning. "It's all right. My father knows I kiss men on occasion."

Leo dropped his hands. "I was about to do a hell of a lot more than kiss you, and on his kitchen counter-top."

"I know." Wasn't her pulse still banging like a kettledrum? Couldn't she see the blind heart of desire in those wonderful eyes of his? "It's a damn shame Dad didn't have to go to work today."

"This is not good." He hissed out a breath, a little unsettled, turned on his heel and yanked a glass out of a cupboard. He filled it with cold water from the refrigerator, considered slashing it in his face then gulped it down instead. It didn't do much in the way of cooling him off, but it was a start. "This wouldn't have happened if you hadn't ticked me off."

Angry, she argued back. "God. Are you going to scold me now?" Then straightened her messy hair. "Ticked you off about what?"

"About that your response to me was so hot it could have set off forest fire, and start making sex noises."

The coffee now wasn't strong enough to calm her down, so she decided to have a glass of wine. "Those weren't sex noises." She wrenched open the fridge, took out a bottle of white wine. "Those were muscle relief noises, which I suppose, could amount to roughly the same thing. Get me down a damn wineglass, because now I'm ticked off."

"You," he slammed opened another cupboard, plucked out a simple stemmed glass, shoved it at her. "You sang so loud."

"I beg your pardon." Her voice cut like ice as she poured the wine, slammed the bottle down on the counter. "This is my house. And I was unaware you were staying over."

"You asked me for stay over, didn't you? It was complicate thing that you started clearly-you intended to be involved in."

"It won't help if we keep blaming each other." She took a long sip of wine and tried to find the control button on her temper. "Yeah, that's right. Can I borrow a knife?"

"What?"

"You don't have a gun handy, but I can use a knife to slit my throat."

"Why don't you wait until you get home?" She sipped her wine again, watching him over the rim. "My mother hates blood on the kitchen floor."

"Your father probably doesn't like his daughter having sex on the kitchen counter, either."

"I don't know. The subject's never come up before."

"I didn't mean to grab you that way."

"Really," she held out her glass. "Which way did you mean to grab me?"

"Not." With a shrug he took the wine from her hand, and downed it in one long swallow to steady his nerves. "You can see this is already getting complicated and jumbled up with the job, relationship, you, me and sex."

"I'm very good at organizing and compartmentalizing. Some consider it one of my best-and most annoying-skills."

"Yeah, I bet." He handed her back the glass. "Steady."

She smiled. "Leo."

He laughed a little, roamed the room. "I've done a lot of screwing up in my life. I worked really hard to change that. I can't put anything of that on you."

"If you could, I think a great deal less of you. If you could, I wouldn't be attracted to you."

He turned back, studying her face. "I can't figure you."

"Then you should rearrange your schedule so that you can spend some time on that matter."

"Yes, I should. But maybe next time it should be happened in my house and pretend there isn't a problem."

To his surprise, she laughed. "Well, that's another alternative. Personally, I'd like to do both. During this time, why don't I leave it to you to handle which part of the solution will we approach first?"

"Why don't we?" He glanced at the clock on the stove, swore. "I've got to go, and you're better get ready. I'll take you to the tour, and show you what we're doing."

"I'll do that." She tilted her head. "Want to kiss me goodbye?"

He glanced at the kitchen counter, the back to her. "I really like your mouth. I could spend hours on it. But I'm not going to touch you again. Your father might have a weapon in his hands now you don't know about."

The fear and regret in his voice only made her smile sweeten. "Well, then, I suggest you'd better hurry."

Hung Bui, author of **Don't believe in tears**, now **Love conquers all** and please read **Love of Love** that concludes his three-part series which will be published in the near future.

Receiving comments and criticism from beloved readers is always useful to help him improve his writing style for stories that have been published or will be added in the future, becoming more stimulating, romantic and thriller.

Visiting him on the website:

authohungquocbui.com
or email: **Hu122@aol.com**.

You can also find him on Facebook. All the information about Hung Bui that you want to find will be there.

Printed in the USA
CPSIA information can be obtained
at www.ICGtesting.com
CBHW031332260924
14965CB00001B/8